THE CURSE OF MOHENJODARO

Maha Khan Phillips is a multiple award-winning financial journalist, and the author of *Beautiful from This Angle* and *The Mystery of the Aagnee Ruby*. She grew up in Karachi, Pakistan. She has a bachelor's degree in Politics and International Relations and a master's in International Conflict Analysis from the University of Kent at Canterbury. In 2006, she completed a master's degree in Creative Writing from City University in London, where she currently lives with her husband and son.

THE CURSE OF MOHENJODARO

Maha Khan Phillips

PAN

First published 2016 by Pan
an imprint of Pan Macmillan India
a division of Macmillan Publishers India Private Limited
Pan Macmillan India, 707, Kailash Building
26, K. G. Marg, New Delhi – 110 001
www.panmacmillan.co.in

Pan Macmillan, 20 New Wharf Road, London N1 9RR
Basingstoke and Oxford
Associated companies throughout the world
www.panmacmillan.com

ISBN 978-93-82616-82-5

This is a work of fiction. All characters, locations and events are fictitious. Any resemblance to actual events or locales or persons, living or dead, is entirely coincidental

3 5 7 9 8 6 4 2

Typeset by Manmohan Kumar
Printed and bound in India by
Replika Press Pvt. Ltd.

For my aunt, Nina Khan, with love and gratitude.

Chapter One

MOHENJODARO, PRESENT DAY.

Even the snakes were hiding in this heat.

Layla felt the sweat slide down her forehead, trickle down the side of her nose and then run past her cheeks. She rubbed the back of her hand across her eyes absent-mindedly, trying to shield her face from the sun. It was almost noon and already about 45 degree Celsius. Definitely time for a break.

She stood up, wiped the dust off her trousers and put her trowel in her back pocket, which was already host to an old dental pick, a small notebook and her battered Nokia. After a moment of indecision, she made her way south, towards the main excavation, the grid that stretched across a hundred yards of terracotta desert. Most of the others were there, digging. Might as well see if anyone needed her to carry anything back before she headed to the trailers.

The ground smelt of baking earth. Looking carefully at the soil as she walked, she was grateful for the first time for the suffocatingly warm steel-toed boots they were all forced to wear. Last week, Denny, one of the field techs, was bitten on his ankle by a king cobra dozing under a rock. Denny almost died, saved only by a quick injection of antivenin. The cobra, with its brilliant turquoise and beige markings, was apparently half dead and had attacked feebly. Too hot for even a cobra.

The locals said not to worry about it too much. But after what happened to Denny, nobody was taking the snake thing lightly.

'Hey honey,' shouted Kat, from her corner of the grid, still a minute's walk away. 'Going back to the mother ship?' She grinned.

Layla smiled. She liked Kat. They had bonded over the past couple of months, and not just because they were the only two undergrad students here. Kat was fun and flamboyant, and never took herself too seriously. Just as well, because there were enough pompous types on this dig already. Kat Mahoney was a small Texan gal with a big Southern personality – her words, not Layla's.

Layla made her way over. 'Hey. I forgot my hat, can you believe it? I'm going to go back before I get heatstroke. You coming in for lunch?'

Kat was crouched three metres in the subsoil, a faded blue plastic dustpan and brush in her hands. Sometimes, even on the most well-funded excavations, the simplest tools were the most effective, although the dustpan had warped slightly in the heat. She shook her head. 'Oh honey, I wish I could, but Professor Webb wants this back soil out of the way. Going to investigate here this afternoon. The gradiometer's picked up something – probably another burial site – and you know the skeletons always get me excited. Besides,' she said with a grin, 'some of us remembered to protect ourselves from vampire-like combustion.' She touched the top of her head, where her black cowboy hat rested lopsidedly over short, thick blonde hair. Kat had a red chequered bandana around her neck and was wearing a white vest – tight across her plum-shaped stomach – khaki shorts and flip flops. Sweat formed a V down her top, and had gathered in beads above her lip. 'I feel like I'm in a damn sauna. But it's totally worth it.'

Totally. Layla looked around. It was crazy how beautiful it was here, and how incredibly lucky their finds had been so far. Two burial sites and a host of writing tablets in only two months. She always knew that archaeology would excite her. But Layla hadn't expected to feel so ... so connected to this place, this land of her father's birth that she had barely begun to explore. Pakistan. The country was going through plenty of turmoil, and yet here she was. She thought about Nadia. She should have called her sister before she left. She should have apologized for her part in their argument, for hanging up on her. Nadia was always going to freak out about her coming to Pakistan, she shouldn't have got so defensive about her decision. For a moment, she felt a sense of unease. But she shook it off, just as easily as she did the fly that had landed on her nose.

Kat scanned the area quickly, put down the dustpan and leaned in, whispering, 'We still got some tequila left in the bottle. Wanna share it with me and Warren tonight? Thought we may even get a poker game going in the lab, if the Dutch are up for it.'

'I can't. Liam's coming back from the Karachi Museum. He promised to make time to talk me through how the Rebus principle might apply to the Indus Valley script.'

Kat rolled her eyes. 'Always such a good girl.'

'The more pertinent question is, you're voluntarily spending time with Warren Carter? Seriously? I'd rather get bitten by that cobra.'

'Don't make light, honey. There are few options at the moment, what with us being in the middle of the desert and all. Plus, not all of us were blessed with the "gorgeous babe" gene. Trust me, I'm the one studying archaeogenetics. We're not all length and legs and boobs. Girls like you should come with a warning label.'

Layla laughed again, but she was pleased. 'I've got to go before I melt.'

She passed Professor Webb, who was standing by the total station transit. Asif Baker, the geomagnetometry specialist who was half-Pakistani, half-English, just like her, and Sara Salima, the ceramicist who had come from Karachi to help date the site, stood close by. As usual, they were locked in debate. Asif was pointing to the north, at the grid known as B-6, and Sara was shaking her head. Layla knew there was still disagreement, and confusion, about what they had unearthed over the last couple of months.

Last summer's floods had devastated the province of Sindh, in southern Pakistan, but they had also unveiled a concealed history. Virtually intact steatite seals, tablets with writing and images, had worked their way to the topsoil about half a mile away from Mohenjodaro, the Indus Valley civilization.

The seals were different from anything seen before. They were bigger, for a start, and they seemed to be lengthy pieces of writing, not just the traditional pictographs archaeologists had come to expect from the Indus Valley. Thermoluminescence dating suggested they were at least four thousand years older than the seals that had been previously found.

From the way Asif and Sara were arguing, the finding was still clearly in dispute. How could the tablets be so old? Only 10 per cent of Mohenjodaro had yet been excavated. Had archaeologists misdated the civilization entirely? Some archaeologists had begun to speculate that this was the case. If there was even a remote possibility of that being true ... well, then human civilization was older than anyone imagined. There were so many tantalizing questions, and not enough answers. Nobody wanted to be wrong about this one.

Assumptions would have to be tested, challenged and stand up to international scrutiny.

No wonder Professor Webb seemed exhausted. He looked up at her and frowned. 'Layla. If you're heading towards the trailers, can you stop by the lab? Warren's not picking up the radio. Tell him that he's needed here, please. He can leave the site mapping for tomorrow. And tell him to bring the KRS. We need to start recording.'

'Yes, of course, Professor.' She headed towards the trailers, about half a mile further to the south. She spotted one of the local village boys, Ahmer, on the way, and waved. Ahmer waved back furiously. She had promised him her bar of Cadbury's Dairy Milk this afternoon. He and Raza ran errands on the site, carrying things in their wicker baskets – mostly water – up and down the ruins. He'd developed quite a sweet tooth since he had met her.

As she walked on, making her way through the part of the ruins of the already excavated lower city of Mohenjodaro, she couldn't help taking a moment to enjoy the view. The place was huge, situated on around 250 hectares of land. It was one of the largest planned cities of the ancient world, and it now stood completely empty. Foreign tourists very rarely felt safe here any more, plus, nobody, except Liam – as mad as he was – would be foolish enough to come out in the noonday heat. Even the locals had taken shelter. Only the archaeologists remained, though most of them would head inside to eat and wait for it to get a bit cooler before continuing their work.

It was a treat to be completely alone in the ruins, and Layla savoured it. She walked through First Street, marvelling at the perfectly laid out fired-clay brick houses, some of them were once two levels high, on both sides of the wide road. Families had slept in the second floor of their houses, she knew, to keep away from the dust and grime of the streets. Remarkably, remnants of some of the second levels had survived, after all this time. Thousands of years ago, this city had great architects.

She turned the corner and stopped for a moment. On the left, the ground floor of one of the houses was almost perfectly preserved. There was a back entrance and interconnecting rooms, as well as an open courtyard for cooking. And she could see the bathing area made with watertight bricks, so that water from the house flowed away into the street drains. Indoor plumbing. The ancient people of Mohenjodaro had had indoor plumbing. There were circular pipes in the brickwork and drains outside. Covered in limestone, the sewage system was an achievement in the Bronze Age. And better still, most houses had deep brick wells to pull in fresh water.

She brushed away damp sweaty hair from her eyes. No wonder there was a dispute about dating the site. These people were so ahead of the game ... Almost unconsciously, she looked up, relishing the view.

The Citadel, the residence of the elite, rested on top of a small hill, its dusty brick structures dominating the skyline. Like many great cultures, the rich and privileged had placed themselves above the rest of the city. The hill pulled at her, for reasons she couldn't explain. Just looking out at the ruins of the great Stupa – the mound on top of the Citadel – with the wealth of cobalt sky behind it, sent a thrill down her spine. Egypt ... Mesopotamia ... and the Indus. This place deserved world attention.

Layla took a deep breath, enjoying the dusty smell of the land as it curled up her nostrils – heady, heavy and tantalizing. It reminded her of something ... like a dream long forgotten. Her fascination with the Indus Valley was one of the reasons she had chosen to become an archaeologist. She felt the ruins permeate themselves through her bones, become a part of her psyche. It was ridiculous. And yet, she couldn't help how she felt. Perhaps she had been here, in another life.

She felt the heat bore into her head, and quickened her pace, walking out of the city and down to the campsite. The Citadel would have to wait. Being here on this dig was a real privilege, not one she wanted to have revoked.

The camp was close to the airport – which was barely more than a runway really – and a few minutes' walk down a long wide paved road surrounded by shrubbery, the road set up by the government for tourists. There was even a small bank, a museum and a souvenir shop. This part of the site was well developed, so much so that it was amazing to think that just a mile away, the dig remained relatively isolated.

The archaeologists lived on a campsite made up of a group of highly sophisticated trailers, jokingly known as 'The Residency'. The trailers stood in a large semicircle on a sandy enclosure just by the airport. They reminded her of wagons circling. A guard manned the trailers twenty-four hours, although Sharif didn't seem to be at his post at the minute, looking intimidating with his bulky camouflage uniform and AK-47. The Indo Foundation, the dig's sponsor, was paranoid about terrorist attacks. It was ridiculous. Who would want to harm a bunch of geeky scientists?

She made her way to the first trailer – the lab – custom-built for the Indo Foundation for this dig. The facility was state of the art. Its walls were made of reinforced fibreglass. It was chemical resistant, had HEPA filtration, fire suppression systems and several brand-new computers and equipment for analysis. It was also host to the team's drying racks, a flotation device for artefact recovery and the weighing and measuring equipment. What made it so impressive was not all the technology, but the fact that it was available to them *here*, in the middle of the desert. Most digs had to make do with sending stuff away for analysis. Archaeologists didn't get comfortable trailers to sleep in either. Not normally.

Layla opened the door of the lab. Damp with sweat, the air conditioning hit her like a blast of ice. Warren had it on at the lowest temperature again. He was using the computer in the front by the door for data analysis, typing into an Excel spreadsheet with one hand and twirling a yellow ballpoint pen in the other, leaning back in his chair, legs crossed over. Layla tried to hide her distaste.

'Hey grunt,' he said, without looking up.

'Your radio is switched off again,' she responded coolly. Warren had taken to calling her and Kat grunts to reinforce the fact that he was a field tech while they were mere students. He was a small, thin man with lanky brown hair and an insipid goatee. Good god, how could Kat possibly enjoy hanging out with this man? He'd hit on Layla only a week ago. She'd told him to get lost and his ego hadn't taken it well.

'Been busy. Forgot to turn it on.'

'The Professor asked me to tell you to bring the cam out, please. He needs you to turn on the KRS. They're excavating the new section in B-6 this afternoon, as I'm sure you are aware.'

Warren sighed and stood up. He stretched his arms, looking annoyed. 'He could at least have waited until the sun went down a bit, or let one of the Neanderthals he's got guarding this place do some filming.'

She didn't reply.

He grabbed the cam and headed for the door. 'Don't go anywhere, I need you to check the connection when I set it up. I assume you can manage that much.'

Arsehole.

Layla sat down and logged in to the Indo Foundation system and opened up the KRS, a program which allowed the camera Warren took to record, transmit and receive video and audio. It was, essentially, a custom-built glorified Skype system. Recordings were sent directly to the Indo Foundation's backup database in London. The KRS was used primarily to communicate visually between the lab and the site. Sometimes, when the team started excavating a new layer in the stratigraphy, Professor Webb liked to keep a record, to establish provenance, the precise location, its features and any artefacts found. Even if the lab computers were damaged, the data feed would be recorded thousands of miles away. The KRS looked like a very small television on a roller base, but it was hardy and able to endure high temperatures. From the lab, Layla could zoom in and out, changing magnification and the angle of the video. The quality was excellent.

Too excellent sometimes because twenty minutes later, Warren's ugly mug appeared on her computer screen. She could see that he was standing in the grid. In the background, Kat was setting up the soil sifter. The Professor and Asif were already excavating.

'Prof says you should eat your lunch and then man the lab. The Foundation wants an update. He wants you to put some analysis together of where we are this week and email it to them.'

'Okay.'

He sneered and disappeared from the screen.

She stretched her back, which ached from the morning's work, and cracked her knuckles, a habit which irritated her sister, Nadia. Now she had to send that email to the Indo Foundation, and she needed to figure out what she was going to write.

She called Liam, procrastinating. The phone rang a few times. She was about to leave a voicemail when he picked up.

'You all right?'

'Yup. Are you nearly finished dusting off old artefacts?' She could picture him as he wandered around Karachi Museum, cataloguing broken bits of Indus Valley seals, stooped over in the basement storerooms, his giant frame awkward in its minute spaces and dark corners.

'Yes. Like, I'm covered in cobwebs, but it's grand. They're all being very nice to me here. I've catalogued all the cuneiform script I can find, all the Mesopotamian and Sumerian texts as well, so I can compare the new pictographs.'

'And?'

'And I think we're close, Layla. I'm fairly certain we are dealing with a precursor to the Dravidic languages, though there's a lot of disagreement about that here.'

He sounded excited. She was glad for him. Liam O'Rourke was a linguistic anthropologist. He had been brought on board to see if he could help decipher the new writing tablets. And he was letting her help. Unlike *some* of the field techs here, he actually cared about the students on the dig and wanted them to learn. They had become unlikely friends. Liam was like a brother figure, constantly teasing, but encouraging at the same time, and she had grown very fond of him.

'Are you still planning on coming back tonight? Please tell me you're not leaving me at the mercy of Warren Carter.'

There was a pause. 'You don't worry about him, sweetheart. If that wanker tries anything, I'll kick his arse for ye.'

'How very old school macho of you,' she teased. 'See you later then.'

The computer pinged, signalling an email update and she caught her breath. She was getting distracted ... she thought about what she would write in the email to their sponsor. Something quick, something cut and copied from the daily reports compiled by the Professor, with a few tweaks and updates. She wanted to go watch the team at work. How would she learn anything otherwise?

Layla had wanted to be an archaeologist for as long as she could remember. The past felt like it was hers, and hers alone. The past couldn't hurt anyone. She wanted to do a good job here so that when she graduated, she could come back and work on other Indus Valley digs.

This time, it was Professor Webb's face that appeared on the screen. He looked tense. 'Get over here, will you? The battery is beeping on the KRS and we need it to work. We think we've found something.'

'Already?' she asked, surprised.

'Bring an extra battery and make sure you've positioned the KRS on the site before you leave.'

'Of course. But what did you find, Prof? Another seal?'

'Just hurry up,' he barked.

It was uncharacteristic, and on another day it might have made her feel insecure, but Layla shrugged. She wasn't going to miss this discovery for anything. Her fingers travelled lightly across the keyboard. Without anyone manning the shop, the KRS would need to be positioned as perfectly as possible. She zoomed in on the team – Professor Webb, Sara Salima, Asif Baker and the Dutch freelancers, Uwe Fikse and Alaric Bauer. They were all huddled around or on top of the grid, staring at something in the stratigraphy. Kat was dusting furiously. Even Warren was there, peering into the earth. It was difficult to see anything with so many heads so close together.

She got up, walked to the shelves in the corner of the room, and stood on tiptoe, letting her fingers do the feeling. Her hand wrapped around the plastic square of the spare battery. She pulled it down and checked that it was charged. She left the lab and went to find Sharif, who was now at his post.

'I need to get to the site quickly,' she told him. 'Can you take me?'

He nodded, and motioned towards the silver Land Cruiser parked by the side of the trailer that was used as an emergency vehicle. Because of the uneven, rough terrain, the drive took about four minutes and they pulled up in a swirl of dust.

Professor Webb looked up, spotted the jeep and waved.

'Quickly,' said the Prof, as she made her way over. 'Replace the battery. We need to record this.' He seemed agitated, pulling at his beard.

She thanked Sharif, who nodded, but didn't seem inclined to leave. He stood by the door of the jeep, observing. She could see Ahmer and Raza making their way to the dig too, curious about their discovery.

Layla walked to the KRS, which was positioned on a small boulder above the corner of the grid, and pulled out the battery cover. The plastic was hot from the sun, burning her fingertips. She replaced the battery quickly, eager to see what was happening in the grid. She checked that the green light flashed on the camera, indicating that it was transmitting. Then she moved towards the others.

There was a skeleton, partially uncovered. In its hands was a large copper box. The skeleton was resting peacefully, it seemed, in a burial pose, inside a metal coffin. Layla looked at it in surprise. The people of the region did not use coffins for burial, preferring instead to wrap their dead in cotton and bury them directly in the earth, as much of Pakistan still did. And yet here the skeleton was, in a coffin which was etched with lines and lines of the Indus Valley script. In life, the skeleton must have been somebody important. Liam would jump when he got back and saw the script on the coffin. No wonder everyone was excited.

'A female,' Kat suggested. 'Of childbearing age. See the hip bones? And look – can you see the discoloration and the fragmentation? This body was burnt before it was buried.'

Nobody said anything as she dusted along the edges of the copper box in the skeleton's hands, gently prying it out of the soil. When she eventually shook it loose, she placed it on the soil sifter by the boulder. She continued to dust off bits of grit and earth.

Layla strained to have a look, peering around the heads of the others. The box was covered in an intricate design. It depicted a woman, wearing a headdress of leaves – thirteen leaves to be precise; she knew there would be thirteen, she didn't have to count. They had learnt from pictographs, toys and carvings on other seals that the people of the region believed in duality, a mother goddess and a male deity who was often depicted with one horn. The mother goddess was worshipped and celebrated in rituals and by children, many of whom would have had a clay icon of her in their bedrooms. She was often seen wearing a headdress made of thirteen pipal leaves. As yet, they didn't know why.

She stared at the box. The goddess depicted on it was wrathful – something that Layla had never seen before. At her feet lay dozens of bodies, dead and dying – men and women and children, some pleading for mercy. The living were climbing on top of the bodies of the dead, their faces etched with misery. The goddess stared ahead, impassive. She was holding something, some sort of lump or tablet, in her outstretched arms. And from it came a ray of light, indicated by expanding, ever longer lines moving out from whatever it was she was carrying.

Layla caught her breath. The box was magnificent. She couldn't take her eyes of it.

'It's incredible,' Asif said, echoing her thoughts. 'Look at the copper, what a piece of craftsmanship. We knew they were wonderful metallurgists, of course, but this is something else. It would have taken real skill to indent those faces. Even the coffin ... I'd wager it's made of lead, wouldn't you? How curious.'

'We're definitely excavating in the right place,' Uwe said, positively beaming. He hugged Alaric, who smiled, but said nothing.

'What about the imagery,' said Warren excitedly, pointing and almost touching the box. 'This goddess is punishing her people. She's killing them. Is this a depiction of some sort of human sacrifice? I've always hypothesized that ...'

'Don't be absurd,' muttered Sara. 'They didn't kill their people. We've never come across anything to suggest that this was a culture of human sacrifice, even ceremonially. This was an egalitarian place, a place of wealth and prosperity.'

'We don't know what kind of place it was,' shot back Warren. 'We're learning new things every day. Kat, is there anything in there?'

'It's heavy,' admitted Kat. 'Look, it doesn't appear to have an opening or a latch, but there's a seam, see? We'll need to X-ray it in the lab, and then open it in a sterile environment, assuming there's a way.'

'Hang on now, let's just pause for a moment,' said the Professor. He cleared his throat. 'I need to make a phone call.'

Layla looked up, curious. The Professor should have been excited. Instead, he looked more than a little anxious.

He caught her staring and frowned. 'Layla, keep dusting the box. Get rid of as much sand from the carvings as you can. But with a light touch, okay? We don't want any damage.'

'Yes, Professor.'

He nodded, then scanned the horizon. 'The rest of you, get to work on exposing the remains of the woman and her coffin. I want the KRS to pick up some of the writing around her, it's clearly important. We can scan some images and send them to Liam at the Karachi Museum for analysis.'

'But Prof,' said Warren, looking confused. 'We need to get the box back to the lab and in a temperature-controlled environment as soon as possible. We don't want an exposure problem. Surely we can clean it up there? Plus, we need to set up a tent around the body. That will take half an hour or so. We'll never get her out before nightfall.'

She watched as the Professor walked some distance away and started punching numbers on his phone, ignoring Warren completely.

Warren looked at her and she shrugged. Pissed off, he walked to the skeleton.

Before she started, she checked the KRS. The battery was still green. Good. It was still on, the feed was live and going to the Indo Foundation. That must be who the Prof was talking to. She picked up a brush. Kat and Sara were already brushing the skeleton's right femur. Warren had started on the coffin with Asif, while Uwe and Alaric were dusting around the hands.

She looked at the box. There was just something so ... compelling about it. It was delicate, its bright copper glinting in the sun, hardly bronzed by its centuries under the ground. It looked like it would fit perfectly in her hands when cupped, although it was too large to carry in just one palm. It was amazing to think that she was going to be the first person to properly examine it. She began to dust around the corners of the goddess's face. She really was beautiful, the deity. There was a hauteur to her visage, an aloofness as well as beauty.

How on earth had they managed to convey so much? Dusting the box wasn't enough somehow. She longed to touch it. She really shouldn't – after thousands of years underground, it had been exposed to the sun, to the oils from Kat's hands.

And the carving was so fine ... But she couldn't resist. Idly, she trailed her fingers along the engraved surface.

She felt a jolt of electricity shoot up her arm. It hurt, causing her to breathe in sharply. What the hell? She looked around. Nobody seemed to have noticed. Everybody was busy with the skeleton, except the Professor, who was walking around the desert, muttering into his phone.

She stared at the box, at the carved figures, at the people who were begging for redemption from a goddess who demanded their fear as she gazed uncaring into the distance. Tentatively, she touched it again. This time, the metal almost burnt her fingers. Something long forgotten stirred inside her. A whisper drifted, somewhere so near that she could almost hear it. She had to open that box. *It's for me. All this time, it's been waiting for me.*

She blinked. Then she rubbed her eyes. What on earth was she thinking? Had she been out in the sun too long? Dehydration made people hallucinate, think crazy thoughts, didn't it? She should have gone in and retrieved her hat much earlier. She forced herself to focus. Live feed images were being sent to the Indo Foundation even now. She'd be fired for disobeying orders if she tried to open the box. She could destroy the whole thing if she was careless.

She moved the KRS so it could get a better angle of the box, trying to ignore the buzzing that had begun in her head. The box wasn't hers, for Christ's sake. It was antiquity and she had to protect it.

But even as she told herself that, the compulsion became stronger. The box. The goddess ... it *was* hers. She knew it, somehow. It was all meant to be hers. She had to touch it again. She had to open it. She couldn't stop looking at it. It was like a *hunger.*

'Stop dawdling,' said Warren, glaring at her. 'You're wasting time. The sooner we get it back to the lab, the better. Why is Prof still on the phone?'

She ignored him. She lifted the box off the rack. Her whole body felt like it was on fire. She'd never felt more alive. And she *burned.*

'Jesus, Layla, that's not funny. You could damage it,' Warren said, walking towards her.

Her fingers played against the grooves. It was almost as if they knew that the face of the goddess would give way when pressed, catching the latch and opening the box. How did she know? How did she know? Every muscle in her body was alight. *I have to open it. It's calling me.* No, that wasn't right. How could that be right?

The buzzing in her head grew stronger. She heard the latch click, and then opened the box with shaking hands. Inside, a jagged red rock. No ... not completely red. It had lines of black, like veins, running through it. Was it her imagination, or were those lines ... yes, they seemed to be pulsating. It should have been a surprise, but it wasn't. The rock that was not a rock ... it was *waiting for her.*

'Jesus Christ,' shouted Warren, from behind her. 'Jesus Christ, what is that thing? No, don't touch it, Layla, you could damage it ...'

But it was too late. She picked it up, she held it in both hands, the box now forgotten. For here was the thing. Here was the thing that had been waiting for her, all this time. She felt ... power. A strange kind of power, rushing through her body, setting it ablaze, every muscle, every sinew taut with expectation. Her mind tingled. An image rushed towards her, taking over, her thoughts somewhere else now. A girl, thousands of years ago, holding the stone exactly as she was doing, right here, right now. A girl with black plaited hair and sharp black eyes who desperately needed help, whose anger and fear stretched across distance and time. A girl who burned with the fire, just like she did now. The girl was showing her what to do. *Reach out, reach out, just like me. Draw from the stone. Feed it. Feed it, and then feel its power.* She lifted the stone in her hands and held it out to the sun. Somewhere at the back of her mind, she could hear Warren shouting at her, saying something urgently.

And then the screaming began.

Chapter Two

MELUHHA, 3800 BC.

A fly crawled across her eyelid.

Half asleep, Jaya blinked and the insect flew away. She turned to her side, her head resting on an outstretched arm, and closed her eyes again. Today of all days, she craved sleep. Let her dreams soothe her for a few more moments at least, before the waking world interrupted. She got comfortable once more, soaking in the smell of the damp earth, anxious for slumber.

But it was not to be. The sun inched its way up the river, light seeping between the leaves of the white mangrove tree under which she lay. She felt the heat on her face. And then that pesky fly was back, buzzing near her ear.

With a sigh of irritation, she sat up, shooing the fly away. She scratched at her chin, and then looked around. Mua was still sleeping, the leaves were denser where she lay, so she was still in the dark. Lucky Mua.

Jaya yawned, then stretched. She would let her mother rest. At least one of them should be refreshed for what was to come, though she knew, from the rustling sounds she had heard all night, that her mother had slept as fitfully as her. She stood up and carefully rolled her bamboo mat, brushing off bits of earth and leaves, and tucked it under her arm. She put on her sandals and headed for the river.

The day was crisp and the air was cool, while the water lapped playfully at her toes. She took a deep breath, enjoying the moment. The Indo river was magnificent at sunrise. There was a stillness to the morning, a calm tranquillity. The mist that hung low above the river this early in the day would soon be gone. Then the fishing boats would come back.

Across the bank, a trio of lawa trees stood so close together that they merged into one another, their lower branches skimming the top of the water in a continuous blanket of green. A cakk bird sat atop one of them, sunning her green and blue feathers, pecking occasionally at the wood. All around, the riverbank hummed.

She tried to calm her nerves. To think that today all this, her home, could be taken away from her ... She closed her eyes. She had to place her faith in Shakari, the Goddess who had blessed her family and her clan with good health and well-being for so many cycles. The river people were strong, though silent. And brave. So she would be brave too.

She pulled her deerskin pouch over her neck and placed it gently on a rock near the water, next to her mat. Then she unclasped her tunic and let it fall to the ground. She stepped into the water, gasping slightly at its coldness, and then felt it embrace her as it had always done. She swam – long, powerful strokes – ducking in and out of the water.

The river was her home. She knew its every turn and peculiarity. Just up the way, the bula – blind dolphins – swam in groups of five or six. They were always young, only a few moons old when they came to this stretch of the water, so close to the city of Meluhha. They lingered for much of summer, eating so much carp and prawn that the fishermen had to row further north to get their morning's haul. The river folk would never hurt the dolphins or prevent them from hunting. Dolphins were blessed by the Goddess. Besides, when the days shortened, the dolphins would move on, old enough to make their own way into the world.

She trailed her fingers along the water, making tiny waves, and then ducked her head under, ignoring the outside world. She continued to swim. She was careful to stay near the bank, far away from the lawa trees. Everyone knew that crocodiles rested under the shade of those leaves in the early mornings. They did not disturb the clan – after all, the clan worshipped them and fed them well – but they would become angry if she went into their territory. Only a moon ago, a little boy had taunted one by poking it with a stick. The boy lost an arm, and part of his shoulder. Amazingly, Meluhha's healers had been able to save his life, though his stump was often red and angry. She stayed on her side of the river.

Eventually, when her body felt fully awake and satiated, she rose from the water and sat on the rock. She hunted through her pouch. She had brought some peelu-tree oil with her, given to her by her father after his last visit to the city. She broke the seal of the little clay vial and rubbed the oil all over her body vigorously and through her hair. Then she lay naked in the sun, letting her skin absorb the oil.

When she was finished, she reached into her pouch for a small wooden comb, and furiously tried to detangle her messy dark curls, which refused to be tamed, no matter what she did. She cursed the One Horned God as she pulled and jerked. Today her hair had to look presentable. *She* would have to look presentable, if she were to be chosen. The combing seemed to go on forever, interrupted only by her curses and the cakk bird, who mocked her from the trees, making nasal-like utterances of laughter.

Eventually, she resigned herself to the fact that she would have to plait her hair, and put the comb away. It would have to do. There was only one thing left in her pouch, and she took it out gently. Her statue of Shakari, small, full-bodied, her belly swollen with the bounty she offered her children. Jaya kissed the icon's head and said a prayer. *Please let them Name me as one of them. I want to be a Crocodile. I was born in this clan, let me die in it also.*

Her fingers lingered over the statue for some time. Then she forced herself to put it back in the pouch. It was time to organize breakfast. She must pretend it was just another day, for the sake of her parents, if nothing else. She got back into her tunic – the new one, bought especially for the Clanning, was on the boat. She scanned the river. The boat wasn't back, though the sun had already risen well into the sky. Apa and Dar must not be having luck with fishing today, but at least it gave her time to light a fire and get things ready.

'What are you doing, child?'

Mala walked to the riverbank, her face still swollen with sleep, her tunic crumpled. 'You should have woken me. Today you are exempt from all tasks. You are supposed to be preparing yourself, remember?'

As though she could forget the Clanning. 'I know, Mua.' But what was the point of meditating when these could be her last few hours here, with her family? The thought made her stomach heavy with sickness.

Mala stroked Jaya's cheek absent-mindedly, then began to pick up pieces of firewood along the shore. It was always difficult, this close to the river, to find dry branches. 'Are you nervous, Jaya?'

'No,' she said quickly, so quickly that both of them knew that she was lying.

She felt her mother's gaze, but concentrated on picking up firewood. 'You should not be,' Mala said. 'We all go through the Clanning, and we are all terrified of being separated from our families. But in the end, these things are usually fairly straightforward. Clans choose their own, above anyone else, except in special circumstances. Besides, your father has already spoken to the Elders of the Crocodiles, and it has been agreed. You will be Named as one of us.'

She looked up, finding it difficult to believe her mother's words.

Mala smiled and stroked her daughter's hair. 'It's true. Today there will be celebration. Tomorrow, we will be back here, living together, as we have always done. Does that make you feel better?'

'The Elders have agreed to Name me? Already?'

'Yes.'

Jaya shook her head. 'But that is not possible, Mua.'

Nobody was allowed to make decisions about Clanning until the day itself came. Until the candidates were all inspected. Otherwise, it wouldn't be fair. 'What if there are other girls, better girls to invite to join the clan? We don't go into the city enough, we don't know how worthy others might be. They cannot choose us all. There are rules, quotas ...' She was aware she was babbling.

Her mother smiled at her sympathetically, even as she struck small pieces of flint and iron together to light the fire. 'The Crocodiles are not the most popular clan in Meluhha, as you have probably understood by now, Jaya, no matter how much we all like to claim otherwise and puff our chests with pride. We never exceed our quota in the Clanning – not like the Tigers who have their pick. Those who do not grow up with the smell of fish under their fingernails are not attracted to a life on the river.'

'But there are so many Unclanned, they would love a chance to take my place ...'

Her mother held up her hand. 'You are strong, healthy, and, since the last cycle, you're of breeding age. The clan Elders have known you since you were a child. There can be no objection.'

'Still, Mua, we cannot know for sure.'

Her mother sighed. 'So little patience, so little faith in Shakari or your family. It has been arranged. Trust me. Everything is possible with a little incentive.'

Jaya looked at her mother curiously. What exactly did she mean? Mala was concentrating on the fire, she seemed distracted. She did not want to talk any more.

Jaya heard rather than saw the boat first. Dar was rowing, the sail was down and he dipped his long oar in and out of the water with small, rhythmic splashes, the oar resting under the crook of his arm. Jaya jumped up excitedly. 'They are back, I will get started on the maize. I hope they have salted the trout.'

Dar waved as the boat pulled to the shore. 'You will not believe it!' he shouted. 'We met Haaes at the market. There is a rumour in the city. The Goddess-Blessed will join the Clanning today!'

His mother stood up and brushed her tunic. 'Don't be ridiculous. The Goddess-Blessed have not attended a Clanning for over thirty cycles, since I was but a babe. They breed their own. They are above politics and clans.'

Jaya's brother stepped down. He tied the boat to the trunk of the mangrove tree. It took some effort – the boat was large enough to sleep all of them and house their supplies and the river trout they bartered with. It was long and curved, with steep bows on each end, making it stable in the water, though heavier to pull. But Dar was barely out of breath. 'Hello Smelly,' he said, smiling at Jaya. 'I've brought you a present.'

He opened his palm. She couldn't help but stare. The brooch was beautiful, a circle made of beaten copper. 'Dar, what did you do? This must have cost you several weights worth. You cannot afford it!'

He kissed her cheek. 'But today is your Clanning. You must have something precious to remember it by. Besides, it will catch the eye of the Goddess-Blessed, and the Seer will pick you, without a doubt, to join them.' He winked.

Her face fell. 'But I want to stay here with you.'

'Tsk,' said her mother, eyeing the brooch with approval. 'Of course you do. But do you know what it means, Jaya, to be chosen by the Goddess-Blessed as one of their own? It means you will become a noblewoman. You will be elevated above all others. The city will bow and scrape, and obey your every whim.'

'I'd rather have the smell of fish under my nails,' Jaya muttered.

Her mother looked amused. 'It's just your brother being a Tuk Tuk again. The Goddess-Blessed never come to Clannings. Their own daughters are born in the way of Shakari – it is in their blood. Why do you think they are the only ones who can read the Bloodstone, and keep the city safe and prosperous? And even if they *did* come, if for some reason they have run out of daughters of their own, then every girl in the city will be vying for their attention. A Crocodile's daughter would have little chance, I'm afraid.'

Dar pushed her. 'Come and get your new tunic, Smelly. It is the softest cotton you have ever seen, you lucky cakk. Hurry, Apa is waiting up the river with the nets.' He held out his hand.

She climbed onto the boat, stepping over the barrels of fish, and bent double to enter the cabin where they kept their belongings and where they slept on cold winter nights, huddled together on their mats. It was cosy, with its assortment of fishing ropes and candles, clothing and blankets, the seeping wood smell that she recognized as home. It was all she knew. And then a thought struck her. 'Why is Apa not back? Why are you still fishing, Dar? It is past morning meal. You should be heading to the market soon, to barter. Why is the haul still outside? I've been waiting to cook the maize.'

Dar hesitated, and looked away.

'What is it, brother?' she asked, taking his arm.

'Nothing.'

But she knew him too well. Her brother would not meet her eyes as he rummaged through their possessions. Dar was strong, muscular and thickset, the bravest man she knew. Very little worried him. But watching his face ... it worried her as well.

'Tell me,' she insisted.

'They won't like it if I do. They don't want to burden you.'

'Well, now you have to tell me, stupid.'

He rubbed a sweaty arm across his face and considered. Eventually, he nodded. 'Apa has agreed to deliver a quarter of our fish to the Crocodile Elders as tithe each day, in exchange for their selecting you as clanswoman. We have so sworn, for a full cycle. It means we need to build more stock, otherwise what we have left will be too meagre to live on, once you take out the cost of the river tariff and clan revenues. So we will work a little bit harder, that is all.'

The pain in her stomach came back in that very instant. Her family had to pay to keep her in the clan? Did nobody want her here, then? Didn't she know all the Elders by name? She knew their daughters and granddaughters, their wives and their boats. She met them at the moorings, at festivals and at the fish market. Would she really not be chosen as one of them? 'Oh Dar, I knew something was wrong. I just knew it!'

'Calm yourself,' he said soothingly, placing a hand on her shoulder. 'This is the way things are done now. It has been thus for some time. You were too young when I was Named, to remember how difficult it was for Mua and Apa. But the Elders are not selfish men and women. They do what they must.'

'I don't understand.'

He handed her the new tunic, but she scarcely looked at it.

'It isn't really their fault. The Elders have to pay the priests a bribe. It is policy, ever since Iaf took over as the High One.' He spat contemptuously.

'Dar,' she said, shocked. 'He is the High One ... anointed by Shakari ... what you just did ... it is treason!'

'And who is going to tell the big man of it, hmm?' He moved to leave the cabin, but hesitated, then turned around. 'Do not get wrapped up in the affairs of Meluhha, Smelly. What use do simple fishermen have for politics and religion?'

'But ...'

'If we do not pay the Elders, then they cannot pay the priests. And then the priests will not let the clan Name any of us, and we will lose all our rights to the river. They'll probably let the Unclanned take our place. It is simply another tax, a way for Iaf and the others to make some money. The Elders take a cut too. But I suppose they would not be human if they didn't.'

'It's not fair,' said Jaya, her face flushed. 'We pay so much to the clan already. Are we being too eager, Dar? Should we not wait and first see what happens, before committing so much in tithe? I'm sure Anarki's parents are not paying.'

He shook his head. 'You really are an idiot sometimes. Anarki's family were the first to pay. They aren't taking any chances with their daughter. She is your friend, Jaya, and you know that she is sick often. Besides, she lay with Hams in fun, became with child and then lost the child. She is barren. There was always doubt about her suitability.'

She was horrified. 'They wouldn't. Her father is one of the most respected men in the clan!'

'And he has ensured that his daughter has a future. And now we have done the same. Even if you are smelly.'

'Stop it,' she muttered, punching his arm. 'It is not funny. Apa and Mua work so hard already.'

He wrapped his arms around her. 'And they will have both of us here to help in this burden, for the rest of their days. All at the cost of some fish. In one cycle, we will be free of this debt and we will be together, always.'

She hugged him back fiercely. 'Always,' she vowed. She would never let anything take her away from them.

Chapter Three

SANTA MONICA, PRESENT DAY.

Nadia's eyes jerked open. She felt her breath; quick, rapid, heart-fluttering, as she lay tense on the bed. The dream. Again.

She pushed away sweaty tendrils of hair and threw back the covers. She needed something to drink. Feeling her way in the darkness, her fingers found the glass of water on the bedside table. Her teeth clinked against the glass as she drank. She sighed with relief and slumped against the headboard. It was better now. It always took a minute or two, before equilibrium returned. *It was a dream, nothing more. I recognize it for what it was. It will come again, and it will go away. It was a dream, nothing more.*

She recited the mantra, over and over in her head, the way she'd been taught to years ago by the child psychologist she'd been forced to meet once a week after they'd pulled her out of the compound. The woman had done nothing but recite platitudes to a traumatized kid. Except this. This exercise had actually worked. Talking to herself, reassuring herself helped her calm down when her dreams became so vivid that they seemed completely real. In a moment, the lingering disquiet would subside and she would be okay.

It was amazing how often the dreams were coming now – the dreams about the young woman from the river. The woman she had always known.

Jaya.

For as long as Nadia could remember, Jaya had been a part of her world. Jaya existed so brightly and so vividly that she felt entirely real – her long black plaited hair, her dark brown skin over a narrow face. Sometimes, Jaya had a blunt, grey tattoo etched into the left side of her forehead, running past her eye. Other times, she would be a child, swimming in the river without a care. Jaya's life was like a movie, playing in the subconscious of Nadia's mind. And sometimes, on a few occasions, it was disquieting.

How she wished that Jaya's story was a fun meandering of her conscious mind – a way to be amused by her own thoughts – and her power to create, almost at will, an entirely different world and the characters that resided in them. But dreams about Jaya often brought on panic attacks these days, as they had done when she was a child. Jaya's life seemed fraught with moments of high stress. Jaya, or whatever part of Nadia's subconscious she represented, was often unhappy. Today's dream had been strange. One minute, Jaya was with her brother. And the next, well, all Nadia heard was screaming.

So much for years of therapy.

She took another sip of water, propped up her pillows and thought about the importance of dreams. Despite the ineffectualness of that pathetic child psychologist – Linda something or the other with the blonde frizzy hair – she'd tried many different types of therapy as an adult. Cognitive behavioural therapy, EMDR, even chanting in groups; the last one had reminded her too much of the Giving of Light Foundation and the compound, so she'd stopped after one session. Numerous shrinks had told her that Jaya was a coping mechanism, a way in which her own brain processed childhood trauma and post-traumatic stress. She preferred to think of Jaya as an old friend. Someone whose story she was now, finally, ready to tell.

Nadia put down the glass and pressed the palms of her hand against her eyes, still feeling disoriented. She looked at the red digital clock on her bedside table and grimaced – 4:53 a.m.

She took a deep breath and turned on the lamp. There was no way she would get back to sleep now. Her sheets were damp and ruffled, she smelt her sweat on them. Out of habit, she pulled out her little notepad and pencil from the bedside-table drawer. She started to write down the dream. It had become a part of her coping process, to keep a record. Writing was cathartic, her way of letting go. It soothed her. And recently, she had decided to write a novel about Jaya, to create something useful from her strange imagination.

Jaya is by the river. Today she is a girl, having to prove herself worthy of joining her family's clan. She has not become a Goddess-Blessed yet, though that happens soon, I think. Must try and work out the chronology of her life. Must also find a location for Jaya's story. Is she in another world? Am I going all Game of Thrones *with this one? Or some place in the distant past? Where should the novel be set? Somewhere real? Somewhere fictional? What time frame?*

When she finished jotting her thoughts, she put the pad back in the drawer. She would read the notebook later, maybe use some of the stuff she'd written down in the last couple of weeks to answer the questions she needed to tackle before she could structure the story. For a moment, Jaya's face lingered in her mind. The dark-skinned woman with the long black hair – hair which was almost always plaited so it rested down her back, her shoulders wide, her body lithe but strong. Jaya had a crooked front tooth and a striking, but hard face. She was not beautiful, but she was arresting.

Nadia yawned and stretched. The more she wrote about Jaya, the more the dreams came. Soon she'd have enough to put together a chronology of Jaya's life, to finish her character sketch and to start thinking about where the novel would be set. Nadia's last three novels had been horror, set mostly in the future. But this felt more historical ...

She smiled. Layla would know. Layla would find an ideal setting, a time and place. Her sister, the soon-to-be-qualified archaeologist ... She should call Layla so they could finally move on from that stupid fight. She'd tell her about this last dream. And Layla would come up with something insightful, she always did. And then she would say something ridiculously motivational, the kind of 'believe in yourself' speech that Nadia would roll her eyes at.

She looked at her phone on the table and bit her lip. It was amazing to think how closely she had reconnected with her sister, considering that Layla had called her out of the blue only four years ago. Layla had been seventeen then, and already so wise, so poised. She'd just left home, she'd said, having graduated early. Despite her mother's unhappiness at the idea, she wanted to get to know her sister, to connect with what little family she had. She was young, idealistic and desperately naive. Unlike Nadia, who, at twenty-four, was trying hard to get sober, already brittle and hardened by life. Layla didn't remember her childhood at the compound. She didn't really remember Nadia and she certainly didn't remember their father. Nadia, on the other hand, remembered the day Layla was born, the first time she held her half-sister in her arms, and how Sohail's second wife, Harriett, had given her the task of feeding the newborn. Nadia's heart had melted. What a joy it had been to have one person to love unconditionally, who asked for nothing in return, who needed her so much. Taking care of Layla was the only good childhood memory she had, though it had been short-lived when Harriett took the little girl and ran away. Her heart had ached for her sister, for many, many years.

There was a thump on her bed and Nadia blinked, surprised. Nelson pushed his fat, furry grey face in her direction and she half-smiled, stroking the cat behind its ears, enjoying the sound of his purring. Nelson had followed her home one day and she'd grudgingly decided to feed him until she could find someone to give him a proper home. He couldn't be with her, she didn't like being tied down. But Nelson looked as though he had been in the wars, with only one good eye and his left ear half chewed off. Nobody wanted him, especially since he was prone to biting on occasion. Even the animal shelter said they would have to put him down because of his age and his arthritic joints. And so they remained together. Nelson and Nadia. The misfits. The cat with no home and the girl with no family.

Well, some family ... She would call Layla and check on her, she decided. She would apologize for shouting at her because Layla had wanted to go to Pakistan to explore the Indus Valley, and even reach out to their father's family.

It would make her feel better to apologize. Over the last four years she had come to love her sister deeply. It wasn't Layla's fault that she only ever saw the best in people, and that she could barely remember Father or his insane cult. Those bastards at the Giving of Light Foundation were relentless. They were always trying to contact Layla to tell her about their father's teachings. They should have told her about his fists, instead. Instinctively, she let her fingers trail against her cheek, the one that had been swollen for many days after the first time he'd left his mark on her. How old had she been then? Six, maybe seven? It didn't matter now.

On her way to the kitchen in the half-light that signalled the coming of dawn, padding on naked feet in grey trackpants and a navy blue tank top, Nadia stopped by the glass patio wall that opened on to a balcony, looking out upon the Pacific Ocean. She couldn't see the waves, not yet. But she could hear the water lapping against the shore. It always soothed her. She loved this house. She'd worked damn hard for it.

She put out Nelson's food – canned tuna, he was very fussy – and turned on the kettle, ready for her morning cup of tea, a habit that over a decade of living in America hadn't been able to drum out, especially since she'd replaced her alcohol addiction with twelve cups of Lipton a day. It was ironic that everyone assumed her love of tea came from her English roots, even though it was her Pakistani father, and not her English mother, who had been obsessed with Lipton tea. He'd let her drink it from a very young age. At six, she had a morning cup before group affirmations, a small infusion mixed with a large amount of milk. How grown up she had felt back then, how much like Father.

The kettle whistled and she poured the water into her mug, lost in memory. Her father. Everything always came back to her father. Daddy issues. She had daddy issues. So said the shrinks and the counsellors during her two-year stint at juvie, and the good folks at AA. And half of her ex-boyfriends, of course. The ones that could spell the word father, at least. She rubbed her tired eyes again and stared out at the horizon.

Five years ago, when *Swamp,* her first novel, became a bestseller, Nadia's editor, Hank, told her it was time she did more publicity. 'People want to know about you. You're too young to be this successful, honey. Nobody likes that, it makes them jealous. You're a fairy tale, kiddo, and you seem too good to be true. And we both know that that's precisely what you are. There's nothing this town likes more than to bring people down, Nadia. Time to let the skeletons out of the closet, before others do it for you.'

She'd refused, of course, but Hank had been right. The Hollywood deal happened, *Swamp* became a blockbuster. And then? Then the media had destroyed her. Her whole life, open to scrutiny and criticism. The girl had been raised in a cult, they said. Her father, the one with the many wives, had got blown up in a gas leak. No wonder she wrote such weird things. So weird that the only people who understood her work were teenagers, who were themselves freaks, according to half the reviewers.

Nadia twirled the teabag listlessly in the mug. '*Swamp!*' was emblazoned across it in olive green, supposedly creepy, lettering. One of the things she'd picked up from the film set on those rare visits. She tried to keep a low profile as much as was possible. Sometimes she wondered if her books sold because of her writing or because her father had created the Giving of Light Foundation, which, for her young adult market, made her cool and mysterious.

Bloody GoL. What was it about her father, Sohail, that had inspired all the crazies of the world? Did none of them realize what a psychopath he had been? How was it that so many people had believed in him? He came across as so mild-mannered, so gentle and caring, when he was in public. And he had fooled them all.

GoL's philosophy was insane, but had the kind of simplicity that attracted people to their cause. According to them, human beings had existed on this planet for billions of years, long before recorded history. Advanced civilizations had been built, and then destroyed, and then built again, centuries before the time of the dinosaurs, but always brought down by greed and desperation. However, they believed that humans were capable of remembering their past, of accessing their collective knowledge to achieve great things. Some had already done so and were using that power to control others. Once the world woke up and remembered its great past, anything was possible. Disease would be vanquished, because people would remember how to self-heal. Famine would be ended, because humans would not require nearly as much food, their bodies would become more efficient. They would be able to fly simply by using the power of their minds. There was so much collective knowledge on this planet, it just had to be remembered.

Well ... Nadia remembered. She remembered those early days, the large, rambling farmhouse in Devon, always full to bursting with new recruits, who seemed to come from every corner of the globe. There was that Chinese couple who always smelt like sour cabbage, and the nudist from Canada. He was nice. He'd given her the book on Peter Rabbit, until her father Sohail had taken it away.

She remembered how Sohail's eyes blazed with fervour and his voice shook with passion as he talked about who really controlled the world, and why. It was the Ancients – humans who were born *remembering,* and therefore more evolved and powerful – who made decisions about which people in the world would live and who would die, which disease would run rampant and which would be cured, who would be president and who would be born to be a slave to television.

But soon, her father warned, the Ancients would be exposed, their knowledge shared with everyone, not jealously guarded, not used to control people. And on that day of liberation, the world would change.

And Nadia's mother, Deborah, would nod and sway, caught up in the power of his words, jacked up on crack, while Nadia cringed behind her mother's skirts and prayed that Father had the power to save them from those powerful, evil beings.

When Nadia was nine, Deborah left the compound, abandoning her child to run away with a heroin addict named Paul. Layla's mother didn't want to be saddled with another kid, and certainly not the daughter of Sohail's first wife. By then she was coming to her senses, and planning to take Layla away herself. So Nadia was left alone.

When the social worker had come and found her in the Basement, Nadia had cried so much, the tears seemed to burn into her skin. To this day she didn't know if it was more from joy or fear.

She watched Nelson slurp greedily through his tuna and told herself that one day, soon, she would stop thinking about the past.

She looked down. She was still swirling the teabag around. She threw it in the bin. Nelson finished his breakfast and perched himself on his favourite spot by the double doors of the balcony. Outside the window, the sun crept up the horizon in hues of dark orange and lilac. Nadia closed her eyes, wanting to rid herself of the memories, to be cleansed by the morning light.

It was the dream. It was that bloody dream that had somehow made her maudlin. She would call Layla. She would feel better. She checked her watch – 5:22 a.m. Just before sunset in Pakistan. A perfect time to call – Layla would probably be finished on the dig. She dialled, but Layla's cell went to voicemail. She contemplated leaving a message, but hesitated and then hung up.

Nadia padded across the hall and into her study, the cup of tea warming her palms. She turned on her desk light and sat down on her racing green leather chair, bought with a small part of the advance on her third novel, *Hellbound*. It was the only piece of furniture she had ever spent any real money on. She'd learnt, a long time ago, that life was uncertain, that it was no use clinging to possessions.

She looked at her watch again. She might as well do some writing, start thinking about where Jaya might be living, and why. Why was she in a clan? Why did she have to be chosen to be a part of them? Her hope was that by writing it all down, she would work out the answers and the dreams would finally stop. And once she stopped dreaming about Jaya, would she finally feel normal? What the hell was normal anyway?

She turned on her laptop and took a sip of her tea, enjoying the warm steam that rose up to her face. She listened to the computer whir into life in the quiet.

She heard the familiar ping of her email and watched the messages download on the lower right hand side of the screen. Her pupils instinctively followed the movement. Okay, well, she might as well check them now that she was here. She clicked on the icon and the first message flashed open.

Google Alert: Mohenjodaro.

Nadia frowned. She had created a Google alert for anything to do with her sister's project, so she could be up to date when she spoke to Layla. Had they made some amazing discovery already?

No ... nothing like that. She looked at the headline. It was a Reuters story about a missing archaeology team in Mohenjodaro, Pakistan. Her heart began to thud. Oh God. Layla. She could barely read the report, her head swimming. Something had happened. The article was vague. Nothing was confirmed yet, except that a YouTube video had been uploaded showing people dying. She read that bit again. Someone had uploaded a video of a group of archaeologists who had died while digging in Mohenjodaro. Nobody was commenting yet, the article would be updated as soon as there was further information.

She spotted the video square with the big white triangle at the end of the article. She clicked on it and watched the screen load.

The image was panoramic. There was Layla, standing in the middle of the site, looking dusty in a pair of blue trousers and a white shirt, wearing a straw hat. In the background, some other people were digging in the earth. Layla had something in her hand. It was difficult to see. A box, Nadia thought, she was opening it, and pulling something out – it looked like a rock or a sculpture. Layla seemed intent on whatever it was she was holding. A guy came up to her, a thin guy with a goatee, gesticulating madly – there wasn't any sound, but he seemed pissed off.

Layla ignored him and raised her hands. Just what the hell was in her hands? It looked red ...

Then there was a bright light. Something flashed and disturbed the camera, because it jerked and went black for a moment. Then it blinked back to life. Nadia couldn't see Layla any more, she wasn't in view.

But all hell had broken loose.

The guy with the goatee was jumping around as though there was something crawling in his underwear. Was it ... no ... that couldn't be right. The guy was on fire. There were actual flames licking his body and he seemed to be screaming, his mouth open in a silent O. Then he was melting, literally, on video. Nadia blinked, stunned. What was this? This had to be some sick joke.

Even as she told herself this, her heart almost exploded out of her chest. The guy was on the ground now, moving feebly with his elbows. He managed to move closer to the camera, he was trying to say something, while globs of flesh dripped on the earth. His body jerked, and then lay inert.

It seemed to Nadia that her heart had stopped entirely. She saw another woman on the left, swatting at her shoulders. Something must have bitten her, she was trying to kill an insect, she seemed so preoccupied. Only it wasn't an insect, because her shoulder caught fire and she looked panic-stricken. A man with a carrot-coloured beard rushed over to help her, and there, on camera, they both burst into flames. They danced, a sick kind of hip hop, clutching onto each other, before they too fell on the ground. An overweight blonde girl in a cowboy hat was next, her flesh literally melted off her bones. There were others, too indistinguishable to make out. The camera caught an arm here, a leg there. One of them must have hit the camera, because the angle turned so that only the ground was visible now.

There were bodies everywhere.

Bones. An eyeball, in the dirt, next to what appeared to be a dustpan and broom. A finger, someone's leg. And lots of lots of skulls and burnt shredded clothes in the distance. There was nothing intact except, in one corner of the frame, a single wicker basket.

The earth was black. Nothing moved. No, wait, that wasn't true. Because in the far distance, almost out of the range of the camera, there were two pairs of legs, two figures who seemed to be walking away. She paused the video and peered closely. One of them was wearing jeans and the other ... it looked like a pair of dusty blue trousers.

Oh God. Layla. Was that Layla walking away? If so, who was with her?

Nadia tried to take it all in. It was a joke. It had to be. People melting and screaming in the desert? It was like something she would write in one of her novels. There was nobody there, no catalyst for ... whatever this was. A terrorist attack? A poisonous gas of some kind? It couldn't be real. It just ... couldn't be real.

Numbly she picked up the phone and scanned her address book. She had the number of Layla's roommate in London somewhere in there. Jay ... what was his last name again? Her fingers fumbled as she skimmed through her contacts. She thought about throwing up but forced herself to concentrate. She found him at last, under Jay Roommate. She called.

He picked up on the first ring. 'Hello?'

'Jay. It's Nadia. Layla's sis ...'

'Nadia. Thank God. I didn't have your number. I've been trying to call your agent, and of course you don't do social media ...'

'What the hell is going on, Jay?' Was this really her voice? She sounded so shrill.

'It's ... I don't know.' He seemed panic-stricken. 'All the archaeologists are missing, they won't tell us if they are dead or not. Nothing official is being said. There were guards too, some local boys who ran errands, and a driver. They haven't told us what happened to any of them. Did you see the video?'

'Yes. Hang on, I just want to be certain ...' Nadia played the video again, trying to make sense of what she was seeing. A brief image of Layla, holding a box, and then a bright light, and then people catching fire. And then, yes, she could see it, just a glimpse, two figures, their legs anyway, in the top right of the frame, walking away at the end. It was over in 1.23 minutes.

She took a deep breath and tried to think rationally. 'Even if this is real, Layla isn't there, is she? I mean, except at the beginning. Maybe she's the one who is walking away. Did you see that? Did you see the two figures, the legs in the corner?'

Jay's voice began to shake. 'She's unaccounted for. They all are, until we get official word. She ...'

'What? What?'

'Well, I spoke to Professor Webb's wife earlier. She was in total shock, but she told me ...'

'Told you what?'

'She told me that they think that maybe Layla is the one who killed everyone.'

Chapter Four

SANTA MONICA, PRESENT DAY.

It took ten minutes to book her flight online, and another twenty to pack her duffel bag, call a cab, pound on her neighbour's door and beg Lennie to feed Nelson, and to gulp down two more cups of tea so quickly that she burnt her tongue. The phone rang, but she ignored it.

Nadia grabbed some Tylenol on her way out, her head was pounding hard. She had almost locked her door when she realized she had forgotten her travel documents. She rushed back into the house, shoved her burgundy British passport into the back pocket of her jeans even as she reached the front door. Screw it, whatever she left behind she would replace.

The phone was still ringing. Someone relentless. She hesitated, but then strode towards the kitchen, where the handset sat on the wall by the fridge. It could be news about Layla. The line was bad, plenty of fuzz and crackle.

'Yes?'

'Nadia?'

'Yes. Speaking.'

'This is your grandmother.'

And here she was, thinking the day could not get any more shocking.

'Are you there, Nadia?'

'What do you want? How did you get my number?' She felt heat spread across her face.

'Have you heard about your sister?'

'Yes, from someone who actually cares about her.'

'There's no need to take that tone ...'

'There's every need. Don't call me again.'

'Wait.' Her grandmother sounded desperate. 'You don't understand. I think you could be in danger.'

She gripped the phone tightly. She wasn't going to play this woman's game, not now. If Jahanara was even a fraction as manipulative as her son – and there was every reason to believe that she was – then everything that came out of her mouth was a lie. 'Even if that were true, you made it clear that I wasn't your problem a very long time ago.'

'It was for your own good, Nadia. There's so much you don't understand ...'

'Don't call me again,' she said and hung up.

She raced out of the house, down the stairs and into the waiting taxi. 'Hurry,' she said. 'We get there in time, I'll pay you double.'

The cabbie saw the expression on her face, nodded and turned on the engine. As he reversed out of the driveway, she sat stunned. After all these years ... her grandmother ...

But there was no time to think about that now. She made a mental list of all the things she would have to do once she got to London. She'd need to talk to Scotland Yard and to the intelligence agencies that were bound to be involved. What exactly had happened? She tried to google more information, thought about calling Hank and finding out about expensive private detectives. Was Layla even alive? No ... she couldn't think like this. Layla had to be alive.

Her cell phone rang, she was tempted to toss it out of the window. Then she saw the UK number and exhaled. 'Jay?'

'Your flight's on time?'

'So far.'

'I'll pick you up from Heathrow.'

'There's no need. I can get a cab.'

'Nadia, you should know. A journalist just left a message on our answerphone. He wanted to know if Layla was your sister ...'

'Bloody bastards!' She didn't mean to shout. She saw the cabbie's eyes slant back at her from the rear-view mirror. 'Sorry.' She raked her fingers through her hair.

It was inevitable that, even though they had different surnames – Nadia had chosen to adopt her mother's maiden name as soon as she turned eighteen – some journalist would find out that she and Layla were related. And if one of those leeches had figured it out, the others wouldn't be far behind. She couldn't believe how fast this thing was unravelling. Missing archaeologists may have melted to death, but one of them was connected to her, Nadia Osbourne, the girl who wrote horror novels and whose father had started that weird cult. The last thing she needed was for the media to reignite that fact; it would take away from finding her sister. Even worse, they would start blaming Layla for whatever had happened simply because of who her father was. It looked like they already were.

'What do you want me to say to them, Nadia?'

'Nothing, please. Say that you have no comment. Don't do their dirty work for them. If they want to find out the truth, they'll have to do it on their own.'

The taxi pulled onto the main road. Nadia spent the next few moments strategizing with Jay, her mind whirring. They passed a man jogging on the path outside her driveway, but she barely noticed.

The man was blonde, muscular and in his thirties. He had a pleasant, well-rounded, ruddy sort of face. He was dressed in a smart blue tracksuit, one which blended in nicely with all the other joggers in the neighbourhood. He bent down to tie the laces on his Nike shoes, and then straightened and leisurely checked his Hugo Boss chronograph watch. He waited for the taxi to disappear around the corner. Then the man stretched and jogged to Nadia's driveway, made his way up the steps leading to the front door. He spent nine seconds playing with the latch until he felt it click into place. He smiled and let himself in.

A couple of hours later, the man made a phone call on a secure line.

'Well?' asked his current employer.

'There's nothing, it's clean. I don't think anyone's contacted her,' he replied, enjoying the view of the ocean.

'The girl?'

'I hacked her email. She's on her way to LAX. Going to London. Chasing up on the sister.'

'Follow her. Report back. I want to know who she sees and what she does. Someone's going to make contact, I'm sure of that. And then we'll know who leaked the video.'

'Understood.'

'Good. And Philip?'

'Yes?'

'Don't get carried away. She's not one of your playthings.'

'I'll touch base with you when I'm in London,' said Philip, as he eyed the books sitting in the shelves on the wall in her study. So many of them were about the evils of cults, about how to help people who had been 'indoctrinated'. Hardly surprising, but so disappointing, an indication of a very simple mind. He wandered around. He liked to get a sense of who a person was, when he was doing a job. It made what happened next all the more enjoyable.

This woman was a loner. There were very few personal touches in the apartment, very little to get excited about. The front of her fridge was bare, no magnets, no reminders, no photographs or to-do lists. The living room looked like it was never used, and the bedroom could at best be described as functional. He picked up a photo of the woman from a table in the hallway. Nadia Osbourne, sitting cross-legged on her balcony, dressed carelessly in cut-up denims and a loose white blouse, cuddling a mangy cat. Her dark hair was long and windswept, and curled nicely, reaching just below her breasts. Her cheeks were pink, her amber eyes sparkled, her nose was just crooked enough to still be attractive and her body seemed limber and lean. Philip smiled. Eventually, this job would bring him many perks. He would just have to be patient. He sat down in Nadia Osbourne's kitchen, phoned for a taxi to the airport and helped himself to a cup of tea.

Chapter Five

MELUHHA, 3800 BC.

The Clanning took place in the main market square, at mid-morning. Not for the first time, Jaya was grateful that they had set out so early to walk to the city. At the gate was a throng of people. Families like theirs had come from neighbouring farmlands and from the river. The children of Clanning age looked nervous and uncomfortable in the shadow of the high, imposing walls of Meluhha. No doubt, like her, they wondered what Shakari had in store for them.

The younger ones seemed more oblivious, running in and out between the legs of the adults, jostling against each other and rolling in the dirt, much to the annoyance of their parents. A group sat on their haunches playing Korkey. A boy, of seven or eight, threw the dice. Then he slapped his head and groaned. He had just rolled a two which automatically disqualified him from the rest of the game, much to the joy of his opponents.

Jaya looked on, curious. The Crocodiles never played games of chance, or gambled in any way. They preferred to lead simpler lives. She had never had an opportunity to play, and yearned suddenly to join the younger children. To be free of all burdens.

But even if she had been allowed, she was conscious that her headdress was easily damageable. Her mother had worked on it for many days, folding strips of keeka leaves tightly around tree vines, interlaced with poppy flowers and bright red berries. Like many in the clan, they could not afford to buy a ready-made headdress and had to make their own. But hers was tight and restrictive. And, she realized with horror, as she watched a farm girl walk by in a headdress decorated with gold-leaf bindings, inadequate.

The wait was long. There were many merchants ahead of them, richly attired in silk and cotton tunics, arriving to sell their wares for the celebrations. They seemed to be irritated at being stuck outside the gates in the peak of the summer heat. They grumbled to one another as they chewed shisa and spat it onto the roads. One of them, a man driving an ox cart loaded with necklaces, shells and beads, cursed as his wheel got stuck in the mud. He jumped out, whipping his buffalo. But the creature seemed not to care, lazily swatting a fly with its tail. It caused delays – behind him a caravan laden with fresh mangoes and dates jerked to a halt.

'In the name of Shakari, get a move on, before I invoke the One Horned God on you,' shouted an angry farmer. Others became involved in the dispute, hurling insults as they waited to enter the city. There was the usual splattering of languages – the rich, soft tongue of Meluhhan, intertwined with the more lyrical dialect of Arrapha, and the harder, coarser mutterings of Dilmun. People from around the known lands came to live in Meluhha, from as far away as Chanu and the North Mountains. It was the greatest city in the world, Jaya knew. She was overwhelmed by it, on the rare occasions that she had been allowed to visit.

They reached the gate at last. A Temple guard checked their seals – her father first, then her mother and then her brother, who wore their clan membership on ropes around their necks. Their clan seal was long and rectangular, unlike most of the others in the city, which tended to be square. It depicted a crocodile eating a bird and above it the name of the seal holder, and the name of the Elder who had Clanned them.

The Crocodile clan were allowed free access to the city until nightfall. After that, they were only permitted to enter certain streets and territories. A Crocodile may have use for the whorehouses, or the Street of Curse Breakers, but what purpose would he have in entering the Citadel, the residence of the gentry? The Tigers, predominately merchants, were the only clan who could go wherever they pleased, as could the priests and Goddess-Blessed, of course.

The Temple guard reached for her seal, and then half smiled when she shrugged at him. 'I have none, I am here for the Clanning,' she muttered, embarrassed.

'Nice headdress.' He smirked, before turning to the family behind them, holding out his arm to stop them for inspection. Jaya and her family walked through the gate.

There was more commotion inside. A group of men were being physically pulled away from the crowd by some guards. A woman was weeping, clutching her child, begging for the return of her husband, who was among the group.

'They must have been begging. They are Unclanned,' muttered Dar, as they were pushed along with the tide of people, the woman already behind them. 'Immigrants, no doubt. As if we didn't have enough of them already. I don't know why the priests allow all our territories to send their downtrodden here, as though we have room for them. Well, they can't clog up the entryways. Not on such an important day.'

'But they can join the Clanning, like the rest of us, can they not?'

Dar frowned. 'They have joined in the past, though few of them are ever selected. The ones with strong backs, perhaps, are sometimes chosen by the Buffaloes to carry bricks and timber – but there is very little building work being commissioned in the city under Iaf's tenure. Sometimes, the younger girls join the Rhinoceros clan, if they are beautiful enough.'

Though she did not know anybody in the Rhinoceros clan, Jaya knew that the clan owned the Street of Dancers and the whorehouses. It was said that the Rhinos only took the most striking and cleverest of women to be concubines. 'It must be a hard life,' she said, careful to avoid stepping on some buffalo dung on the ground.

'Pay attention there, nobody will choose a girl with shit on her sandals. Yes, hard, but at least the girls in the Rhino clan are guaranteed a hot meal at the end of the day, which is more than you can say for the Unclanned. They are lucky to get the odd jobs they do, and that's without clan wages.'

'Lucky,' she agreed, distracted by a family who was pushing past her, anxious to get ahead, the boy looking determined and terrified at the same time, his headdress already slightly askew.

Dar glanced at her sharply. 'Don't feel sorry for the Unclanned, Jaya. They don't respect our traditions and they don't make any effort to learn our ways. The clan system is here for a reason. It makes us all equal, it offers us protection. If I fall ill tomorrow and I am unable to work, the Crocodiles will always pay me a ration of their earnings. That is why the clans are so important. Those who are Unclanned are not worthy enough to earn a place amongst us.'

She had heard it all before, many times. But it didn't help the sickness in her stomach, or the fluttering in her heart. She had to concentrate on the Clanning, not on politics.

But they were interrupted, just then, by an old woman. She placed her body between them and the family ahead. She must have been at least fifty.

'You are here for the Clanning, yes?' The woman was thin and gaunt, her hands twisted and gnarled. Her grey hair was wild and knotted. She wore a necklace of chicken bones over a dirty tunic. Jaya tried to pull back, but the woman had gripped her hands and would not let go. 'Yes ... the Clanning. I see now. You are a beautiful one, aren't you, dearie? For one cube's worth of copper, I can call upon the powers of Shakari and her children. I can cast a spell so that you are chosen by every clan in the city, my lovely. What is one copper piece for such a precious outcome, eh?' She stroked Jaya's hands and winked. 'Take your pick of 'em. Choose the Tigers, they'll give you a life of luxury or them Rhinos, if you want to spend a lifetime on your back.' She laughed. Jaya flinched. The woman was making her skin crawl, but would not release her.

It was her father who stepped in this time. 'Get away from her, Soothsayer. We want nothing to do with your magic.' Tur'un looked furious, his strong face dark and angry.

The woman snarled, but dropped her hands. 'So be it then, old man. But be warned. Without my help, your daughter is destined to a life of misery. What is one cube of copper to save her from that fate, dearie?'

Her father laughed. 'One of your kind said the same thing to me when I was being Clanned, many cycles ago. I didn't pay then and I won't pay now. Go back to the Street of Curses where you belong.' He pushed her, to move her along.

The woman hissed, and disappeared in the crowd.

Jaya felt ill, and leaned against her father. 'It's all right,' he said gruffly, patting her shoulder. 'There are all kinds in the city. We'll be home soon enough, my girl.'

They left the chaos of the entrance and headed to the main market, following the wide streets and the direction of the slow-moving crowd. There was a bottleneck at the entrance of the square. They had to show their seals once again. A Temple guard blocked the way, looking tall and imposing in his black-and-orange sarong, holding a sharp spear. 'Only those participating in the Clanning may enter the square,' he informed them irritably. 'The rest of you should go find seating, if you can, on the rooftops.'

Mala looked anxious for the first time, scanning the lines of people waiting to climb ladders and step onto the roofs of houses, and of the Tiger storerooms and granaries surrounding the square. 'But it is so busy! We want to be able to see our daughter be Named.'

'So does everyone else,' the guard said. He seemed harassed, motioning for another girl to pass by. Then he looked at Jaya and sighed. 'Look, go find a Tiger merchant. Offer him a copper weight or two, and he will make sure you have a good view. It's their market, after all. But if you can't pay, there's nothing I can do about it.'

The next few moments passed in a haze of hurried goodbyes, of her mother hugging her so tightly that she couldn't breathe, smelling of the river and the earth, of her father patting her head awkwardly, and of Dar smiling and winking, reminding her that her new clasp would be the envy of all. She was aware then of her family disappearing, of being pushed into the market square, its regular shops closed to make more room. There were girls and boys everywhere, trying to get their bearings.

Girls and boys. When they left here, they would be Clanned. And they would be men and women with their own bread to earn, and their own futures to make. If Shakari was willing to bless them with her bounty, that is.

She looked around. There were some priests, dressed in traditional orange-and-black robes with swirling patterns, their heads shaven, moving everyone into lines. The boys stood on the left, the girls on the right. She found herself in the second row, and craned her neck, looking for Anarki, or her other friend, Mela. She could see neither. The sound of a fruit vendor shouting about his wares obscured most of the noise in the square. In the distance, she could just make out the figures of family members scrambling onto the rooftops.'Name?' A priest stood beside her, looking expectantly. Beside him was a scribe, a small, unblinking man holding a tablet of fresh clay and a long copper wire.

'Jaya, daughter of Tur'un, of the Crocodiles.'

The scribe began to record her name but the priest looked her up and down, and pursed his lips. 'Another Crocodile. You people breed like rats. There must be something potent in those fish of yours.'

She was unsure of how to respond, so she said nothing.

He simply smirked and moved on. 'Name?'

Her body slumped with relief. Nobody had prepared her for how difficult this was going to be! Was that part of the test, to see how she would react? She could not see her parents or Dar on the roofs, the glare of the sun preventing her from making out any features. She started to sweat, her headdress weighing her down. The girl next to her ignored her and stood tall. Nobody seemed to want to talk to one another, to compromise themselves in any way at this critical moment.

And then something was happening. She could tell by the way that the line seemed to suddenly straighten itself, by the hush of the crowds and the stamping of feet against the brick ground. The Temple guards were marching into the square. Iaf had come.

She had never seen the High One before, except from the little statuettes they sold in the market, but here he was, surrounded by his priests, all of them wearing robes of perfectly pressed orange stamped with swirling patterns of black. The priests had red pigment on their palms and on their foreheads. The pigment, she knew, symbolized their devotion to the Bloodstone and Shakari. Jaya shivered. They looked pale and imperious, as though they had never been kissed by the sun.

Iaf walked to the wooden platform at the head of the square. It was wide enough for a dozen people or so to move on freely. Even Jaya, with her limited knowledge of the city, knew that at night, the dancing girls came here to sell sexual favours. They were famous in all the known lands. The dancing girls moved their bodies provocatively, their bangles tinkling in the moonlight as they showed off their wares. People came from all around to offer money to bed with them. It was a symbol of a person's stature, to have lain with a dancing girl. They gathered so much wealth that they retired young, enjoying a life of leisure. In the light of the day, the stage was used by visiting theatre troupes, performers and jugglers.

But not today. Today there was Iaf, climbing onto the platform. He was a tall man. Tall and thin, with a wispy beard. Still, he commanded attention. A simple raising of his hand and the entire square went still.

He spoke quietly, and yet, it seemed to Jaya that everyone could hear him. 'Welcome, brothers and sisters of Meluhha. We come together, as we have done for hundreds of cycles, to celebrate the Naming of our children into our clans. It is an auspicious event, symbolizing the continuity of our city and its prosperity. Let us pray to the Goddess, and to her children, and ask her to bless us in our efforts today.'

The entire city clapped their hands once, and then brought them together against their chests, as Iaf led them in worship. 'Seven hundred cycles ago, there was a great battle in the sky, and the Goddess Shakari was flung down to the land, wounded by the One Horned God and his followers. The One Horned God burned with anger. Shakari had spurned his advances, and he punished the people here, the people who she loved and who loved her back, by burning the land and drying its rivers.'

He paused, his eyes sweeping the crowds. 'Only one woman dared to help Shakari against such evil and tended her injuries in secrecy. That woman was Meluhha and we praise her name, just as we praise those who will be Named today.'

He raised his hands. In perfect synchronicity, the city responded, raising their hands and then bringing them together once more in a single clap to their chests.

Jaya stood still, hands on her chest, her eyes trailing the crowd as the people listened to Iaf, enthralled. The ritual had a rhythm of its own. And Iaf was the best of storytellers, the way he paused in the right places, the way he looked at his audience as though imploring them to listen. She couldn't help but stare. She would never stand so close to the High One again. What an honour it was!

The tale of Meluhha and the Goddess was as old as the city itself. It was repeated at every Clanning, and at every Feast Day. Children learnt the story while they were still being weaned on their mothers' breasts. And yet, today, the people listened as though they had never heard it before, clapping as though for the first time.

Jaya knew the tale as well as she knew her own mind. Meluhha was a young girl whose village was starving. There was a drought. The wild boar, tigers, asses, peacocks and jackals had starved long before, and the great Indo River had dried up. Crops had shrivelled and died in the heat. People were fighting one another for scraps of food. Only the strongest survived, preying on the weak. Some left the village, preferring to walk across the great desert, to die trying to find food, rather than be slaughtered by those more powerful.

And then, suddenly, came the Great Battle. The sky opened up. Gods and goddesses came to the land of men. They fought each other, giants in the clouds, throwing lightning bolts and burning stars across the sky. The One Horned God was furious that the Mother Goddess, Shakari, had spurned his offer of marriage, and had begun the war. He had turned his fury on to the other immortals, and on the people. He captured Shakari, and stabbed her with a lightning bolt. Shakari fell like a stone from the sky, into the hollow trunk of a pipal tree, where thirteen leaves obscured her from his furious gaze.

While the rest of the village cowered in fear, Meluhha raced to the Goddess's aid. She tended to her wounds and offered her friendship. She hid her from the One Horned God, even as her own family starved. She watched them die, one by one, and though it broke her heart she would not give up the Goddess.

Without Meluhha, Shakari would have been returned to the One Horned God, whose wrath was insurmountable. And so when the Goddess finally healed, she gave the villagers a great gift in gratitude. She Named them. Before she travelled back to the Upworld, Shakari created the clans. Men and women were divided into groups and given powers of their own. The Tigers were given cunning, to master their enemies, and the Jackals were given wanderlust, so they might explore the great lands and bring back knowledge and bounty to the village. The river was given to the Crocodiles, who could communicate with it, and understand its rhythms. The Buffaloes were given superhuman strength, the Peacocks great skills as artisans, and the Cobras were given bravery and the desire to protect others. Each clan had a particular talent, ensuring that everyone was equally powerful, that everyone worked for the benefit of the whole. That way, there would never be disagreement again, and nobody would be stronger or weaker than anyone else. Together they would prosper, Shakari told them. But without each other, they would die.

To Meluhha herself, the Goddess gave a very special gift, a gift beyond imagination. Shakari took out a piece of her own heart. She gave her the Bloodstone.

The Bloodstone gave Meluhha the ability to see the future and to know the world's secrets. By using its power, Meluhha helped her village prosper. They escaped many raids from warring tribes and planned their crops around the rains. They knew which lands were rich with boar, and when the crocodiles would leave the banks of the river, ready to be speared for their meat.

As Meluhha had daughters, they too, used the Bloodstone to predict the future, although their powers were not as strong as hers. Meluhha helped them. She taught them how to see with new eyes, and they, in turn, taught the daughters that followed, who became the first Goddess-Blessed, the first among all the clans in the village. The most important clan.

In order that the Goddess-Blessed could do their work, to predict the future without interruption, Meluhha's sons were anointed as priests to help them apply their visions and protect them and the people from the One Horned God, who grew more and more angry with those who had helped Shakari, and tried as much as he could to bring back drought and war upon them.

Meluhha lived to be over three hundred cycles old. When she died, the people were overcome with grief. The village had become a thriving city-state, and it was renamed in her honour. In other lands, kings and despots ruled their people with iron fists. In Meluhha, all were equal. The clans ensured it was so.

Over time, with the Bloodstone's help, the people learnt to bake bricks, to become architects, to understand geometry and develop fire technology. They wrote poetry and created music that astounded and mesmerized the known world. Then they built boats that could sail far into the seas and began to prosper through trade. Their knowledge superseded that of any other known land.

One summer, Meluhha's descendants, the Goddess-Blessed, told the people that a great plague was coming, one which could only be avoided by strict cleanliness. And so wells and baths were built across the city and in every household. The city heard, some moons later, that many in Dilmun and nearby towns had perished from sickness. But not Meluhha. The Bloodstone had warned them of what was to come. From that day, Dilmun agreed to pay an annual tithe to Meluhha in exchange for knowledge of any catastrophic event which would come in the future.

The Purification baths were built as a symbol of Meluhha's new power, in gratitude of the Goddess, next to the Temple. The baths allowed the Goddess-Blessed to honour Shakari, the Great Mother, with water rituals. None of the other city states had such powers or rituals. Many were envious. But most agreed to pay tithe to the great city, in exchange for its protection and its warnings of the future.

After two hundred cycles, the city grew crowded with nearly fifty thousand mouths to feed. Following the advice of the Seer of the Goddess-Blessed, a woman who saw great cities being born around the Indo, the people moved far and wide, and built towns of their own, like Chanu and Arrapha, always remaining under the guidance of the priests, always paying an annual tithe to Meluhha for its help and protection. The priests brought forth peace and harmony to all the lands, as they would always do, Iaf was now saying. They would always care for the welfare of the people. Even the Unclanned would always be given food in Meluhha at any of the free food stalls down by the Street of Boat Makers.

'And so we live in gratitude to Shakari, for all her blessings upon us. Today, we continue to keep faith with her by Naming our children into the clans that she once created,' Iaf said, finally lowering his hands.

Jaya felt sick in the heat. Her headdress was too heavy and she was sweating profusely. She dropped her hands to her sides with relief.

There was some murmur on the wooden platform and then the clan leaders were called forth – thirteen clans to symbolize each leaf of the pipal tree which hid Shakari from the One Horned God. Twelve clans were represented today. The thirteenth, the Goddess-Blessed, were born into their clans and did not embrace newcomers.

The leaders of each clan left the platform and stepped into the square. They were mostly male and elderly, save a few. Each of them wore a headdress representing their clan's power. The leader of the Buffaloes was well muscled and young, and wore a headdress made of buffalo skin. The head of the Cobras – the clan which served as Temple guards – wore a headdress depicting a set of serpent fangs. There were two women, the leader of the Rhinoceros clan, who wore a turban of silver and gold, and had bangles going down the length of her arms, and the leader of the Asses –

the clan of the scribes and teachers – who was a plump, white-haired woman with a headdress made of donkey hair.

The priests walked along the lines of girls and boys, placing bowls at their feet. Jaya's pulse began to race. This was it. The clan leaders would now inspect the candidates. This was the moment. If they liked her, they would place a coloured stone in the bowl in front of her. If not, they would walk past. If, by some miracle, she had more than one stone in her bowl at the end of the day, then she would be able to choose which clan to join. But if she had none, then she would have to leave her place at the river and fend for herself without a home or a family.

The marketplace fell silent. The leader of the Buffaloes, Al-Zenn, came first, his arms resting casually on his hips. He walked along the lines of the boys, inspecting slowly, asking one or the other to step forward as he examined their bodies and pressed on a muscle or two. She watched several boys slump with relief as he pulled purple-painted stones from his pocket and dropped them into their bowls. Others stood more rigidly, becoming anxious as he passed them by without so much as checking their teeth.

He then moved to the other side of the square, unhurriedly. Jaya watched as he walked by the first line. The girl in front of her stiffened as Al-Zenn leant forward and squeezed her breasts, and then her stomach.

'Are your bleeds regular?' he asked her. She nodded. 'Have you laid with a man yet?' She shook her head. 'I have only had my bleeds for two cycles,' she replied shakily. He pulled her chin to the side, examining her neck and head. Then he put his hand between her legs and stuck his fingers inside her, feeling, as she tried to stand still against the onslaught.

Eventually, he seemed satisfied, nodding to himself. He wiped his hands on a piece of cloth, and dropped a purple stone into her bowl. He moved on. Jaya sucked in her breath when he reached her, but he barely gave her a second glance as he walked by. She didn't know if she felt relief that the man's hands would not be inside her, or trepidation that she did not have a stone. Some of the girls he smiled at, and placed purple stones in their bowls immediately. Clan girls, obviously.

It went on like this, throughout the day. The Asses were next, the Elder was the woman Hessa. She asked the assembled group many questions about their ability to read and write, but did not conduct any physical examinations. Anyone who could read the clay tablets from Dilmun, Magan and the Northlands, or write the scriptures of Meluhha was chosen, even the girl with the club foot in the corner, who had been shaking with anxiety up until then. The Jackals came after. The Elder was a man named Jaezead. He wanted to know about how many languages each candidate spoke, how long they had ever gone without eating, and then gave them each a problem to solve. To Jaya the clan leader asked a stupefying question. 'What would you do, girl, if you were part of a caravan travelling east through the desert and a violent dust storm came from the south? But from the north, a band of brigands were riding Magani horses trying to intercept you, anxious for your supplies? What if the way to the east was suddenly blocked, leaving only the west, where you had come from, open? Where would you go?'

She hesitated. 'I would turn back and go home,' she said at last. 'It would be the safest option.' The man looked disappointed and walked away.

What, she thought, was the answer to such a riddle? How was she supposed to make herself sound intelligent with such difficult choices? She closed her eyes and prayed. Please let it be over soon.

Much to her shock, the head of the Rhinoceros clan, the woman Annaba, stopped in front of her. 'When you close your eyes,' the woman said softly, 'you miss the most important things in life. What is your name?'

'Jaya, daughter of Tur'un, from the Clan of the Crocodiles, Lady.'

The woman smiled. 'You are far too beautiful to be a fisherman's daughter. That's a pretty clasp.' And with that, Jaya received her first stone. It fell into her bowl and swirled around, bright red, before settling at the bottom. The woman had already moved on.

My blessings upon your children, Great Mother. Even though she would hate to sell her body at a whorehouse or dance in front of strangers, at least she now had a future.

Things got better after that. Jarun, head of the Crocodile clan, smiled gently as he placed a blue stone in her bowl. And, after she was able to successfully guess at the ingredients that would go into a poultice to stop a putrid wound from seeping, she received a green stone from the clan of the Cranes, who apparently had very few candidates of their own this cycle, and needed to fill their quota from elsewhere. The Cranes were healers. If she had not been selected as a Crocodile, she would not have minded joining their clan instead.

The day wore on. The lines relaxed as futures were decided. She could see a few of the boys become cocky, their bowls full of stones. Jaya longed to turn around and look for Anarki. If her father had truly paid the Crocodiles, she would be fine.

Sunset came and then it was over. All twelve clans had chosen. She heard soft crying behind her. It chilled her, but she did not turn around. Someone had not been Named. She invoked Shakari's mercy on whoever it was. The girl would be Unclanned and would have to leave the city with no rights or privileges. She shivered and thanked the

Goddess for the blessings she had received. She could picture the river already, waiting for her, the water against her body as she swam, her family sitting down to the evening meal, her life as it had always been.

But something was amiss. She felt the ripple of human movement in the square even before she heard the drums. They beat slowly, thud, thud, thud. What was happening? From the Street of the Temple, a procession was making its way down towards them, she could see it if she craned her neck. Thud. Thud. Thud. The sound of many sandals, slapping the brick road. Fire breathers came first, dancing on the edges of the newly Named, blowing fireballs into the crowds, much to their delight. Then some maidservants, handing dates to the people in small straw baskets. And walking slowly behind them, a group of women in green, wearing headdresses so elaborate that they took her breath away. Gold. They were entirely gold, intricately carved depictions of a pipal tree with thirteen leaves fanned across the headdress, each with silver-tipped veins.

Nobody had bowed for Iaf. But the people bowed now, going down on their knees, as the women walked into the square. The Goddess-Blessed had come.

Jaya went down on her knees like the others. She had never seen a Goddess-Blessed before. They kept to themselves, it was said, rarely venturing beyond the city. And now, after all these cycles, to attend a Clanning!

A woman separated herself from the others. She was tall, and by far the most stunning creature Jaya had ever seen. She had fierce grey eyes and sharp cheekbones. She was about her mother's age, Jaya guessed. The tattoo of the Goddess-Blessed, the branches of a pipal tree, was etched into the skin on the left side of her forehead. The woman stared at the girls in front of her for some time, searching, it seemed, for something.

Eventually, she spoke. Her voice was cool. 'Do not be alarmed. I am Sarema, Seer of the Goddess-Blessed. From time to time, we expand our numbers not through birth, but through the absorption of girls from other clans. This is one of those times.'

All at once, the crowd began to murmur. Such an honour! The girls stood tall once more, anxious for their chance.

Except her. Jaya did not want to be Named amongst the Goddess-Blessed or any other clan. She wanted to go home, on the river. She searched desperately for her parents and for Dar. But the rooftops were full of people, and she could not spot them.

The crowd was growing more and more excited, as two of the Temple maidservants carried an intricately carved wooden box between them. They knelt before the Seer, who opened it slowly.

And from it, she removed the Bloodstone and held it high.

The city went wild. People cheered and shouted. Others began to pray, following the lead of the priests who had closed their eyes and were chanting, clapping their hands rhythmically at the same time. Jaya simply stared. It looked, on the surface, from what she could see, to be a jagged ruby, full of sparkling richness. But then its veins became apparent, lines of pulsating black which seemed to breathe, almost like it was a living thing, a thing which was *aware*.

Jaya felt like she had forgotten how to breathe. The heart of Shakari. Here, at her Clanning!

Sarema placed the stone back in the box and looked up at the crowds. 'The Bloodstone will choose who is Named, not I,' she said aloud. 'Praise Shakari. Praise the Named.'

'Praise Shakari,' the city roared back.

The other Goddess-Blessed moved among the girls, who stood in a single line.

Sarema turned to them. 'You are about to do something that is unimaginable to most people. To almost anyone who has ever lived. You will touch a piece of the Goddess's heart.' She paused, her sharp eyes resting on each and every one of them. 'You will hold it in your hands, if only for a moment. Even such a thing will bring you blessings and joy for all of your cycles. Each of you will have your turn to hold the Bloodstone,'

Sarema said. 'Those who are most worthy will feel its power, and will join us as a sister.'

The Bloodstone was once again held out. The girls were brought forward, one by one, all trembling with excitement. Each girl held it tight, some cradling it, others polishing it with their fingers, hoping against hope that they would be selected. Jaya craned her neck. She could barely see. What was meant to happen? Each time Sarema would shake her head and the girl would be dismissed. She waited her turn anxiously. What if she dropped it? What if she destroyed Shakari's heart?

There was a girl holding it now, who very nearly dropped it, save for the quick thinking of the Goddess-Blessed who took it from her hands. The girl didn't even seem to notice. She stood still, her eyes closed, almost as though she were in a trance. 'There will be many rains this harvest,' she said suddenly. 'We will need barriers to stop the river flood from destroying the crops. We need fresh bricks. The ones made last year will crumble at the first sign of water.' And then she opened her eyes and blinked, looking confused.

A cheer went up through the city. The girl was a Goddess-Blessed. She had to be.

'What is your name?' Sarema asked, eyes narrowed.

'Nene, daughter of Arune, from the clan of the Cranes, Lady.'

'Do you wish to join us, Nene?'

The girl did not hesitate to answer, though her eyes swept the rooftops once, perhaps looking for her parents.

'Yes,' she said loudly, looking back at Sarema. 'I do.'

'Then take your place amongst us. Soon you will be branded and Named as sister.'

Nene walked slowly into the group of Goddess-Blessed as the crowds continued to cheer.

The others had their turns, each holding the stone, each feeling, or rather not feeling, something. A few of them tried to hold on to it for longer, thinking that more time would allow them to wield its power. But the Goddess-Blessed were stern and the Bloodstone was taken away. Far too soon, it was Jaya's turn.

It was such a small thing, she realized in shock. Such a small rock. And yet here it was, the fate of an entire city. The Bloodstone was placed in her trembling hands.

And then there was only darkness. She was in a tunnel, racing, her body exploding into thousands of little points of light. It burned, oh Goddess, it burned! What was happening to her? She saw herself, *felt* the searing pain of hot iron pricks touching her flesh – the marks of the Goddess-Blessed being branded into her temple. Iaf was watching, as were the Goddess-Blessed, while one of the women held her head down as her flesh was seared.

And then the vision was gone, and she opened her eyes, aware, suddenly, of how quiet the city was.

The Seer, the woman Sarema, held the Bloodstone now. When had it been taken from her? 'What did you see?' she was demanding.

Jaya shook her head. The ground was spinning. She felt ill. 'Nothing,' she whispered. 'I saw nothing.'

Sarema frowned. 'Speak louder, child.'

Jaya doubled over and vomited. And then the world went black.

Chapter Six

LONDON, PRESENT DAY.

Layla and Jay lived in a flat just off Hackney Road, on a side street made up of a seventies' high-rise of cheap student accommodation, a pub and a dingy kebab house. The kebab house, Neem's Grill, had a lopsided placard with an image of a pink hookah, advertising its Monday night shisha evenings. The pub next door was derelict but functional. Black paint was peeling from the doorway and along the bricks in the front.

Nadia stood by the window of the fourth floor walk-up. Somehow, despite the washed-out yellow paint, vinyl floor and the shoebox of a living room, Layla and Jay had managed to make this place a home. They had framed posters of art on the walls and there were large scented church candles and dried lavender in a long vase on a side table in one of the corners. They'd thrown a Pakistani carpet over the worst of the floor. A hefty stone Buddha sat next to a small blue plate full of incense sticks amongst some plants in another corner, while a soft burgundy blanket covered most of the sofa, hiding a multitude of years of use, no doubt. They could do nothing to disguise the lingering scent of fried onions, however, which seemed to be perpetually wafting up from their downstairs neighbour's place.

In some ways, it was amazing to be here, to be reminded of how her sister lived her life, Nadia realized. When Sohail had died, he'd left his earthly belongings to Layla, on the proviso that she come and live on the compound in Devon and learn about GoL's work. Their father had made millions, mostly by funnelling GoL money, given to him by his followers, into real estate and keeping a chunk of the profit for himself. Then there had been the embezzlement scandal ... Layla could have inherited enough money to live the most luxurious of lives. But she had declined to accept the inheritance.

Layla had been only four when her mother had taken her away. She barely remembered anything about the compound, or about their father, Nadia knew. Though it pissed her off, she respected the fact that Layla wanted to keep an open mind about GoL. But Layla had a very strong sense of right and wrong, and to accept the money would be unfair, she felt, if she didn't intend to carry on Sohail's work. Layla had told Nadia on many occasions that she wanted an anonymous life, a simple life, one that would interest nobody but herself. In their own ways, they were both looking for peace.

On the worn-out and scratched wooden coffee table there were photographs of both Jay's and Layla's families. Layla's mother, Harriett, and her stepfather, Andre, the aid worker. Nadia stared at the photos and felt a sudden ache. Sometimes it was hard not to feel the sharp pangs of jealousy. Layla's mother had come to her senses. She'd put GoL behind her and Layla had grown up with a more or less normal life.

And because she hadn't known him well enough to hate him, Layla had a picture of their father, Sohail, on the table. It captured him perfectly, and was a shock to see. That crooked, wide smile that lulled you into a false sense of safety, his hair shoulder length, his beard longer than she remembered. He was wearing his classic white kameez with jeans, looking every bit the leader of a cult – benign and thoughtful, his two index fingers coming together to suggest that he was in a meditative mood when the photo had been taken.

There was even a picture of her, looking stilted, annoyed and tense, taken shortly after they'd first come back into each other's lives. Back then, she had still been prickly with her sister. She had just started the process of recovery, and everyone seemed to be against her, even the sister she had longed to see for so many years. With pain, she realized how much time she'd wasted, being unapproachable.

In any other circumstance, Nadia thought, being here, getting to share Layla's life, would be special. Instead, she stared grimly out of the window at the pub below. There was nothing special about this. Two days in and she had nothing to show for it. She had not been able to find out anything about Layla, the Brits had been useless. She would leave for Pakistan soon, if she couldn't find out anything more here.

She'd watched the news with Jay, right after she'd landed and barged into the flat. The Pakistani government had held a special press conference, staging it directly by the ruins of Mohenjodaro, instead of Karachi or Islamabad, the capital city. Perhaps they wanted to be seen to be in control of the situation.

But they weren't. She could see from the televised images that the police were struggling to hold back the swarm of journalists and onlookers who had gathered by the makeshift boundary of cement blocks and rope they had put up to stop people going to the ruins. In their dark grey uniformed shirts and khaki trousers, linking arms, the police had looked like an imposing wall. Yet the people were looking antsy. She could understand why.

It was always the same, wasn't it, whenever there was tragedy and violence anywhere in the world? People came, partly to enjoy the spectacle, and partly because they were all burning with curiosity. Someone's car crash was someone else's entertainment.

Nadia understood people. It was a trait she had inherited from her father. And she knew that for the public, it probably didn't get any better than this. Foreigners burnt alive? That's what the rumours were. She had done some research on the flight. Larkana, where Mohenjodaro was situated, was a poor district. None of the locals would have enough money to own a computer. It was unlikely that many even had electricity. Nobody knew what YouTube was, and they couldn't access it even if they wanted to since the government kept shutting it down. But the locals understood politics. If white people had been burnt, there was sure to be a reckoning.

The press conference had been a farce. A politician with a long moustache came out to the podium, and gave a speech about how the video on YouTube was fake. Something about experts having assessed the video and found key markers where things had been doctored. He'd circled things on blown-up photographs of the video. He'd even brought along representatives from the countries whose citizens had disappeared – the US, the UK and the Netherlands. Ambassadors and Consul-Generals, sweating in the heat, half-heartedly agreed that the video was a forgery. There had also been representatives from Oxford and the University of Pennsylvania, the two universities that had taken the lead on the project. All of them gave brief statements about how the upload was a badly doctored piece of theatrics designed to cause friction and conflict in the region.

Journalists had begun to shout out questions and the politician continued to talk, ignoring them. Sixteen people were still unaccounted for from the team that was stationed in Mohenjodaro. Five of them were security guards from Links, a Karachi-based firm. There was a cook, two boys from the village nearby, and the eight who were part of the international expedition. The names were not being released, at least not yet. This was a terrorist attack, the assumption was that these people had been kidnapped by the Taliban.

'Bullshit,' Nadia had muttered, frowning at the TV. The story reeked of a cover-up. But why? Had the Pakistani government been trying out some stealth technology? Had the team stumbled upon some secret weapons stash? Where was Layla? What had she had in her hands? Was it Layla who she had seen, walking away from the camera, along with someone else, after the burnings? Was she still alive? Her stomach turned on itself. She could not afford to think like this. Of course Layla was alive. And her sister needed her.

Nadia looked out of the window. London was streaked with grey clouds, as usual. It was typical summer weather, spitting with rain one moment, sunny the next, light even at this time of evening. The pub was doing brisk trade, students gathered outside, clutching pints of beer in clear plastic cups or drinking wine, smoking cigarettes. She caught the occasional smell of a joint, carried by the breeze. A couple was making out against the black brick wall.

She pulled her cotton cardigan tighter across her chest, cradling her tea for comfort. Four years sober, but alcohol was still so tempting.

'Are you all right? Can I get you anything else?' Jay, ever solicitous, hovered around. Nadia turned and managed a weak smile. She was glad Layla had someone like Jay in her life. When she had first met him two years ago, she'd assumed he and Layla were an item. Until Jay had mentioned an ex-boyfriend, that is.

He was young, probably in his early twenties, she guessed. Around the same age as her sister. Jay was tall and thin. He wore skinny jeans and a pastel green T-shirt. The front of his head was bleached blonde, the rest was brown. He was kind. Since she had arrived, she'd relied on him heavily. He'd insisted that she stay with him, in Layla's room and not in some 'uncaring' hotel. With some surprise, she found herself agreeing.

Jay was another archaeologist in the making. She wished him luck. She suspected he would need it. He seemed to be one of those people that could easily be stepped on by other more ambitious characters. He cared about Layla, his best friend in the whole world, he'd informed her.

They had been busy since the press conference. First, they went to Scotland Yard, where the head of the task force responsible for the 'Mohenjodaro 8', as the press had begun to call them – conveniently forgetting that other Pakistanis on the site had also disappeared – offered her sympathy but very little else.

Scotland Yard's head of public relations, a middle-aged man with a serious case of dandruff, came to talk with them. He offered them nothing in the way of detail though, and raised his hands every time she asked a question. 'There is a meeting of the missing's families tomorrow. I'd like to address your point then, if that is all right? It wouldn't be fair to the others.'

No, it was not bloody all right. It was an absolute brush-off, which left Nadia incensed. How could they treat the families of the victims like this? Victims. It was a horrible word.

The man had provided the usual platitudes, the 'doing everything we can' speech. Layla was officially registered as missing, presumed kidnapped, and since the video posted on YouTube was a fake, it was unlikely that Layla would have uploaded it or been one of the people walking away in the last few seconds of it. Scotland Yard was satisfied that Layla Hussain had not been responsible for the incident – the faked incident – in Mohenjodaro. As though that was supposed to be some kind of consolation.

Someone, some terrorist, most likely had them. At least, that was the working theory. The Taliban had been upping its game recently, trying to recruit young men who were flocking to that other, newer, brasher terrorist group which was the ISIS. They wanted to show the world their brutality, and kidnapping foreigners would give them great media exposure. Scotland Yard was working closely with Pakistani intelligence, following leads, tracking extremist groups, waiting for news. And no, he insisted, when Nadia pressed him, they did not know what the video was all about, only that it was a forgery. Who knew what kind of game the Taliban were playing?

He invited her back the next day, to attend the 'organized' briefing for the families of the British missing, the emphasis being on the organized bit – clearly, Nadia was being subtly rebuked for just showing up.

She thought the guy was an idiot, and in any other circumstance she would have made a scene, but today she let it pass. The only thing that mattered was finding Layla.

And so she and Jay came back the following morning for the briefing, learning nothing new. The worst bit, Nadia thought, was running into Layla's mother, Harriett, who was inconsolable and completely unwelcoming. Hardly a big surprise. The woman could barely tolerate her even when she had been a little girl. Apparently, she looked too much like her father ... what was more surprising was her own need to connect, the instant yearning when she saw the older woman. As dismissive as Harriett had been, she had always treated Nadia better than her own mother ever had. And then running into the press, who laid in wait outside for the families, anxious to grab a photo of a grieving mother, a bewildered brother, a distraught sister.

The connection between her and Layla hit the newspapers the next morning, as she'd feared. The weird woman whose books teenagers read obsessively, who made millions off the back of the *Swamp!* franchise and who was born and raised in a cult, was connected to the Mohenjodaro 8, according to the tabloid she picked up. The bastards. Layla had chosen an anonymous life, a quiet, normal life away from the media spotlight and the GoL. Not any more. God, how she hated the bloody press.

She did her best to dodge them, but somehow, her US cell phone number had been leaked, and the phone calls requesting interviews began. She simply turned it off. Let Tamara, her UK agent, deal with all the vultures.

After Scotland Yard, Jay took Nadia to the main campus of University College London to meet the head of the archaeology department, a tetchy woman named Jane Davies. The meeting only left Nadia more confused. It seemed that almost nobody at UCL had even known that Layla had been given a place on the Mohenjodaro summer archaeology programme. For one thing, the Indo Foundation sponsored Oxford and Penn, not UCL, and the Mohenjodaro dig was Professor Webb's baby. Webb was based out of Oxford, not UCL. He and Davies seemed to have a past history, some kind of rivalry, so why hire someone from her university? Davies admitted that she had been surprised, but happy for Layla and had given her some time off the course to do a four-month placement at the dig.

So how on earth did Layla get into the programme? The Indo Foundation's only stipulation for sponsoring the dig was that anyone, from any university, be allowed to apply for a summer position. Something about fostering diversity, sharing insights. Nobody expected anyone besides Webb's undergraduates and a few of the Penn students to get selected. Layla's acceptance was a surprise.

Jay was looking at her now, expecting a response. She raised her eyebrows questioningly.

He gave her a sympathetic smile. 'I asked if you wanted more tea.'

She shook her head. 'No thank you. It's still warm. At the rate I'm going, I'm going to die from caffeine overdose.' She began to pace the room, restless. What next? How to figure out what was going on? 'Jay,' she began, trying to think, to understand. 'Did you apply for a place on the dig?'

He sat down on the edge of the sofa. 'Sure. We all did. We never expected to get in though.'

'So how did Layla get a place? Was she getting better grades or something?'

'Her grades are good, but not spectacular, if that's what you're asking. Even she couldn't believe she had got the spot. Digging in the Indus Valley is like hitting the jackpot.'

'Why?'

'You've heard of the ancient civilizations in Egypt and Mesopotamia, of course.'

'Of course.'

Outside, the couple who had been kissing against the brick wall were now shouting at one other. She could hear the girl screaming expletives – they carried in through the window.

'Well, the Indus civilization is just as important. There were only three written languages in the third millennium and the Indus script was one of them. The civilization spanned the entire region, not just Pakistan. There are sites in India, in Afghanistan and Iran, even as far as Oman. So far, archaeologists have identified around 2000 sites. This was the biggest civilization of all time, Nadia, and probably far older than either Egypt or Mesopotamia. And we know barely anything about it.'

The truth was Nadia hadn't even known that Mohenjodaro existed, not until Layla had phoned her up to tell her where she would be spending her summer, and then they'd had that fight. Jay got up and began to rummage through the bookshelf in the corner.

'It's incredible how little people are aware of the Indus civilization, and that's because there haven't been many excavations there. The Pakistani government hasn't allowed anyone to dig there in almost thirty years.'

'Why?'

He shrugged. 'They don't have the facilities to do conservation work, to protect the exposed sites, I think. Mohenjodaro itself has only ever been partially uncovered, because the high water mark means any further excavation could risk damaging the site. The parts of it that are exposed are already eroding because of the salt content in the ground and because of bad conservation work. The place might not even be around in twenty years' time.'

'So there's time pressure?'

'Absolutely. Archaeologists are dying for clues to help decipher the script before it's too late. That's why the Indo Foundation was able to offer the government considerable funds in exchange for the chance to do some more excavation. A bribe really. You let us play and we'll make sure the place survives kind of thing.'

'What is the Indo Foundation exactly?'

He walked over and handed her a book. It was an anthology entitled *The Priest King: Relics from the Indus Valley*. The cover had a picture of a statue – the bust of a bearded man who was richly robed.

'They believe in bringing history to life. They're a charity dedicated to helping antiquity survive in places where governments don't have resources. Keep the book. It belongs to Layla. It will answer most of your questions about Mohenjodaro.' He sat down on the sofa again and began massaging his brows. He was clearly exhausted. 'Do you mind if I smoke? Layla doesn't let me smoke in the flat. Or fry bacon, though she just about stomachs the smell of chicken in black bean sauce.' When she nodded, he lit a cigarette. 'I usually crash at Jim's place on the weekends. He's a smoker too. But we broke up just after Layla left.'

'Sorry to hear that.'

'Thanks. You want?'

She shook her head. 'Quit four years ago.' The day she had first reconnected with Layla, in fact.

He gave her a rueful smile. 'Bet you're dying for one today.'

'Yup.'

He exhaled the smoke, using a glass of water as an ashtray, and put his feet up on the coffee table. He had long elegant hands, Nadia noticed. Artist's hands.

'Tell me more about this Indus script then, and why it's important. I want to understand why Layla was so excited about this place.' But Layla had always been interested in Pakistani antiquity, hadn't she?

'Language,' Jay clarified, waving his cigarette about. 'They found seals – pictographs, with images and written symbols – made out of a variety of substances. I think clay, steatite and copper.'

'What were they for?'

He inhaled deeply. 'At best guess, they were administrative, used to keep track of grain and other agricultural harvests. At least, that's the theory. Layla had to write a paper on the place, did you know? For the application. It should be around here somewhere. I'll have a look. She was excited because the images are tantalizing, and she wondered why the seals would be only administrative in nature. Her hypothesis was that the seals are some kind of identifier, some sort of affiliation of different groups in the city. Interesting theory, but hardly backed up by anything concrete.'

Jay took another drag and smiled properly for the first time. 'Layla made me read her paper, over and over, every single draft, before she submitted it. She has been obsessed with it lately. There were rumours floating around at school that after the floods in Pakistan, many new seals were discovered in the topsoil in the area. But they were all rumours, a few blurry images on the net. The Indo Foundation swooped in quickly and paid the Pakistanis rather a lot to have proprietary excavation rights. That's what they do, they effectively bribe local governments to let them safeguard antiquity. Sad really, that it has to happen this way.'

Nadia sipped her tea, brows furrowed. Something didn't make sense. None of it made sense, Goddammit. 'What's your Wi-Fi password? I'd like to look them up. The Indo Foundation people.' She pulled out her phone from the pocket of her jeans and turned it on, grimacing when she saw the number of missed calls and voicemails.

Jay blew out smoke rings. '"IndianaJones". All one word. The I and J are capitalized.'

She looked up. 'Seriously?'

He shrugged. 'Layla thought it was funny.'

It was so typical of her sister, she thought, as she did a search for the Indo Foundation. She read quickly, both the Wikipedia entry for the Foundation, for whatever that was worth, and their own website. The Indo Foundation looked like it had charitable status in the UK, an organization that raised money for the preservation and excavation of ancient ruins around the world. The website was slick, far slicker than she had expected. It had an almost corporate feel. She clicked on the biography of the chief executive. A woman named Marianne Riviere. She looked surprisingly slick too.

'Do you know her?' She flashed her phone at Jay and he nodded. 'She spoke at the university earlier this year. She's a conservationist, quite inspiring, actually. They've saved a number of sites in Peru and Bolivia. More recently in Iraq, where locals were pilfering ancient bricks and the ISIS had blown up many structures.'

Marianne Riviere looked to be in her late forties, sophisticated, dressed in a navy blue suit with a red and blue scarf. Her expression was serious and unsmiling.

That's who she should be talking to, Nadia realized. Marianne Riviere. If the Indo Foundation had invested a great deal of money in the dig, then they would be kept abreast of any developments in Pakistan. She searched some more. The Indo Foundation had their headquarters in London, just by Green Park. Perfect.

'We should go to their office,' she told Jay, pointing at the map on her phone. 'We should go talk to them.'

'I doubt we'll get anywhere.'

'All the same, it's worth a try, isn't it? This is my last shot. Then I'm going to fly to Karachi.' The very idea filled her with dread. What would she find there? Would she have to make contact with her grandmother? No, she refused to do that. Jahanara had abandoned her in her darkest hour, when she was a terrified eleven-year-old trying to escape the compound. She couldn't imagine why her mother even had Jahanara's number in her diary, considering that her father and her grandmother were estranged. But she'd made the call – the long-distance call – desperate for help. And what had

Jahanara done? Told her never to call her again and hung up on her. And then *he'd* found out, and she spent two and a half weeks in the Basement, in 'Reorientation', alone in the dark, the complete and utter dark.

Jay threw the end of his cigarette into the glass of water. It went out with a mild hiss. She blinked, caught up in her own thoughts once again.

'All right, if that's what you want,' Jay said. 'We'll head down there in the morning.' He yawned. 'It's been a difficult couple of days. Why don't we call it a night and wake up refreshed?'

She looked at him and felt a pang. Jay was exhausted. She could see it from the hollows under his eyes. She cleared her throat. 'Look, I'm not much of a cook, but I can rustle up a decent omelette. Why don't I make you one? You look like you need to eat.'

He came and hugged her. It was unexpected, and for a moment she fought the instinct to pull away. She had never been relaxed around spontaneous intimacy. 'You know, you're really not as hard-nosed as you think you are. Thanks for the offer, but I'm not hungry.'

'Goodnight, Jay.'

''Night. See you in the morning, love.'

She watched as he made his way into the bathroom and pulled on the string that turned on the light and the extractor fan at the same time. The fan whirred crankily as it spluttered around without any rhythm. That damn thing needed to be replaced, it was way too loud. Then the tap was turned on and an electronic toothbrush buzzed.

Time to leave Jay alone. She made her way down the narrow hallway to the second door on the left. Layla's cubbyhole. For some reason, the idea of being among Layla's things gave her peace.

Layla had a small, narrow bed and a desk in the corner. The rest of the room was crammed with books and photos. The books were mostly academic tomes, stacked high in different piles. *Linguistic Man. What Does It Mean to Be Human? Collapse: Why Some Societies Fail and Others Survive. Archaeology and the Raj. Early Deities In Mesopotamia.* There was the odd novel – literary fiction from around the world, a couple of thrillers and all of her own books, Nadia noted, pleased to see that *Hellbound* looked very well thumbed. Then she glanced at the books below hers and frowned. There, among them all, was their father's own contribution to the writing world – a piece of vanity publishing he had entitled *Awakening the Light.* Layla had read it, Nadia could see that from the coffee stain on the title page, from the curled edges of the lilac cover. It was not until she flipped through it that she remembered that Sohail Hussain had dedicated the book to Layla, the child he cared about, the one who was taken away from him. Nadia turned the pages reluctantly. She had not seen this book for years, but it evoked so many memories. It had been stacked in hundreds against a wall in the compound in Devon, given out to potential recruits and anyone Father wanted to impress. It was Sohail's rationale for why human civilization was older than previously thought.

In the first chapter, he challenged Darwinism. She rolled her eyes. Talk about delusions of grandeur. Her father had thought he was more intelligent than the most celebrated scientist in history. In *The Origin of Species,* Darwin argued that the first apes and monkeys appeared about forty or fifty million years ago on earth. The first ape-men, called Australopithecus, appeared about four million years ago. This was followed by Homo habilis, Homo erectus, and Neanderthal man. The first identifiable human beings – Homo sapiens – appeared only around two hundred thousand years ago, with 'civilization' being only ten thousand years old. It was all there, in Darwin's book. But then her father had decided, in all his glory, to cast doubt on the theory of evolution. She snorted.

Of course he had. His writing was pompous, a diatribe against any kind of establishment. According to him, until Darwin came along, most scientists – those that were not afraid of the religious implications anyway – were happy to subscribe to the view that human beings had existed on the earth for two billion years *at least*. But then Darwin had published his work, and any evidence, any fossil records that conflicted with his thesis, were slowly lost over time, even hidden by his supporters. The fact that no solid 'missing link' has ever been found in evolution showed the fragility of Darwin's theory, as far as Sohail was concerned. Civilizations were old. Humankind was even older.

The rest of the book examined some of the ancient civilizations unearthed throughout history, and used them to argue that human beings were in a period of *devolution,* not evolution. Sohail had pulled several 'mysteries' from archaeology, dressed them up as academic analysis and written about them. One chapter was dedicated to an early Palaeolithic skull on display at the Natural History Museum in London, which dated back 38,000 years and was excavated in 1921 in what is now modern-day Zambia. On the left side of the skull was a perfectly round hole, nearly a third of an inch in diameter. How had this Neanderthal man died? Not by an arrow or spear – there was no radial split-line around the hole. According to her father, there was no shattering effect and the cranial damage could not have been done by anything other than a high-speed projectile. A bullet, in his opinion, and the opinion of various other 'forensic experts' he had been talking to, had done the damage. Human beings had been running around the earth with some sort of gunfire weaponry before they could even read and write.

She knew this, she had read all this before, and yet, she couldn't resist turning the pages. Here was another chapter about the discovery, in 1938, of a six-inch-high pot of bright yellow clay dating back two millennia, in Baghdad, which contained a cylinder of sheet copper. The copper cylinder was soldered with a lead–tin alloy. The bottom of the cylinder was capped with a crimped-in copper disk which was sealed with bitumen or asphalt. There was an iron rod suspended in the centre of the cylinder, which showed evidence of having been corroded with acid. This ancient artefact was, according to Sohail, nothing short of an ancient electric battery. Forget that there was no evidence to support his claim.

But much of the book was a rant against the Ancients. Wasn't it strange, suggested Sohail, how the 1 per cent managed to keep their fortunes, while the poor never succeeded in rising up? Why did capitalism still exist even though it suppressed so many people? Why, every time there was a moment of peace, a new threat would be identified, a new paradigm of world politics would begin? Who was really controlling the world?

She shut the book with a thud. Reading it had given her a headache. She should have known better. She put it back where she had found it, curious, all of a sudden, about what Layla had thought of it. Had she read it simply because she wondered who her father was? Or was she interested in GoL? They didn't talk much about Sohail, not to each other. Thinking about him made Nadia feel raw, it set her teeth on edge, and Layla had respected that. But still. What did her sister really think about their father?

She looked around. How different they were. In spite of the small space, Layla had mementos everywhere. Dried, faded roses pressed on the side of the mirror just above her desk. Birthday cards. A collection of small elephants, made out of paper and crystal and plastic and everything in between, walking in a line along the desk. There were pictures too. Pictures stuck to the mirror, next to an invitation to a UNESCO lecture on World Heritage and what it meant, and a Post-it note which simply said 'Don't forget to smile', as though cheap motivational psychology would solve every problem in the universe.

With nostalgic irritation she thought about Layla's constant Facebook updates – inspirational quotes from the Buddha and from Eleanor Roosevelt, comments about sunsets and nature and why living life was important. Nadia had joined Facebook only because Layla had insisted. She never looked at the bloody thing, except to check in on Layla from time to time.

The whole room smelt of lavender, probably because of the aromatherapy oils on the bedside that Layla must have lit while she was studying. On the desk were several photos of Layla, one of her at a charity run, of her hugging a group of children at what looked to be an orphanage or a school, probably in Lima from that summer when she worked for Habitat for Humanity. There she was with her arms flung around a group of women, on a hot summer day in a park, and here was one of her with Andre, her stepfather, the aid worker, somewhere in the desert. No boyfriend though.

How could she be so nice, so ... normal, Nadia wondered. Sohail had lost custody of Layla when Harriett divorced him. He hadn't managed to mess his younger daughter up before he died. Layla Hussain was a living, breathing advertisement for humanity.

Living ... breathing ... how Nadia prayed she was both. Her head began to throb, and she realized just how exhausted she was.

She lay on the bed, not even changing her clothes, shut her eyes and waited for the dreams.

Chapter Seven

MELUHHA 3800 BC.

She opened her eyes. Her mother was pressing a damp cloth against her forehead. Jaya sat up quickly, and then fell back again as the world began to spin.

'Shh ... daughter. Stay calm. All is well.' Her mother patted her shoulder reassuringly.

'Mua ... what happened?'

'You fainted. But everything will be fine.'

Her mother sounded nervous. Jaya slowly pushed herself up on her elbows. The last thing she remembered was the Clanning. She had become a Crocodile, hadn't she? Then the Goddess-Blessed had come and she had touched the Bloodstone ... What had happened after? She had seen herself ... she had seen herself being tattooed. Being branded. As what? A Goddess-Blessed?

Gingerly, she touched her forehead. It was smooth, slightly damp from the cloth, but clear of any scars. Had she dreamt of the branding? It couldn't have been a vision, could it?

She was lying on a bed. A proper rope bed with thick cotton coverings, not her usual mat on the ground. Where was she? For the first time in her life, she was in a proper bed. Somehow, the thought made her panic. The softness felt uncomfortable, a reminder of how strange things had become. The air was cool and dry, she was nowhere near the sun.

She looked around. They were in a room somewhere, a richly gilded room with wall hangings, bronze and gold carvings, a small fire heater and a plate of fresh fruit placed on a side table. A whole plate of an assortment of fruit, not just bananas, but oranges too, and grapes. And some things she had never seen before, dark red in hue. Even as her mind processed the fact, Sarema, the Seer of the Goddess-Blessed, stepped into the room.

She looked different, though still as beautiful and haughty as before. She had taken off her veil and was dressed in ochre and black now. Ochre and black. The colours of the Temple. Jaya felt her throat constrict. Was she in the Temple?

Sarema smiled at her, though her grey eyes were not warm. 'And how is our little patient? Feeling better now, my child?'

'Yes, my Lady, I thank you,' Jaya said, sitting up straight.

Mala became flustered. 'Please, Lady, sit down, won't you? Jaya get up, make some room on the bed.'

The Goddess-Blessed raised her arm. 'Do not trouble yourself, Mother. Jaya, do you know where you are?'

'I ... I am not sure.'

'We have brought you to my house, on the Street of the Pipal Trees. Has your mother told you why?'

Jaya shook her head.

'Leave us,' Sarema said, without so much as looking away from Jaya.

Mala hesitated, but the Goddess-Blessed turned her gaze on her. 'Please,' she said, though somehow, Jaya knew, her mother would have left her anyway. Sarema was not a woman to be trifled with. What did she want with her?

Mala nodded. She gave Jaya a watery smile and then got up. Jaya heard the door close. She brought up her knees and crossed her arms over them, watching the older woman carefully.

'Would you care for some mulberries, Jaya?'

Jaya shook her head. She did not know what a 'mulberries' was. It would be better to decline rather than demonstrate her ignorance.

'No? A shame. They have come all the way from the Northlands, I'm told, in wet bales of cotton, because they are easily crushed. A true delicacy, rare, even for us.' Sarema skimmed her long, elegant fingers over the fruits, picked up something that looked like a dark red caterpillar and put it into her mouth. 'Perhaps later then. Do you know what happened to you in the market square, my child?'

'I ... I fainted, Lady. I am sorry for the difficulty. If you would just let me go now, I'll return home and will not trouble you any further.'

'You did not faint, you had a vision.'

She swallowed. No, that couldn't be right, could it? It was over so quickly, and it hadn't made much sense. How could that have been a vision? She did not want to be a Goddess-Blessed. She wanted to live and die by the river. She summoned her courage.

'Please forgive me, Lady, but you are mistaken. It was the heat. My headdress was too tight, it caused some misery. Mua made it for me, you see, because we were not able to buy something ready-made. My friends made their own as well, but I think their mothers did not bind the vines so tight. All the city girls bought theirs and they did not get dizzy.' She was aware that she was babbling, but she wanted to go home. Even if it meant lying to the Seer of the Goddess-Blessed.

Sarema said nothing. She just watched her for a moment. Jaya scratched her chin, uncomfortable.

Eventually, Sarema came and sat on the bed next to her, and put a hand on her knee. Once again she smiled, but there was a hardness in her expression. Jaya shrank away. The Seer was not a welcoming woman. There was something ... something so calculating about her.

'You do not strike me as stupid or frivolous, Jaya. I'm sure you are aware that any girl in the city would feel honoured to be in your position now, their futures open to great possibilities. But not you.'

Her eyes narrowed and held the question.

Jaya stared at a spot near the fruit plate. There was a fly hovering around it. Someone should really swat it away.

'You may as well tell me. You put your soul in jeopardy by lying to one who is chosen by the Goddess, child.'

She felt the tear slide down her cheek. 'It is only ... I want to live with my family, on the river.' She turned her head away and looked down.

Amused, Sarema stood up, smoothing down her tunic. 'Such a simple ambition.'

No, thought Jaya, not simple at all. It was proving far from simple.

'Well. You are still young and have had a happy life. Perhaps too happy, for your family has not schooled you in your options for the future. You do not seem to understand, my child, what honour has been bestowed on you. That will change.'

'I fainted, Lady. It was simply the headdress, you see.'

Sarema headed towards the door. 'Rest now. We'll talk later. There is much to say.'

Jaya slumped back on the bed, heart racing. She had seen nothing! Nothing of consequence, at least. Her own skin being tattooed, being burnt. Had that been a vision, sent to her by the Bloodstone? Surely the Goddess-Blessed would not keep her here against her wish?

Anxious and worried, she tried to calm her mind. Her parents would not allow them to force her to stay. They had rights. They were Clanned. It would be all right. She would leave and return to her old life. This was Meluhha. Her rights were sacred, now that she had been Named. She had been Named, hadn't she? Just because she hadn't officially had time to pick up the blue stone, to take it back to the Crocodiles and officially accept the clan, it wouldn't change anything, would it?

The thoughts churned in her head, as the room fell into darkness. Night had come. And yet, somehow, she was still here.

Chapter Eight

LONDON, PRESENT DAY.

They arrived at Green Park just after 11 a.m. It was a bright and sunny day. A grey-bearded homeless man with a paper cup in his hand was dozing in a sleeping bag, against the window of Marks & Spencer's Food Hall. Nadia stopped and slipped a ten-pound note into his cup. It was bad enough being homeless, but even worse sleeping rough outside a shop window that advertised pastries and bagels and three for two deals on baked goods. The man mumbled something in his sleep. It sounded like *fuck you.*

Tourists were already prowling the streets. Some walked in the direction of the Royal Academy and others towards Fortnum & Mason, the department store whose famous turquoise awnings were glinting in the sun. Jay had pulled out his phone and was searching for the Indo Foundation's headquarters on Duke Street, and they stopped to take a look at Google Maps.

She did not notice the tall blonde man, dressed impeccably in a charcoal suit and sky blue silk tie. The man leant against a lamp post. He sipped his latte and watched her, amused as she looked around, trying to get her bearings. He admired her long-limbed body, now hidden in jeans and a tailored black linen jacket. He liked that she had dressed up a bit today.

She was normally so grungy. Philip watched her push a lock of dark hair from her face, curling it behind her ear as she huddled next to that irritating boy. Together, they were looking up something on his phone. He stared at the upward curve of her lips, enjoying the way her brows came together when she frowned in concentration. He smiled.

Nadia looked up. She'd just had the strangest sensation. She felt chilly, despite the warmth of the morning and folded her arms across her chest. That was London for you. Inconsistent weather, perpetually feeling unprepared for the day.

'Got it,' said Jay. 'Just there on the left. It's only a few minutes away.'

They walked through the crowd, she let him take the lead. They cut through Jermyn Street, passing several men's tailoring stores, each looking other-worldly and discreet – she imagined them to be full of the scent of old tobacco and even older money. Outside a hat shop, an old man watched them go by. They turned left onto Duke Street.

She would never have guessed that the building in front of them hosted a charitable foundation. It was as fashionable and expensive-looking as all the others. It also had a distinctly corporate feel, with its glass entryway, security punch code and buzzer. The Indo Foundation did not go out of its way to advertise itself, there was no sign to indicate its presence, just the building number – 143. It was nestled between a bank and the offices of Arrapha Capital, whatever that was.

'Shouldn't these guys be in a dilapidated building somewhere, saving every penny for their cause?' she wondered out loud.

Jay shrugged and chewed the nail on his thumb, leaning against the glass. She pressed the entry phone buzzer.

The speaker crackled alive. 'Can I help you?'

'Yes, hello. I'm here to see Marianne Riviere, please.'

'Do you have ...' The voice was muffled. It faded in and out, made worse by the noise of the traffic, but she got the gist.

'No, I don't have an appointment.'

'I'm afraid she's very busy. If you'd like to ring up for an appoint ...'

'Tell her that my sister is missing in Pakistan, she's one of the Mohenjodaro 8, and that I'm not going anywhere until she speaks to me.'

There was a pause, the static stopped. Then, a few seconds later, it started again. 'What is your name, please?'

'Nadia. Nadia Osbourne.'

The door buzzed and she pushed it open, looking at Jay. 'Come on.'

Inside, colourful modern art graced the walls of the chrome-and-steel lobby. A receptionist with a tight smile asked them to follow her. In a very clinical fashion, Nadia and Jay were photographed and then presented with an ID swipe card which would allow them access through the glass security barriers.

She looked at Jay, who seemed as confused as she was. What was this place, a charity or a bank?

They swiped their cards and took an elevator up to the third floor as they had been directed. There, another receptionist escorted them to a series of black leather sofas and asked them to please wait. There were newspapers, magazines and brochures about the Indo Foundation. There were also envelopes, inviting people to donate to help preserve ancient treasures, around the world, in any currency of their choosing. The place was briskly efficient. They were asked if they wanted coffee or tea.

Jay took coffee, but she asked for water.

'Still or sparkling?' asked the receptionist, smiling.

'Erm ... still, please.'

'Would you like ice and lemon with it?' The woman's smile was still plastered on her face.

'Okay.' It was like a bloody hotel. It was disconcerting.

They waited about ten minutes, saying very little, drinking their drinks, conscious of the receptionist only a few feet away. Then, Marianne Riviere came out to greet them. She looked harassed. 'Ms Osbourne?'

Marianne Riviere was a handsome woman, who looked every bit the successful executive, dressed in a chic suit and Hermes scarf. Nadia had given away much of her budding fortune to charities in the last few years, and none of their executives had looked like this. Nadia and Jay stood up. 'I'm Nadia Osbourne. And this is my friend, Jay McKenzie. Thank you for seeing us.'

The other woman shook hands with them both, but pursed her lips, making her annoyance clear. 'You didn't give me much choice. Had you phoned, I would have been happy to meet with you at a convenient time. Of course, I understand that these are trying times, for all of us, which is why I agreed to see you. Please come with me. I can give you ten minutes.'

They followed her to an office down the corridor. It was large, the size of a boardroom. A mahogany desk stood at the back of the room, and there was a brown leather sofa in one corner next to a coffee table, with two armchairs on either end. Side tables held elegant displays of orchids. On the wall behind the sofa, protected by a thick glass covering, was a map, torn and jagged on its edges. Jaya peered at it. It was ancient, beautifully drawn with ships and images of compasses. It seemed like there should be a giant squid and mermaids coming out of the ocean, it was so other-worldly, like a Jules Verne novel. Marianne Riviere cleared her throat, offered them the sofa and then leaned against her desk, arms crossed. Waiting.

'Thank you for accommodating us,' Nadia began. 'I know our approach was unusual. You'll understand, I'm sure, that we are desperate for information about my sister.'

Marianne sighed, all traces of defensiveness gone, and came to sit down on one of the armchairs, tucking her crossed legs under her in the manner of elegant women everywhere. 'I'm very sorry to hear about your sister, Ms Osbourne. About all of them. Such an anxious time for us all.' There were still traces of a French accent, underneath the polished English.

'What news can you give us? The police have been useless.'

'Not much, I'm afraid. We are speaking to all parties, of course, but we have no answers, not yet. We can only pray that they are all safe. The Foundation has insurance for excavations. We can pay almost any ransom, should it come to that.'

'Ransom ... so there's been a ransom request?' The thought was disquieting, but also relieving in a way. If there had been a ransom request, then the video was no doubt a hoax and she had been wrong.

'No. Not officially. There is some suggestion that this is a splinter group of the Pakistani Taliban getting nasty, taking an opportunity to swap political prisoners for the team – for prestige. They may be proving themselves to the Islamic State, looking for another group to join. I am sorry, I wish I had better news. When we know anything for certain, we will contact all the families. For the moment, it would be appreciated if you could keep this information to yourself. All governments concerned are working hard to stop people from panicking.'

Nadia's hands trembled. 'How do you know this? From Scotland Yard?'

'No. The information came to us from a reliable source in Pakistan. But we are yet to hear it officially, as I said.'

So they had been kidnapped, after all. Layla was in the hands of some crazy terrorist group. 'But that means ... the video ... that was definitely a forgery. Why would somebody put that out? Shouldn't that be your primary priority right now?' She heard the shrillness in her voice.

'Wow. I must ask, Ms Riviere, is that Shiva?' Jay had gotten up and was peering at another set of display shelves in the corner. Nadia looked at him curiously. They needed to focus. Yet, Jay was acting like a child let into a toy shop at Christmas, his eyes were gleaming.

'Yes,' replied Marianne, walking towards the shelves, clearly grateful for the change in subject. 'It is indeed the Hindu god Shiva, found in the Katas Raj temple in the Punjab, in Pakistan. On the shelf below, do you see that large Buddha? That was from a stupa in the Cholistan desert, it is over a thousand years old. And that golden bird is from a new excavation, one of our sponsored ones actually, in Peru. This icon is a fertility god from Iraq, we've recently supported an excavation there too.'

Nadia craned her head. The shelves were well lit, like a museum display. The Shiva statue was beautifully carved, the deity in a posture of meditation, wearing a garland of snakes around his neck. The bird was interesting too, it was nearly two feet tall and appeared to be solid gold. How had the Indo Foundation ended up with these? 'I thought any discoveries you found belonged to the countries where you work?'

The Riviere woman waved her hand dismissively. 'Of course. That is indeed the case. These are just on loan. It helps with funding if our donors can see that their hard-earned assets are making a difference, no?'

She stood up. 'And what exactly do you do here, Ms Riviere? Dig for buried treasure?' She was being deliberately provocative. The Indo Foundation seemed to have plenty of cash. Where had it all come from?

Marianne Riviere looked annoyed. 'I set up the Foundation in 2001, after the Taliban destroyed the Buddhas of Bamiyan in Afghanistan. I'd been a banker until then, but I have always been passionate about antiquity. Our history often defines our future, don't you think? We support projects that protect and safeguard ruins around the world. You have to understand, this is heritage that would be destroyed by climate change or war or lack of funds – look at the destruction the ISIS has caused in Iraq and Syria. We support excavations in new areas as well. In the case of Mohenjodaro, Professor Webb's team was shedding much-needed light on the Indus Valley civilization, and we were happy to support him.'

'You haven't explained ...'

Marianne Riviere raised her hand to cut her short. 'I refer you to our website for more information. It is all there. We are fully transparent. We are not archaeologists, Ms Osbourne. We simply help others do good work by providing them the funding.'

Something about this woman did not smell right. 'And where does this funding come from exactly?'

'A variety of donors, wealthy individuals and institutions.'

'I see. Is that why you need all this security?'

For one brief moment, Marianne Riviere dropped her mask of politeness, her face full of contempt. She pointed at the shelf. 'Look at these treasures, Ms Osbourne. They are worth a fortune. Pieces like this come in and out of our office all the time, either on loan or to be studied by the British Museum or exhibited somewhere. We facilitate their transfer. We need to be careful about who we let into this building, especially now, with everything that is going on. But, je suis désolé, I have a board meeting upstairs I simply cannot be late for. If you'll excuse me ...'

It was Jay who spoke this time, his tone deceptively casual. 'But one more thing, please. How was the video even shot? How did it get on YouTube?'

'It was a hoax, clearly,' she replied, walking them to the door, which she opened.

'Yes, but, please bear with me. Some of it had to be real, someone had to have filmed Mohenjodaro, and the team there. A video can be manipulated, but only if there is something to work with in the first place, like images of the team going about their day. Any visual arts student would be able to tell you that.'

Now Marianne looked really pissed off and closed the door again. She walked behind her desk, fiddling around with the papers on it. 'We have a system. It is called KRS. It allowed them to transmit audio and video to our databases, to keep a record of the discoveries the team made. That way, the whole process can be transparent and recorded for posterity.'

'Records?' Nadia looked at her, amazed. 'You're saying you've got the video, a record of what happened?'

Marianne shook her head. 'No, not of what *happened*. Our feed was cut off sometime before the event. Our system may have filmed the kidnapping, or whatever happened before the video was altered and edited, but we'll never know, because it was never transmitted here. Someone must have reprogrammed the feed. The hardware, the actual computers ... well, those have been seized by the Pakistani authorities. If there is any data on them, we don't have it.'

'I want to see the tapes,' Nadia said.

'What tapes?'

'The feedback, whatever, your system. The images.'

Marianne shook her head. 'I'm afraid it's just not possible. We've sent all of it to Interpol and to the Pakistani intelligence, the ISI.'

Jay crossed his arms. 'And you don't have backups? I'm afraid I find that hard to believe. I mean, you have a priceless Shiva behind your desk and a solid gold icon from Peru. As you say, you are clearly diligent about protecting the things you discover.'

There was silence. Eventually, Marianne nodded. 'We will make copies for you and give you the CDs. But you should know, there are hundreds of hours of content. Plus, they've been watched, over and over, both by my people and by the authorities. I'm afraid you'll be wasting your time.'

'With respect, it is ours to waste,' Nadia said firmly.

'Yes. Of course. If you would be kind enough to return to the lobby, I will have someone bring you the CDs. It will take some time, however.'

'We'll wait.'

Marianne opened the door once more. 'As you wish. I really am sorry about your sister. About all of them. Let us hope that Mohenjodaro does not live up to its name.' She looked at Nadia pointedly.

Nadia stopped. 'What do you mean?'

'Don't you know?'

'Know what?' Jay put a hand on her shoulder. 'Nadia, you don't need to trouble yourself ...'

'Mohenjodaro is a Sindhi word,' Marianne cut in. 'It means ... Mound of the Dead.' With that, Marianne Riviere closed the door firmly behind them.

They sat there for nearly two hours before the receptionist came towards them, her heels clicking on the hard floor. She handed over the CDs without comment.

It had been three days since Layla had vanished. Didn't they always say the first twenty-four hours were crucial? Nadia felt like she was running out of time. Why was the ancient civilization called Mound of the Dead? Was it because those who came after knew that their ancestors had once lived on the land and had left traces? Or because of something else? Had it always been a place of violence and destruction?

'Thanks,' Nadia muttered, putting the heavy manila envelope in her satchel. The woman flashed a brief, clearly insincere smile, and then turned around, continuing to click all the way to the elevator.

When they left the building, Nadia was grateful for the fresh air and the sunshine. The Indo Foundation had felt oppressive. The woman, Riviere, had been less than forthcoming. Why? Jay followed her out, and lit a Marlboro Light.

'Well played, my friend,' she told him.

Jay smiled at her. 'You weren't going to get anywhere, she was close-minded and antagonistic. That's why I asked about Shiva. But now what?'

'We can't go through all the footage right now. It would take forever, like she said.'

'Maybe just the last day, then? The day they were kidnapped?'

He steered her out of the way of a man who was talking angrily on his mobile phone, and almost ploughed into them. 'Careful.'

They walked towards Green Park tube station, until Jay stopped her again. 'Listen, my ex is studying mass media and communications at UCL. Why don't I take the CDs to him? We can go over them. They've got all kinds of fancy equipment, he or his mates could tell me if the feed was tampered with, and what might have happened to it. Why don't you go home and take a nap or something? I'll come and find you after.'

'I can't,' she replied, restless. She could find an AA meeting, couldn't she? She could definitely use one. She was exhausted, she hadn't been sleeping, those bloody dreams about Jaya were getting worse. In the last one, Jaya had been separated from her family, and she was anxious, which meant Nadia woke up anxious too. And now, the tension of all this ... it would be so easy to slip up, to walk into a bar and never leave. 'You're right. I'm going to get myself together a bit. Here, take them.'

She pulled the manila envelope out of her bag. The envelope wasn't sealed and the CDs fell to the ground. They both scrambled on the pavement, picking them up.

'Damn,' she muttered.

Later, she would wonder if it was instinct or pure serendipity that made her look up. Because just then she spotted her. Marianne Riviere. The woman was wearing a beige mac and scurrying down the road at the traffic lights, carrying a ratty black backpack. What the hell? Marianne Riviere had not seemed like she would be caught dead with something so unfashionable.

She nudged Jay in the ribs. 'Look.'

He stood up slowly, the CDs in his hands. 'She said she had a board meeting in her office. I wonder where she's going?'

'You go. Find your friend and look at the feed. I'm going to follow her.'

'I'll come with you.'

She took his arm. 'No. Please,' she said urgently. 'We can't waste any more time. You check out those CDs. We can compare notes later.'

'If you're sure ... maybe we should call the police?'

She shook her head. 'Over what? She's just walking down the road, we have nothing to tell them.'

'Okay, well, if you're sure ...' he repeated looking at her dubiously, but Nadia was already halfway down the pavement.

Jay turned and walked towards Green Park, oblivious to the blonde man in the charcoal suit who passed by him, whistling a tune.

Chapter Nine

MELUHHA 3800 BC.

Jaya did not learn until some days later that her parents and Dar had left the river. Left and moved away. Such a simple thing, as though their lives – as though *her* life – meant nothing.

She listened to the news in horror, though it was not Sarema who told her nor any of the other Goddess-Blessed who brought her food and checked on her well-being as she lay on that rope bed, refusing to get up. She had learnt it from Kaul-Tu, the Temple fishmonger, who had been instructed to inform her by the head of the Crocodiles, presumably with the blessing of Sarema. Because here he was, in her sleeping chamber, still smelling of the trout he had brought, looking uncomfortable as he scratched his beard. The man who had probably not washed in days, was now being allowed into the inner sanctum of the Seer of the Goddess-Blessed.

'It's true, Cakko. I would never lie to you. The Goddess-Blessed are very generous with the families of their Chosen Ones.'

'But my parents would never just leave me!' She felt sick. Sick and numb at the same time.

At least he had the grace to look sympathetic. 'It is as I said. Your father has been given a high-ranking position as Crocodile Elder in Dilmun.'

'He would have told me ...'

Kaul-Tu shook his head. 'The position needed to be filled urgently. If they had not left when they did, he would have lost the opportunity. And do you know that, as an Elder, he will get a percentage of each clan member's stock? A truly eminent position. Your father will become a wealthy man.'

'But ...'

'They sent their love and hope to be reunited with you soon.'

He wasn't meeting her eye. Why wouldn't Kaul-Tu look her in the eye? 'Why didn't they leave me a message then? Dar could easily have gone to the Street of Carvers, or left a token for me here, and ...'

'I'm sorry, Cakko, there was no time. It all happened so quickly.' He took a step towards her, but then hesitated and stepped back to where he was, standing by the door, head bowed. 'You know that our vassal states are all grumbling about the tithe they pay Meluhha and about our right to select their Elders. The position had to be filled before the Dilmunis decided to create problems. So Tur'un packed up the boat and they sailed away, but they promised to be back as soon as he had established his authority there.'

Dilmun. They had gone to Dilmun. Kaul-Tu would not say it if it was not so. It would take her seven or eight days by boat to reach them. How could they just leave her? How could they just abandon her here? It made no sense.

'Swear that what you speak is the truth!' she demanded.

He looked miserable as finally he looked up at her. Her father had been his friend, no wonder his eyes were red-rimmed. 'I swear it, Jaya. You are better off here, with the ... the noble people. You will have a rich life, a life without cares or illness. This is the will of the Goddess, after all.'

'I will leave here soon, Kaul-Tu. And then I will need your help in finding them again.'

He shook his head once more. 'It is better that you don't,' he said quietly.

'What do you mean?'

Once again he seemed to want to come closer, and once again he pressed back against the door.

He's frightened, Jaya realized, her heart sinking. *I am in the bedroom of the Seer of the Goddess-Blessed. I am not the child who used to ride on his shoulders at the fish market any more.*

'The priests have been generous to your family with this new posting. It is rare for them to intervene, to place a Meluhhan in another city. It is a high honour, bestowed on the father of one who will soon be Goddess-Blessed. If you leave, then your father's blessings will be taken away. Think about Dar and his future. He should marry soon. Now he will have wealth to offer his bride. He can choose who he wants. Even ... even someone from another clan if they agree to pay the new Naming price.'

She said nothing. The light was fading now, casting everything in shadow.

'They said they would be back soon to see how you are faring,' Kaul-Tu said desperately. 'Give them a chance to return. Is that not the best course of action?'

He was right, of course. If she left now – even if she had the ability to travel so far without any gold – she would jeopardize her father's new position. But she could not believe that he would leave her here, not without a choice! How long would it be before they returned for her?

Kaul-Tu estimated four moons at least. But that seemed an interminable length of time. She didn't know what to do.

The next days were swallowed by misery. No further messages arrived, not even to say that her family had settled or arrived safely. 'Your father must be busy,' Sarema said one night, trying to soothe her. 'Perhaps the weather has delayed the boats travelling the river. You will hear from them soon enough. But they are not coming back, Jaya, whatever the fishmonger told you. They would not give up everything simply to take you away from a comfortable life. When you have been a Goddess-Blessed for some years, perhaps you can lead a pilgrimage to Dilmun. It will be a good opportunity to remind Dilmun that we are the true daughters of Shakari. You will see them again then.'

But still she hoped, as the sun rose and set a multitude of times, that there would be some news. She could not believe they had forgotten about her. She would not believe it. That left only two possibilities, she decided. Sarema was keeping her family away from her. There was something about the woman that made her skin crawl, no matter how nice she was being. And if it wasn't Sarema, then something had happened to her family on the way to Dilmun.

The day she realized this, she got out of bed and joined the others. The Goddess-Blessed – soon they would be her sisters, she accepted that now – were all kind to her. But though unspoken, it was understood that she was simply adjusting to her new reality, before taking her place among them. Well, let them think what they wanted. She loved her family. If they were being kept away from her, she would have to find them on her own. She would not accomplish that by lying in bed. She needed to learn as much as she could about where they might be. And she might have to become a Goddess-Blessed before that happened. She watched, and waited.

Sarema was away from the house for much of the day. The Seer was busy, attending to matters of state and helping the High One, Iaf, with the daily rituals and cleansings. There was Feast Day – Karani – to prepare for, Jaya was told. Thousands came to the city and it was the Seer's responsibility to organize the blessings and all of the logistics, from taking on dozens of cooks, to building a stockpile of crows and lentils for the soups, to housing dignitaries from other city states and organizing the festivities.

Jaya spent those first moons as a stranger, learning their ways before she was to be branded, before she officially became one of them. During that time she made discreet enquiries about who she could pay to gain passage to Dilmun. But there was no one. It was a treacherous passage, particularly in the monsoon cycles, and the oarsmen required six cubes of gold in compensation, gold which she didn't have. She could join a caravan, of course, but none would take her unless she had goods to sell or the physical strength to lead the buffaloes. Besides, the journey over the desert would take nearly three weeks, and it was dangerous.

So she continued to wait. As the days passed, she watched the Goddess-Blessed with growing amazement. They were all so lovely, so accomplished and beautiful. They seemed serene and so noble. Her sisters-to-be spent their mornings involved in cleansing rituals, from bathing in the Sacred Pool in rose petals to meditating in the Temple. In anticipation of Karani, they were also busy practising the Uncovering Ceremony, a dance of thirteen veils which covered their naked bodies, symbolizing the leaves of the pipal tree which had saved their Goddess. The dance was long, languorous and sensual. It was ritualistic as well, a form of prayer, a way to honour Shakari. Only the Goddess-Blessed were allowed to learn it. It was performed each year for visiting dignitaries and was fairly complicated, each movement of the arms expressing a different emotion, each twist of the ankle made in rhythm with the slow drummers.

In their free time, the women would meet at each other's houses. Each was allocated a large abode in the Street of the Pipal Trees just beyond the Temple, further down from the Citadel. Bored, they would lounge together, eating fat meals of buffalo milk and dormouse, surrounded by an army of serving girls, who catered to their every whim, from washing their hair in almond milk or softening it with mustard oil, to rubbing their body with mud to soften the skin.

None of the Goddess-Blessed seemed particularly pious or devoted to the Bloodstone. Instead, they gossiped about one another, about the priests and about the new silks that had come in from the market. In the afternoons, they sometimes sat on the rooftops, dousing their hair in lemon juice to make it lighter, surveying the world from their high vantage point.

With shock, she learnt that Nene, the other girl who had been selected to apprentice as a Goddess-Blessed at the Clanning, had not had any vision at all when she picked up the Bloodstone. Nene was a tall, lithe creature with long silky black hair which reached her buttocks. She knew exactly what she wanted out of life. She had a playful personality and befriended Jaya with ease.

'Of course I didn't see anything, silly! Do the river folk have fish stuffed between their ears? Everyone knows the Bloodstone ran out of power many cycles ago, if it ever had any to begin with. A lot of it is just old tales, passed on by the priests. They're so outdated, with their ridiculous superstitions.' Nene was examining her nails as she said this – one of the serving girls had soaked them in almond oil and blunted them.

Jaya gaped. 'If anyone heard you ... how could you speak such things!' She had her hands firmly by her sides, refusing to let anyone touch them.

'Ha! You think that because we are going to be Goddess-Blessed that we have to believe? What a foolish child you still are, Jaya! The Bloodstone does not speak to anyone. There are no visions! Those are just stories they tell the masses. But if a girl is clever enough, like I was, she can worm her way into this cushy life.'

'But the vision you saw ...'

Nene winked. 'Oh, when the floods come and the brick walls along the river have to be strengthened? That happens every year, does it not? It was clever of me to think of it. But not as clever as you were, pretending to faint like that. The fainting spell was mysterious, the whole city was gripped by it. And here we are, living this wonderful life,' Nene said, opening her arms wide, grinning.

'Wonderful,' Jaya echoed, her heart sinking.

She must stop thinking about her family, she realized. For here was a world far more complicated than the river. A world she had yet to understand. She had to live in it, at least, until she found a way to buy her own passage to Dilmun.

Chapter Ten

LONDON, PRESENT DAY.

Nadia followed Marianne Riviere into the Ritz Hotel in Piccadilly, nodding awkwardly at the smartly uniformed doorman who let her in. She looked around, trying to get her bearings, deliberately not catching the eyes of the receptionists, trying to look as though she had a purpose in standing there. Marianne had already disappeared. Wait, no, there she was, striding through the hotel foyer as though she were in a train station, still clutching the black backpack. Nadia followed as close behind as she dared. She crossed the circular reception, the small table full of elegant pink roses and watched Marianne walk to the Palm Court. For a moment, she wondered if she was being paranoid. The woman had a board meeting, perhaps it was taking place at the Ritz. Then she considered how unlikely that would be, for a charitable foundation to meet at one of the most expensive hotels in the world. What was Marianne up to?

Almost every table at the Palm Court was full, people sitting down to have the Ritz's famous afternoon tea, abundant with scones and clotted cream, cucumber and smoked salmon sandwiches, and delicate little pastries. There was a lingering smell of expensive perfume and an unassuming piece of music was being played by a small man at a grand piano, amongst the noise of chatter and clinking porcelain.

Marianne did not sit down. She bypassed the tables and turned right at the end of the room. Nadia hastened to catch up, once again ignoring the eyes of the wait staff, hoping she wouldn't be stopped. The other woman was now walking down a long corridor, resplendent with a crimson carpet and what looked to be Louis IV gold-gilded furniture. Nadia hesitated. There was nobody else here. If she followed any further and the other woman turned around, she would be spotted. She watched Marianne pass some bathrooms, hesitated, and then decided she had little choice but to continue. She walked slowly down the corridor and then stopped short. Some distance away, Marianne was handing in the backpack at a coat check and was given a ticket. She put the ticket into the pocket of her mac, which she clearly didn't plan on removing, nodded her thanks and turned to head back the way she had come.

Nadia dashed into the nearby bathroom, hoping she hadn't been seen. She waited a couple of minutes and then tentatively poked her head out of the door. Marianne was gone.

It didn't seem like there was any board meeting after all. She had to get that backpack and see what was inside. She waited in the corridor, uncertain. She could see from the corner of her eye that there was only one woman manning the coat check, dressed all in black, trying her best not to look bored. Could she bribe her, perhaps?

She smoothed down her linen jacket, put on her best anguished face and walked up to the counter. 'Please,' she said, 'you've got to help me.'

The woman, who was probably in her mid-fifties, stood up, looking concerned. 'What's the matter, luv?'

'My ... my boss is about to fire me. She's got a meeting upstairs, but I left some important papers in her bag. She's really angry, she's a lawyer and she's negotiating a big deal. If

I don't bring the bag up to her in five minutes, she said I'm fired,' Nadia wailed.

The woman smiled kindly. 'Well, that's not a problem. Just give me your ticket and I'll bring it out for you.'

'That's the thing,' said Nadia, sniffing. 'She gave it to me only a minute ago. I could have sworn I put it in the pocket of my jacket but it's gone. I don't know what to do!'

The coat check woman frowned, clearly torn between sympathy and her job. 'I'm sorry, luv, I'm not allowed to hand things over without a ticket.'

Shit. What now? There was a tip tray on the counter. What if she casually placed a few notes on the tray and asked again? Then she spotted the book of ticket stubs sitting next to the tray. Everything before the number eighty-three had been ripped off. She exhaled. The tickets were sequential and Marianne Riviere had been the last person here.

Nadia said quickly. 'I can describe the bag to you. It's a black backpack, and I can tell you the ticket number was eighty-two. I saw it before I put it in my pocket. Please,' she implored. 'I really need that bag, more than I can possibly say.'

A few minutes later she was back in the bathroom, in one of the stalls, unzipping the backpack.

Inside, there was a clear plastic folder with a wad of A4 sheets and a small rectangular object, wrapped up in black velvet cloth. She hesitated. The object was heavy though small, roughly the size of a mobile phone. She laid it on her lap and unwrapped the cloth. Then she stared, amazed.

It was something ancient, that much she could tell. There were lines etched on it, like lines in a notebook. And on those neat straight lines, there were hundreds of tiny symbols. There were arrows and stars and squares and fish shapes. There were a lot of triangles, of varying lengths and groupings. And underneath all that, a large scratched line, after which there were other symbols, different symbols that looked like scratched lines and wheels, the letter U and a stick man. This wasn't Egyptian, she had seen enough hieroglyphs to know that. Just what the hell was she looking at?

Just then her phone rang and she jumped in surprise. Quickly pulling it out from her jeans pocket, she saw that it was an unknown number. She ignored it. She wrapped the object back up carefully in its velvet cloth. She placed it in her own satchel. Then she pulled out the folder from the backpack and scanned the papers quickly. There were numbers, a series of numbers, in columns. On another page, a series of addresses. What was this? She stuffed the papers into her satchel and paused, considering. She didn't want to keep the backpack, in case she got caught. Somehow, this ancient writing was connected to Layla's disappearance and if it was a bargaining chip, a way to get her sister back, she wasn't going to hand it over to anyone. The backpack was empty, apart from the papers and the relic. She double checked. After a moment's hesitation, she lifted the lid off the sanitary towel disposal unit on the side of the toilet. She shoved the bag inside and put the lid on again. And then washed her hands and flushed the toilet for good measure, in case anyone was waiting outside, listening.

She tried to be casual as she left, walking normally, passing through the Palm Court once more. Her heart was pounding. She thought about her options. This was important, what she had in her satchel. It had to be important. How was it connected to Mohenjodaro and what was Marianne Riviere doing with it? Nadia walked outside into the sunshine and hailed a cab.

She gave the cabbie Layla's address, climbed in the back and breathed a little easier. Her headache had returned, probably from all the stress.

She massaged her temples. Sleep. She desperately needed to sleep, it would help make the headache go away. Her body moved with the easy rhythm of the car, her limbs felt heavy and rebellious. With a sigh, she let her head rest against the back of the seat, wrapped her arms around her satchel and closed her eyes.

Chapter Eleven

LONDON, PRESENT DAY.

Philip answered his phone, saying nothing.

'Is your mother at home?' asked the voice.

It was code, used by his employer, to check if the line was still secure, if Philip had been compromised in any way. 'Yes,' he replied. 'She is. She's reading a magazine now though.' His response let his employer know that he was in a public place, that nothing overt could be said by him.

'Fine,' said his employer. 'Have you been keeping tabs on the woman?'

'Of course.' He could see her now, stepping out of the taxi, paying the man some money and walking into her sister's building.

'She was at the Foundation today.'

'As was I. I believe she has recovered our missing ... merchandise.'

There was a pause. 'So it *was* her. Riviere.'

'It would seem to be the case, yes.'

'You know what has to be done?'

'Of course. Your instructions?'

'After you've dealt with Riviere, I think it is time we found out just how much the girl knows. And get the tablet back.'

Philip smiled. 'As you say,' he said. Finally, he could have some fun. The job had been mindless up until now.

There was a pause. 'Don't go overboard,' said the voice. 'Not with the girl. We might need her later.' His employer hung up.

Whistling to himself, Philip put his hands into the pockets of his trousers and walked down the road. He looked up at the fourth-floor window of Layla Hussain's living room. The light was on. He smiled and imagined himself waving from the pavement. *Goodbye for now, Nadia. I'll see you very soon.*

Chapter Twelve

MELUHHA, 3800 BC.

The branding ceremony began when the sun was in its highest point in the sky. It was a private affair. Only the priests and the Goddess-Blessed were in attendance. Branding was a hallowed event, a sacred ritual that could only be shared by those who had been initiated into the ways of the Temple.

Jaya and Nene stood naked at the Purification baths, just outside the Temple. The sun beat down on the water, the onlookers had taken shelter in the shade under the roofed colonnades that ran along the length of the pool, near the large, wide drains.

Not much about the ritual had been explained to them, other than that Shakari would welcome them once they had cleansed their bodies and their souls. Some of the priests stepped forward and the High One gestured that they should get into the water. His countenance, as usual, was aloof and superior. He was the High One and would not broker opposition.

She had never thought this day would truly come, no matter how much she prepared for it. Somehow, she thought, somehow her parents or Dar would have made contact with her. She had hoped that by now she would have found out where they were and found a way to reach them. But it hadn't happened.

Quietly, Nene and Jaya stepped into the pool. The priests began to chant blood oaths to Shakari, walking round and round the pool, heads bowed. Jaya immersed herself, dipping her head under, letting the sounds fade away. How she longed for the river! This water was perfumed, still and cold. It was lifeless and nothing like home. By now, the riverboats would have been at the market, and the women would be trading with each other and with the caravans for ingredients for the evening meal. Children would be swimming in the water. There would be laughter and adventure, and so many things to see – the Yoke swans teaching their little ones to swim, the Goh lizards, larger than a little child, waddling in for a drink, only to be swallowed whole by a hungry crocodile, or just the steady banter of the people, at ease with their surroundings, grateful for the simple things, for the catch they had made that day, or health that they were blessed with. She wanted that life. *Oh Shakari, what purpose have you in taking me away from it?* Her family had never come. They had never even sent her a message from Dilmun. Where were they?

She felt arms reaching into the water, pulling her out. Her sisters. The Goddess-Blessed were her sisters now. They wrapped her in a white tunic and placed a jasmine flower in the palm of her hand. 'A symbol of our purity,' Lal, her new sister, whispered, as they were led towards the colonnade.

Jaya swallowed. A clay cauldron was resting on a coal fire. A firesmith stood by, a set of thin, long metal reeds in his hand.

It was the tattoo, she realized with dread. Just like in her vision. Those reeds would be heated against the coals. They would sear into her flesh thirteen times, to obscure her from the gaze of the One Horned God, just as the thirteen leaves of the pipal tree had obscured Shakari from the One Horned God. She would be blessed, charmed and free from the powers of dark magic. But at what price?

She stepped forward reluctantly, even though the other Goddess-Blessed had been quick to reassure her and Nene the night before. 'They are only small burns,' Lal had said, laughing. 'Like mosquito bites. You will forget about them before long. Besides, the healer makes us a special poultice, and will give you an amulet that will protect you from disease and from curses.'

And after the branding, she would be a Goddess-Blessed. Forever.

The night before, her nerves getting the better of her, she had begged Nene to run away with her and travel to Dilmun, no matter what the cost. They would steal if they had to – steal from the Temple even. There was plenty of gold there. Her friend had looked at Jaya as though she had lost her mind, pointing out that the punishment for theft was to have one's hands chopped off or be hanged outside the Temple. Besides, they had no food stored up. How would they survive the perilous journey on only their wits? The truth was, Nene was happier than she had ever been. She had never belonged with the Cranes, for theirs was a life of service, of healing others, of learning. It was not in her nature to stay still, she could not wait to officially become a noblewoman with a house of her own, with little to occupy her except the archaic rituals of the Temple.

'You go,' she'd said to Jaya. 'But you'll regret it. The journey is long. Treacherous even. Young women without support are treated brutally, no matter how much you have paid for passage, even if you could get the gold together. They'll rape you before you're out of the city gates if you go without a protector. Is that really what you want or what your family would want for you?'

And so she had stayed. Her father would be horrified at the idea of her stealing from the Temple, what had she been thinking? Shakari herself would curse her and Nene was right, the journey was too treacherous. She would have to find one of the few caravans that crossed the vast expanse of the desert with women accompanying it. The Jackals rarely took women with them on their trading routes. She could take a boat, of course, but it would take her many, many moons to gather the gold for the oarsmen. The thought had preoccupied her for most of the night. Oh, why had she not had the strength to just run away and take her chances! She was the worst kind of coward.

And now, here they were ...

They were given something to drink in heavily decorated clay cups, with images of cranes, dipping their necks in the river. She stared at her cup suspiciously. The liquid was the colour of swamp water. It tasted bitter and she frowned. But Nene drank hers in one go, desperate for her life to begin as one of the Blessed. Under the watchful eyes of the priests, Jaya swallowed what was left of hers.

Iaf walked towards them. He and the priests had once again covered their faces with red pigment. No, not pigment. She knew now that it was goat's blood that was used in the rituals of the Temple. He was talking about the importance of the Goddess-Blessed, of their obligation to learn the ways of reading the Bloodstone. As he talked, he dipped his finger into a bowl of the very same blood. He then ran that finger down her cheek. She tried not to flinch, aware that the whole Temple was watching. He dipped his finger back in the bowl, and smeared her other cheek as well. Sarema was at his side, proud and beautiful in a tunic dyed a colour that Jaya had never seen before. It looked like the evening sky just before dusk. The tunic was expensive, no doubt. Expensive and rare.

After many days living as her guest, Jaya was beginning to understand Sarema. The woman enjoyed fineries. She was a selfish creature, who doted on her own daughters, Aashti and Taali, but ruled the others with an iron hand. Everyone feared her and bowed to her every whim.

Lal had warned Jaya and Nene very clearly. 'There is one thing you must remember above all others. Do not anger Sarema. If you do as she says, you will enjoy a life you can scarcely begin to imagine. A house of your own, plenty of servants and amusements. But if you cross her ... I have seen what happens, my soon-to-be sisters. You cannot imagine how destructive her anger can be. Take heed of my advice.'

It was good advice and she meant to heed it, but now, Jaya began to feel dizzy. It was the heat, no doubt. How strange. Everyone seemed to be moving very, very slowly.

'It is time,' said Sarema.

Jaya was brought to the firesmith.

Iaf placed her hands in his, his eyes narrowed. 'Do you swear to live and die for the honour of Shakari, the true Mother Goddess, and her children? Do you swear to uphold the laws and rites of Meluhha, and place yourself in the service of the Temple?'

Did she? No, she didn't. Why should she? She was a Crocodile! But it seemed enough that she remained silent, unfocused and dizzy. Iaf carried on talking regardless. She was seeing double. Two High Ones. What a scary prospect. She was about to point it out when one of her new sisters cradled her head. What on earth was she doing? The world tilted to one side.

Then the pain came. She had not even seen the firesmith approach her, but there he was, poking her forehead with those sticks of his. Lal had lied. It wasn't like mosquito bites at all. It was like giant lightning bolts striking her head. She started to shake, hearing her flesh sizzle. Was that her, shouting out like that?

But then it was over. Somebody was wiping away the blood on her face, some of it was the animal's, but now, some of it was hers too, and people were embracing her, calling her sister.

The whole situation made her feel strangely giddy. Was she really one of them now? Was it that easy to say goodbye to her former life? Perhaps she was dreaming, for why were the priests sipping from the bowl of blood, painting their lips red with it? And then the bowl was in front of her and she was drinking too, a smell of rust against her nostrils. But suddenly, here was Nene, hugging her and crying at the same time, blood still trickling from her own wound, blood on her lips. 'Sisters forever,' she whispered, as they were whisked away and taken into the Temple.

There the women applied the poultice given by the healer, which helped ease the pain. Both girls were given amulets to protect them from all ills, which were placed around their necks, and new tunics, dyed ochre and black. She tried to focus, but the day faded in and out like an old memory.

Afterwards, they ate in the Temple with all the priests, a succulent meal of venison, spinach and apricots, washed down with buffalo milk, wine and barley beer. Jaya drank more of the beer than she ordinarily would have done, letting the servants fill her cup time and time again. She wanted to continue feeling the sense of other-worldliness that this day had brought her. But it did not seem to take away the pounding in her head, and soon, she was ready for bed.

She stared at the others. They sat in a haphazard circle on mats on the floor. They seemed to be talking as though they were under water. It was a game Dar and she used to play as children. Dive into the river and talk to one another through moving liquid. Guess what the other was saying as the bubbles floated out of their mouths. She tried to sit up straight. If this was the game tonight, she was doing a bad job of playing. What was that bit? About the legitimacy of the priests to make decisions for the people? There was some talk about how the Unclanned had been grumbling, complaining about their lack of rights, and how it fell upon the priests to protect the people from them, to make it clear that they should leave the city.

There were many speeches to endure and she had difficulty guessing what was being said. Iaf, Sarema and Iaf's most favoured priest, a man named Kul, talked about what an honour it was to serve the Goddess. Kul also talked about the beneficence and greatness of Iaf, the High One, who, if it was the will of Shakari, would lead the city for many cycles to come. Everyone clapped at that and Iaf tilted his head and raised his cup, looking bemused. She shut them out, watching only Nene, whose eyes had lit up at the sight of the grapes, mangoes and pears that were served along with the venison. Nene ate them all, beaming, even as little beads of blood gathered at her wound. What a strange sight she was, sucking on a piece of fruit, as a trickle of red ran past her eye.

When the meal was over, Jaya was more grateful than she could possibly have thought. She needed to lie down, to close her eyes and let go of the world for a moment or two.

But again it was not to be. Someone was saying something and she was on her feet. Why?

They were led down the hallway to the antechamber, to the room where the Bloodstone lay in its box, on a high podium. What would happen now?

Iaf was saying something and Nene was nudging her in the ribs. What?

'As part of your initiation, you will both offer your first visions as one of the

Goddess-Blessed,' he was saying. 'Jaya, you will begin. We praise your name, and your deeds, and your actions.' They all clapped, bringing their hands together to their chests and bowing their heads.

'We praise your name, and your deeds, and your actions,' the others were intoning.

What deeds, what actions, she wondered, as she walked towards the Bloodstone. Somebody had already taken it out of its box. Others were throwing rose petals on the floor as she walked, she felt their softness on the soles of her feet. There was a drum beating slowly, though she could not identify where exactly the sound was coming from. She crushed roses as she walked.

Then, the Temple went silent.

'You will ask the Bloodstone for a vision to help us understand the structure of the new granary,' Iaf was murmuring. Had he always been walking next to her? 'The foundation keeps cracking, how do we stop it? You must ask this.'

Is that how it worked? She was supposed to *talk* to a piece of Shakari's heart and it, in turn, would answer her? This was it then, the moment they would all realize that she had no value to them, that the last vision had been a one-off thing. What would they do, throw her out? Make her Unclanned? The others seemed to be surviving on false visions. She must be creative enough to do the same.

Iaf took her hands and placed them on the Stone. She closed her eyes, wanting the world to stop spinning. But instead she was transported, physically turned inwards to a place within herself, it felt as though her stomach had flipped over. She was her own body, her own muscles, her own frantically beating heart. And the Stone was there with her. And it was *alive*. She felt it probing her, felt it probing every joint and every organ, every muscle and sinew, and she felt its black veins in her blood, in the very essence of her.

Slowly, she felt it pulling from her core, pulling pieces of her away. And in that moment, when she protested, when she willed her body to let go of it, the Stone played with her mind.

It let her understand that she could take her thoughts anywhere and see anything in the realm of possibility. She learnt then that the earth was both far, far bigger than she could ever have imagined, and much smaller, in the great expanse of life.

It made her so happy, this sudden power, this sudden knowledge. She felt giddy, heavy with it. But somewhere, some part of her was being told that the Bloodstone demanded payment in kind – it would take her life in exchange for knowledge, if she lingered to spend time with it. She had to keep her thoughts from wandering. She forced herself to focus on something that would help the city, what the structure of the foundations for the new granary should look like.

As she concentrated, it came to her, such a simple thing, the layers of brick, patterned with limestone, how they should fit and be baked together with bitumen, the geometric shapes, the width and diameters of the baked clay and how it should be fired in the kiln and at what temperature to keep from getting brittle. They had not lined the brick with limestone, in their first attempt, and the bricks needed to be bigger to support the structure. How did she know this? How could she suddenly understand geometric patterns and the weights and depths of the stones? And yet she did. She understood it all.

In that moment, holding the Bloodstone, with only some small part of her still conscious of the outside world, she realized that she must truly be a Goddess-Blessed. Was this the life she was meant to lead after all? Was she not meant to search for her family? She had to know. They were not allowed to ask personal questions, to gain knowledge for their own purposes. It was said, in ancient times, that all selfish requests angered Shakari. A Goddess-Blessed would be cursed for putting herself before her people. She would be damned and go mad from the knowledge she was given, if she used the Bloodstone for her own desire. Still ...

Where is my family? When will I see them again? Show me what the world has in store for me.

An image appeared immediately – a vision of a man who lay upon her. The man hurt her. He treated her violently, grunting and pounding into her like she were a slab of meat, biting her flesh and pushing her down so her head crashed into the floor and she cried out in pain.

That man was Iaf.

In her shock, she let go of the Stone. The impact of the separation while her mind was still connected to it caused her so much physical pain that she fell and convulsed on the Temple floor.

They pulled her up, giving her no time to recover before the onslaught of questions. 'What did you see?' Iaf was demanding.

She shrank from him, her mind turbulent. She had to protect herself. How could she protect herself? Her mind was not working properly!

'Well?'

She tried to focus. What to say? She told him about the foundation then, about the bricks and everything she could remember, and he in turn barked an order for the city architects to come to the Temple, so she could help them record what she had seen. She spoke with the architects at some length, answering their questions, her body still trembling, her voice worn, until at last, they thanked her and left.

'Did the Bloodstone show you anything else, Jaya?' Sarema was asking, stroking her hair with an expression that seemed concerned, but which Jaya knew was full of calculation.

She did not hesitate. Her senses had returned and she understood that Sarema's eyes were too sharp, her countenance too eager. 'No,' she said. 'Just the granary. Now please, help me, I feel very unwell.'

Sarema and Iaf exchanged looks, she watched the unspoken communication between them. What had they in store for her? She had to leave this place as soon as possible. If only the Bloodstone had shown her family!

'Come,' said Lal soothingly, placing her hands on Jaya's shoulders. 'It has been a long day. Rest now.'

Jaya was taken outside, to the Temple's large courtyard, and given a bed amongst many others, set up, no doubt, for the ritual. 'Sleep here,' Lal said. 'Tomorrow you will have your own house, and your own servants, and a generous allowance of credit to use in the market. You may not realize it yet, Jaya, but today has been the luckiest day of your life.' Lal stroked her arm and smiled briefly. Then she went back to join the others.

Jaya lay down. She had to think of a strategy, a way to leave without getting caught. She should leave now, when everyone was distracted with Nene's reading of the

Stone. But there were people and guards everywhere. Could she sneak out in the cover of darkness? She rubbed her aching head. She had to think. But her head ... it hurt ... Sleep overcame her so quickly that she barely had time to close her eyes.

Chapter Thirteen

LONDON, PRESENT DAY.

Sometimes, she was a glutton for punishment.

Nadia sat in the pub across the road and nursed her Sprite, looking longingly at the bottles of Jack Daniels behind the counter. It was easy, far too easy to remember what it tasted like, the sour, rich malt seeped in oak. Whisky on the rocks. That had been her poison of choice. And God, how she had loved it. Had? There was no past tense about it, was there? She *did* love it and being here was a really bad idea.

She tried to content herself with her soft drink. She hunched over the bar counter, smelling the stale ale that had seeped into the wood over the years, enjoying the noise of the students and the clamour of voices. The pub might be a bit of a dive, but it felt comfortable, a place where you could be left alone, if you wanted. A place where you could meet up with people who liked to stay anonymous, like hackers who had once helped you research a novel, for instance.

While she waited for Apollo to get there, she looked around. Despite the many groups of students, the Lion was a typical old gents' pub, with several scratched wooden tables scattered around a couple of large fireplaces. Little red curtains covered small Edwardian windows, full of dust and grime. There were figurines on the black ledges and some large copper boxes. A string of brass horseshoes made a daisy chain on the walls. This place looked like it hadn't changed in a century.

Behind the counter, rows and rows of alcoholic beverages were lined up on the glass shelves. The bartender was pulling a pint for an old man at the other end. There was a dart board and a trivia machine in one corner, the latter in use by a trio of young guys who cursed good-naturedly each time they got a question wrong, and a chalkboard advertised the Lion's Tuesday night Pub Quiz.

It was the perfect place, as far as she was concerned, for her meeting, even with the booze. She should probably have met Apollo somewhere alcohol-free. But Apollo – she didn't know his real name, only that he was a big fan of *Battlestar Gallactica* – didn't like crowds. And she was a big girl now, plus four years sober. She wasn't going to throw that away, no matter how tempting or how much pressure she was under.

She'd just about finished her Sprite when Apollo showed up.

'Typical,' he muttered crossly, shooting her a sideways glance as he struggled to get up on the bar stool. 'The skinny girl never thinks of the fat bloke, does she? Couldn't you have picked a table or something, Nut Job?'

She looked at him sheepishly. Apollo weighed over three hundred and eighty pounds. He'd once told her that his version of exercise was to pick up the remote for his Wii with one hand and a slice of pizza with the other. But she also knew that he hated it when people treated him differently, simply because of his size.

She gave him a sweet smile. 'What happened to that aqua aerobics class you were going to sign up for?'

He shrugged, moving his bulk around the stool in an attempt to get comfortable. 'Pint of cider please, love,' he said to the woman at the bar, who nodded. He turned to Nadia. 'They made me dance. In the water. Like I'm going to go around wasting my time prancing around a pool like an underwater ballerina. So, what was so important, Nut Job, that I had to drop everything and travel halfway across London?'

He'd called her Nut Job when he had first contacted her, after she'd started posting messages online about wanting to talk to hackers for *Blaze*, her second book. He'd told her she was an idiot, and she'd realized he was right when her computer was hacked nine different times as a result of those messages. 'You practically put a target on your back and invited us to shoot the arrow,' he had said. Of course, he'd also meandered through her laptop. He'd seen the appointments with all those shrinks, the crazy dreams she'd recorded over the years, the friends and family of GoL members who had reached out to her for help and guidance. It was GoL that had grabbed his fancy. He decided it would be amusing to help the daughter of an infamous cult leader.

Most of their relationship had been conducted online, though in the last couple of years, as he trusted her more, they'd met a few times, in person, on her London trips. She'd gotten to know Apollo, to recognize his handiwork in the news. He was a libertarian. He had shut down bank websites and left messages about the unequal distribution of wealth in the banking system on their home pages. He'd messed with the algorhythmic trading model of a successful hedge fund which had made a profit from shorting subprime mortgages. That had caused chaos. She'd read about it in the papers for over a week, and Scotland Yard had come close to catching him.

Apollo was idealistic. He hated corporations, politicians and well-meaning champagne socialists, he said. He had morals, even as he hacked into bank accounts and used the money to support his own lifestyle – not that he required much. He took little, unnoticeable amounts, and used it primarily for his gaming addiction.

Apollo had lanky black hair which almost reached his shoulders and a beard that never quite grew thick enough to be considered proper. He was wearing a crumpled green shirt which looked like it hadn't been washed in days, and in its front pocket were several ready-to-smoke rollies. He was hardly minting it.

'You need a housekeeper, my friend. Who does your laundry?'

'Yeah, yeah, enough of the pleasantries. You said it was urgent. I'm assuming it has something to do with Layla's disappearance? I was gutted to hear about that, by the way. I saw you've been researching the place, but you aren't getting far on finding her on your own, are you? I should've called.'

Of course, he had hacked her phone. He trawled through her life whenever he was bored or curious. Or concerned. But she didn't mind. Apollo would never share what he found with anyone else. There were few people in the world that she trusted, but he was one of them, with his misguided morals and deep passion for what he believed in. She passed him the papers she had found in the black backpack. 'What do these look like to you? Bank accounts, maybe?'

He scanned them quickly and nodded. 'Yes. Bank accounts routing into other bank accounts. See these addresses? They're all offshore tax havens. Someone's trying to hide their cash, I reckon.'

'Can you find out who?'

He winked. 'Do you doubt it?'

She smiled in relief. 'Thanks. You want to take the papers with you?'

Apollo snorted and rolled his eyes. 'You really are so old school, love. Guess they didn't teach you much about technology at that compound?' He pulled his mobile phone out of his pocket and scanned the papers. When he was done, he handed them back.

'Keep 'em, I've just turned them into PDFs. I'll track these down when I get home, okay?'

'Thanks Apollo.'

'Is this going to help you find your sister?'

'I hope so. I don't ... I don't really know how it's related to her yet.'

He looked at her with sympathy.

She hesitated. 'There's something else.'

'What?'

She looked around, making sure they were not being watched. 'I found something. It's like an ancient tablet or something.'

He nodded his thanks to the bartender, who'd put the pint of cider in front of him. He took a sip. 'Show me.'

'Not here. Someone might notice.'

'Nut Job, we're in a dive in Hackney. Nobody's going to notice anything.' It was true. The students were laughing in the corner, giggling over their cider and blackcurrant, while the old man was reading his paper, his glasses hanging delicately on the bridge of his nose.

Nadia pulled the relic out of her bag and, placing it on her lap, unwrapped it slowly. Apollo leaned in and peered at it. Then he whistled. 'That looks authentic, for sure. Not that I'm an expert or anything.'

'Do you recognize the writing?'

'Do I look like a history professor? But let me take a photo of it, I'll find out for you. If it's a well-known piece ... maybe it's been stolen. How did you get it? No, no, don't answer that. The less I know the better. If they haul my arse to jail, I want deniability.'

She placed a hand on his shoulder. 'Thank you. You're a good friend, Apollo,' she said. 'Fuck the water aerobics.'

'Fuck it,' he agreed. He winked, finished his cider, gave her a kiss on the cheek and left.

She ordered another Sprite. She should leave, go back to the flat. But she liked the vibe in the pub and it wouldn't hurt to just sit, for a few more moments. To gather her thoughts.

'You all right there?'

A man took the stool next to hers, cradling a pint in both hands. He smiled, and she assessed him coolly. He was attractive enough, she supposed. A good chiselled jaw, a slightly gaunt, shaggy look about him, with sandy brown hair that curled up a little at his neckline. Tall, very tall, and muscular – she could see that even through his blue shirt and jeans. Penetrative green eyes, with just enough unkempt about him. Interesting.

'Another evening, perhaps,' she said, looking away, aware, suddenly, of the Sprite in her hands and how out of place she was sitting there alone.

He seemed confused and scratched at his stubble. 'Another evening for what?'

She turned on her seat to face him. 'Look, I've had a crappy day and the mother of all crappy weeks, okay? Please don't take it personally. I'm just not in the mood to flirt with you. I'm going to finish my drink here and head home. So please, don't waste your time.'

He half smiled, but shook his head. 'A crappy day? I've had a crappy day too. More than one, actually. A whole lot of the buggers. Do you know, I've just flown halfway around the world for reasons I can't fathom?'

'That's an interesting accent. Irish?'

He nodded. 'Northern. Belfast.'

'Oh. Well, I'm sorry for your crappy day, Mr ...'

'O'Rourke. Liam O'Rourke.'

'Well, I'm sorry for it, Mr O'Rourke. There's far too much crap in the world at the moment. But I'm not going to sleep with you, if that's what this is all about.'

'And if a man were to bid you hello, he'd be wanting to get in your pants, is that it?'

'Isn't that what men do in seedy pubs? They take a chance on a woman who is sitting alone? Men are fairly single-minded in my experience.'

He drummed his fingers irritably against the counter. 'Well,' he said eventually. 'Your experience aside, I'm not here for that. You can believe me when I say that sleeping with you would be the last thing on my mind.'

She looked at him more carefully. He had lines of fatigue etched across his face. And he seemed stressed. His fingers continued to drum on the counter. They were long and tapered, but his hands looked solid, well used. She took a sip of her drink. 'Look, I know this sounds callous and bitchy, but I'm not the touchy-feely type either. You've clearly got a lot on your mind, and I'm not the best shoulder. Those girls playing pool over there are giving you fancy eyes – why don't you try your luck with them?'

He looked amused now. Amused and cross, as he took a sip of his pint, shooting her a sideways glance. 'Well, now, of all the things I imagined you to be, I never thought obnoxious would be one of them. Stands to reason, of course, that you'd be standoffish. How could you not be?'

She shrugged. 'You're entitled to your opinion, Mr O'Rourke, especially after what I've said. But you don't know me. And you're the one who approached me. I did you the courtesy of being honest, of letting you know that I'm not interested in any kind of dialogue with you. Like I said, there are plenty of other proverbial fish and plenty of shoulders. One of those girls is winking at you, did you notice?'

He didn't even turn around. 'You're wrong,' he said, his green eyes turning harder. 'I do know you. I know that your coming here was a stupid move, for instance. Stupid because alcoholics should never visit pubs in moments of high anxiety.'

She caught her breath. 'How did you ...'

He leaned forward and said, 'You're Nadia Osbourne, born Hussain, but like most little girls with an arsehole for a father, you took on your mother's maiden name. I don't blame you for that, I would have done the same. And we need to talk. It's important.'

'Who are you?'

'Like I said, my name is Liam O'Rourke. We need to talk about Mohenjodaro and Layla.'

She felt the anger take over. 'I see. Well, I know exactly who you are now. I don't talk to the press. Excuse me.' She got up to leave, and he put his hand on her arm.

'I would advise you to listen to what I have to say, Nadia. I've come a very long way.'

The bloody media. They would do anything to get a story. Had he overheard her conversation with Apollo? She hoped he hadn't seen the ancient tablet, or whatever it was. And damn the jerk, now he was crowding her. 'Listen, I don't know who you think you are or what kind of story you're publishing, but you'd better get out of my face this instant. I have no comment.' She pulled away. She didn't like being touched by strangers.

He raised his hands. 'Just so you know, I'm not a journalist. Bastard maybe, but journalist no.' He sighed. 'I'm sorry, I was out of line. You pushed my buttons, and I'm tired and a mite stressed. You've got a bark on you, lass. I don't blame you. But I'm here to help you, Nadia, please believe me.'

'Go to hell.'

'Listen to me, you damned woman. I'm here for Layla.'

Several pairs of eyes turned in their direction. She raised her voice, making it clear to the whole pub that he was not welcome. 'Like I said, go to hell. And if I see you again, I'll call the cops.' She marched out of the door as the man watched, looking bewildered and frustrated.

Chapter Fourteen

MELUHHA, 3800 BC.

When Jaya opened her eyes again, it was late at night. She could smell the woodsmoke from the kitchens. The air was dusty and dry. Jaya sat up. She was alone in the courtyard. How long had she been asleep? She shivered, rubbing her hands across her arms. It was dark. Now was her chance to leave, before the others found out. She still had friends amongst the Crocodiles. She would seek sanctuary with Kaul-Tu and ask him to protect her until she could pay for passage to Dilmun. He would take her in, wouldn't he? He was her father's oldest friend, after all.

'Are you cold, child?'

She recognized the voice and her heart sank. She turned around. How long had Iaf been standing there? Oh, Goddess protect her, but Iaf was a tall man. Tall and imposing, despite his slender frame. And now the vision came flooding back, the images that the Bloodstone had shown her. Iaf, rutting on top of her. Hurting her.

He came towards her and held out his hand. 'Come, there is much to discuss.'

She shrank back and he frowned. 'I said come, child.'

'I am fine where I sit, though I thank you, High One.' She felt shocked at her own bravery.

He looked at her strangely. 'You have nothing to fear from me, child. We have much to celebrate, do we not?'

She forced a weak smile and put her hand to her head. 'The branding. I'm afraid I have become too intoxicated, High One. I am not fit to be in your presence.' She tried to keep the nervousness out of her voice, though she could hear it all too well. The slight quiver in her tone, the edge of it. He must know that she feared him. How was she to run away now?

He dropped his hand. 'The branding ... yes, indeed. I forgot about the branding.' He looked contemplative. 'It was not the branding I refer to, Jaya. It is my excitement at seeing you here. I always knew there would be others who could read the Stone. It has taken me a long time to find you. I asked the Stone to help me. I have seen your face in it for many moons now.'

His words confused her.

'Come,' he said, more urgently. 'We must talk privately about your vision. This is not the place to linger. My chambers are a better option. There are far too many spies in the Temple.'

'Spies, High One?' He was blocking her way, she could not see. Everything was dark around them, save a spatter of starlight.

His eyes narrowed. 'The priests in Dilmun and Arrapha ... even in Chanu, they are all plotting against us. They invoke their own new laws and they want to stop paying tithe to Meluhha. As though such a thing could even be contemplated. We are strong because we have power. And power comes from wealth, does it not? They say we have not given them any protection or warnings for several cycles, that they are paying us for nothing. But then their people come here expecting work, expecting a better life. The Unclanned.' He spat on the ground. 'And now the Unclanned think to question our laws. Do you know, they've started to demand rights and privileges? If my father were alive, they would never have dreamed of questioning him thus.'

He frowned at her, waiting for her to respond. But she said nothing, lost in his words. Eventually, he shrugged. 'But what do you know of such things? You have much to learn. There is time yet. The architects tell me that your plan will work perfectly for the new granary. They are already laying the foundations and it is holding. I have waited a long time, as I said, to meet someone like me. Someone with real power.'

Like him? What did he mean? The High One was smiling, but that terrified her even more. 'The other Goddess-Blessed,' she said desperately, looking behind him for the way out of the courtyard. 'They have power ...'

Iaf scowled, walking the length of the courtyard, looking out for eavesdroppers, before returning to her. It was getting chilly now, but he seemed oblivious to the wind. 'You and I both know that the others are useless, no matter how many chances I give them or how much they pretend. Their visions are hollow. Cheaper than the broken shells that the merchants sell in bulk in the square. But what is one to do? We must have the Blessed, the masses demand such traditions.' He came towards her. He smelt of the camphor that burned inside the Temple. It was stifling and made her stomach churn once more.

He seemed puzzled. 'What is it, child? Why do you get so anxious?'

'It is ... nothing, High One, I am just ... overwhelmed, that is all.'

He frowned. 'Perhaps reading the Stone has taken a toll. I know all about that. I was the only one who could read the Stone for many, many cycles. Until now. I was Chosen, and so are you, don't you understand? Nobody else in this city has proven worthy enough for the honour.'

She shook her head. His words made no sense. Everyone knew that men could not read the Bloodstone, that the gift was passed to Meluhha's daughters, not her sons.

He sat beside her now and was trailing his index finger along her shoulder, causing her to start and grit her teeth. 'Oh, I begin to contemplate this. You think what I am saying must be an untruth. It is not for men, this business of visions. It is what the Goddess-Blessed are for. For that is what we teach you, is it not?'

She shivered. 'I am not accusing you of lying, High One.'

His breath smelt strange. Rancid. 'Indeed. For that would be heresy, punishment by torturous death. Do you know what we do to heretics, Jaya? To the followers of the One Horned God? We hang them from the pipal tree outside the Temple, leaving the noose just loose enough so that they can draw the faintest of breaths ... in the end they die of thirst, but not before the crows and vultures feast on them. For how else can we ensure that our people follow the path of Shakari faithfully? Oh, do not look so alarmed, my dear, I do not wish any harm to befall you.'

He looked so calm, so rational, so *normal* as he talked of torture and death, still smiling away. Just what did Iaf want with her? Oh, Goddess help her, she did not understand. Had she cursed herself by demanding that the Bloodstone show her a vision of her own future? Was this the result? Was she to be damned?

'In actual fact,' he continued, 'men have always been able to read the Stone. I think, many hundreds of cycles ago, someone – perhaps the priests – made it so that only women could be Named as Goddess-Blessed.'

'Why ... why would they do that?'

'An interesting question. You are Chosen, so perhaps you already know. Prolonged use of the Stone will weaken you. You will sicken and you will die. We do not know why this is so. But my father, may his soul reside forever in the Upworld, hypothesized that perhaps the priests knew of this and decided that only women should be subjected to that fate, as the strength of the men was needed to protect the city. He was a strong man, my father. Before your time. None would have dared to question the power of Meluhha under his tenure. The answer is, I really don't know, for we have nothing written about it in our tablets. Even I cannot divine the will of the Goddess all the time, Jaya.'

His fingers reached her neck, and he continued to stroke her. 'I ... please ...' she said, feeling sick.

'It is frustrating, but there you have it. The sad fact is that I cannot use the Stone any more, it weakens me too much and my responsibilities are too great for that. And so I sent Sarema to search for others who could read it. I knew I couldn't be the only one. I used the Stone one last time and do you know what I saw, Jaya? I saw you. And your power. It will be a great power, once you understand how to use it. I looked out for you at the Clanning. Holding the Bloodstone was a test. I knew you'd pass.'

'Please ... High One. I ... I don't ...'

'At the next Clanning, perhaps we will find more women to join us. It has to be women, don't you see? Another man with my powers would grow too powerful. He might have thoughts about taking over. I cannot have that. You must ask the Stone to find these women for us. Do you like history, Jaya?'

Had the High One been touched by madness? Is that what was happening? How could anyone talk like he did, changing ideas so rapidly. 'I ... no. I don't know.'

He was caressing her cheeks now and trailing his fingers through her hair. 'Our great stories have been written on tablets for many cycles. They are in the priests' private chambers, many in languages so obscure that even our best scholars do not know what they say. I know, because the Stone has told me. Stories of war, of famine, of ingenuity and creation. Of how our ancestors claimed this city from the dust. They made it real, tangible. Imagine how much power the Bloodstone gave the people then when there were many who had the visions!'

What should she do? What *could* she do? How could she leave with him sitting next to her? She saw a figure enter the courtyard, hesitate and then walk away. It was one of the serving boys. She was tempted to shout out, but he left so quickly ...

Iaf continued in his conversational tone. 'Would you like to see them? Or can you not read? You clearly have an affinity for the river, but the Cranes saw something in you also, which means you must be clever as well.' He stopped. This time his fingers ran down her thigh. He chuckled. 'Ah, but the Rhinoceros clan offered for you also. What does that tell me? The Rhinos only choose temptresses, did you know that? Women with the capacity to seduce men. It is no wonder the Stone chose you as my equal.'

'No,' she said, standing up quickly. 'You are mistaken in that. Please, leave me alone.'

He stood up as well, looking less than amused. 'All I ask is that you read the Bloodstone, Jaya, as you are meant to do. Show me the visions that I seek. But fail to comply with my wishes ... well ... you would not like the outcome.'

'According to you, if I seek out too many visions, the Stone will kill me.' She moved backwards, looking to follow the serving boy's way out of the courtyard.

He shrugged, as though it were of little concern. 'Eventually. In time. If we are careful, you will live long enough for others to take your place. We will use the Stone sparingly, so that you have strength to give me daughters. Daughters with my seed in them. Imagine how much power they will have, if my seed bore the child in your womb. The two of us combined ... our daughters will be my greatest army. I have seen this in my visions, and I have plans, Jaya, many, many plans for this great city of ours, and my place in the known world. Meluhha grows weak. Others are questioning our supremacy. Our own vassal states want freedom from us. Unimaginable, is it not, after all the knowledge we have shared with them? And what do we get in return? Their squalid and their poor. The immigrants that arrive here every day disgust me, for they do not have our blood in their veins. They are not made from the dust of this city, as you and I are. They will never read the Bloodstone. And yet here they are, demanding rights, demanding free passage across the city, as though they were entitled. Meluhha needs a strong man to lead the city in this difficult time. I will be that strong man, like my father was before me.'

He was mad. Totally mad. Later, she would wonder why she did not stay silent. Why she did not let him rant. What it was that possessed her to speak out. Somewhere at the back of her mind she had been thinking about Dar. 'But Meluhha is never supposed to have a leader, High One. Is that not so? We are all equals in the eyes of Shakari. One man has no right to make decisions for the many. It is the Council of Clans who decide ...'

His face was full of contempt. 'You are a foolish girl. A very foolish girl.'

Was that the way out? That little brown gap in the wall? A hall or doorway? She could not see in the dark. She ran towards it, but he was faster. He pushed himself against her. They fell to the ground and she felt his hands all over her.

'You can't,' she gasped, remembering her vision. It was forbidden for the Priests and the Blessed to lie together. There were sacred rituals for fathering a Goddess-Blessed. 'Get off me!'

He pressed his body onto hers, so that she could not move. He was not weak at all, why had she ever thought that? 'Any other girl would be honoured to lay with me. I am the High One. You are so far beneath me as to be a beetle in the dust of my footsteps. And yet, I seek to elevate you, though I wonder now if your mind is even weaker than those who are Unclanned.'

'I will tell Sarema ...'

He laughed. 'Tell her what? That the High One does as he pleases? What would you have her do? Summon the Council of Clans to make a decision for me about whether I can bed you? She would have you whipped before you could finish talking. Stop squirming so. It is our obligation to give life to others who can read the Stone. Even the Council would agree.'

She could not lift him off. She tried desperately to draw breath as he pressed his body on hers. 'All right,' she croaked, raising her hands in supplication. 'All right. You do not have to hurt me. I will do as you wish ... High One. Please. Forgive me for being so foolish. I still do not understand the ways of the noble-born.' She felt the tears, hot and salty, flowing down her cheeks.

He released her, but only long enough to untie his tunic and lift hers. Then, he pressed his fingers deeply into the sockets under her eyes until she screamed.

He smiled again and parted her legs. 'If our daughter is to be helpful to me, she must be born from a mother who knows her place in the world. You,' he grunted, as he rammed himself inside her, 'will learn your place tonight.'

She screamed again, the pain tearing at her insides. She looked at the heavens in the night sky as he moved inside her.

Shakari, why have you abandoned me?

Please, make it stop. I swear I will never use the Bloodstone for my own gain again. I will never ask selfish questions. Take me home. Please. Do not curse me for my sins.

Shakari? Great Mother?

But there was no answer.

Chapter Fifteen

LONDON, PRESENT DAY.

By the time Nadia got back to Layla's, she could have wept with fatigue. Her head was still pounding from how angry that journalist had made her feel. She dumped her bag and shoes in the living room, and headed to the kitchen. Jay had left a yellow Post-it note on the fridge:

> *Got home, you weren't back yet. Vegetable curry on the top shelf, so eat it! There's a bottle of non-alcoholic beer too, in case you like that kind of thing. I need to get some more ciggies – be back in a bit. Call me if you need anything from the shops. We'll swap notes later, but I've left the CDs on your bed. Jim made copies, so these are your originals. Jay x.'*

God bless the man, she thought. It was late and he had been thoughtful. She'd eat, but later, when he got back from the store, so they could talk and catch up. It had been a long day and she wanted to get clean, to curl up in her PJs and give her brain and body a chance to unwind. She picked up the CDs, put them in her satchel, made herself a cup of tea and headed down the corridor to the bathroom. She had a quick shower, ignoring the loud knocking of the pipes and the whirr of the broken extractor fan, her head under the hot water. Feeling marginally better, she changed into her sweatpants and tank top, and then turned on the TV in Layla's room, sitting cross-legged on the bed, drying her hair with a towel. The news was still full of the Mohenjodaro 8, and speculation about where they had been taken and who had them. Some smug reporter had found out that the word Mohenjodaro meant 'Mound of the Dead' and was commenting on how appropriate that title was.

Nadia turned off the TV. She rubbed her temples and pressed her palms against her eyes. She didn't want to think about all of this now. She hadn't slept properly in two days, and that jerk reporter in the pub had really pissed her off. She needed a round or two of kick-boxing in the gym ... some way to blow off steam.

She drank her tea instead. Then she turned on her phone, ignoring the pinging of messages and voicemail. Bloody reporters.

First she called Lennie, checking in on Nelson. Stupid idiot cat. She should have dumped him when she had the chance. He was fine, apparently. Had started bringing mice back to the apartment, which she considered reasonably enterprising of him. She told Lennie she owed him one, and would repay him for the expensive tuna he had to buy.

When she hung up, she dialled her sponsor, Sarah, who lived in LA and had supported her through the worst of her rock-bottoms. Then she heard a loud thump and she frowned, hanging up. What was that? Layla didn't own any pets, did she? Jay would have mentioned that. It was probably Jay then. He must have come home when she'd been in the shower. There was another sound, something like scuffling and a moan.

'Jay?' she asked carefully. 'You back?'

She made her way to the living room. Everything looked exactly as she had left it, though the lights were off, which made her skin crawl. Hadn't she left them on? Of course she had, she never turned off the lights. Not completely. Her stomach began to churn. Could Jay have switched them off and gone straight to bed? She hated the darkness, it made her hyperventilate. Too many memories ...

Thankfully the curtains were pulled back, providing a kind of half-light that allowed her to see shapes. Her bag was still tossed on the sofa, black travelling boots were by the door. Nobody here. It was nothing. She exhaled.

She made her way to the kitchen to turn on the lights and make another cup of tea, using her cell phone torch to guide her. Where was the switch again? She shone the torch on the wall. There it was. She pressed, but nothing happened. Shit, had a fuse blown? She felt her bare feet stick to the floor. It was not the vinyl ... no ... there was something wet here. She turned the torch towards the ground.

She almost tripped over him. Jay, his eyes closed, forehead gashed, red and furiously swollen, the left side the size of a tennis ball. His mouth was slightly open, as though he had been caught by surprise, his lip was bleeding profusely and his left arm was bent the wrong way at the elbow. She shouted or would have, if she wasn't suddenly gasping for breath. Someone grabbed her from behind. An arm snaked its way across her neck, she felt her windpipe compress, her scream sounded like a kitten mewling. She fought maniacally, twisting her body, but she had no air in her lungs. He was strong, she could hear him breathing roughly against her ear. He simply increased the pressure on her windpipe, and barely moved while she flayed around.

'Who are you?' she gasped, when he finally let her breathe. 'What do you want?'

The man reached down to her left hand and pulled at the cell phone. She held it tight, but he simply yanked her index finger back until she cried with pain and dropped it.

He chuckled and pressed his body closer to hers. With his free hand, he cupped her breast. He whispered roughly in her ear. 'Oh, the things I would do to you, if we had the time. Where's the tablet, Nadia?'

'I don't ... I don't know what you ...'

'The tablet.'

'I don't know what you're talking about.'

She clawed frantically as he increased the pressure on her windpipe again. 'Let's not play games, darling. You won't like what happens next, trust me. Where's the tablet? The ancient artefact you took from Marianne Riviere, the one which doesn't belong to you.'

She felt the tears trickle down her cheeks. 'It's in my bag, okay? Take it. Take whatever you want. Just tell me what's going on. Where's my sister?'

'That's better. You're cooperating. See how easy that was?'

'Who are you?'

He let his fingers caress the side of her cheek and she winced. 'Someone you'll never forget, Nadia.'

'Is ... is Layla alive? Take what you want, okay ... just please, please tell me that much. How do I get her back? I'll pay any ransom you want.'

He pulled her backwards, back into the living room, never letting go of her neck. 'This bag of yours, where is it?'

She didn't reply and he squeezed, tightly. 'It's on ... on the bloody sofa, okay?'

'Now, there's a good girl.' He let go of her, and she whirled around. She had a brief glimpse of a figure in black. She turned and started to run. He pulled her back by her hair as though it were the easiest thing in the world. 'Not yet, not quite yet. I haven't got what I need just yet. Who told you about the tablet? Have you read it?'

She clawed frantically as his arm circled her windpipe once again. 'Do you know what it says?'

Jesus ... the pain. 'I don't know, okay? I don't know anything about it.'

'Then how did you know that Riviere had it?'

'I ...'

'How?' he demanded.

She couldn't breathe. She tried to speak, but she couldn't breathe. He relaxed his arm slightly, and she began to cough, gasping. 'I saw her ... walking down the street. I decided to follow her and see what was in her backpack. I didn't know what I was looking for, or why. I still don't know what that bloody thing is, okay?' She could hear it in her voice. The desperation. The fear. It made her feel sick.

'Excellent. Well done. See what happens when you behave?'

'I've told you all I know, I swear. Please, where's Layla? What have you done with her?'

'And here we were, getting along so well.' He held her down and she felt him press something against her face, a cloth, a cloth with a cloying sweet smell. She struggled, kicking her legs as hard as she could. But he only chuckled again. 'Sweet dreams, Nadia. You and I are going on a little journey,' he whispered. Her head began to swim and her legs turned to jelly.

And then the cloth was gone, and so was the man, his weight lifted off her. She could hear grunts and a curse, the sound of a fist smacking flesh. There was someone else here. Her legs and arms barely worked, and the world was spinning. But she forced herself up and reached towards the lamp next to the sofa, praying it would turn on. She hit the switch, and then her legs collapsed beneath her again.

Light flooded the room. The man in black had blonde hair. She couldn't see his face, not very clearly. With shock, she realized that the other man was the guy from the pub,

Liam somebody, the reporter. He had jumped on top of the other, who was trying to shake him off. They fell to the floor, wrestling and grunting. Then Liam punched her assailant in the face. She heard the crack as the other man cursed and put a hand to his nose. Blood spouted through his fingers.

She tried to get up, tried to get out of the apartment. But there was something wrong with her legs. As soon as she stood up, they buckled and she fell on the floor. She started to panic and curled up, unable to do anything but watch.

The man from the pub – Liam – was grunting now and gasping with pain. His assailant had somehow managed to stand up and had landed several swift punches to his stomach, before slugging him in the jaw. Liam groaned, but twisted his body and moved backwards. For a moment, they circled each other warily, until the blonde man dived forward and slammed the other into the wall. Then his eyes darted in her direction. And beyond her, to her bag.

He dived towards her. Liam seized the moment to grab him by the collar, pulling him backwards.

'Fuck,' grunted the blonde man. But he managed to extricate himself and turn around, his hands pressing into the other man's face. Liam did not stop though. He rammed his body into her attacker, pushing him head on into the stone Buddha in the corner. There was a loud cracking sound. For a moment, the man seemed stunned. He lifted himself off the floor and moved his hand to the back of his head. It was covered in blood. With whatever strength he had left, he pushed Liam aside and ran out of the flat.

'Are you all right?' A set of sturdy brown boots came towards her. She looked up. His breathing was ragged and there was blood on one of his knuckles and his chin, which was already starting to swell. His shirt was speckled with blood too – whether it was his or the other man's, she did not know.

Instinctively she recoiled, hating that the panic had overtaken her so completely. She couldn't speak.

He watched her for a moment and then crouched down beside her. 'Look, I know you've had a big shock. I'm not here to hurt you. I'm a friend.'

She shook her head. She remained curled up, watching him.

He rubbed his jaw. 'Christ, this hurts like a motherfucker. Look, Nadia, that man, whoever he was, could come back any second, you understand? We're only lucky he didn't have a gun. He wouldn't have been expecting much resistance.'

Her eyes instinctively went to the kitchen, where Jay lay in the same position, his body twisted like a marionette. Was he ... was he dead? Who was that man? Why would he hurt a boy who was so sweet and kind? She started to shake, her whole body started to shake uncontrollably. She couldn't stop herself. She needed to run. She needed to run and get help for Jay, but she could not stop shaking.

Liam looked at her and then behind him. 'I'm guessing that would be Jay there? Layla's friend?' He walked over quickly, knelt down and put two fingers against Jay's neck. Then he looked up and frowned. 'There's a pulse, but it's weak and erratic. He's been bashed in the head. We need to get him to the hospital quickly. Layla will kill me if anything happens to him.'

She looked at him sharply.

He hesitated, and then came and hunched down next to her. He kept his voice low, his tone even. 'Listen to me, Nadia. I know you're scared. Your body has gone into shock. We have to get you warm, but first, I need to see about helping Jay. So you'll be needing to stay where you are, all right?'

As though she had any choice. She watched him pull a phone out of his back pocket and dial for help in calm, measured tones, requesting both an ambulance and the police. Then he went back to Jay and bent over him.

'Stay away from him.'

He looked up. 'I am a friend, I promise. Didn't you just hear me call the police?'

She watched him warily. 'You could have called anyone. You could be the one that did this to him. You ... you and that other guy. Just stay away from him until they get here.' She could hear the hysteria in her voice.

He frowned again. 'Look, if I was in cahoots with that mentaller, he wouldn't have tried to smash my head in now, would he? I'm on your side, Nadia. Just take a deep breath and think for a moment.'

'Just ... stay away from him.'

'I can't, he needs medical attention. My name is Liam, like I told you. I came to find you because I'm trying to help Layla and the others. She's my friend. We worked on the dig together these last two months in Mohenjodaro.'

He didn't look like an archaeologist. He certainly didn't fight like one. 'You're lying,' she whispered, shaking her head. 'Everyone on the dig is missing. What do you want? Did you hurt Jay? Are you playing some sort of sick game with me?' Her voice was raspy. Talking was painful, but her sense of self-preservation had kicked in. Jay was hurt and she couldn't trust anyone.

He rubbed his hands through his hair in frustration. 'Jesus. Hurt Jay? No, it was yonder man there, the blonde one who ran. He was going to hurt you too, remember? I'm the one who pulled him off. Listen to me,' he said urgently. 'My name is Liam. Liam O'Rourke. I was one of the team in Mohenjodaro. I just happened to be in Karachi when ... it happened, whatever it was. So I wasn't kidnapped. You can google me, Nadia,' he said gently. 'They've stuck my face in the papers and all. But now you have to listen to me and do as I say. You're in danger. The police will be here soon. We'll make sure Jay is safe, but then we'll have to go. You'll be needing to trust me.'

'Go? Go where?'

He hesitated. 'We have to go to Pakistan.'

She laughed, the sound hollow and slightly hysterical, trying to see if her legs would start goddamn moving. 'To Pakistan. Sure. Jay's in a bad way, he was nearly fucking *murdered* by a psychopath who wanted a stupid piece of stone. Now you're here, making up stories. It's in my bag, all right? Take it. Just take it. I don't know why it's so important and I don't care.' It came out like a half-sob.

'I'm not sure what you're talking about. I'd offer you a whisky to calm you down, but I can't now, can I? Layla told me you drink too much. Now can I trust you to wait there, while I make sure this kid is okay?'

She looked at him again, startled every time he mentioned her sister's name.

His expression was intent. 'I am telling the truth, Nadia. I'm checking Jay out, but only to see what kind of shape he's in. I'm not going to hurt him. Come here and supervise if you want.'

She tried to get up, but her legs were still shaking.

He looked at her for a moment, assessing. 'What did he do to you? Did he drug you?'

'I don't know, something ... there was something over my mouth.' And she couldn't breathe. She pressed her hands and her head against the wall.

He looked around, spotted a damp rag on the floor by the Buddha, sniffed it and winced. 'You'll be all right, you didn't get a strong enough dose to knock you out, but it's going to take a few minutes before your legs feel normal again. It'll be chloroform that he used on you. The headache will be intense, but the adrenaline will help make it all go away faster. You need to drink some water. We have to flush it out of your system. I'll get it for you in a minute, once I've finished here.' He was gently pressing Jay's limbs.

'If you're an archaeologist, how would you know all this?' She regretted asking the question the moment it came out of her mouth. Why wouldn't he just take the tablet and leave?

He stood up. 'The boy's in bad shape. His arm is broken in two places and I'm pretty sure he has several fractured ribs as well as a serious concussion. The ambulance better get here soon.' He went to the sofa, pulled off the throw and covered Jay with it.

Then he brought her a glass of water. 'Strictly speaking, I'm an anthropologist. But before that I was a mixed-up kid in a gang in Belfast. We used to get into a lot of fights. The kind of fights where people got knifed. There was stealing too.' He handed her the glass, but she remained where she was, her head pressed against the wall.

'You don't believe me? It's true. Lucky for me, I got caught trying to grab Professor Webb's briefcase one day. Best mistake I ever made. Like, I owe the Professor my life, Nadia. The man is like a father to me. I'm only telling you this so you will understand. I need to help my friends. If there's even a chance they are still alive. Now drink, please. It will help.'

She tried to steady her breathing. She tried to make sense of everything, but it was too much. It was all too much. 'Even if I believed you for one second, why would you come all the way to London – to find me?' If she could just get her legs working again ...

She could see his jaw clench as he put the glass down on the coffee table. 'A good question. One I've been asking myself all day. Because she told me you were in danger. And that no matter what I said, you wouldn't believe me, that you were too much of a survivor to take any story for granted.'

'Who? Layla? Why would Layla say that to you?' She was so confused. Her head hurt so much.

'No.' He shook his head slowly. 'Look, I know this doesn't make much sense, but it wasn't Layla. It was your grandmother. She's been trying hard to contact you, but your phone was turned off, and the first time she tried to call you, you didn't listen ...'

She was stunned. Jahanara? He was here because of her grandmother? 'I don't even know her. She isn't a part of my life. Don't come any closer,' she said quietly.

He stepped back, raising his hands. 'I don't know anything about that, to be honest with you. She contacted me after my team went missing in Mohenjodaro. But she wouldn't tell me anything, except that you were in danger and that I had to bring you back. She seemed adamant that you were the only one who could help Layla and the others. She told me that if I brought you to Pakistan, she could tell us exactly what happened to them. I can't imagine that a little old lady would make up a story like that, can you? She seemed to know a lot about the dig and was entirely sane.'

The man was making no sense. 'I'm not going back with you, okay?' She looked over at Jay. She was going to be sick. She clutched the wall and moaned.

He said nothing further. Instead, he was reaching into his back pocket, and she forced herself to pull her body sideways. What was taking the ambulance so long? What if he had never called it? If she could find her phone, she could dial 999.

He pulled out a small piece of paper from his pocket and handed it to her. It was folded in half. 'Jahanara told me to show you this sketch. She said you'd know what it meant.

If you'd care to share with the rest of the class, I'd be most grateful, for I haven't got a clue. But she's a good artist, your grandmother. She whipped this up in a couple of minutes.'

She hesitated, and then took the paper reluctantly and turned it over. She inhaled sharply. How was this possible?

He was staring at her, his expression curious. 'She gave it to me last night and then made me catch the next flight out. She said you would know her, this woman. And that she is the reason that Layla is missing. She didn't explain any more. But she said that she would be able to help find Layla and keep you safe, if I brought you back with me. That's the message I am supposed to pass on.'

Nadia stared at the picture. She couldn't stop staring. A dark-eyed, gaunt face stared back in rough lines of pencil. A girl with long black hair, braided from behind, wearing a tunic and a necklace made of lapis lazuli. A girl with a crooked tooth and a lithe, hard body. It was Jaya. The girl from her dreams.

Chapter Sixteen

MELUHHA, NINE YEARS LATER.

Jaya rested the damp cloth against Nene's brow. She wiped away fat beads of sweat and made soft, cooing noises in an attempt to console her. It was futile. Nene continued to scream, the sound ripping through the Temple walls, made worse by the silence that followed.

Nene's face was ashen as she lay there with her legs splayed open. She was panting heavily.

'She's lost a lot of blood,' grunted Enia. The midwife was up to her elbows inside the other woman, trying to turn the baby.

Jaya nodded. She opened her deerskin pouch and pulled out the small shaved pieces of willow bark that she had managed to purchase from the old man in the Street of Healers the night before. She chewed on them, pressing hard, until they became soft and yielding. Then she placed them on the floor. From her pouch, she also took out a pinch of poppy seeds and some keekar sap and quickly mixed them into the bark, creating a paste. She rolled the paste into a small ball, opened Nene's mouth and placed it inside. 'Suck on it, sister. The pain will ease.'

It was difficult to ignore the blood pooling on the pallet or the smell of rusted iron and putridness that came from inside her friend, despite the lingering smoke of the mustard oil used to light the lamps. There was a babe tearing its way out of her body. Shakari herself would have to intercede if Nene were to survive.

Jaya dipped the cloth back into the earthen bowl and gently wiped her friend's face, quietly cursing the High Priest and Sarema, and the nine years of pain and misery they had been put through. She could not hold the tears back any longer and felt the damp saltiness on her cheeks, flowing hot and fast. 'Shh ... you must be calm, Nene. Shakari is with you always.'

Nene laughed then, or let out something like a laugh that was more like a wince of pain. 'You always did know how to make me smile, Jaya. There is no Goddess – I have told you that for many years. I have never understood how it was that you kept your faith, despite it all.' She gasped and gripped Jaya's hand. 'Do you remember ... how ... how clever I thought I was, joining the Goddess-Blessed? I was so proud. But we have been damned, sister. Damned by Sarema and Iaf and the priests. Damned by the whole city.'

'Shh ... do not think of it now, Nene. There is still time to leave. We will leave this place together. I will pray for it.'

'You and your prayers ... it's all because of the Bloodstone.' She coughed. 'Why did it work for you and not for the rest of us? If only it had been silent. You would finally understand that there is nothing left to pray for.'

'That's not true, the Goddess ... she will help us. I do not know why she has not helped us already, but she must help us now. She *must* help us. She gave us the Stone, Nene, and she made it possible for me to read it. It has to be for a reason. I must pray to her,' she said, a little too desperately. 'I must pray for her to remove her curse, to set us free.'

'If you must pray, then pray that it is a girl.'

Jaya nodded. She closed her eyes and took a moment to calm her thoughts, asking Shakari to bring the babe into the world safely and for Nene to recover. *And above all, please, let it be a girl.*

She opened her eyes, hating that they were in the darkness of the Temple, where the giant, oppressive images of each of the city clans were painted on the walls to loom over Nene while she suffered. The Tigers, Rhinoceros, Jackals, Cobras, Peacocks, Buffaloes and so many others, each coloured with red paint, each looking menacing in the lamplight, flickering like the shadows of evil spirits.

This was the place he brought them to most nights. Iaf. It was not only she who suffered, night after night after night. Iaf wanted to lie with all the Goddess-Blessed, to have as many daughters as he could to increase the chances of having children who could read the Stone. He was not a kind man, he enjoyed bringing pain to women. He enjoyed it so much that many of the Blessed could not have children any more, which only made his anger grow. She had learned much about Iaf, since those early days. It was whispered in the Temple that the High One cowered under the shadow of the memory of his father. Danoor had been a strong, fierce leader. Iaf would do anything to garner the same respect, to hold the loyalty of the people. But respect had to be earned. Danoor had built the Temple and the boat yard. He had increased trade tenfold and opened poorhouses. What had Iaf done in his tenure? Bribery and corruption had increased. Merchants were taking over everything. And the Unclanned were voicing their dissent, flexing their muscles, angry at being denied access to the Street of Healers, when mosquito sickness was still rife in their camps. It was said, by some of the priests, that Iaf's father had beaten him so often when he was a boy that he had never recovered. She could well believe it.

The High One enjoyed inflicting pain on others, it gave him a sense of power.

The bitterness threatened to overwhelm her. The Goddess-Blessed were prisoners. The world thought they were Shakari's honoured ones, but they were nothing more than playthings. They sat in their beautiful homes being pampered. But they were subject to Iaf's whims. Sarema, curse her, helped him in his pursuits and was compensated with new pieces of land and settlements every time a girl was Named and brought to him. She had grown fat and indolent, while Iaf, the man the entire city looked to for guidance, for piety, for hope, was a monster.

They had endured, learning why the Goddess-Blessed had been so keen to increase their numbers from outside the clan. It was the youngest ones Iaf tormented the most. To stop him from lying with their young daughters, to stop him hurting them and to continue their blissful lives, the Goddess-Blessed had brought in others from the Clanning. Idiot girls who thought they were being taken into a life of abundance, but instead had to endure his touch, his pain. His control. Iaf, in turn, grew increasingly disappointed, as no one else had proved to be able to read the Bloodstone. Jaya had lied to him, time and time again, to protect those who the Stone had shown her had abilities. There were several girls in the city. Little girls, too young to be trapped in this nightmare. And she had suffered for it, suffered until finally, she had given birth to her own daughter. A daughter who Iaf would one day turn to – to read the Bloodstone. A daughter she had to protect.

Aal. Every time she thought her misery could not be compounded, she thought about her daughter. She would endure, for the sake of her child.

Nene coughed and Jaya gripped her friend's hand tighter. Nene should not be forced to give birth in this place, this hollow place devoid of Shakari's light, no matter what the priests claimed.

The midwife lifted her head, looking exhausted. 'It's turned. It's coming. Be ready.' Enia was a gifted healer, a truculent, wizened woman of nearly forty-one, who had brought many souls into the world. If it were at all humanly possible, the child would live.

'Push now, Nene. Push hard.'

'I can't,' whispered Nene. Her body slumped. 'What a cruel world it really is. If it is a girl, then raise her as your own, if the priests allow it.'

Neither of them wanted to speak about what would happen if it were a boy.

The midwife cursed. 'The child is coming now. I will have to pull. Try to keep her from getting agitated.'

There was no need. Her friend had lost her strength entirely. Jaya ignored the midwife, who was pulling and straining, and held Nene's hand. 'You must fight, Nene. You must fight to stay with us. Your babe will need you.'

Nene gasped.

There was a brief cry, a wail so fleeting that Jaya wondered if there was a jackal outside the Temple, not an infant newly born. But the midwife had saved the babe and was examining it, even as it moved its arms feebly in protest of the violence of its birth. Pulling a small knife out of her robe, Enia quickly cut the cord that bonded the child to its mother. There was a dark expression on her face. She looked up and shook her head.

Jaya knew then that the Goddess Shakari continued to curse them.

'Is it a girl?' Nene whispered, resting her head on Jaya's knee, her long curly hair damp and glistening, stuck to her gaunt face.

Enia wrapped the baby quickly in a clean white cotton robe. Jaya understood the gesture. 'It is a girl,' Jaya said, turning to gaze at the panting woman on the floor. It was clear that Nene would not last long in this world. 'Rest, Nene. It is a girl and I will love her more than a mother ever could. I will tell her stories about who her true mother was, and the dreams and hopes she had for her child.' She felt a lump in her throat.

Nene strained to see the babe, and Enia placed the child on her chest. She would not have the strength to remove the wrapping around her son. She would never know.

'A girl ...' Nene sighed, raising a shaky hand and pressing it to the child's head. The babe was so small and so perfectly formed. Jaya could not bear to look at it. She took deep breaths, trying to calm herself.

'She will live,' Nene said, her voice barely more than a breath on the wind. 'My child will live. Maybe you are right, sister. There may be a Goddess after all.'

And then she died, her hand still resting on her baby's head.

Jaya felt her heart shatter into pieces. She closed Nene's eyelids and stroked her cheek one last time.

'You must kill the child,' the midwife said, looking up briefly as she collected her things. 'You can suffocate it by placing your palm against its mouth and nose. It will not suffer for long.'

Jaya shook her head. 'I cannot ...'

Enia spoke sharply. 'Better that than the alternative.'

'No!' she said. Is that what Nene had done the last time she had conceived a boy, three cycles ago? The one that supposedly had been stillborn? Had she suffocated her child to save him from Iaf? Iaf, who, it turned out, ensured that the masses in the city continued to believe that the Goddess-Blessed only ever produced daughters, who did not want a son to one day challenge his supremacy. Something he had seen in an early vision – a male child of his seed – destroying his legacy.

'I will not do it for you,' muttered Enia, as she folded the bloody sheets, to be washed and used again. Shakari had shown them, hundreds of cycles ago, that old blood carried disease and must be cleansed away.

The midwife's face was grim. 'I cannot do it, child. I have killed too many in my time and have not the strength for another. But I have counselled many a Goddess-Blessed as well. You must harden your heart. Save this child from his fate. They will not suffocate him. They will not want to risk the evil spirits that might come upon them if they murder an infant. Instead, they will leave him out in the blazing sun, letting the heat shrivel his skin, letting him die of thirst and leaving his bones for the dogs. It will be an agonizing death.'

She felt her stomach turn. Enia was right. She would have to kill him. Just as one day, she might have to kill her own son.

She placed her hand on the babe, feeling the rise and fall of his stomach as he drew breath, her mind racing. Perhaps, if she left the Temple now, she would have time to go home and collect Aal. They could disguise themselves as pilgrims ... if they could buy some milk or find a wet nurse for the babe, make their way to the gates and convince the Unclanned to help them escape ...

No, it would not work, not with the symbol of the pipal tree on her face. How many times had she considered escape? How many times had she taken those first steps of leaving her house and running to the gates at the end of the city, surrounded by the human tide of misery and sickness that lived there in the slums? But nobody would offer them sanctuary, they were all too scared to risk the anger of the priests. She was branded and leaving the city was punishable by death. Not just her death, but her daughter's as well, and that she could not countenance. The Goddess-Blessed were guardians of the Stone. They were not allowed to travel outside the Citadel without Iaf's permission and without bodyguards from the Temple to escort them. How stupid she was not to have run away the day her parents disappeared!

Her thoughts all jumbled up, she barely registered Enia shake her head and walk away. What if they left the city entirely and took their chances on a riverboat? It was a seven- or eight-day journey to Dilmun. Despite all attempts, over nine cycles she had not located her family. She had sent messengers to Dilmun. But her family had vanished. Her father had never taken his post as Crocodile Elder, she had learnt that much. Dilmun had refused to pay tithe to Meluhha and all Meluhhans in leadership roles had been asked to leave. Trouble was brewing in the vassal states. But her family had never returned to the city.

She had stayed, curse her, because leaving was so dangerous for her daughter. But now ... could she bribe the oarsmen to take her even further away, further into the Northlands perhaps, and risk the wrath of the Temple? How much gold and sesame oil had she already stashed away to trade ... enough to buy them a guard or two to protect them on the journey? But Iaf would be watching her, as he was always watching.

'You are not thinking clearly in your grief,' said Enia, pausing at the chamber door. 'Do it now, quickly. It is your last chance.'

For another moment, she hesitated, watching the babe open its mouth, searching instinctively for his mother's breast. And then, hands trembling, she placed her palm directly over the child's mouth and nose, feeling his soft breath, barely a whisper on her skin. *It is the will of Shakari. It has to be.*

But it was too late. The doors to the inner sanctum opened, she heard the footsteps echo on the walls. They came then, in their ochre robes, alerted, perhaps, by the cessation of Nene's screams. Two of the Temple guards escorted Iaf, and she saw, sickened to her stomach, that in his arms he held her own child, Aal, who was half asleep and curled against his shoulder.

Aal was only seven, confused to be out of bed and in the sanctum of the Temple at this hour. Iaf had brought her here to remind Jaya that she could not take the babe and flee, not if she wanted her own child to survive. How many times had he used Aal as a hostage against her? Too many to count. She tried not to wince as he approached.

She forced her face to reveal nothing as Iaf placed Aal on the ground. He observed the dead woman with a dispassion that was chilling. Then he peeled the babe from her body. He unravelled its bindings, though the act was a mere formality. Had it been a girl, Jaya would have brought her out straight away to be blessed by the priests.

He frowned, but said nothing.

'Nene will be honoured,' he said eventually, handing the babe to the Temple guard. 'As a Goddess-Blessed, her gift to this city was beyond measure. We will mourn her passing.'

Jaya fought down the seeds of rebellion, fought hard to keep her head lowered for the sake of her own child, Aal. It was his own son he was so ruthlessly handing over! All because of a vision the Stone had once given him – a son of his line would one day destroy everything in his path, including his family. And so the boys were left to die and the girl babes were raised in privilege, so that one day they could read the Stone for him and carry on the myth of the Goddess-Blessed.

There was silence. Something was expected of her and so she looked up. She had her own daughter to think about. 'I thank you for honouring her, High One. Shakari will welcome Nene into her arms even faster with our prayers and offerings, and guide her journey.' She swallowed the bile that came as she said the words.

He inclined his head graciously. He knew he had won, as he always did. Theirs was a strange relationship. He needed her for the Stone, but he had been true to his word. Before Aal had been born, he had not forced her to read the Stone more than once a moon. But now, since she had not produced any more children, he took her to meetings with merchants and traders. They all wanted to know which caravan routes to take, which to avoid in case of bandits, which gems would fetch the most money in the markets of Ocha. The Goddess-Blessed were only supposed to use their power to help the city, not the merchants. But Iaf called them, time and time again, to the Temple, where she held the Bloodstone and made her predictions. In turn, the merchants paid Iaf and the other priests a fat bribe, which they used for their own purposes.

As long as Jaya did what he asked, she was left to herself at her house in the Street of the Pipal Trees. Unlike the other The Goddess-Blessed, she had dismissed all her servants. She knew they were all in the employ of the High One, all spies doing his bidding. Better to live alone, to cook and clean for Aal without others reporting her actions. As long as she continued to use the Stone, Aal was not touched by the monster. But she had sacrificed everything, including Nene's son, to make sure her daughter was safe.

Perhaps it was she who was the monster, after all.

Aal yawned. She lay curled up on the floor, near the body. Did Aal not realize that Nene was dead? She must have thought her to be only sleeping. How would she tell her, Jaya wondered. How would she tell her child that the only other person who had protected her in this world was gone?

Iaf clasped his hands behind his back and surveyed the room. 'Tomorrow some pious men are coming to the Temple. You will read the Bloodstone for them.'

She bowed her head. 'An honour, High One.'

'Good.' He nodded, his eyes calculating. 'Prepare Nene's body. She will be buried at midday.'

She watched him leave, watched the guard carry the squirming babe, still looking for something to suckle and now starting to cry in frustration. He looked so small, nestled there in the muscled arms of a full-grown man. And even though it burned her heart, she remained completely still and kept her head bowed.

What kind of woman would let an infant die, and not do anything to prevent it? She took Nene's lifeless hand in her own, the tears flowing down her face. 'Forgive me, forgive me,' she sobbed.

Chapter Seventeen

KARACHI, PRESENT DAY.

It was the heat she noticed first. The heat, and then the humidity. Crowds of people gathered outside Jinnah International Airport, all of them sweating, standing uncomfortably under the glare of the sun. Arrivals was packed. Several flights had come in at once, but there was a kind of chaotic method to the process of leaving the terminal. They walked through.

A large group of men blocked the exit, holding garlands of red roses and green political party flags, waiting for some VIP, Nadia presumed. As one of them spat tobacco onto the pavement, Liam guided her through them with surprising ease. Perhaps it was his height – he could see past the mobs while she couldn't.

They walked by a mother who was craning her neck, looking out for someone, her four children tugging at her shalwar kameez impatiently. Then there was a little boy in green dashing in and out of the legs of the crowd, and a group of porters in white uniforms, who expertly wheeled overstacked trolleys all the way down to the car park. Already the air smelt different, heavier, more pungent.

She took a deep breath. Karachi. The birthplace of her father, the place she swore she would never come ... and now here she was, having done exactly that, getting ready to meet a woman she had promised herself she would never speak to, a grandmother who seemed capable of reading her mind.

It was difficult to process the last few days. It felt as though her brain had simply shut down. Her neck felt swollen and raw, and she was exhausted. Layla was still missing. There was an ancient artefact burning a hole in her satchel, her hand resting not quite casually against it, protecting it from opportunistic bag snatchers. She had worried all the way through security at Heathrow that the relic would be scanned, and she'd be asked what it was. But they had boarded the flight without a problem. What choice had she had though, but to bring it with her? The artefact was important. Whoever had Layla had attacked her in search of it. Whoever had kidnaped Layla had killed for it ...

She could not stop thinking about Jay, even here, standing in the heat of the noonday sun. Especially not here, as she watched families reunite, friends pat each other on the back and pick up each other's luggage, and the mother of four rush to greet her husband, weeping, as he beamed, soon overwhelmed by the number of children who had jumped on top of him. Jay. Oh God, Jay.

'You all right?' asked Liam, as he guided her through the people. 'Almost there. We leased a Land Cruiser while we were on the dig, I left it in the parking lot.'

No. No, she was not bloody all right. How could she be? 'Sure,' she replied, wishing that she'd pilfered some of the little booze bottles that the stewardess had been handing out before the flight. 'Just dandy,' she muttered under her breath. Her arms felt itchy. Her whole body felt ... she just wanted to drink. To drink and to sleep. And to find out what she was carrying in her bag.

She hadn't told Liam about the relic. She wasn't sure yet if she could trust him, though she knew now that he was a linguistics expert. He could probably tell her what kind of writing was on the stone and why the bloody thing was so important.

Not that she *mistrusted* him either. She had done everything he'd asked her to, up until now. On his insistence, once she really had googled him, they had hidden the chloroform-soaked rag left behind by her attacker and concocted a simple story. They told the police that they were old friends. Liam had come to meet her at the flat, and discovered a burglar had attacked Jay and was trying to assault her. She and Jay didn't know who the burglar was, but he had initially demanded cash, jewellery and phones, only turning violent because they had not complied fast enough.

The rest was a haze of exhaustion. Nadia received medical attention – it was impossible to hide the swelling on her neck and arms. They took her to the hospital, and she sat with a police artist. The artist created a facial composite of the blonde man, his fingers working quickly on a laptop. It was like watching clay being moulded, the way he manipulated images with the click of a mouse, until some overarching aspect of her assailant appeared to come together on his screen. His high forehead, his round face, the wide-set blue eyes and thick eyebrows ... she had not realized how much of the man she had been able to see, but there he was, looking rather bland and expressionless, like he could be *anyone,* in blurred black-and-white lines and grey shadows. Seeing him made her feel sick.

The doctor had cleared her medically, after which she had been interviewed by a smartly dressed police inspector from the Hackney station named Sarah Blake. Blake asked her several questions about her relationship with Liam, and Nadia had been anxious that the police were going to blame him for the attack. But then Jay had woken up, long enough to confirm that a blonde man had rammed his way through the front door and come straight at him.

That was pretty much all Jay said. He was only conscious for a matter of minutes, asking the nurses if Nadia was all right, worrying about *her* instead of himself. Doctors confirmed that he had a subdural haematoma, trauma from his injuries, and they had decided to induce a coma to help combat the swelling in his brain. But it hadn't worked. Three hours later, Jay's body had given up and he had died.

Perhaps it was the shock, but as soon as it happened, as soon as Jay was gone, she and Liam left London. She wept silently, so aware that even as they did so, somebody – some hospital member or police officer – would be calling Jay's family. All those photos on the coffee table ... the mother with the lopsided smile, the sister who was a nurse ... they would be devastated. And they would have questions, questions for her and Liam. But Jay was dead. She couldn't help him. The blonde man was still out there, however. She was still in danger. And her sister ... Christ, she prayed she could help Layla.

'Just down here and to the right,' Liam muttered, shaking his head when a porter asked him if he required any help. 'No, we have a ride, thanks.' He turned to look at her. 'If you're okay, we'll go straight to your grandmother's. I know she's desperate to see you. She insists that she knows what happened in Mohenjodaro, and that your family is connected somehow. I'm not sure why I believe her, but she was right about you being in danger. Maybe we'll both get some answers now.'

Her grandmother ... another piece in the puzzle of insanity. She'd quizzed Liam on the drawing that Jahanara had given him on the flight over. He'd insisted that he had watched

Jahanara make the sketch herself. It was so surreal. To see a visual representation of Jaya somewhere outside of her own head was just ... what was it exactly? Impossible? Was her grandmother truly a mind reader? How was a fictional character born of her subconscious someone that her grandmother would know about? The only explanation was that Jaya was not fictional, after all. But if not, what was she? Some kind of family psychosis? She wouldn't be surprised. Her father had been insane, after all. But what could any of this possibly have to do with the events in Mohenjodaro?

'You're exhausted,' said Liam, reaching over and trying to take her bag.

She shook her head and gripped it even tighter.

'Just offering to help,' he said, raising his hands, looking at her oddly.

'I'd just prefer to carry it myself, if that's all right.' It wasn't just the relic. It was that everything she had was in the large satchel. An extra pair of jeans, a couple of T-shirts, her tracksuit bottoms and tank top, her toothbrush and her iPad. Her passport. She had always travelled light, hadn't she? Always had the instinct to flee.

'Of course, whatever it is you're wanting. That's me told off for being a gentleman. Watch out, that porter is trying to cross in front of you.'

A man scowled as she nearly went headlong into his line of collected trolleys.

She could only imagine what she looked like to him right now. Wild hair, faint bruises and shadows under her eyes, cheeks hollowed. Irrational foreigner, out of her depth in the big bad world. She apologized as they sidestepped him. Liam told her to wait, that he would get the jeep and pick her up.

She watched him go, aware, suddenly, of how alone she was. She wrapped her arms around her chest, thinking.

The last day was a blur. They had spent much of the journey in silence. Each had questions. She wanted to know how Liam had met her grandmother, and why he was not there at the dig when the ... incident happened. But it was too much, all too much to be answered during a journey that was fraught with tension and grief, especially since the most important question of all was one she would have to meet her grandmother to have answered.

Was Jaya real?

Rather than let her mind churn, she'd spent most of the flight reading the book Jay had lent her – Layla's book – on the Indus Valley civilization. Jay's summary in the flat that day had been very good. The people of Mohenjodaro were advanced for their time. They had a sophisticated social structure, a priest king or council which ran the city, numerous technological capabilities such as heated plumbing and metallurgy, a perfectly planned city on a grid, and some very interesting games for children, which was important because in most cultures, 'childhood' was not a concept which existed until the 1800s, according to the authors. But in reality, not much was known about the culture, for the Indus language was still undeciphered. She peered closely at an image, a copper seal with a picture of a buffalo on it and some writing above. Why did the image of the buffalo look so familiar? She realized as well that some of the writing on the artefact she had in her bag matched with the writing in the book. Some, but not all of it. What did that mean?

She closed the book and decided to use the airline's Wi-Fi service to check her emails before she tried to get some shut-eye. A couple from Hank, asking her how things were going. One from Lennie, her neighbour, who'd taken a picture of Nelson sitting in his favourite place by the balcony, and one from Tamara, asking her which of a dozen interviews she wanted to do. The last was from Apollo. Encrypted, of course, but he'd given her a rather complicated password to open his messages.

Nut Job,

Where are you? I've been trying to call. I traced the accounts. It's a web all over the blooming world, in the Caymans, Bermuda. Jersey. A lot of money in Dubai too. You should know that many of the accounts are directly linked to the Indo Foundation. Others belong to a hedge fund named Arrapha Capital. And interestingly, Arrapha Capital is the investment manager for some of the Giving of Light Foundation's assets. That's right, your daddy's freaky cult. Coincidence? Personally, I think not. I did some poking around on the Indo Foundation's internal servers. Check out the website Marianne Riviere just bookmarked a couple of days ago. A link below. Call me when you get this.

The Indo Foundation and GoL. She blinked, stunned. There was a link between the two? How was that possible? Was Marianne Riviere a follower of GoL? Was GoL funding her? Why? In the crowded, dry airplane cabin, as a baby screamed and a harassed-looking stewardess offered her a drink, she had tried to think it through. Her father had been obsessed with history. Had his followers continued that obsession and decided to pay for a dig in the region of his birth? Some sort of historical memorial to him? No – not memorial, the crazies had decided that Sohail would be resurrected at a time when GoL would take over the world, so there was no memorial to him. But why else would they be operating in Mohenjodaro? And why be so furtive about it? She looked at the link Apollo had sent her. It was an article on a website entitled 'True Conspiracies'.

Why on earth would Marianne Riviere be reading junk like this? She scanned the article.

What Happened to the Mohenjodaro 8?

While government officials desperately try to hide the truth about the events that took place in Mohenjodaro, Pakistan, on August 16 of this year, 'True Conspiracies' can reveal that this is not the first time that bodies have burnt in this ancient city. In 1931, archaeologists excavating down to the street level of Mohenjodaro found the skeletons of forty-four people fleeing the city. The skeletons were in odd positions. There were adults covering children in protective postures, people holding hands, some falling where they stood, all facing some immense catastrophe.

Were those bodies burnt? 'True Conspiracies' can reveal that the bodies were highly radioactive when they were found, as radioactive as those found after the bombings in Hiroshima and Nagasaki. What caused that level of radioactivity? And why were the bodies left on the streets and not buried, perfectly preserved, without ever being touched by scavengers? Could it be that this ancient city has some sort of powerful nuclear technology? Is that why our governments are keeping us in the dark about it?

Nadia frowned. She nudged Liam in the ribs.

'Ach,' he complained, waking up. 'What is it?'

'Have you seen this?

'What?'

'This article.' She handed her iPad over, watching him read. He glanced at it and then rolled his eyes. 'Oh, that old chestnut. Pay it no mind.' He handed the iPad back, and closed his eyes once more.

Was the man crazy? There was a photo of the bodies, right there in the text, black and white, skeletons clutching each other, holding hands, some simply collapsing forward, as though they had been overcome by some malevolent force.

Next to them were markers, rulers, indicating where and how they had been found. 'Are you telling me these aren't real?'

He opened his eyes again. 'Of course, they're real.'

'So?'

'So what?'

She waved the iPad in front of his face. 'Liam, it says here that the skeletons were just there, lying on the streets, like they were running away from something. So what happened? How did the Mohenjodaro civilization end? Who are these people? There has to be a link, especially if Marianne Riviere is looking into it.'

He frowned. 'Marianne Riviere? At the Foundation?'

'It's a long story. Please, just answer the question.'

He stared at her for a moment, his eyes searching hers. 'The truth is, we don't exactly know how the civilization declined, Nadia, but that doesn't mean that we have to rush to conclusions. There are some who would argue that the Indus river changed course, that the city flooded one too many times, and then people abandoned it. I'd not be a big fan of that theory, only because I think there would be more evidence of water decay on the structures themselves if that were true. But there could always have been an Aryan invasion. One race kills another and their civilization disappears into the dust.'

'But wouldn't there have been some sign of war? I mean, wouldn't there be ... be wounds on the skeletons or some remnants of ... I don't know, spears or daggers or something?'

Liam shook his head. 'Well, we've only explored so little of it ... perhaps these were the people who were fleeing and got caught in something. When we excavate the rest, we'll know more. But you need to stop reading gob shiite like that. It's all tall tales, Nadia, like the fact that the bodies were contaminated and that around them there were signs of vitrification. Trust me, we get asked about stuff like this all the time.'

'What the hell is vitrification?'

He rubbed his eyes. He looked exhausted. 'It's the transformation of a substance into glass. In Mohenjodaro, lumps of black glass were found, clay melted under immense heat.'

'Is this some sort of joke?'

He shook his head. 'I wish it was. So many people take this conspiracy stuff seriously. It's a nightmare for the mainstream archaeology community. In 1979, an archaeologist named David Davenport wrote a book about Mohenjodaro, about the radioactive skeletons, about the clay objects found that appeared to be fused, glassified in heat as high as 1500 degrees Celsius, followed by a sudden cooling. He called the book *Atomic Destruction in 2000 BC*. No doubt that is the source of "True Conspiracies's" ground-breaking and attributed research, hmm? There's a reason this stuff doesn't make it into the mainstream media. It's all nonsense which will distract us from finding the team.'

She almost forgot how to breathe. 'A nuclear explosion?'

He put his hand on her arm. 'Calm yourself. It's bollocks, of course. The usual conspiracy rubbish that people make up about ancient cities. You'll find them everywhere.'

'But the bodies *were* radioactive?'

He looked at her intently. 'Listen to me, Nadia. Once you start playing this game, you'll never get off the Ferris wheel of fantasy. You of all people know how easy it is for people to believe mistruths and delusions.'

'Because I grew up on the compound, you mean?' she asked, cheeks flushed.

'That's not what I said ... look, don't glare at me like that. Yes, they had some level of radioactivity. Most bodies do, when they decay. Why it was higher than normal? I don't know, perhaps the devices used in the 1930s were faulty. There's no bloody source for this information, don't you see? It's all hearsay right now.'

'What if they are right?'

He sighed. 'If they were right, it would be better. Then we'd know what we were dealing with. But this misinformation, it's dangerous. Do you know, it was rumoured that Adolf Hitler sent people to Pakistan to search for ancient technology?'

She shook her head. She hadn't known that.

'It's true. Long before Davenport wrote his book, Mohenjodaro was famous for the forty-four bodies, and Hitler apparently wanted to find out what killed them. And my guess is that now others are trying to do the same. That's why this kind of nonsense is dangerous, Nadia. Maybe the government or one of the intelligence agencies of Pakistan bought into all the crazy conspiracy theories, and started poking around, doing tests, using chemicals or other materials that are combustible. Maybe that's what happened to Prof and to the others, some experiment that went wrong. I hope to God I'm wrong, that they are still alive. But I owe it to the Prof to find out.'

She nodded slowly. 'Some sort of weapons test, that's what I was thinking too.' But maybe ... maybe it was GoL who were behind it. Because they were just about crazy enough to believe in nuclear bombs and radioactive bodies.

'Not ancient,' he said quickly. 'I don't believe in ancient weapons. But I do believe in modern ones. And I believe that it is easy for those who covet power to try to claim the past. But what I can't figure out, Nadia, is why I was *waylaid* on my way to Mohenjodaro by your grandmother, and told to come and find you before I tried to find my friends and colleagues. I can't figure out why that sketch is important, or how you know what Marianne Riviere is reading on her computer, or why you even care. You owe me some answers. So does your grandmother.'

'I owe you about as many answers as you owe me,' she shot back. 'Why the hell would you listen to an old woman anyway?'

He looked irritated. 'I'm beginning to wonder the same thing. She's pretty persuasive, which you'll soon see for yourself. I suggest you get some sleep, 'cause we're going to be pretty busy when we get there.'

Chapter Eighteen

MELUHHA, 3791 BC.

When the sun rose from its slumber, Jaya went to the market. She took Aal with her. Her daughter's curly black hair bounced up and down as she half skipped, half raced through the street, barely paying mind to where she was heading. She managed to sidestep a washerwoman, who was balancing a basket of laundry on her head, and ran past a man selling barbecued corn, spiced and grilled over a charcoal fire in the ground, making the street sizzle with the smell.

It was amazing, the resilience of a child, Jaya thought, as she followed behind at a normal pace. Nene was dead not two moons and Aal was already back to her old self, her youthful exuberance could not be contained, especially as she now spent most of her days cooped up in the Temple, with Iaf giving her special lessons on meditation. Goddess, how she hated the High One!

Aal was running now, and disrupted a game of Korkey by racing through the chalk circle drawn by the group of boys, who were now slapping their foreheads and groaning. One glared fiercely at the receding figure. Aal didn't seem to notice. She was caught up in her speed, in the easing warmth of the morning and the rare freedom of being outside. She continued to run, until she collided with a stall keeper selling necklaces of lapis lazuli and carnelian. Jaya winced, moving faster to catch up.

The man cursed as he dropped his precious jewellery on the ground. 'Stupid creature! This necklace costs more than your worthless skin.' His face was plum with anger and he pulled at her tunic. Aal in turn tried to move backwards, uncertain.

Jaya reached them then, and caressed her daughter's frightened face. She picked up the necklace from the ground, brushed it off and handed it back to the man. 'It appears undamaged.'

He started to curse again. Then he saw the tattoo – the thirteen lines running down her left temple. His expression became fearful. He bowed. 'Lady. Forgive me.'

'There is nothing to forgive. My daughter was careless.'

'Your daugh ... but then this child is Goddess-Blessed! Ah la, Shakari will punish me for my anger!' He looked as pale as the ivory in his necklaces.

She smiled gently, feeling sorry for him. 'Calm yourself. It is nothing. The Goddess does not anger so easily.'

'You must accept this lapis as my apology,' he said desperately, holding out his hand.

The piece was beautiful, a necklace in rich hues of blue and red stones, interlaced with delicate carvings of ivory. She considered. It was undoubtedly expensive and it would cost the man to lose it. But to refuse would be worse.

'I thank you,' she said graciously, inclining her head. 'I will ask Shakari to bless you.'

The man beamed, looking relieved, and continued to bow as they walked away.

'Mua,' said her daughter, taking her hand. 'Why do they treat you so?'

'Because I am Goddess-blessed,' she replied. 'As are you. They set us apart.'

'Will the people give me necklaces then, when I come of age and have my face marked? Will they love me like they love you?'

'Perhaps.'

'Well, then I cannot wait until I take my place among the Blessed.'

Jaya stopped, her daughter's words causing her physical pain. She sat on her haunches, stroking her daughter's hair, there in the street, enjoying how it curled against her fingers. She looked at the eagerness in her expression. 'There is so much you don't understand,' she murmured.

What point was there in scaring the child. Her life would unveil itself to her soon enough, though by then, she prayed, she would have garnered enough gold to take them far away from here. Just thinking about it made her nervous.

Ever since Nene's death, she had been playing a dangerous game. With Enia's help, she had been offering blessings to people at her home at night. They came, asking her to pray to Shakari to heal a loved one or find a missing brooch or help them in their business ventures. She prayed for all of them, in exchange for half a copper weight. It felt wrong to take payment for her blessings. But it was desperately needed.

Jaya had been buying gold, in very small pieces, burying it in the courtyard of her house. Soon, she hoped, she would have enough that they could escape from here. It would take half the wealth in the city to bribe someone to help a Goddess-Blessed leave, but she would do it. She had spent long enough being afraid.

'Mua, look!' Aal exclaimed, bending down.

Jaya glanced at what her daughter had just picked up – a small clay-burned dice that had been left on the road, probably by the children playing Korkey. She smiled as her daughter held it tightly, relieved to think of happier things. 'Come,' she said, 'let us go to the Street of Dancers. A caravan has just returned from the North. I am sure there will be many tales being told.'

Aal smiled and took her mother's hand.

The Street of Dancers lay beyond the Citadel. It connected to the merchants' square, the very place where she had once been Clanned. The Tiger clan administered this part of the city, and she saw them now, their markings of clanship visible by the clay seals around their necks, hung over robes in rich hues of purple and green. They walked amongst the others, hands clasped behind their backs, ensuring that everyone behaved themselves, and that none from the Jackal clan had gained admittance while the two clans were still in a trading dispute.

The Tigers were merchants. They were affluent and powerful, aligned with Iaf and the high priests. The Jackals stood little chance of addressing their grievances. Iaf would never let another clan gain prominence over the Tigers, not when they paid him so well.

A crowd was gathering in the square. Children danced around the edges. Some were playing Korkey, others pushed toy carts and bullocks along the brick road. Women from the alehouses were selling barley beer from wooden trays which hung from their necks, and slices of oranges were on display at a fruit stall in the corner, though few could afford the steep prices. All around, the steady hum of excited voices. The street was awake and alive with possibility.

In the middle of it all was the raised platform where the dancing girls came at night to sell their bodies. Today, a caravan had arrived, so there would be stories to barter instead.

The platform was currently occupied by Nor, an Unclanned man from the North, who was well known and widely loved in the city. He was gaunt and long-limbed, wearing a brown robe and a rope belt across his waist, on which he had attached his many treasures – an eagle feather, a string of agate, a jade dagger given to him by a lord in the North.

Nor was an adventurer. He had accompanied many a trading caravan over the cycles, journeying the length and breadth of the Northlands, and even to the West, where the light-skinned tribes would sooner kill a man than ask his name.

The man lived by his wits and was popular with caravan leaders because of the many tongues he could speak. He had survived being Unclanned, a rarity in Meluhha, though many clans would have him, if he wanted. Nor liked to go his own way. There was no price too high for freedom, he was often heard saying. Surprisingly, nobody had tried to kill him for it.

'Gather around,' he shouted, his eyes gleaming. 'For today I have a story that will amaze you beyond your comprehension. It is a story of anger, of jealousy, of true passion, when a blue-eyed witch tried to curse the young Prince of Choll.'

Aal raced forward excitedly, diving into the throng. Jaya watched her and smiled. Her daughter should enjoy herself while she could. She would be safe enough.

She took the opportunity to slip away for a moment or two. She preferred to wander to the stalls further down the street, to enjoy the time away from the Temple in relative obscurity, while the crowd was distracted by the tale. She felt the sun tickle her skin and tilted her head up so her cheeks burned with the heat. Unlike the rest of the Goddess-Blessed, she refused to wear a veil in public. In some respects being without a veil gave her anonymity – at least until the passers-by noticed her tattoo. Much to the surprise of the others, Iaf did not censure her for it, perhaps because she was giving him the predictions that he wanted. There was plenty of time to wallow in the cool darkness of the Temple. She longed for the sun's kiss.

She paused to admire a chessboard for sale, trailing her fingers lightly against the ivory and clay pieces. Perhaps it was time to teach Aal, as her mua had taught her all those cycles ago. She had been so diligent about filling their coffers. A little something to keep the two of them amused in these dark times would surely be no bad thing.

'How much?' she asked.

The merchant saw her tattoo and stuttered. 'For you, Lady, I beg only that you keep me in your prayers. Please take it, with my good wishes.'

'But I must pay something,' Jaya protested. 'It is a fine piece of craftsmanship. You must have worked hard to polish the pieces to shape them so.'

The man looked down, embarrassed.

Jaya sighed. As usual, she would have to take matters into her own hands. She lifted the merchant's scales, which rested on the corner of the table. She pulled out three copper pieces from her deerskin pouch and placed them on one of the scales. Then she picked two of the cubic measures from the table and placed them on the other scale. It did not balance, her copper raised slightly. So she added another small copper piece until the scales were even. She looked at the combined weights and nodded, satisfied.

'Two cubes worth. Enough for a deer's shank or a wild boar, including the tusks. You can use the tusks to make your next board if you like.'

'Lady ...'

'I will not have your family go hungry simply because I wished to play a game of chess. Take it, and take my blessings with it.'

The man looked up, smiling with relief. He shovelled the copper pieces into the folds of his tunic quickly, as though he were worried she would change her mind.

He wrapped the chessboard and pieces into a square of old cloth and tied a knot on top. He handed it to her, and she nodded her thanks and moved away.

The board was heavy in her hand, but she didn't mind. Since Nene's death, she had not allowed herself to purchase a single thing. Iaf gave her latitude in many things, but unlike the other Goddess-Blessed, he had never given her a credit line in the city, knowing, perhaps, that she would use it to run away. Even the food they ate came from the generosity of the people who left offerings outside her home – though they were always welcome to eat at the Temple. It was a mutually beneficial agreement. Iaf left her alone to fend for herself, as long as she read for him. Today ... today she just wanted a moment of happiness, something she could share with Aal, a chance for them to forget about their worries and cares.

She looked up the street. Nor's crowd had grown now, and he leaned forward, gesticulating madly. He was talking about horses – she could tell by the way he was using his fingers to mimic their gallop. Most Meluhhans had never seen a horse, but they had heard about the large, magnificent stallions of Dilmun and Choll. Men and women alike dreamed of riding those horses through the desert with the speed of a lion.

Jaya could not see Aal in the crowd, and frowned. That child could get into all kinds of mischief. Perhaps she had been wrong to leave her alone. She made her way back.

Something was happening, she could see it from the way the crowd almost rippled, before people started jostling against each other. There was a shout. Then another. Then many voices were raised. Panicking, Jaya ran. If anything happened to Aal ...

But her daughter was there, away from the crush, running towards her. Her eyes were flushed with excitement. 'A thief, a thief!' she shouted from across the street. 'Mua, they have caught him and his little apprentice!'

When she reached her, Jaya hugged her daughter tightly. Together they walked towards the throng and up the three steps to the stage, where Nor's little performance had abruptly come to an end. Nor stood on the platform, smoking his pipe, looking amused. Jaya looked down.

A child was being dragged into the heart of the crowd, and a bearded man struck him a blow across his face, causing him to fall, weeping, on the ground. 'Thief! This little bastard stole my pouch. He's a pickpocket. Little shit. You'll see what we do to thieves here. Get up. Which clan do your parents belong to?' He grabbed the child by the scruff of his neck and shook him. 'No answer? Unclanned, are we? In that case, you'll wish you were dead by the time the priests get to you. We don't let Unclanned filth into Tiger territory.'

Another man, young, with long dark hair, broke through the mob and launched himself at the man with the beard. 'Leave my brother alone!' he shouted.

And then things happened very quickly. The two men started wrestling, surrounded by the excited crowd, while the child stood up and howled, his hand pressed against his cheek. Amazingly, a monkey appeared amid all the chaos, and hopped onto the child's shoulders. The monkey was an agitated brown little thing, who held a pouch in his paws.

Jaya hesitated. The pouch was similar to her own, though it appeared to be goatskin, and not deerskin. Such pouches were used to keep copper pieces and other precious things, and were sold by the dozens at every street corner. She had heard of monkeys who were trained to pick pockets. Nor himself had talked about being robbed by a monkey in Chanu once. It was true what the bearded man had said. The Unclanned boy would be shown no mercy when the priests were called in.

'Stop,' she shouted, but it did little good over the noise of the cheering crowd.

Nor picked at his teeth and then spat on the ground, showing little regard for her rank. 'Don't get involved. They won't thank you for it.' He motioned towards the other side of the street, where the Tigers had gathered some men and were marching towards the crowd.

She looked at him coolly, assessing. Then she made her decision. 'Stay here,' she told Aal, hoping her daughter would listen. She stepped down from the stage and pushed her way into the gathering. She would not let another child suffer.

A stray elbow connected sharply with her cheek, causing her to reel backwards. There was a collective gasp, as recognition slowly grew and the implications of what had just happened sank in. Very quickly, people disappeared. A Goddess-Blessed had been struck. Someone would lose his life over this.

Seeing her, the bearded man released the other with a jerk, his face streaked in sweat and dirt. 'Lady, it was not me, I swear it. This man is Unclanned. He is responsible.'

She raised her hands. There was little time to deal with the situation, before the matter went out of her control. 'This man was protecting his brother, a child who you struck without proof.'

The bearded man was panting even as he spoke. 'Without proof, Lady? His monkey has my pouch, even now, in his hands!' He spat on the ground and pointed to the child.

'Then the monkey should be punished, not the boy.'

'No! Not Pinar!' The boy began to howl again and gripped the monkey tightly in his arms.

She could see the boy clearly now. He was about ten cycles old, but something wasn't quite right with him. His eyes were too close together, his face crooked and his jaw deeply misshapen. He stood with a stoop, and one of his hands was much smaller than the other. It curled up slightly, into his chest. She looked then at the brother, the young man with the long dark hair, who was well muscled and seemed normal. His eyes burned with fury. Right now, much of it was directed at her.

'I am certain the monkey took the pouch in jest, is it not so?' She directed her question to the dark-haired man.

He hesitated, his dark eyes searching her face. Then he nodded, running the back of his hand across the side of his lips, smearing blood. 'It is so. The monkey is my brother's pet. He is from Chanu and is still untrained.'

'But this is not good enough,' said the bearded man, shaking his head. 'They are lying, clearly. There were witnesses ...'

Witnesses who had all but vanished when a Goddess-Blessed had been struck across the cheek, which was a good thing, Jaya decided. The Tigers had reached the stage now and were looking at her questioningly. She ignored them and placed a hand on the bearded man's arm, which startled him. 'Look at the child,' she said gently. 'He is not capable of deceit. Let him be. The Goddess has already punished him enough. He is but half-human.'

The dark-haired man scowled at her words and pulled his brother closer to him. But such words were necessary, for the other man capitulated.

'It is as you wish, Lady. If you will kindly ask the monkey to return my pouch ...'

The dark-haired man whistled under his teeth. The monkey came leaping into his arms, and he plucked the pouch from his paws.

The bearded man turned red. 'See ... see ... do you see that? He has trained it to obey him. He is part of it – he is a pickpocket ...'

She turned to the man and said, 'Are we to revisit the reasons why the boy is innocent, my friend? Do you think a Goddess-Blessed would know more about the truth of the matter, or you? Tell me, was it your hand that struck me earlier?'

The bearded man backed away. 'I ... I will take my pouch and leave, Lady ... thank you, Lady, for your kindness.'

With one last look of hatred towards the boy, the bearded man took his pouch and hurried down the street.

Jaya exhaled. She had overreached, she knew, for this crippled child. The Goddess-Blessed were not supposed to get involved in the day-to-day affairs of the people. That was what the priests were for. It was ironic how powerful the people thought the Blessed were. But there was no power here. If Iaf found out, he would be angry with her. He may even take it out on Aal, and that she could never survive. Yet ... she could not bear to see a child have his hands cut off for thievery, or worse, because he was Unclanned, sold into slavery to one of the whorehouses on the outskirts of the city. She could not let another child suffer. Not again.

'Everything all right?' one of the men from the Tiger clan asked. They stood around her, curious and alert.

She nodded and smiled. 'Just a misunderstanding. I am sorry you wasted your time.'

The man frowned. He had seen the mark on her cheek. But he did not press the matter. 'It is as you wish, Lady. Perhaps we can escort you and your daughter back to the Temple?'

'Yes, in a moment, please.'

She turned to the dark-haired man and smiled. Lowering her voice, she asked him, 'Where do you come from?'

He stared over her shoulder, looking at the Tigers as he spoke. 'Arrapha. Our parents died of sickness before I was Clanned, and so, after some time, we left. I was told there would be work here, even for the Unclanned, because it is such a big city. But that was a lie that the head of the caravans told me to convince me to hand over everything we owned in exchange for passage.'

'Where are you staying?'

He shrugged. 'We sleep on the street by the main gate, like the other Unclanned who cannot feed themselves without resorting to thievery.'

She could feel the bitterness. It all but seeped out of him.

'You look strong. You may not have the funds to bribe your way into the Tigers or Jackals, but there are other clans who would take you. The Buffaloes, I am sure, need more bricklayers. Surely, even in Arrapha you would have found work.'

He said nothing, but she saw his eyes dart towards his crippled brother. She understood. No clan would take the boy, not the way he was, and he was not prepared to desert his brother. It made him noble in her eyes. She made a decision, sudden and surprising.

'I have a house, it is on the Street of the Pipal Trees. You will recognize it by the blue door, and by the tree outside. Its roots have spread the length of the pavement. You and your brother can find shelter there, and some dried meats and water.'

His eyes met hers then. 'We are Unclanned. We have no seals to show the street guards, no permission to pass. I cannot allow my brother to be caught again.'

She hesitated. 'Wait till nightfall. Stay out of sight. Then we will talk.'

'Why?'

'Why what?'

'Why help us?'

She looked at his brother, the way he was showing off his monkey to Aal, the foolish grin on his face, now that the worst was over. She looked at his stooped figure and how he limped alongside her daughter.

'I don't know ...' she began. But it wasn't good enough, because she did know, didn't she? 'This city has ... has destroyed enough innocents already.'

'Come, Lady, we must be going,' said the Tiger leader.

She picked up her daughter, who was already protesting about leaving her new friend and the monkey, and followed the Tigers down the street. She felt the dark-haired man's eyes bore into her back as she walked.

Chapter Nineteen

KARACHI, PRESENT DAY.

The house was timeless and palatial, like a forgotten relic of the British Raj. It had large, sweeping gardens full of orange and pink roses, lilac snapdragons and rustling coconut trees. The property itself was single-storeyed and painted a faded eggshell, which did little to hide the long cracks in the cement. Tall columns stood sentry around an elegant veranda. The tops of its long windows were shielded by a mass of red and white bougainvillea which overflowed from the roof, and an old dusty blue Cadillac sat idle by the gate. The place reeked of faded grandeur.

Nadia felt a familiar sense of resentment build in her stomach. Her grandmother lived in Clifton, with the rest of the well-heeled gentry of Karachi. The people around here were affluent and connected. They lived in their large secluded houses surrounded by servants. They didn't care about what happened to the rest of the world. To their own grandchildren ...

Nadia remembered when she had first made contact with her grandmother. One of the new recruits had smuggled a portable TV into the compound, and Father had caught her watching cartoons. Watching cartoons ... a simple thing, a normal thing, she learnt later. Not a sign that evil had infested your mind. Televisions were strictly prohibited at GoL. They were considered to be instruments of thought control, of illusions created by those with higher knowledge to keep humanity from questioning its existence. Nadia had never listened to a radio station. She had never used a computer.

When Father had caught her, he had slapped her and left a hand-shaped bruise on her cheek. Father brokered no disobedience. It was the weekend, she should have reported in to work, and he was incensed that his daughter was such a bad role model for the others. That day, she remembered, the kids were going to be out in the fields, lifting heavy stones and wheeling them away so that the land could be planted. The work was hard and they would be at it until sunset without any breaks. Even her friend Simon, with his asthma, would be there, wheezing and spluttering. Simon's inhaler had been taken away the day before, because, according to Father, medicines were just another conspiracy created by pharmaceutical companies. All it took to heal the body was belief in oneself, a natural diet, meditation and ... the Light, of course. Nothing worked without the Light. Without him.

What had happened to the new recruit, the one with the TV? She tried to remember now. He'd accepted his penance, hadn't he? Three days in Reorientation. It was a mild punishment, doled out so that he would not be spooked away before they got their claws properly into him. That was right ... he didn't even get thrown into the Basement. Instead he spent the time in meditation with his Light Guide. And afterwards, he'd stayed and become a fully fledged devotee of her father.

It was amazing how many people bought into Sohail's New Age psychosis. As a child, Nadia had desperately wanted to be touched by the Light, as her father had been, praying that his healing hands had passed into her genes as well. All the miracles he performed, the people he saved ... it wasn't until she had been rescued from the compound, had grown up and learnt how cult leaders manipulated the truth, manipulated people, that she saw just how fraught her childhood had really been. She'd come across many child survivors of cults over the years. The Scientologists. Children of God. Even the Moonies. They'd all had one thing in common. They had all *believed*. Fervently. And then they had stopped believing, and afterwards, when they entered the 'real' world, they became the most screwed-up people on the planet. Like her.

At least, she thought, surveying her grandmother's imposing house with contempt, at least she had given back. At least she'd done something. She'd spent years publicly fighting GoL, trying to warn people about them. It was a common misconception that only stupid people joined cults. In fact, the opposite was true. Often it was highly educated, high achievers who made the best members, because the clever ones were convinced that they were intelligent enough not to be outsmarted. Uneducated people tended to be more wary of what they didn't understand. GoL was full of clever people – people who initially thought they were joining a group of New Age hippies. They thought they had found some sort of happy medium through meditation and yoga, a way to navigate life's hardest challenges. And then they found themselves moving into the compound so they could better learn which meditations to use and better experience Sohail's teachings. After that, they would quit their jobs, because their jobs did not give them any spiritual fulfilment and the Light had *plans* for them. And then they'd be isolated from their families and friends, the ones who didn't understand what it was that Sohail was trying to achieve. Finally, they'd sign over their earthly belongings to GoL. And then? Then they never left. Even the ones who woke up one day and realized just where the hell they were. There was nowhere to go. They didn't have family, they didn't have money. And any discord was brokered with a harsh punishment. Reorientation. Days of darkness and isolation in the Basement, kept half-starved and desperate for water by her father's goons, the Exemplar Militia. The EM were Sohail's personal bodyguards. They were the most devoted, the most physically strong and the most unquestioning. They guarded the Basement and the compound walls.

The Basement ... Even now, with the sun on her back, amidst the roses and the bougainvillea, thoughts about the Basement made her feel like she couldn't breathe. People used to tell horror stories about it all the time, but it was only when she had actually been there that she had truly understood what terror was.

Initially, the Basement was just that, the lower-ground floor of that first rambling farmhouse which had served as her father's headquarters. But later, when the money came in, it became a purpose-built set of tunnels and rooms under the new buildings. People could get lost in there. One family who told Sohail they were leaving simply disappeared one day, and was never seen or heard of again. The Exemplar Militia's handiwork presumably. Had they been sent for Reorientation? Left in the Basement for months? Or worse?

That Saturday morning of the illicit cartoon watching, she was taken by the Militia to Public Confession, a forum in which the sinner stood in the middle of a circle of people, begging forgiveness for his or her misdeeds from the entire group by touching their feet. Evidently, Nadia did a poor job when it was her turn, for afterwards, she was thrown into the Basement.

How to describe what it was like? How to explain the depths of hell that one reached from being alone, in isolation, as a young child? Three days of aloneness, that was what that first time had been. Three days of sitting on a concrete floor in complete silence and utter, utter darkness. The mind slowly unravels when it is tortured, and so did hers. It was only the briefest of threads – the dreams about Jaya – that brought her any solace or companionship. That, and the stories she started making up in her head. The stories that kept her sane.

When she was let out, she thought about the one thing her mother had left her before she ran off. A phone number. A number for her grandmother, Sohail's mother, in Pakistan. 'This woman will help you if you need anything,' Deborah had said. And silly, silly Nadia, she hadn't understood what was really being said. *I'm running away in the middle of the night. I'm abandoning you, so here's a number that will assuage my guilt.*

And then she was gone, her wayward, drug-addled mother, gone on the wind. Luckily for her, Sohail had not noticed her absence until the next morning. Nadia had kept the phone number, the spidery scrawl in blue ink, knowing that one day, it might be useful.

Being in the Basement was enough to destroy anyone's soul. She was meant to come out broken, ready to be moulded and be forgiven. But she had come out with a plan instead. She would contact her grandmother. She would beg her for help, for money, for anything that would get her away from GoL.

So late one night, she had braved the darkness one more time, broken into the visitor centre at the new compound and made the phone call. She had spoken to her grandmother. And her grandmother had made it clear that she should never have bothered calling her.

'Please,' Nadia had whispered, cradling the phone, her voice breaking. 'Please, can you help me?'

'Nadia, I'm sorry, but I don't know you and I don't have any relationship with your father. We have an agreement, he and I. I will stay out of his life, and in return, he will not come back to Pakistan. I'm afraid there's nothing I can do for you.'

'He ... he hurts us. He hurts us and I don't know what to do.'

'Call social services. The police.'

She stayed silent. If she did that, they would find nothing. It had happened before, several times. The compound was good at covering its own tracks. And then her father would kill her.

'I'm sorry, Nadia, but I can't help you. Please don't contact me again.'

That had been it. She'd been caught, of course. Someone had seen her. And how was she to know that Sohail recorded all phone calls that were made at the compound? She had many sins to confess to the group after that. And two and a half weeks to think about them in the Basement. Two and a half weeks of porridge and water, and a bucket to piss in. Two and a half weeks of sitting in her own filth and muck, of hallucinating new friends and letting her mind ramble with stories in the dark. And then one day, by which point she'd started to babble incoherently to herself, the place was raided, and she was set free ...

No thanks to Jahanara. What kind of woman ignored a desperate child? Christ, what was she doing here? She felt sick.

'Come on,' said Liam, motioning her forward. Nadia closed her eyes and took a deep breath. Then she followed him in.

Inside, the house had an air of neglect. A housekeeper escorted them to a dusty study and offered them green tea, which Nadia ignored. After he left, they sat in silence, nothing except for the rattling of a ceiling fan to offer distraction. Nadia was grateful for the quiet. It allowed her time to quell the chaos in her head, to pull herself together. She looked around. The room was tasteful and refined. There were hundreds upon hundreds of books, all stacked in shelves along two of the walls, their subjects ranged from philosophy to astronomy, including the odd work of fiction. Some of them looked to be ancient.

With a start, she saw her own books, all hardbacks, in one of the lower shelves. So Jahanara knew that she'd made something of herself, without her help. Good. *I hope she regretted her decision.*

Another wall held various framed maps and pictures. Some black-and-white photos of bygone family, a few reproductions of antique cartography. She stared at them, eyes narrowed. 'I've seen this before,' she said, pointing to the map in the centre. 'I remember all these beautiful ships painted around the continents, thinking there should be mermaids and a giant squid in there too. I think the original is in Marianne Riviere's office, in London.'

Immediately, Liam was at her side. 'I wonder what it is,' he murmured.

'I can explain, if you'd like?' said a husky voice.

It was her. Jahanara. A long, sharp face with shrewd tawny eyes, weathered with age. Wrinkled lips. A hooked nose and white hair, pulled back in an elegant bun. The strong chin and the haughty stare – a stare that Nadia had seen so many times on her father's face, when he wanted to intimidate someone.

She wore a white sari which hung loosely from her bony body. She seemed small and tired. Seeing her took Nadia's breath away.

Jahanara walked towards her slowly, heavily dependent on her stick. They paused, looking at each other. Each one measuring, each one weighing. There was no hug, no effusive welcome.

Then Jahanara turned, lifted a shaky arm and pointed at the map. 'This was created by Hadji Ahmed Muhiddin Piri, a Turkish Admiral and cartographer, circa 1513. It is known as the Piri Reis map. It is one of the oldest world maps in existence, although much of it is missing, we only have parts of the original parchment left. This map is a copy. Hello Nadia.' Her voice was a little unsteady.

Nadia didn't trust herself to speak.

'Does this map hold some significance?' asked Liam.

'More than you realize. Sit, please.'

Nadia felt the bitterness rise. 'Why did you ask Liam to bring me here? Where is Layla? I think you owe us some answers.'

Jahanara pursed her lips, placing both hands on her cane. 'I suppose I must be an impolite host and seat myself first. I am an old woman, after all.'

She wasn't going to be intimidated. Not by this woman. Nadia raised her own chin, and gave her own haughty stare. 'Nobody's stopping you from sitting down. Do what you want, it's your house.'

Incredibly, Jahanara's face relaxed into a smile and she nodded. 'You have some fire in you. Good. You'll need it.' Then, with difficulty, she made her way to a leather armchair by the window. Liam went to help. 'Thank you.'

'Where is Layla? Who has her? Tell me about the dreams.'

Liam turned and frowned at her. 'What do you mean dreams?'

'Sit. Please. Have a biscuit. First, I will tell you more about the map. It has a fascinating history.'

'I don't care about the bloody map,' Nadia snapped.

Liam went to Nadia and rested a hand on her shoulder. 'Jahanara, Nadia is tired. She's had a terrible shock and this week has been hell. I think you owe her some answers, and me some too. I brought her here because you said she would be the key to finding the others. How? Where are they?'

Jahanara looked at them and shook her head. 'I am not here to waste your time. I cannot talk about Layla, without talking about why and how we got here, to our current ...

predicament. Do you think that it is a coincidence that Nadia's eyes were drawn to the map? The map is at the heart of it.'

Nadia snorted, but crossed her arms and sat down.

'Something to drink?' asked Jahanara.

Nadia shook her head, waiting.

Jahanara relaxed in her chair, her eyes on her granddaughter. 'Did you know, Piri used several older maps and resources in his cartography? One of them supposedly compiled by Christopher Columbus himself. And another from the library in Alexandria.'

'So?'

Jahanara nodded, almost as though she understood her granddaughter's sullenness. Her eyes washed over Nadia's face ... and lingered.

She's taking me in. Why? It would be too much if her grandmother actually thought they could be friends.

'Feel free to look at the map closely. What land mass do you see?'

Liam stood up and peered. 'It's the Americas, right?' he asked, eventually. 'South America in that corner? I'm not sure how that's relevant ...'

'What else do you see?'

Nadia got up and had another look, letting her eyes scan the intricate map. 'Antarctica,' she said. 'This land mass here, next to all these illustrated ships, it's Antarctica, isn't it?'

'Yes.'

It was Liam's turn to sigh in frustration.

Nadia stared at her grandmother, who was delicately nibbling on a biscuit, and made a decision. She started to walk to the door. 'Ignore her, Liam. What she's trying to get us to see is really not going to help Layla, or get you any answers. Trust me. We're on our own.'

Jahanara cackled. 'Figured it out already? I knew you would. I do read your books, you know.'

'Would you mind telling me what she's on about?' Liam said.

Nadia turned back towards him. 'She's showing us the Piri Reis map, a map that was created in the 1500s, right? But Antarctica wasn't discovered until 1819. I know, because I researched it for *Hellbound*.'

'That would be your novel?'

Nadia nodded. 'Yes. The novel is set in the future, but there's a section about the history of Antarctica. I'll never forget the date, because I had to research the period.'

Liam looked at them both. 'But what's the point here? That a cartographer got lucky and found a continent that was supposedly unheard of? If Piri used multiple sources, maybe Antarctica existed on one of them. Maybe it was lost to people for centuries, but our ancestors knew about it. One of the lost secrets of the library at Alexandria, for instance. I hardly see what this has to do with anything.'

'He's right,' said Nadia, looking at her grandmother. 'I don't see what this proves.'

'It would prove nothing, if this were a representation of Antarctica as we know it. But it isn't. Please, come and sit down again,' said Jahanara.

'I'm getting tired of these games,' Nadia warned. 'I want to know about Layla.'

'And I'm trying to tell you about her,' Jahanara said, with a hint of steel in her voice. 'But you need to have the background, as I've said before. Otherwise, you won't be prepared ...'

'Prepared for what, exactly?' The room was hot. The fan whirred at a glacial pace, moving heavy dust around, more than anything else. She ached for a smoke, something, anything, to inhale or digest or swallow that would take her away from the insanity of this moment. Her grandmother. Jahanara. All this time, she had been here.

'This map, Piri's map, is a scientifically accurate scale representation of Antarctica ... before it was covered in a sheet of ice 4 kilometres thick. Its measurements are precise and unmistakable.'

Nadia snorted. 'That's impossible. That would have to make the sources of the map, or the knowledge it is derived from, tens of thousands of years old, before the Ice Age covered and changed the continent's shape. Our ancestors were living in caves, eating berries, discovering how to make fire. Precise scientific measurements of Antarctica? Did Piri have some land mass X-ray machine we've never heard of?' She heard herself laugh bitterly.

Jahanara said nothing, and quietly sipped her tea.

'It's not possible,' said Nadia, but she sat by the window, looking out at the garden. A small beige lizard darted up a palm tree, shimmying past rough green fruit until it was lost in the foliage. She felt sweat on her palms and rubbed them against her jeans. None of what her grandmother said made sense and yet, part of her, some part of her knew the answers to her questions would take her further than she would ever want to go. Who was Jaya? Why did she dream about her?

She heard Liam pace around. 'How would humans have had knowledge of Antarctica from before the last Ice Age, Jahanara?' he asked.

'Are either of you familiar with the work of Charles Hapgood?'

'No.'

'Hapgood used aerial photographs of Antarctica, taken by the US Air Force, to do his research. He compared Piri's map with an azimuthal equidistant projection of the world. Do you know what that is?'

'No, we don't. But I suppose you'll tell us it's some sort of ancient technology and that's why this is relevant.'

Her grandmother shook her head. 'It is a map projection in which all distances measured from the centre of the map along any latitudinal line are accurate. Hapgood's projection centred near Cairo. In the 1950s, he was able to ascertain that Antarctica was accurately represented on the Piri Reis map. Just not as we know it now. But as it was then, before it was covered by 90 per cent of the ice currently on our planet. The shape underneath all of that ice remains the same, you see, but you cannot tell without the imagery.'

'Well, Mr Hapgood was clearly off his rocker,' said Liam, folding his arms across his chest.

'You might think so,' said Jahanara, nodding philosophically, 'although, Hapgood was respected in his field. There was a notable theoretical physicist at the time, one who was so impressed with Hapgood's work that he wrote the foreword for one of his books about earth crustal displacement theory, and embarked on a long correspondence with him. That physicist was Albert Einstein. Would you argue that he was "off his rocker" too?'

'Just what are you trying to say?' said Liam, turning around. 'That human beings are older than we think? That somehow we had access to technology that was only invented fifty years ago, tens of thousands of years ago?'

'Jesus Christ,' burst out Nadia, running her hand through her hair and pacing. 'You're as bad as *him*. Your son. My father. He believed in the Light, the metaphysical. Transcendence through knowledge. The idea of knowing all human knowledge because you were born with the ability of remembering what had passed. He thought mankind had evolved to the point where we could fly, where we could go to other planets, where there was no illness or famine. But then we messed it up, right? We killed each other. But that's okay. Because we get to *remember* and become masters of the universe once again. Jesus. I always thought he was insane. Maybe it's in the genes. He obviously got it from you.'

'Sit down, please,' said Jahanara. 'I'm not talking about your father. Right now, I'm talking about science.'

'I've had enough,' said Nadia, heading for the door again.

'And yet you know I'm right,' said her grandmother, holding out her arm as Nadia walked past. 'You've had the dreams, you've seen for yourself our past in your visions. Don't lie to me, girl. I've known you had the gift. I knew it when you were born. You sister never had the dreams though, did she? It often works like that, skipping some and landing on others in each generation.'

'You know nothing about me,' hissed Nadia. 'You raised a monster. Father told me once that I would die, that I had not embraced his teachings and so I would be punished and suffer the same fate as the rest of the unenlightened. I was six-fucking-years-old, Jahanara. I loved him and when he was happy ... it was wonderful. But when he went crazy ... And where the hell were you? Here, in this room, probably. Drinking green tea surrounded by servants.'

'Nadia,' Liam warned. 'Don't upset her.'

'Why?' demanded Nadia. 'Because she's elderly and frail? She can't play that card, I'm sorry. She's done enough damage already.'

'Do not presume to know my life,' snarled Jahanara suddenly. The old woman got up and pointed a shaky finger at her granddaughter. 'You think I haven't watched out for you. Cared for you. Loved you. But I did the best I could. I stayed away, because *he* would have destroyed you otherwise.

Trust me.' Her voice wobbled slightly. 'Trust me. He is my own flesh and blood, but God help me, it's truc.'

'I think you better sit down,' said Liam, taking Nadia to the sofa. 'And Jahanara, you better explain just what the hell is going on.'

Chapter Twenty

MELUHHA, 3791 BC.

The bathing rituals and Temple work had taken up most of the day. Jaya and Aal took their time walking home, enjoying the coolness brought on by the sunset. Aal was quiet. Her sandals slapped the road, bringing up dust. Jaya glanced at her daughter, whose hand lay clammily in her own. Her little girl was tired.

They had worked on arrangements for Karani, the day of Feasting. Even though it was over two full moons away, there was much to be done. Spices had to be sent for, all the way from Chanu, and harvest collected so that the traditional fare of barley soup, smoked river trout, venison stewed with cardamom, spinach boiled in mustard pods, fresh mango, cakes of bread and glasses of buffalo milk thick with foam were available to the people when the time came. All of Meluhha celebrated Karani, even the Unclanned, and nobody went hungry or had to pay for their fare. It was the one day of the year that the city came together to enjoy the bounty of Shakari, and it was a day that was the envy of the known world. Meluhha stood above any other city in its greatness and generosity to its people. And, as had been decried many hundreds of cycles before, it was the Goddess-Blessed on whom the burden of organization fell, under Iaf's watchful eye, of course.

Just today, Sarema had met with clan leaders to discuss who would provide the extra labour that would be required. She had taken Jaya with her. Jaya had been given the relatively mundane job of hiring cooks for the Feast. She had been trying hard to seem complacent, willing. A good sister. She wanted no one to question her actions or her loyalty. Not now, when she was so close to leaving. Her strategy was working, because Sarema was trusting her more and more.

With Enia's help, Jaya had already reached out to one of the oarsmen in the river. He'd promised that he would risk his life to take her and Aal away. But the price ... the price was still too far out of her reach, though she had saved what she thought was a whole city's worth of gold. The man was not stupid. He knew what would happen to him if they were caught. A traitor's death, hanging from the pipal tree outside the Temple.

These were uncertain times, and the man wanted to make his fortune before he left. The clans had been fighting more than usual. The Crocodiles had raised the price of river fish by a whole cube's worth, arguing that the priests had forced them to sell the fish at a cost that left them with meagre provisions for themselves. This had prompted the Tigers to raise the tariffs they charged merchants to sell spices in the market. Inexplicably, Iaf had banned the Crocodiles from trading by the river, as they traditionally did, and insisted they trade at the main square ... in Tiger territory. The Tigers agreed, but for a large commission on the sales. The Crocodiles were not happy, having lost any compensation they had made by raising their costs. The Tigers and the priests both made money by the arrangement – the Tigers paying the Temple a hefty share of the profits each week.

It made her feel even more bitter. Iaf had always controlled everything in her life. And now he was making the Crocodiles suffer. He was all-powerful, there was nobody who could stop him.

Aal's hand grew heavy in her own and she looked down at her daughter. The poor thing had had to spend the day sitting in the stifling heat of the Temple, listening patiently to each squabble and petty grievance. Jaya would have happily traded it for a day by the river, throwing stones in the froth and watching the fishermen head to the market.

Jaya liked to be free and unconstrained, just like her daughter. Despite what Nene had said, she had always believed in Shakari, for how else was it that she had the visions? The power of the Bloodstone came from somewhere ... where else but from Shakari's heart? She could not understand why Shakari had not listened to her prayers. Perhaps the Goddess wanted her to endure for a reason she did not yet comprehend. Perhaps she was still cursed for her disobedience, for using the Stone for her own selfish reasons. She did not know.

But she did know that the Goddess could be found in the warmth of the sun and the sound of a strong wind, the collection of a harvest and the ripening of fruit. Not in negotiating with clans or discussing grain, especially not with Iaf lurking, making his own arrangements on the side, striking deals to grow the wealth of the priests and his own dominance.

It helped that he had Jaya, whose visions had been growing more powerful every time she used the Stone. The others continued to offer up 'visions' of their own, but so far only hers had proven to be accurate. Using the Bloodstone tired her, often deeply. Sometimes she fainted, as she had done that first time.

But she had never made the mistake of asking for a vision of her own future again. She had angered Shakari with that request, that was why the Goddess had sent Iaf to lay with her. She had sworn never to question the Goddess's will again. She had kept to that promise, no matter how badly she was tempted to break it. Shakari had given her the power to see the visions. There was purpose behind it, even if she did not understand what that purpose was. But she could not risk angering the Goddess even further. Well, soon it would not matter.

They turned down the road away from the Temple and towards the Street of Sorrow. Jaya hesitated. It would save them a few minutes to take the shortcut, but she was superstitious. The Lamenters were paid to weep and cry at funerals and sombre events. She did not like these women, who shaved their heads and made little cuts in their bodies as they howled, to show that they would shed blood for the person who had moved on to the Upworld.

The sound of wheels on brick brought her attention back to the road. A merchant, a man she recognized, was lazily flicking his whip against the flank of the bullock pulling his cart. The man was Bahaud, he sold jugs of beer and Sura, an intoxicating liquid made from rice meal, to the Temple and to the taverns and whorehouses. He was amiable enough, though struck with a disturbing skin ailment, which left part of his face covered in small red pustules. She pressed Aal closer to her side, as he stopped and offered her a greeting. She nodded, patiently waiting for the bullocks to move past. The roads were so crowded these days, the merchants came in and out of the city like flies to the lychees that the fruit man sold for exorbitant prices in the summer.

By the time they reached the house, the moon was high in the sky. She unbolted the door and ushered her daughter in.

She jumped as a figure came towards them in the darkness.

Rafe raised his hands. 'I did not mean to scare you, Lady.'

She put a hand on her chest. For a moment, she had forgotten about this man, this one quiet rebellion of her own, away from Iaf's prying eyes. 'Not at all,' she replied, trying to keep her voice even. 'I was distracted.'

Aal was suddenly smiling again and launched herself at Rafe, hugging him tightly. 'Thank the Goddess we are home at last! Where's Al-Mien? I want to show him my new spinning top.' Rafe laughed and put her down gently. 'Always so eager, little one. He is in the courtyard, preparing the evening meal.'

Even Jaya had to smile at this. Who would have thought that the crippled boy she had met in the market all those moons ago would turn out to be such a fabulous cook, among his several other talents? Al-Mien could do many things, despite his misshapen body. He had a strange affinity for animals and would sit quietly in the courtyard for hours, with his left arm outstretched. The birds would flock to him and perch on his arm companionably, kingfishers, blue jays, cakks and even parrots. Mostly, he would let them go. Sometimes, when they were low on supplies – closer to Karani, the people were less generous in their tithes to the Goddess-Blessed, saving much of their food for their offerings to Shakari – Al-Mien would catch one and boil it with lentils or maize, making a delicious stew. Jaya had become deeply fond of him.

A thought struck her suddenly then. Why should the boy not use this skill to learn a trade? If he joined the Unicorn clan, he could cook on Feast Day. And now, since she had responsibility for the cooking at the event, she could make it happen ... She felt the excitement grow within her. Finally, she could help Rafe by finding a place for his brother. Then Rafe could join his own clan and be free. *And she could focus on leaving. She had put it off long enough, letting the boy and his brother distract her from her purpose.*

He was looking at her in that intense way of his again. Rafe. He was such a contradiction. A man who spent much of his time being angry, at the world, at the city and the way it worked. But he was also a man who would not join a clan because it would mean deserting his brother. He was a man who fed a monkey to keep Al-Mien happy, even when there was scarcely enough to feed himself. He was a man who looked at her with such intensity sometimes, it made her stomach turn on itself.

He took her parcel of oranges – the ones she had pilfered from the Temple – from her hand, and led the way to the courtyard. 'You are tired. You must eat, Lady. From sunrise to sunset you are at the Temple these days. Surely those bloated fools can spare you.'

It made her uncomfortable when he talked like this. If Iaf ever found out Rafe was staying here ... she was putting Aal in jeopardy, and yet, it seemed, Shakari had brought them to her, for what purpose, she could not yet fathom.

'Come, drink some tea, my Lady,' urged Rafe, handing her an earthenware bowl with jasmine flowers seeped in boiling water.

'I've asked you before, please stop calling me that. We are friends now, are we not? I am Jaya, not Lady.'

He looked pleased, but said nothing. For a few moments, they sat in companionable silence, sipping tea, gazing at the Upworld, where Shakari's many tears gathered to shine on the world. Nene was there, watching over her. Would Mua or Apa be dead now, she wondered? Would they have survived all these cycles? Was one of them watching over her too? That life seemed so far away now, that blissful, peaceful time by the river where there was no politics, no Bloodstone, no Iaf and no Sarema to dominate her life. And yet, the pain of losing her family was still so very raw.

Jaya watched Al-Mien as he gently stirred a cauldron of soup, offering a spoon to Aal to try. The little girl took a sip and grinned, nodding back, happy with the fare. The night was still, only interrupted by the occasional braying of a neighbour's donkey.

In moments like this, she thought, I could be happy. If Aal could live a free life, have children, and enjoy the sun on her face and the wind on her back, I could be happy here.

But she had never been happy here, wasn't that the point? Her life, her world, moved in and out of favour on the whim of the High One. He had lain with her, many times, always bringing her pain. He had given her Aal, but he had nearly torn her apart. And Aal would always be in danger as long as he was alive.

What would the world look like if Iaf was gone, if the priests did not rule things, if there were no Goddess-Blessed? What would she do if her life were her own? She shut her mind to such things, taking a sip of her tea instead. It was no good thinking of what would not be.

'I have never seen my brother so happy,' said Rafe, as he sipped his tea. 'You see how much he is thriving here, despite the secrecy, despite the fact that we have to leave so early each morning to avoid being caught. I thank you, Jaya.' He said her name shyly.

Jaya put down her bowl and looked at him. 'The festival of Karani will be upon us soon. There will be high demands for cooks and those who are handy with food. I think even Al-Mien would find a place in a clan now.'

Rafe snorted in disbelief. 'You say that, Lady, because ...'

'Jaya. Please call me Jaya,' she gently reminded him. For reasons she didn't fully understand, she didn't want her rank to be a barrier between them.

'You say that, Jaya, because you are sheltered from the harsh reality of this city. Thousands of the Unclanned will be applying for jobs in the kitchens of the Temple and the big houses around here. Able-bodied men and women who can cook well, or learn. Al-Mien doesn't have a chance, not against them. They would sooner cut off their arms than give up an opportunity to join a clan.'

She frowned and tucked her chin into her knees. 'Well, if he already has a job cooking in the Temple, the clan will have him. If they won't, we will simply find another way. The head of the Stone Carvers was a friend of my father. Perhaps, he will simply make you some seals for me.'

His eyes sought hers. 'Forgeries, then? To allow us to pass through the city?'

She shrugged. 'I suppose so. I haven't really thought about it.'

'You know the penalty for stealing a clanship?'

She nodded. 'He would do it for me. He is a good man.'

'You would risk that. All that? For us? Why?' Once again, his dark eyes were suspicious.

She hesitated. Could she trust him? Why not? She had already said and done enough to damn herself. 'The truth is, Aal and I are leaving. I have some gold hidden away under the bricks in the courtyard. It will not be long now, I have nearly enough. We will go, and I would like to see Al-Mien protected before I leave. I have grown very fond of the boy. Fond ... of you both.'

He turned away from her, looking at the Upworld. 'You would leave? Would not the High One be angry with you? Or do the Goddess-Blessed have so much power that they can do as they please?' He said the last with scorn in his voice.

He was such a bitter man. It was foolish, but she wished she could take away some of that anger, and replace it with ... with what, exactly?

'We do not live the indulgent life you seem to think we do, Rafe,' she said as lightly as possible. 'Life as a Goddess-Blessed ... it is ... difficult.'

He rolled his eyes.

'Truly. You do not understand ...'

'I do not understand all the sleeping? Or the neck aches you get from all the jewellery you wear? You are right. It must be a challenge to decide which maidservant will bring you your food for each meal, or the fruit you eat all day while gossiping in each other's houses. I know you are working hard now, in the Temple, but it is nothing to what most of us endure.'

'If you just listened ...'

He shook his head. 'You cannot run away from a life of ease just because you have been forced into organizing Karani. You have no idea how harsh life can be.'

It was enough. His stubborn refusal to listen was enough. 'Don't I? Don't I know? It is you who know nothing about what you speak,' she hissed. Then she looked down, embarrassed by the outburst.

He wiped his face with his arm and stared at her for a moment. 'You are right,' he said at last. 'You have been nothing but kind to us. You have risked much, hiding us here each night and sneaking us out each morning before the others come. I should not begrudge you your life simply because it is an easier one than most.'

'It is not easy,' she said hotly, feeling the flush spread across her face. 'Why can't you understand? You think that being a Goddess-Blessed is all about luxuries and fineries. You and the rest of Meluhha.'

He shrugged, looking bored. 'Perhaps. But nothing I have seen has made me feel differently.'

'Then it is you who should open your eyes.'

He said nothing, his fingers trailing the bricks in the courtyard. Eventually, he sighed. 'Forgive me,' he said at last. 'Sometimes ... sometimes I have no patience left. I know it is a failing. My father often told me so. But when I see such horrible things in this city ... it would shock you, Jaya, if you saw how ugly things truly are.' He clenched his hands, and then looked at her once more. 'Please,

please tell me about your life.' He crossed his legs and put down his tea.

Shadows from the fire under the cauldron danced around the courtyard, and mosquitoes hovered above her head. Al-Mien and Aal laughed and sat in the corner cooking soup. But in that moment, the world seemed so still. In the end, it was not a difficult decision. She felt the burden of secrets lighten as she told him about her childhood on the river, about growing up with the smell of fish under her fingernails and swimming with Dar. She told him how the rest of the Goddess-Blessed could not read the Stone, but how the Stone had taken her to a whole other world when she had touched it, proving that Shakari existed, that Shakari had cursed her for her selfishness. She told him about Iaf and his frequent visits to her bed, about the pain he brought her, about how trapped she was, when Aal was born, how she would do anything to keep her daughter safe. Then she told him about Nene and how she let Nene's son die. The last confession brought her so much shame that she hung her head, unable to look at him any more.

Al-Mien called them to eat, but neither of them moved. The night was hazy now, smoke from hundreds of cooking fires reaching up into the sky.

He reached out and held her hand.

'When will you leave?' he asked.

'Soon,' she replied, watching Aal rush to eat. 'I have collected gold, enough to bribe the oarsman, except he has asked for a little bit more, another three cubes' worth, because helping me is such a great risk. Then I hope to find my family.'

He frowned. 'Jaya, the mighty arms of Meluhha reach out in every direction. You will not be safe, no matter where you go. Your face ... your tattoo ...'

'I will tattoo the rest of my face. Like the women from the Northlands. Nobody will recognize me as Goddess-Blessed. Not once we leave here and are far enough away.'

He shook his head. 'The women from the Northlands – your hair is not light enough. Neither is your skin. Even if it was, they are nothing but chattel to their husbands. If you leave here unprotected, one of their men will claim you as his own. What will you do then?'

'I will find my family before that happens.'

'You and I both know that it is unlikely that you will, not when they are so far away. This plan is not well thought through.'

On the contrary, she had thought of nothing else for many cycles. 'What else would you have me do?' she said at last, squashing the folds of her tunic in the palm of her hands.

He brought his body close to hers. 'Stay,' he replied.

'Aal will be in danger. Perhaps not today. But soon, when she is old enough to use the Bloodstone.'

'I will take care of you both, I give you my blood oath. I will not let anyone hurt you any longer.'

His expression was so serious, his eyes so intent, that for a moment she almost believed him. Then she shook her head. 'You cannot stop Iaf from hurting me or my daughter. I must go.'

'Stay,' he whispered again. This time, his hand rose up and his palm rested against her cheek. 'Please.' He leaned forward, and his lips were where his palm was, leaving soft kisses all over her face. Then his lips found hers and she was kissing him back, basking in his woodsmoke smell, in the roughness of his cheek against her skin, in the safety of his body.

When they broke apart, she trailed a finger along his jawline in wonder. 'Come with us. You and Al-Mien.'

He shook his head. 'You will not have enough gold to take four people to Dilmun. Not if we must pay extra to ensure secrecy.' He hesitated. 'Will you give me some time, some time to work and save some gold or precious jewels to barter?'

'Yes.' She caressed his face, her heart suddenly lightened. 'Yes, I will. We will save our gold and we will leave together. After Karani. The boats will be leaving in flocks then, and someone will be willing to accept our wealth.'

He grabbed her and kissed her with so much passion that she felt giddy. Something new bubbled up inside her. Something sudden and strangely wonderful. The world had righted itself, at least for the moment. Hope, she realized suddenly. It was hope. How strange, until that moment she had almost entirely forgotten what that felt like.

Chapter Twenty-One

KARACHI, PRESENT DAY.

Jahanara talked well into the night. Nadia and Liam sat there, in the dusty room, amongst the flickering shadows and the whirr of the slow ceiling fan, listening to a woman who seemed to be unburdening herself of years of pain.

Her husband Komail Hussain had died shortly after their marriage, killed in the riots of Partition, when Pakistan became a separate nation from India. She was six months pregnant when she heard the news.

Jahanara found herself alone with a newborn child, one on whom she lavished attention and adoration, trying to compensate for the loss of his father. Sohail. The name meant the second brightest star in the sky. His father would always be the first. Sohail was her second chance at life.

Sohail was spoilt, not just by her, but also by his father's family. The Hussains were devastated by Komail's death. But then the child was born. Here was life, at a time when so many had lost family and friends in the darkness of Partition. They obsessed over him.

Sohail had always been highly strung. As a boy of five or six, he would wash his hands, often ten to twenty times, to protect himself from germs. He'd close his eyes and sing to himself, and then yell at anybody who interrupted. He cried at the smallest thing: the dead ant on the veranda, the fact that there was a power cut, or that his mother hadn't smiled that morning. She took him to the doctor, who said they were simply childhood tantrums. The boy was very clever and would grow out of it. Give it time, the doctor counselled.

And she did. The doctor seemed to be proven right. At school, Sohail was popular and charming, and vice-captain of the cricket team. But at home, he was often moody. He preferred to be alone with his thoughts. He loved to read. He could sit in his room with a mountain of books on philosophy and religion and pore through them, forgetting to eat dinner unless it was brought to him on a tray. He became scholarly.

One day, he asked his mother about dreams.

Jahanara looked at him, slowly putting down the sewing she had started. 'What do you mean?' she asked carefully.

He seemed embarrassed. 'There are some things ... stories that I see. People. There are some people in a strange land. I see them all the time.'

Jahanara was stunned. She had never talked about the dreams to her son. She never imagined that he would be born with the same abilities that some of the women in her family had, for as far as she knew that gift was passed down from one woman to another. Jahanara had dreamt of Jaya since she was a little girl. So had her grandmother. Jaya's life was a part of their own existence, they discussed her, as they would any member of the family. It was said, by her grandmother, that Jaya was a memory of their ancestor, one who had lived perhaps thousands of years ago, and who had come to them because her spirit was restless.

In those days, Jahanara explained, women were not educated and so everything was born from superstition. Jaya was a ghost, a djinn-like creature who invaded their thoughts but who they were happy to share their lives with. For she was a clever, brave little thing whose fate was never really made clear to any of them. The dreams had no chronology. One day she was a child, on another, a grown woman. And she never, ever died. What had happened to Jaya? Nobody knew. Nobody knew why some of the women in the family dreamt of her, while others didn't. It was inexplicable, but also such a normal state of affairs within the family that no one ever thought to question it.

So Jahanara told Sohail of her own dreams, of Jaya, of the place where she lived. Probably the Indus Valley, the family had guessed, for that is where their ancestors were said to have come from, where they had land. Had Sohail been having dreams of her too?

'Forget it,' he muttered, clearly frustrated. 'I knew you wouldn't understand. You never understand anything.'

He'd left, and she had remained there, with the sewing in her hand and a feeling of complete confusion.

When he was fifteen, Sohail disappeared. They found him, the following night, sleeping at the shrine of a pir, a religious leader. He had taken opium. He was stoned, too stoned to even recognize her. That's when the drugs became an issue. Sohail had inherited a great deal of land and money. His father's family allowed him access to it whenever he wanted. He used it now, disappearing for chunks of time without accounting for his whereabouts. Jahanara didn't know what to do, the family was unhelpful. He'd often be found with one of them, complaining that his mother was tight-fisted and controlling. They would take his side because they were devoted to him. Then his father's brother proposed that Sohail live with him, so that things might improve.

She should have stopped him, Jahanara told them now. She should have locked him in a room if that was what it took. But he was still attending school and still doing well, despite his tantrums. So she let him go. She'd been convinced that he would be happier that way, that maybe he would talk to his uncle about his problems. Perhaps he needed a male authority figure in his life.

But the opposite occurred. At his uncle's house, Sohail was allowed to do whatever he wanted. He ordered a lot of books about dreams, about the occult, about spirituality. She knew he was taking drugs, she could see from his eyes that he was high all the time. But mother and son had become out of sync, and he wouldn't even talk to her. It was strange, but it was almost as though he hated her. It was disconcerting. And she lost him, one day at a time.

His father's family continued to protect him. When he had finished school and wanted to travel to India, they funded his trip, even though she was adamant that he must go to university. He did not return to Pakistan for two years, sending nothing but an odd postcard. Three in total, to his uncle. None to her.

When he did come back, he was sporting a beard. He had spent time with Hindu nationalists who passionately believed that Indian civilization had flourished many millennia ago, that India had once been a centre for space science, genetic technology and health innovation. Sohail also brought along an American girlfriend who wore flowery dresses and spoke of free love. He'd met Deborah in an ashram outside Bombay. He was going to marry her, he said.

For the first time ever, his father's family baulked. They wanted him to settle down with someone they approved of, not this odd American woman who seemed to take even more drugs than he did. And why had the boy turned to Hindu nationalists for answers, the very people who were responsible for his father's death? Everyone was disturbed, nobody knew what to do.

Sohail and Deborah spent much of their time in Karachi ingesting LSD, listening to loud music and swaying around in the garden, sometimes in their underwear, to the horror and shame of everyone. There was no more talk of dreams. Sohail had found his spirituality. 'There is no God,' he told his shocked family. 'There is no Allah, no Shiva, no Buddha. There are only humans. Humans and more evolved humans. Those of us who are evolved ... well, we have all the power.' Often he made little sense.

But he had theories and ideas. 'We are the sum of all our knowledge. And that knowledge is vast. There are others, others who were born with all the knowledge of the world. And they control us, don't you think? They control what we eat, they put mind-altering drugs in our food, did you know that? They control what we see on television, in the media. And they control who we are, what we think. The Ancients control everything.'

His father's family suddenly realized that Sohail had problems. Real problems. They came to Jahanara. What should be done? First of all, that woman, Deborah, had to go. She was a bad influence. We will support you, they told Jahanara, when you ask her to leave.

Jahanara had done just that. She had told her son that it was time for Deborah to return to America. They fought. Deborah left, refusing to ever come back to Pakistan.

Sohail was high and in his anger, he pushed his mother into a wall, screaming that she was evil. The force was enough to give her a concussion.

When she was recovering in the hospital, he was grief-stricken, apologetic. It was because she didn't understand, he told her. She hadn't let her mind evolve. If she would only try LSD, if only she would let her mind expand ... she would understand ... the world was not what it seemed. It was all mind control. He cited the example of Francis Crick, who discovered the double helix structure of DNA while he was high ... it was the only time the Ancients couldn't control the scientist's thoughts, didn't his mother understand? They were always out to get anyone who challenged their supremacy.

Jahanara had had enough. She told Sohail to leave, to take his father's money and follow Deborah if that was what he wanted.

Sohail cleaned out his father's old accounts and got on a plane the next day.

She heard of him infrequently, through his father's family. He'd apparently bought a farm in Devon, in England, and was trying to grow apple trees. He was doing some university courses in Philosophy. Deborah was pregnant. They were settling down. Her heart began to ache for him, but she did not contact her son.

When Nadia was three, Sohail returned to Pakistan. He had wanted to show his daughter his roots, he told his family. He wanted to mend bridges. Deborah had come along too, very sullenly. At first, Jahanara's heart lifted at the idea of being reconciled with her son. But she soon realized that Sohail had come to sell all his landholdings, everything he had inherited from his father. He was cutting off all ties with his homeland. And something was very, very wrong.

The little girl, Nadia, was quiet, so quiet that you could have missed her in a room. The mother, Deborah, was a nightmare. She hadn't been able to smuggle drugs in with her from London, and so she was paying the bootlegger large amounts of money for vodka instead. She spent her time wandering around the house, rather reeling around the house, sneering and suggesting that everything in it should belong to her husband as it was his inheritance. And Sohail? Sohail was beatific. He had figured it all out, he said. He had spent his childhood having strange dreams, dreams which he finally understood. It was his job to bring people into the Light. Humans had existed on this planet for hundreds of thousands of years, he said. He had seen the visions. Human civilization flourished long before the Ice Age. People made great strides in science, art, technology and medicine, just as the Hindu nationalists had once told him.

But then they destroyed themselves with their greed and their violence. Civilizations turned to dust in apocalyptic circumstances. Nuclear bombs. Climate terrorism. Chemical and biological weapons. Then, as time passed, they began all over again with the few human survivors who were left. Those survivors passed on no memory of what came before them, they could barely stay alive and memories were lost over the ages. And so legends were born instead. But, while humanity was struggling to regain simple skills like building fires, some people were born more evolved than others. They were born with the breadth of past human knowledge inside them. They could *remember* and so they were special. They used this to their advantage, gaining positions of power, manipulating those less evolved. They were the creatures of the Dark, for they banded together and sought to keep the rest of humanity from learning the truth. That they could heal themselves. That they could use their mind to increase their psychic powers, that they could create incredible things just by the strength of their will. That they could even fly. All of these were skills their ancestors had once known. There was no need for violence. For bloodshed. For any kind of suffering at all.

That was the beginning of his philosophy, Jahanara explained. What followed was an ever-changing mass of contradictory beliefs. He had already begun to get followers, sharing his pretend amazement with his family, that anyone would want to listen to what he had to say. He started to run meditation courses, offer yoga retreats at his farm, alongside his preaching. But there was a mounting ego there too. Perhaps, that's why he had returned, to show them all how important he was beginning to realize he could become.

He talked about Light Guides, about helping people evolve to a point where they could guide others to finding the Light. About how he would need an army to protect himself from the naysayers and the Ancients. For how else would they make money, if nobody needed medicines, if there was no longer any need for the armaments of war?

Sohail babbled all the time. His father's family thought he had gone crazy. Jahanara noticed that he often excused himself to go to his room, and came back with red-rimmed eyes. Her son was still a drug addict.

Naturally, her thoughts turned to her grandchild. She was such a small, quiet, strange little thing, with dark, watchful eyes. She was jittery too, and who could blame her? One or the other of her parents was always angry or high or incomprehensible. Their bedroom stank of smoke and booze and pot. They had trashed the house. Nadia woke up often at night, rubbing her eyes, looking bewildered and talking to people who weren't there. Her grandmother would always be by her side, watching, protecting. Jahanara realized then that her granddaughter had taken after her. She was seeing Jaya in her dreams.

'Whatever you do,' she whispered to the sleeping girl, 'don't tell your parents that you see her. Keep your dreams to yourself, child. Keep her safe from them.' The child would not remember her grandmother's words, of course. But perhaps some subconscious part of her had always known that Jaya was sacred, for she had never mentioned her dreams to her parents, though her father had asked her, on many occasions, if she had them. Perhaps it was his tone, his sharpness, his eagerness that put her off.

When it was time for them to leave, Jahanara had begged them to leave the child with her. 'You have such a busy life ahead of you and so much to teach others, Sohail. Why not leave her here? Collect her when you have built this new world of yours?' She didn't want to antagonize him. Not with so much at stake. But Sohail had become incensed at the very thought and looked at her with intense loathing. 'Why? So you can teach her about Jaya? So you can perpetrate the myths of the Ancients?'

'What Ancients?' she had asked, confused. 'What has this to do with Jaya? I don't understand this new philosophy you have.'

'You're one of them,' he had hissed at her. 'You *are* one of them, aren't you? You want to keep us all in darkness. You tried to do it to me my whole life. Well, you can't have Nadia. I will bring my child to the Light, no matter how much you try and stop me.'

'You are truly crazy,' she whispered, moving away from him.

'Come,' he'd barked at his family. Nadia hadn't wanted to leave. She was crying. He had become furious. 'If you come near her again, I'll kill her,' he told his mother. 'I'll kill her, rather than let you have her. I swear it.'

She didn't understand it. She could never understand it. But she could see the intent in his eyes. He hated her. He was fully capable of hurting his child just to spite her.

And so she'd watched them go, her heart full of pain. The girl with the dark eyes looked out of the back windowpane of the car, lifting her arm in a half-gesture of goodbye.

When Jahanara finally finished her story, her voice was gruff and heavy. 'You see,' she whispered, her eyes glistening, 'I didn't leave you because I wanted to. I left you because he might have hurt you. Your life would have been harder if I was in it. When you called me ... it nearly broke my heart. But I knew he'd be listening. So I refused to help. I hired a private investigator instead. He told me your father had locked you up in the dark. So we took that evidence to the British authorities. That's when they acted, when the compound was raided. I'm sorry. I'm so sorry. I should never have let you go with him. I should never ...' She started to cry.

Nadia began to cry too. It was all too much. She didn't know what she was crying about. Was it for her lost childhood? For all the times she was alone? For the years, after the compound, when she had had nobody? For a grandmother who had loved her, after all? But something didn't make sense. 'Why didn't you ... why didn't you find me after? Why didn't you reach out after he died?'

Her grandmother straightened, wiping her eyes, looking gruff once more. 'There's more to the story that I must share with you. I want to show you something,' she said, standing up with the support of her cane and hobbling to her books. She struggled as she pulled at a large green leather tome.

'Let me help,' Liam said, and she nodded gratefully. He put the book on the coffee table. 'What are we looking at here?'

'This is a translation of both the Mahabharata and the Ramayana. You are familiar with these?'

Nadia nodded, confused. 'The two are allegorical epic tales of Hinduism, poems and folklore written in Sanskrit. I've always meant to read them, I just never got around to it.'

Jahanara shook her head. 'Allegory? It is amazing, isn't it, that anything we can't rationalize is turned into folklore? The story's recordings date back to the fourth and fifth century BC, but the tales are far, far older. They were passed down orally from generation to generation, long before they were put to paper. It's where the Hindu nationalists get their ideas from, though these stories are far older than even they imagine.' She started to turn the well-thumbed pages. 'Your grandfather had bought this book. Your father read it many years ago. Liam, if you would be so kind, perhaps you could read from here?'

He did as she asked, following her finger to a paragraph in the middle of the left-hand page. He cleared his throat, and began,

> '"Gurkha, flying a swift and powerful vimana,
> hurled a single projectile
> charged with the power of the Universe.
> An incandescent column of smoke and flame,
> as bright as ten thousand suns,
> rose with all its splendour.
> It was an unknown weapon,
> an iron thunderbolt,
> a gigantic messenger of death,
> which reduced to ashes
> the entire race of the Vrishnis and the Andhakas.
> The corpses were so burned
> as to be unrecognizable.
> Hair and nails fell out;
> Pottery broke without apparent cause,
> and the birds turned white.
> ... After a few hours
> all foodstuffs were infected ...
> ... to escape from this fire
> the soldiers threw themselves in streams
> to wash themselves and their equipment."'

'It's just a story,' said Nadia. 'Isn't it?' But what about the forty-four bodies they had found, she wondered. What about those?

'It's not just a story,' insisted Jahanara, shaking her head. 'After Sohail left, after he took you, I dedicated my time to learning just exactly what it was that he thought he was talking about. My son is crazy, but I don't doubt that he was having dreams of his own. And ... and I think some of what he rambled about might be the truth.'

'Was crazy,' Nadia said automatically. 'Was crazy.'

Jahanara was quiet for a moment. Then she said, 'Nadia, I think that Mohenjodaro is one of the ancient cities described in the Mahabharata and Ramayana. A city with great power, with a technology so powerfully destructive that it cannot even begin to be contemplated. I think Jaya had access to that technology. The Stone ...'

'The Bloodstone, yes ... I've ... I've seen it in my dreams.' She touched the book with her fingers, tracing an image of an angry god, his eyes blazing red, a thunderbolt in his well-muscled blue arms.

'Yes,' Jahanara nodded. 'I don't know what it is, exactly. Something from ancient times, perhaps, from a human existence that we don't remember any more, when we were more advanced? Something much, much older than Jaya's civilization. I don't know what it is, but neither did the people in Jaya's world. They thought it was something from their Goddess. All I know is that it gave Jaya visions. Now I'm beginning to wonder if it burned people as well. What if it's exactly what the Ramayana describes? What if Mohenjodaro was destroyed because of the Stone? And what if that's what Layla found, in the box, before all hell broke loose?'

'It's not possible,' replied Nadia, wrapping her arms around her body. 'It makes no sense. None of this can be real.'

'You're right,' said Liam, shutting the book with a thud. 'This is the biggest pile of gobshiite I've ever heard. Professor Webb didn't just go up in flames in the middle of the desert because of an ancient stone. That was a hoax, and you'd be adding to all the hysteria if you talk like this.' He sounded furious.

'And yet here we are,' Jahanara insisted. She put an arm around Liam. 'I'm sorry, I should have told you this from the beginning. I don't see how the Professor could have survived. But I think that Layla did, and I think we need Nadia to find her.'

'Me?' Nadia shook her head. 'What could I possibly do to help?'

'Did you know that some years ago, scientists at the Emory University conducted research on genetic memory? They experimented with mice, and found that they could pass on learned information about stressful or traumatic experiences – in the case of the experiment, the smell of cherry blossoms – to their offspring. In effect, they proved that it was possible for information to be inherited biologically through chemical changes that occur in the DNA. The results, they suggested, may help explain why some people suffer from irrational phobias. It might be that they have inherited the experience of their ancestors.'

'So what are you saying?' asked Liam, his arms crossed. 'You're saying that you and Nadia ... and possibly Sohail, *inherited* Jaya?' Nadia could hear the scepticism in his voice.

'We inherited some memory of what had happened to our ancestors, yes,' Jahanara replied. 'There is so much that science is beginning to understand that has yet to be explained. Fifty years ago, could anyone have imagined that the Hadron Collider would prove the existence of dark matter? Memories in our genes ... it is only now that science is beginning to understand how that works. What if Sohail was right? What if we – our family and others like us – are more evolved in that sense? That we dream memories that others don't?'

'You're wrong,' said Nadia, feeling sick. She began to pace the room. 'We're not evolved. And we're not taking over the world. There are no Ancients out to subjugate others, to stick Kool Aid in the water fountains, to keep us in the dark.' She looked at her grandmother. 'There is no conspiracy. GoL is evil, not a force for good.'

'I agree with you about GoL. It is simply a product of your father's madness. But maybe Sohail is right about our memories. Maybe that's what pushed him over the edge,' Jahanara insisted.

'Was right,' said Nadia, her voice sounding shrill, even to her. 'Was right. Why do you keep referring to him in the present tense?'

'Sit down, Nadia.'

'Why?' But she knew. She knew the answer. Why was GoL funding the Indo Foundation to dig in Mohenjodaro? Why had her grandmother never contacted her, if she claimed to care about her, after Father died?

'It's him, isn't it?' she said dully. 'It's always been him. I should have known.'

Jahanara hobbled to the chair. 'Your father wasn't killed in that explosion. It was a cover-up. He was facing criminal charges for the abuse of children, and for money laundering. It was convenient for him to disappear and so he did. Sohail is alive, Nadia. He came to Pakistan years ago. *That's* why I never contacted you after you left the compound. I knew he was still capable of tracking you down. He let you go because he thought you were inconsequential to him. And I didn't want any reason for him to focus his attention on you ever again.'

With some difficulty, she sat down on the chair. 'He's alive, Nadia. Sohail is alive. And he has Layla.'

Chapter Twenty-Two

MELUHHA, 3791 BC.

The days that followed were some of the most blissful she had ever known. Being with Rafe invoked something new in Jaya, something unspoilt and precious. Every moment spent with him made her feel more alive, almost as though she were a different person altogether.

In contrast, each moment spent in the smoky darkness of the Temple was an eternity now. It was agonizing to be away from him, to be imprisoned under Iaf's oppressive gaze. Jaya spent her days dreaming of returning to Rafe. They would lie together under the soft gaze of the moon, and she would feel the heat of his body, the tickling of his hair against her skin, the strong contours of his muscles and the smell of the earth in his pores. She lived for these moments. He made her feel safe. She had forgotten what it felt like to have someone cherish her. She did not think it was possible to lie with a man and to feel joy, but there it was. Such a bewildering feeling.

They were a happy, productive group, in the small house on the Street of the Pipal Trees. The days were busy for all of them, but they would assemble at sunset, after the street was clear of onlookers, Al-Mien cooking in the cauldron over the fire, Aal playing with her toys or watching her friend as he stirred his stews. She was exuberant and often bounced around under the stars, asking a multitude of questions, grateful to be away from the Temple.

But Rafe would always come home tired. Jaya, Aal and Al-Mien would gather there before his arrival. They would brew the tea and wait. Finding work was not easy for a man who was Unclanned, though he toiled very hard, picking up the odd job – moving cargo at the river dock or sweeping the streets, the sweat pouring off him, his face streaked with lines of dust and fatigue, being paid half the wages of the Clanned men and often not even that. At first, she worried that their dream of leaving together would never be fulfilled, not if they had to rely on Rafe to earn the gold they needed to take four on the journey.

But then things improved. Nor, the Unclanned traveller who had been telling tales in the market the day Al-Mien got caught, helped by introducing Rafe to some of the merchants with stalls on the Street of Jewellers. Jaya had not realized that Nor and Rafe knew each other. The former showed such irreverence towards everyone, it was surprising to see that he cared about the fate of his Unclanned brethren.

Nor had relationships with all the merchants because of the time he spent travelling with the caravans. The jewellers relied on Arrapha for their supply of amethyst and ivory, which would later be taken to the main market at Ocha, and from there, across the oceans, to lands almost unknown. However, few spoke the Arraphan dialect well or understood the cultural nuances required to barter successfully with its people. Arraphans, it was generally agreed, were thick-skinned and stubborn, and any attempt at bargaining was seen by them as an insult to their honour. And so Nor had managed to get Rafe a job as a negotiator. The work was not regular, but it was something, and Rafe seemed to grow in confidence with each passing day, talking to the traders from his home.

Jaya did not know what he did in his spare time, when there were no bargains to be made or no odd jobs to be done. He came home later and later in the night, his cares seemed heavier, but he wanted nothing more than to fill his belly and lie with her. Every time she tried to talk to him, he would sigh and close his eyes. 'Not now, Jaya. Another time. We can talk another time.'

'But is everything as it should be?' she had insisted once.

His finger trailed along her cheek. 'Yes. Everything is as it should be.'

She decided not to press him further. Rafe was doing everything he could for them. He would share his burdens when he was ready.

It was a shock then, when she went to the market one morning and spotted him, amongst the crowds. She was there to buy beautifully decorated vials of kohl in bulk, bargaining with the stall holder, who was so intimidated by her that he would not accept payment for his goods. She was trying to ascertain a fair value – the kohl was for all the Goddess-Blessed and she would need thirty vials at least – when she noticed that Aal had disappeared. As usual, the girl had gone off in search of adventure, getting underfoot of the adults, chasing a small mangy cat which had appeared on the cloth covering of the stall.

She sighed and asked the merchant to forgive her. She had to retrieve her daughter. He bowed deeply, looking both relieved and disappointed.

'Aal,' she called. 'Come back here at once.'

But Aal was rushing now, the cat had meandered down a narrow alleyway towards the Street of Scribes, and Aal, giggling, had followed it. The alleyway twisted through a series of old houses and shops. Jaya frowned. She had not come this way before. It would not do to lose her daughter in an unfamiliar place.

'Aal,' she shouted more furiously, turning the corner, pushing past some cotton tunics that had been hung up to dry on a gnarled piece of rope across the alley. The tunics were still dripping wet. She pushed them out of the way in irritation.

It was then that she spotted him. Rafe was further ahead, standing in the alley. Nor was with him. They knocked on a door several times in rapid succession, then waited, and knocked again, several times more, almost rhythmically. She grinned and was about to call out, until she realized that it would be difficult to explain her relationship with him to onlookers. And if anyone found out, they would both suffer. Her eyes narrowed. What exactly was he doing here, looking furtively about like that?

Jaya pulled the hanging tunic back towards her to shield her face. What was Rafe up to? He seemed to be arguing with Nor now, until the door opened suddenly. A grey-haired man she did not recognize ushered them in, looking in every direction before shutting the door again. She hid behind the tunic and waited several heartbeats. When she looked again, the alleyway was empty.

She shook her head, feeling silly. It was nothing, obviously. A trader, a friend, someone who had invited them to break a meal. But she felt unsettled by it. Why had they all looked so tense? And ... well ... the truth was, they were Unclanned. Did they have permission to be on the Street of Scribes in broad daylight? Nor would have, of course, but Rafe was limited in where he could go. Why would he break the rules when it would be so easy to be caught here?

'Mua,' shouted Aal, from further up the alley. 'Come and see. This cat has kittens. Oh please, can we take one home, Mua? Please?'

She retrieved her daughter. 'Come, child, it is time to go home.'

'But I want a kitten, Mua, look, they are so beautiful. I will take care of it, give it food and water. Mua? Please, Mua?'

'Do as I say,' she snapped, squeezing her daughter's hand tightly as they left the alley. Aal sulked all the way home.

Later that night, she asked Rafe where he had been. His answer was vague. 'There were no traders today. So I walked along the Street of Boat Makers, to see if they needed help hauling lumber. But there was no work there either.'

'And then?' she prompted gently. 'What did you do after?'

He paused for a moment, pulling down his sarong before joining her in bed. 'Nothing much,' he replied at last. 'Nothing that would be of interest, in any case.' He wrapped his strong arms around her. She lay there, quite still, full of confusion, listening to his breathing deepen and turn into heavy snores. Try as she might, she could not fall asleep.

Chapter Twenty-Three

KARACHI, PRESENT DAY.

Sohail was alive. Perhaps she was in shock, Nadia thought. That's why she felt numb ever since she had heard the news.

She sat on the veranda overlooking Jahanara's garden, her feet resting against a grey cane and glass table, trying to get warm in the noonday sun. Despite the summer heat, she had wrapped one of Jahanara's shawls around her. She cradled her mug of Lipton tea, which had long since gone tepid. Nadia had not slept the night before, and she hadn't eaten anything since the flight. She felt the fatigue rest on her like a second skin. Would she ever, ever be rid of her father?

He haunted her. She closed her eyes, imagining him sitting on this very veranda, growing up in this very house, surrounded by the beautiful gardens. She could smell the jasmine flowers and hear the rustle of something in the coconut trees – some small creature moving around – and a soothing whispering of the leaves. Her father had come from this peaceful place. He had had a family who loved him and wealth enough to ensure the most comfortable of lives. Were monsters born then, instead of being made?

Sohail was alive. Sohail was alive, and he had Layla. Why?

She sipped the tepid tea, grimacing slightly. She had tried to answer that question all night. And she wasn't the only one. Liam was suffering, she could see it all over his face. He was exhausted and he didn't understand these dreams of theirs. He couldn't wrap his head around the idea that something from an ancient civilization, one long gone, might have killed Professor Webb and the rest of the team. He demanded proof from Jahanara that Sohail was still living. He wanted to go to the authorities immediately. He had paced and snarled around the library like an angry caged animal.

More to shut him up than anything else, she had taken the ancient relic out of her satchel, unwrapped it and showed it to him. He'd simply stared at it, shocked. 'You've had this all the time? They were after this?' He walked towards her.

She nodded, suddenly ashamed that she hadn't trusted him right away. She watched as he lightly trailed his fingers along the writing, saying nothing.

'It's Sumerian,' he said at last, picking it up in his hands. 'At least, the first half is. It's the cuneiform, logosyllabic script used in the Early Dynastic IIIa period. The second half is ... it's the Indus Valley writings.' He inhaled sharply and looked at her. 'Do you know what this is, Nadia?'

She had shaken her head.

'It's the bloody Rosetta Stone all over again! The same message, written in both Sumerian and the Indus script.'

'So?' She came to stand beside him, peering at the relic.

'So ...' He jabbed at some of the symbols. 'We understand the cuneiform. We can use that understanding to translate some of the Indus Valley script, if we had the time. This is the key to unlocking everything. I can't believe you had this in your bag. Jesus Christ, I can't believe they *found* this and kept it a secret.'

She watched as he took the relic to a side table and turned on a lamp, examining it under the light.

'Do you think that my ... do you think Sohail found it in Mohenjodaro?'

Liam shook his head. He was pulling out his phone now, and was taking pictures of the thing from every angle. Perhaps he was scared she would take it away from him, or demand it back. 'It can't have come from Mohenjodaro. There haven't been any communications in any other languages that we've found so far. It has to be Sumerian in origin, from somewhere in Iraq probably, excavated along one of the caravan routes or at an ancient trading capital.' He was turning it over in his hands in wonder.

Iraq. Hadn't Marianne Riviere said that the Indo Foundation had recently excavated there? And then she wondered, had the Indo Foundation always been just a front for GoL? How much time had her father spent searching for ancient weapons? And did he know about the Bloodstone itself before financing the dig? He must have, surely? Some of the picture was beginning to make sense. Jay had told her that Layla was stunned to be selected to join the team in Mohenjodaro. Sohail – she refused to call him Father any more – he must have wanted her there, and ensured that Layla was chosen. Why? She cleared her throat. 'Can you translate it?'

Liam looked up and nodded. 'That bit's easy. But deciphering the Indus script will take time. Months, probably, assuming there is enough to compare the two languages here.'

'What does it say?'

He frowned, concentrating, his fingers running along the ridges. 'It advises merchants that the city of Meluhha has turned to ... to banditry, and it is no longer safe to trade there or travel the roads. The ... priests have all been slaughtered and the city is in revolt. Merchants are warned that there is a great evil there, that a terrifying power was unleashed on the people and that ... that ...' Liam stopped. He scratched his stubble, looking stunned. 'Mary Mother of Christ!'

'What?'

He took a ragged breath and looked up. 'That many of the people of Meluhha have been burned alive by a powerful Stone, given to the city by their Goddess. Those who are left are dying, struck with a plague. The Sumerian king has decreed that all trade must end with this dangerous place.'

No one said anything for a moment. Jahanara had been so quiet up until then that Nadia had forgotten she was even in the room.

'I've heard that name before, Meluhha,' said Jahanara. 'It is what Jaya's people called their city. I've dreamt the name.'

Liam looked like he was going to be sick. 'It's ... we've hypothesized that it is what the Sumerians called Mohenjodaro. It's true name. They certainly traded with a city called Meluhha that was famous for its lapis lazuli, and was near the Indus, we think.' He looked back at the writing, brows furrowed. 'It then goes on to say that refugees ... I think this word is refugees ... though it really says, those who have no clans ... from Meluhha are banned from settling in the kingdom as well, in case they bring their curse with them. Perhaps that's why the text has been rewritten in the Indus language as well, to warn them off. Jesus Christ!'

He sat down heavily, his head in his hands. Then he looked up. 'If this is real ... if it got out ... after what happened to the team ... there would be mobs in Mohenjodaro. People would demand to know what other secrets the government was hiding. But I don't understand why your father wants this so badly. Does he think we'll try to hide the evidence? If this got out, he would be proven right, wouldn't he? It would prove that mankind is more advanced than we ever thought and he'd have more followers than ever.' He shook his head. 'I can't believe you kept it from me. I can't believe any of this.'

She stared at her feet. The man had just shown up, for God's sake. Just shown up and demanded to speak to her. She bit her lip. Just shown up and saved her life, more like it. 'There's more,' she said, feeling guilty. She rummaged through her bag and pulled out the envelope of CDs. 'I don't know if there's anything worthwhile on these, but I got them from GoL. From Marianne Riviere. It's all the video feed from the site, up until the incident. Jay showed it to a friend of his, but they didn't spot anything. Perhaps you can.'

He got up and took the envelope from her, his expression dark. 'Is there anything else you're keeping from me?'

She shook her head. 'This is it, I promise.'

'Well, then, I'll have a look at the discs. You never know.'

Jahanara offered them beds for the night. Nadia was shocked to realize that somewhere, in the last few hours, she had let go of all her hatred. Now she felt something akin to pity for the old woman. Years ago, Jahanara had left Nadia to her fate, knowing full well that her son was crazy. She should not have done it. She should have found a way to protect an innocent child, to have kept her away from her parents. And yet, her grandmother's instinct *had* been to protect her. Could she have foreseen what a disastrous decision that would be?

Jahanara offered them some food as well, but Nadia shook her head. She had gone straight to her room, declining everything but a warm shower. She had lain there, on the bed, willing sleep to come, but it hadn't, of course. There were too many questions. She tried to map it all out in her head. Sohail had faked his own death, knowing that the authorities were closing in on him. He'd locked his own child in a basement, for Christ's sake, though it was the matter of GoL's accounts and dodgy finances that he'd been arrested and was out on bail for. So he'd decided to disappear, she supposed. Who had really died in that gas leak? She felt sick to her stomach. A willing follower, giving his life for Father, as they all called him? Someone else? They'd pulled a body out, she knew that. There was a skeleton. It was identified. How had he managed that?

She didn't really remember when Sohail had 'died'. She'd been in care then, and nobody had bothered to tell her. But later she learnt that he had never had a funeral. It was simply announced that Father had temporarily left his physical state to ensure that things would be ready for when GoL would take over running the world from the Ancients. This time, referred to as the Enlightenment amongst followers, would be a new renaissance period. Father would return, and his return would be a sign that it was time for action. Together they would destroy those who were hiding the truth about human history from the world. They would teach the Enlightenment to everybody. There would be no more war, not once their enemies had been destroyed. There would be no more famine or disease, because their bodies would 'remember' how to cure themselves.

He had planned this, she realized, feeling even sicker. For over fifteen years, he had planned and plotted his great return. Perhaps, he had always known about the Stone. Perhaps, he had found that ancient tablet and realized that the Stone was real, and that with it he could burn people. Who else would be crazy enough to believe in something like this, to try and dig it up? Who else had the resources to find it?

Her mind continued to churn all night, thoughts refusing to settle. If only she had brought her notes on Jaya with her. She tried to remember as much as she could, tried to remember dreaming about the Stone. But the dreams often made little sense. Jaya was one of only a few people who could use the Stone, as far as she knew. Is that why Sohail had wanted Layla to be at the dig? To see if that ability was inherited? Surely not. Surely, there were millions of people now, descendants of those who had once lived in Mohenjodaro? Who had once shared DNA with Jaya, assuming Jaya's line continued?

She thought about the ancient tablet. Why did Marianne Riviere have it? Who leaked the YouTube video? And why did Sohail want the relic? To stop anyone else from deciphering the Indus script? Presumably, he knew what was on it. He'd probably seen it, even deciphered the language himself. Or ... did he want it back because it warned about bodies burning? Perhaps he didn't want anyone else to know about the Stone's power? She frowned. In her dreams, Jaya used the Stone to predict the future. She never once used it to kill anyone.

There was a noise outside the gate. A man, a street vendor pushing a cart, called out and offered his wares. It brought her back to reality. She ignored the man and walked back into the house, rubbing her arms, which were full of goose pimples despite the heat.

Her grandmother was in the library, sifting through a cardboard box, in which there appeared to be several old leather-bound journals and some notebooks.

'You said that I was the key to finding Layla.' She put down her cup and raised her eyebrows enquiringly.

Jahanara looked up and nodded. 'Not to finding her. Saving her.'

'How? Why?' She crouched down next to where Jahanara was seated.

Jahanara emptied the cardboard box on the coffee table next to the sofa. The notebooks and journals poured out. Some of them looked to be really old, the papers brown and crisp, weather-beaten.

'What are these?'

'Records, put down over the years, of the dreams our family has had about Jaya,' replied Jahanara, picking up a notebook. 'This black diary belonged to my grandmother, if you can believe it. She recorded her visions of Jaya for over twenty-three years. I have translated some of them into English, for she wrote in Persian. Some of them are mine. Others belonged to my aunt. She didn't enjoy writing, so she made sketches instead. I did a bit of both. Not every woman in the family had the dreams, Nadia. But many of us did.'

'That's crazy,' Nadia said, staring at the pile.

Jahanara was rubbing her eyes, looking tired. 'The problem is, some of the dreams are so obscure. Jaya dancing as a child or praying in a Temple – see? They aren't enough to understand what happened to her. No one in the family ever bothered to establish a chronology. We have to compile them, if we are to know.'

Nadia turned over the journals in her hand. She flipped through the pages of one. There she was again. Jaya. Captured so perfectly, a girl of about ten, her feet dangling in the river, her head tilted towards the sun, eyes squinting, a hint of a smile on her lips, her tooth already chipped. She had seen her like that, once or twice, in her dreams. It was still so strange, to see her subconscious, rather what she thought had been her subconscious, open for public viewing.

'How are these going to help?'

'What's your last memory of Jaya? How old was she?'

Nadia frowned. 'I can't really ... I can't remember. She had such an unhappy life. Wait ... no ... I've seen this man before.' She'd picked up a picture. A young man in a sarong, with dark eyes and wavy black hair, his expression angry. 'I've dreamt of him. She met him once, in the square. And then ...'

'They became lovers,' said Jahanara softly, taking the sketch from her. 'Rafe and her. They became lovers.'

'Did they? I've dreamt of them together sometimes, but just by the river.'

Her grandmother's hands were shaky, she noticed, as she put down the notebook. 'They were in great danger, both of them. There was a rebellion in Meluhha. I've seen it. There is a battle. They had been separated, and I could sense her great anxiousness. But I have never seen more than that.'

Nadia looked up sharply. 'That's more than I've ever dreamt of her. I've seen ... worse things though.'

Jahanara nodded. 'You mean the High Priest.'

'Yes.'

Jahanara opened the black diary, flipping the pages. 'My grandmother wrote about it in here. What he used to do to her. She had nightmares about it, she often didn't sleep. This man ... it seems he was a psychotic monster. I never dreamt of him with her, isn't it strange? We all seem to have different memories. My aunt, Aisha, only dreamt of Jaya when she was a girl. Who knows why. Perhaps, we all pick up whatever emotional state our subconscious wants us to. My grandmother talked about the rebellion quite a lot. She saw much of it. We will find answers in her writings.'

'But I still don't understand how this will help.'

Jahanara put her hand on hers. It felt strange to see it resting there, the leathery contours, the spidery veins. But she didn't shake it off.

'Listen to me. Jaya knew how to use the Bloodstone. The Bloodstone killed people, according to everything we can deduce. Unless we are wrong and there is another ancient power that existed in Meluhha that we haven't come across yet. But there has to be a link. We have to learn what happened.

How she used it. How we can prevent it from being used again. The answers to helping Layla are here.'

'All right,' said Nadia, nodding slowly. 'I suppose ... I suppose I can make some notes of the dreams recorded here, and the things that I recognize from my own dreams? Then we can use it to build a timeline.'

'That sounds like a start to me,' said Jahanara, smiling tiredly.

They sat in companionable silence, Nadia scribbling notes in the margins of the diaries. Here was a dream about Jaya with Nene, a dream her great-grandmother had recorded on paper. She shook her head. Her great-grandmother. It was hardly believable that she could have this connection with her ancestors, and yet here it was, the blunt, faded strokes of pencil on thick cream paper showing the truth of it.

Nene was heavily pregnant. Nadia had never dreamt of this, of Nene walking around with a swollen belly, but she did know what followed, an event which was not recorded in her great-grandmother's diary. Nene died. Her child died with her, killed by the priests for being a boy. She made a note of it and, on a separate piece of paper, started the timeline. It was long, tiresome work, but it absorbed her and gave her a sense of purpose.

Some hours later, her phone rang and she looked at it in irritation. She recognized the number immediately, the 0000 that meant the call was being rerouted and encrypted along the way. She picked up. 'Apollo?'

'Why the hell are you in Pakistan?'

'How do you know where I am?'

'I pinged your phone, you idiot. Listen to me, this shit is getting crazy. Marianne Riviere's body washed up on the banks of the Thames this morning. It's being ruled a probable suicide, they found a note on her computer and everything. But it's connected to you, isn't it? I think you should come back. It's safer here.'

'What? Oh my God!' Riviere was dead. Had Sohail something to do with that? She felt compelled to tell Apollo the truth. 'My father is alive, Apollo.'

There was a pause, and then, 'Well, I'll be the dogs bollocks. That's big. Are you sure? Of course you are, you wouldn't say so if you weren't, not about this.'

She walked up to the window, massaging her lower back. There were too many shocks. Too many shocks for one day. She felt numb. 'That's not all. He's after me. And he's after the relic I showed you. He might have had Marianne Riviere killed. You have to be careful. You took pictures of it. If he knows that ...'

'Nut Job, don't you worry about me. I'm a ghost. Those GoL fuckers will have better luck finding a leprechaun pissing under a rainbow than me.'

'I think he killed Layla's housemate, Apollo. He sent someone to kill Jay. And he has Layla too.'

There was another pause, and then a slow whistle. 'For real?'

'I'm afraid so.'

She watched from the corner of her eye as Liam walked into the room, looking pissed off. 'I'll call you back, Apollo. Thank you. For everything.'

'Just take it easy, Nut Job. You know how to reach me.'

'I owe you one, my friend.' She hung up.

Liam was pacing the room. 'We are wasting time. We need to go to the police. To the authorities.'

She shook her head. 'I don't think that's a very good idea.'

'Why not?'

'Because Marianne Riviere is dead.'

He stopped and looked at her in shock. Then he ran his fingers through his hair. 'This has to end, Nadia. The authorities are the only people who can help us now. If we tell them that your father is alive. If we tell them that he ...'

'Tell them what exactly?' Jahanara interrupted. 'That there's an ancient stone which we think might have powers to kill people? Oh, and give them visions, too? We can't prove anything.'

He crossed his arms. 'They might consider it. They obviously shit their cacks about Mohenjodaro and covered up what had really happened there. They'd be wanting answers as much as we do. We can start by telling them that Sohail Hussain is alive. How did you know that, by the way?'

Jahanara looked like she was going to be ill. 'I saw him watching me, one day when I went to the Sunday bazaar. It was a few years ago. At first, I thought it was the heat, that I'd imagined him amongst the crowds. But then, a few weeks later, I saw him again, standing against a market stall, smirking. He had followed me there. He wanted me to know that he was alive.'

Another shock. Another pain in the pit of her stomach. 'You should have told us,' Nadia said quietly. She and Layla had let their guards down. They thought they were safe. Would Layla have come to Pakistan if she had known that Sohail was living there? Would any of this have happened?

'It was an impossible situation,' said Jahanara desperately, watching her. 'I had no proof, and I had no authority in your life. You were doing so well, as a writer. You were getting sober. And Layla was happy and at school. What good could have come of it?'

'Well, that's not important now. Right now we have to come up with a strategy to find Layla.'

'Here, look at this,' Liam said suddenly. He put the relic on the coffee table, once again examining it. 'Do you see this? It mentions the Bloodstone in cuneiform. I think I've managed to isolate the corresponding pictograph in the Indus Valley script. If I'm right, it's mentioned all over the place. In at least half the new tablets we found at the site. The Bloodstone was the focal point of the whole city.'

'So?'

'So it means there's something that we need. Something in Mohenjodaro.'

Nadia frowned. 'In Mohenjodaro? What could we possibly need from there?'

He looked grim. 'Jaya. We need Jaya's body.'

Chapter Twenty-Four

MELUHHA, 3791 BC.

Someone was pounding on the door. Jaya opened her eyes and sat up, blinking. Beside her, Rafe muttered something and turned over in his sleep. Moonlight cast a long shadow through the window of her bedroom. Everything was still and silent. It was just her imagination getting the better of her.

She had just lain back down when she heard the knocking again. Her eyes flew open, her body tense. She put on her tunic, shivering slightly from the dampness that had settled through the house, and padded down the steps into the courtyard. Who was it? What could be happening? She opened the latch and peered out.

She was startled to see Nor standing there, looking grim, his face haggard and his eyes darting in every direction. 'Are you alone?' he asked.

She took a step back, confused and uncertain. 'What are you doing here? You are Unclanned. If the Temple guards see you ...'

He put a finger to his lips and let himself in, closing the door quickly behind him. She winced as she heard the wood scrape against the ground.

'It took you so long to answer, I had to knock several times. Let's just hope I have not woken your sisters on the rest of the street.' When he spoke of the Goddess-Blessed his face showed contempt, which confused her even more, amidst all her tiredness. Nor was well liked in the city, by everyone in fact, Clanned and Unclanned alike. He had never before shown any disdain towards the Goddess-Blessed. What could he possibly want with her?

It was not her he wanted though.

'I must speak to Rafe. It is urgent.' His dark eyes were inscrutable.

She felt the panic begin in the pit of her stomach. 'I'm afraid you are mistaken. I do not know anybody by that name.'

He simply arched an eyebrow and waited.

She sighed. 'He should have known better than to tell you about us.'

'To trust me, you mean, Lady?'

She said nothing. There was something about Nor ... she felt uncomfortable. The man was a friend to all, a great storyteller. And yet ... and yet it seemed that he was obligated to none. He would do whatever pleased him and that made him dangerous. Now he was picking his teeth, walking around the courtyard, examining the chiku tree in the corner, glancing in her direction every once in a while. 'If you will not rouse him from his slumber, I will do it myself.'

'I will go and wake him,' she said at last.

He waited, warming his hands on the embers of the previous night's fire, and she raced up the steps and shook Rafe.

'Nor is here,' she whispered furiously, anxious not to awaken the children. 'Nor has come.'

He sat up immediately, his expression alert. 'Nor?'

'Yes.'

He hurriedly put on his sarong and went downstairs. She went with him.

The men embraced and then broke apart. 'Faros has been arrested, along with two others, for stealing a gold icon of Shakari from the priest's seminary,' Nor said.

Rafe glanced at her quickly and then turned to his friend. 'Faros? Why would he do something so stupid?'

Nor spat on the ground. 'The Cakk was going to sell it, to buy medicines for his daughter. She is dying of mosquito sickness. The seminary guards say he will be hanged for treason. It is an icon of Shakari, used in worship. It is sacred.'

She watched Rafe's expression change to the angry, haunted look so familiar to her now. 'He had no choice,' Rafe said furiously, adjusting his sarong. 'They must see that. He was driven to it by fear for his child. The Unclanned are not welcome at the Street of

Healers, and so we must pay exorbitant rates for medicines to the traders outside the gates. What else could Faros do? Surely the priests will see reason if it was about saving his daughter's life.'

Nor said nothing, his expression impossible to read in the shadows.

'Who are the other two?'

'His cousins, I think. We both know that Iaf has been looking for a reason to punish the Unclanned for a long while, Rafe. He wants us out of this city, and this is his chance to send a message.'

Rafe looked at her again. 'Go to bed, Jaya. I must go to the seminary to see if I can intercede. Faros is a good man. My friend.'

She crossed her arms. 'I do not know this man of whom you speak. And I am sorry for his troubles. But you will not be able to stop the seminary guards, Rafe. Not if they have orders from Iaf.'

Rafe shook his head. 'We must try.'

'They will hang you alongside the thieves for interfering. Please, there is nothing you can do.'

He hesitated and then he turned away from her, lifting the latch on the door. 'I'll be back as soon as I can,' he whispered. The two men left the house, silent conspirators in the moonlight, and disappeared down the road.

There were a thousand words that she wanted to say to him. *Come back now. Don't be a fool. Think about us. Think about me.* But she said none of them.

She waited for him with a heavy heart for the rest of the night, eventually sending Al-Mien out just before daybreak, to hide by the river alone, for Rafe had still not returned. After the morning meal, she had no choice but to go to the Temple. There was much still to do and her absence would arouse suspicion. It was all she could do to hide her anxiety from Aal, who was grumbling about having to leave her bed when she had not slept well the night before and was walking sulkily down the road.

They turned left on to the Street of Sorrow, and then right on to the Street of the Temple, trudging down the long length of the road, which was busy at this time of day. They walked past several bullock carts, overladen with supplies, and a group of washerwomen who were hauling laundry to the wells, their faces already plum with sweat from the loads on their backs. She smiled tightly at the men and women who stopped to bow or wish her good fortune, but her mind was distracted.

Outside the Temple, there was already quite a crowd and her heart sank. Men and women had gathered by the large pipal tree, the one with the heavy branches. The one which was used to hang those accused of treason or blasphemy. The men had been hanged, then. She prayed that Rafe was all right.

She quickened her pace, so much so that Aal almost had to run to keep up. She stopped short of going through the crowd. She could see enough, through the gaps among the people, to know that Rafe was not among those who had been condemned. Because she was at the fringes of the throng, Aal was not tall enough to see the faces of the men, no matter how much she craned her neck. It was better that her daughter came no closer, for the image was a haunting one.

There they were, the three men, swaying in the breeze, their ropes creaking, their mouths gaping like fish, their hands tied behind their backs. They were not dead yet, still enough space in the noose, just enough to breathe, little good it did them. One of them was twitching, his face contorted in agony. They were not able to speak, but their bulging eyes showed their torment. Shakari had abandoned them.

Jaya whispered a prayer and asked the Goddess to show them mercy now. They had been punished enough for stealing her icon. Let them die quickly. Then she offered a prayer of gratitude that Rafe had been spared the fate of his friends. Was he all right? Had he taken up their cause? Had he been arrested?

The whole day passed in a blur of worry and anxiety. She could barely concentrate on the tallies of corn bread she was supposed to be calculating, or on the bathing ritual in the Purification pool. She wanted to get home. She took Aal and left, even before the sun went down. She pleaded a headache to Sarema, who let her go with an irritable wave of the hand. They hurried out into the street. She moved purposely away from the pipal tree in the other direction, preferring the longer walk home.

They had not got far before they saw it. Jaya stopped and stared, bringing Aal close to her. There was a curse written on the side of a house on the Temple road:

Let those who watch while innocent children die have their necks twisted and their bones buried separately.

They walked past slowly, horrified. The wording ... it was a harsh curse and powerful magic. For a person's bones to be separated at death ... the person's soul would never be able to find its way to the Upworld, it would be condemned to walk the lands in spirit, doing the bidding of the soothsayers.

She wondered if the curse was meant for the priests, if it was a reaction to the hanging of the three men. But surely the Unclanned would not risk Iaf's wrath further by writing something like this? And surely they would not risk using dark magic to show their anger? Curses were powerful, and often harmed the curse bearer as much as those who they condemned. Besides, if the man who wrote this was caught, the priests would not simply kill him. They would torture him, every day, until he was old, and had a broken mind as well as a broken body.

They moved on, her thoughts in turmoil, her daughter's hand tucked firmly into hers. Then a few steps later, they came across more writing painted across a dusty brick wall in white chalk.

Death to the High One

'Mua, what is that?' asked Aal, pointing.

She gripped her daughter's hand tighter in her own. 'It is nothing. Nonsense. Come, we must be getting home.'

'But Mua ...'

'Hurry up, Aal,' she snapped. 'I'm tired of you not listening. Do you want to feel the slap of my palm against your cheeks?'

Aal flushed, looking hurt and mortified. They did not speak further.

When night fell, Rafe returned to them, and she threw herself in his arms and sobbed. 'Never,' she cried, 'never do that to me again, do you understand?'

He held her close. 'I won't, I swear it. I am sorry, Jaya. I had to try.'

'At the risk of your own life? Our lives together?'

He shook his head, looking bitter. 'I risked nothing. The priests would not even hear our petition. I failed. I could not face myself afterwards. I could not face you.'

Clouds obscured the moon, plunging the night into darkness. 'It's all right,' she whispered, pulling him to her breast. 'It's all right.' She held on to him as though she would never let him go. They remained that way, standing together. 'It's going to be all right,' she said once more. But no matter how hard she tried, she could not stop thinking about the curse on the wall.

Death to the High One.

How would Iaf respond to such an insult?

Chapter Twenty-Five

MOHENJODARO, PRESENT DAY.

They could no longer see the lower city. Nadia glanced behind her from her vantage point at the top of the Stupa. The early morning mist rendered everything into a haze of light and dark shadows. The only thing visible were the tips of some overgrown olive-coloured bushes, which pockmarked much of the desert around the ruins. In the distance, a solid line of white reflected the path of the Indus river, also completely shrouded in the morning mist.

She took a deep breath. The air smelt moist and dusty at the same time. It was fanciful, but she imagined that it smelt of home or a homecoming, if such a thing was even possible. If Layla wasn't missing, if people hadn't died here, she would never have believed that it could be anything other than a happy place. A beautiful old ruin, secret and still, and covered in early morning clouds. No people, no wildlife, just a quiet immobility, the smell of the earth and the slowly dissipating fog. Jaya's home, not hers, she reminded herself.

Beside her, Liam took a swig from his bottle of water and wiped his mouth. He put the bottle in his backpack and pointed to the north. 'That's where they were digging when it happened. We'll need to be quick. They'll be back patrolling soon. We're lucky the fog is as thick as it is.'

She followed him cautiously, thinking through the events of the last twelve hours. Liam had found something on the CDs. The body that the team was digging up, the body that he hypothesized was Jaya's, because of its proximity to the Bloodstone, had been buried in a lead box with many carvings and writings etched onto it. One side had been partially uncovered and dusted by the team, and the camera had panned into it, briefly, only moments before the KRS had stopped working.

'See that?' Liam had shown her, freezing the frame on his laptop. 'Those symbols behind the right femur? It's the same pictograph which we see on our own relic. I think it means Bloodstone or Stone of Blood, or something like that because it corresponds to the writing in the Sumerian script.'

It was an oval, with several spherical designs inside it.

Liam had then pulled out the relic Nadia had found and shown her and Jahanara the cuneiform writing on it, pointing to a section in the middle. 'This is the bit that speaks about the destruction of Meluhha in Sumerian. If I look at the Indus Valley writing and isolate the pictographs that I know are often used in small administrative seals all over the city, I can eliminate the ones which I think are generally fairly unimportant. Then I eliminate any with derivatives of this marker, the Bloodstone, and I'm left with these two, which probably mean destroy or ending or something similar, given the context of the Sumerian writing, which talks about how the Bloodstone destroyed the city of Meluhha. You see, the Indus script is probably logophonetic, it has signs which have meanings and other signs which are used for their phonetic values. At least, that's the theory.' He had shown her a funny-looking upside-down U with a slash going through it, and a set of zigzag lines which he thought was a symbol for destruction.

She'd shaken her head. 'English, please.'

He'd jabbed a finger at his computer. 'Look again at the screen. Look at the inscriptions in the burial ground, the ones we can read anyway. Do you see that both the upside-down Us I just showed you and the symbol for the stone are being used, over and over, in etchings on the tomb?'

She nodded. He was right. At least, it seemed like he was right, based on what little they could see from the grainy image they had frozen on the laptop. The writing was, Liam hypothesized, warnings, buried with the body to let future generations know how to destroy the Bloodstone, should anyone dig it up again. Either that or warnings about the Bloodstone's destructive power, that it should not be tampered with. There was no way to know which, but, he suggested, either way, the writings would provide some information on what it was they were dealing with. The coffin was lead-lined. It meant that the Meluhhans had understood the Bloodstone worked by exposing people to energy, possibly even that it exposed people to radiation. They had understood enough about metal to know that lead was the best containment source they could find. If they were that advanced, what else might they have buried with the Stone? Often tablets – writings and accounts of a person's life or poetry written in their honour – were left with the bodies, at least in the burial sites they had unearthed recently. Anything like that, anything that could tell them what they were dealing with, was worth retrieving. Plus it was evidence about what had really happened at the site. They could take that evidence to the authorities to try to get them to listen.

Nadia had another suggestion. She wanted to make contact with GoL and offer a trade, her sister in exchange for the relic. They had all accepted that there was little hope that any of the others were alive, not once Liam had translated the writing on that tablet, but Layla had been on that video, she had been seen walking away.

In any case, Jahanara had vetoed her immediately. 'It's too dangerous. We can't trust them.'

Liam still wanted to go to the authorities, but Nadia was the one who argued against that decision. Had Liam never heard of Edward Snowden? The government had lied about what they'd found in Mohenjodaro. If they thought the Bloodstone was real, they'd kill everyone in their pursuit of it, including Layla, who was probably on some terrorist watch list now.

They then agreed to give themselves twenty-four hours to gather more information, to see if they could find some leverage, before deciding what to do next. Unfortunately, because the KRS only filmed Jaya's tomb for a minute or so, Liam couldn't read all of what was excavated. Plus it had not been fully dug up. He wanted to expose the rest, to see if there was anything that could help them. What if there was a way of containing the Stone, and they could find it?

As far as plans went, it was a long shot. But it was all they had.

Nadia had left Jahanara to read the diaries and accompanied Liam, despite his protests that it would be safer for her to stay at home. They'd driven all night to get to Mohenjodaro, through one of the most treacherous regions of the country, armed solely with a pistol that once belonged to Jahanara's husband, a shovel and some brushes, and a thermos of tea. Thankfully, they hadn't encountered anyone on the way.

When they got to the ruins towards dawn, they found the place shut down. The police had built a bunker of sandbags and ropes to mark the territory as off limits, and the army was patrolling the airport.

Thankfully, Liam had friends in the little village nearby.

Nobody paid attention to the villagers. Nobody cared that two of their boys, Ahmer and Raza, who'd run errands on the site, were also missing. Ahmer's father, Mushtaq, burst into tears when he saw Liam at his doorstep. Mushtaq used to deliver groceries to the site just before dawn each morning. Since Liam was an early riser, the two had taken to drinking tea, thick with buffalo milk, and watching the sunrise together.

Mushtaq agreed to smuggle Liam and Nadia into the ruins, for he was bringing in supplies from Larkana for the police now, and was allowed to make his way past the sandbags and cement blocks to the police tents set-up in the area. The man was half mad with anxiety, not knowing what had happened to his son. 'Whatever the truth is, I will get you an answer,' Liam promised him.

And so they'd slipped into his cart amid burlap sacks of potatoes and onions – in the predawn shadows the police hadn't given the cart a second glance – and jumped out once they were past the barricade. They looked around and realized that they were near the encampment kitchen. Mushtaq started to offload his supply of potatoes, whispering to them that they should go.

But a sleepy cook was awake, scratching at his hairy belly under a grey vest, wearing only a shalwar and lighting a cigarette. They all stood still, unsure of each other. With a finger on his lips, Liam then approached the cook and handed him some money. Nothing was said, but the man stared at them for a moment. Then he quickly pocketed the money, nodded and walked away.

They, in turn, headed up the hill, towards the excavation site. The area was vast and steep. As long as they kept their heads down, they would not be spotted from below. At least not until the sun rose properly. The cops were all asleep anyway. They were not expecting any trouble. Liam and Nadia set out, making fast progress.

'This way,' said Liam, taking her hand, forcing her to pay attention.

She let him help her up and down the rocky terrain, brushing off bits of grit from her jeans as she nearly slipped among some rubble.

'You all right there?'

She nodded. They made their way to the new dig, weaving in and out of the streets of the old city. 'I hope you know what you're doing,' she muttered, not for the first time.

'We need to know how to stop the bloody thing, don't we?'

'No, we need to find my sister.'

'I've been thinking about that,' he said, as he walked past a grove of acacia bushes and stopped, waiting for her to catch up. 'Your idea about contacting GoL. Do you know that GoL has a massive building in Karachi? It's in Lyari, isn't that interesting?'

'You say that like it should mean something to me,' she said, grunting as she skid on some pebbles. She reached into her own pack and pulled out her water bottle. Christ, it was hard work. And the sun hadn't even risen properly yet.

Liam scanned the horizon, and then looked at her.

'Lyari is not a particularly safe part of the city. Gangland violence, drugs, gunrunning and so on. Not somewhere anyone would go for the fun of it. It got me thinking, why headquarter yourself there unless ...'

'Unless you don't really want anyone looking at you too closely?' She took a swig of water and then closed the lid of the bottle.

'Exactly. Shit. Get down, quickly!' He pulled her onto the ground and then cautiously lifted his head above the bushes. 'Fecking hell, we're too late. Bollocks.'

She lifted her head too and gaped. There was just enough early morning light to make out what was happening. There were men at the site. Men in bright orange hazmat suits. There was a digger too, and an army truck. The whole thing was one gigantic hole in the earth, everything was mud. The burial site, the whole excavation, was gone, razed to the ground. 'What the hell?'

'Radiation,' said Liam tensely, pointing a finger. 'Yonder man's got a Geiger counter. We have to get out of here.' He put his arm on hers, to help her up.

'No,' she said, shaking it off. 'We need to wait and then follow them. They can't have destroyed the evidence, they would have catalogued it first, sent it off for analysis or something, wouldn't they? We have to find out where they're going with it.'

But another army truck rolled on to the site, making it impossible for them to talk further. More men jumped out, this time with shovels and fresh sandbags. They began cutting open the sandbags and refilling the hole.

'Nadia, it's the bloody Pakistani government,' he whispered. 'Hiding the evidence. They're covering it up, to stop panic. What do you think they're going to do to us if they find us here?'

'But ...'

'Come on,' he said urgently. 'There's nothing for us here.'

They scrambled back up the hill, towards the direction of the village. Another dead end. More time wasted.

Mushtaq had promised to be waiting with his cart before the checkpoint on the other side. But he wasn't there. He had clearly not found an excuse to talk his way past the guards yet. He wouldn't have expected them back so early either.

'Bollocks,' said Liam again, wiping sweat off his brow. 'Bollocks.' He stood with his hands on his hips, looking around. Nadia followed his gaze. The whole place, miles of ruins, was encircled with sandbags and ropes and concrete stones. It was easy to walk through the makeshift barriers – they were flimsy over such a large space – but not without being spotted. They couldn't go through the police encampment, they would be detained right away. And if they walked down the hill and tried to slip through the sandbags, they'd probably be caught by the sentries, now that the sun was higher up. Even if they weren't, they'd end up on the main airport road, which was being patrolled by the army, not a bunch of sleepy local cops. The same army that was even now destroying the evidence. In order to avoid them, they'd have to make their way around the desert for several miles, looping back towards the village where they'd hidden the car.

She was just about to ask Liam for his opinion, when he put his hand on her arm, his expression wary.

Three cops were coming up the hill, distinctive in their grey shirts and khaki trousers. One had an AK-47 strapped across his chest, the others were holding revolvers. They had dressed in a hurry, Nadia realized, because one still had his shirt buttons undone, while another was patting down his hair. That damn cook. He'd ratted on them.

'Christ,' muttered Liam. He hesitated for a moment. Then he raised his hands and waved, waiting for the cops to arrive. 'Smile. We're tourists, okay? We got lost, that's all you tell them. We're tourists and we're lost. We didn't know this place was off limits.'

The cops reached them then.

'Hiya,' said Liam, shooting a cocky grin. 'Thank God, youse all are here. We got lost, can you believe it? Our car ran out of petrol, we were looking for someone to help us. Lucky you came along.'

The policemen exchanged glances, but said nothing for a moment. Then the one with the AK-47 lifted his gun and trained it on them. The second one, the one with his shirt still unbuttoned, stepped forward and began to search Liam. When he found nothing, he pushed him to one side and grabbed his backpack. He unzipped it, sticking his hand inside.

'What are you doing?' protested Nadia. 'Please, it's like he said, we're just tourists ...'

The cop pulled out the pistol they had brought with them, and held it up.

In an instant, the other two stepped forward and forced Liam's arms behind his back.

'What are you doing here?' grunted the cop with the AK-47, in English.

'No, listen, the gun is mine,' Nadia said desperately, watching as Liam winced. 'You can let him go. We're just tourists, but the gun belonged to my grandfath ...'

'What government do you work for?' insisted the cop.

Liam shook head. 'It's like she said. We're just tourists.'

But even as he spoke, two of them hauled him away, down towards the encampment. He kept looking back at her, his eyes making it clear that she should say nothing. Then she was alone with the one remaining policeman. His gun remained pointed at her, his finger on the trigger.

She stood there, shocked. 'What are you doing? Where are they taking him? Why have you separated us?'

The cop looked at her coldly. 'Name?'

'Marianne Riviere.' The man's eyes appraised her, his gun still raised.

She took a step towards him, raising her hands. 'Listen, please. Why have they taken him?'

The cop said nothing.

'I'm a British citizen,' she blurted, realizing how stupid that sounded when the cop narrowed his eyes, looking amused.

A voice squawked on his radio, which was attached to a pocket near his shoulder. He tilted his head, listened and then muttered into it. The voice squawked again and she heard her own name, her real name, being broadcasted. For a moment, she forgot how to breathe.

'Move,' said the cop, motioning with his gun.

'Where are you taking me?'

He pushed her forward.

'All right, okay.' She raised her hands. 'I'm coming.'

They made their way down the hill, past the police encampment, but did not enter it. She couldn't see Liam anywhere. She turned to look at the cop again. 'Listen, I don't understand, where are we going? Where is my friend?'

A single poke in the ribs with the gun was the only response she got. She prayed fervently that Liam was okay.

When she saw the blue van parked behind the tents, her heart sank.

Chapter Twenty-Six

MELUHHA, 3791 BC.

She waited at the waters for Rafe.

Rafe. Her tongue curled as she said his name – invoked his name – because just then she saw him approach from the darkness of the riverbank.

Rafe.

Six moons ago that name had meant nothing to her. *He* had meant nothing to her. He was just the brother of a misshapen child who had needed her help on the Street of Dancers one day. Now she truly loved that child, Al-Mien, as though he were her own. And Rafe ...

Rafe she loved as though she were his.

There was a chill in the air, the river breeze making it known that winter had come, and she wrapped her arms around herself, feeling the goosebumps.

Rafe.

Had she lost her mind? Was she really risking it all for him? If they were caught together ...

He reached her then, his long, muscular arms giving her warmth, his breath hot against her cheek. At once her body relaxed, the fears slipped from her mind and there was only him. They stayed that way for several precious moments, under the light of the moon and the scattering of the stars.

'Is everything as it should be?' he asked eventually, stepping back. His eyes were assessing, as they always seemed to be. Rafe seemed to understand everything about her, this dark-haired warrior from Arrapha.

She stroked his arm. 'It's just that I'm worried about Aal.' About Aal, about the city and about him. But mostly, she supposed, about Aal. She was losing her child. Thank the Goddess it was finally time to leave.

Aal was always at the Temple these days, barely ever away from Iaf's gaze. It was unnerving how much interest Iaf had suddenly taken in the child and more than disconcerting to realize that Aal seemed to hang on his every word. She could not blame the girl. Iaf could be charming and she was but seven cycles old.

'Ever since the troubles began, Iaf has wanted her with him.'

'With him?'

It was incredible how much had changed in just over one moon. How she missed those days when Rafe and Al-Mien had rested with them in the house on the Street of the Pipal Trees, those days of intimacy, where she did not have to explain things because there was an immediacy to their conversations. But ever since the Unclanned had started protesting in the city, Iaf had increased security. He had placed a Temple guard outside Jaya's house. It was no longer safe for Rafe and Al-Mien to live with her, and so they had moved to the river, hiding themselves from the Crocodiles, in the spots Jaya hoped would still be shielded from curious eyes. Because of the guard's presence, Jaya could no longer offer blessings. They were dependent on Rafe now to raise whatever else they needed in order to leave. But tonight, come what may, it was over. It was time to go. That is why she had needed to see him, to tell him. They would have to get by on what gold she had.

He pulled her towards a large boulder at edge of the riverbank, and they sat down. The sound of the water frothing as it passed, the cold pebbles at her feet ... it was peaceful.

He was looking at her, concerned. Expectantly.

What should she tell him, about Iaf and Aal? How badly she had protected her child? She gazed at the black waters, the expanse of infinite space the darkness provided. She took a deep breath.

'Iaf is in trouble. He is losing his grip on the city. Have you seen some of the slogans being painted on the walls of the Temple? The curses aimed at him? It has made him very angry. He needs more people who can read the Stone, I am not enough any more. He is drawn to Aal, because he has learnt what I have always known. Aal will be a powerful Seer, I feel it in my heart. The others know it too, for she often makes comments about things that will pass in the future as though she has knowledge of them already.'

'I know this,' he said, nodding seriously. 'She told me not to take that job with Nak the butcher, she said he would try to cheat me, and he did.'

She felt her eyes grow moist. 'I shielded Aal from Iaf, but not from my sisters. I should have been more careful.'

He waited, his expression sharp.

She sighed. 'Someone told Sarema, I do not yet know who, of Aal's ... abilities. Yet Aal has never used the Bloodstone, she is too young. Iaf was not interested in the child before. He was waiting for her to come of age so that she could read the Stone for him. But now he realizes how powerful his daughter could become one day. And so he seeks to forge his own bond with her, especially with things so turbulent in the city. He realizes that he will need her, that she is the child he always hoped he would have.'

'Tell Aal not to listen to him.'

She shook her head. 'If I say anything, he will simply have me removed from her life. We have to leave now, Rafe. Forget waiting for Karani. This is the time, before it is too late.'

She did not want to tell him that, as it was, Iaf was making her read the Bloodstone almost daily, so that he could acquire more gold from the merchants. She felt tired all the time. At night, her bones ached. They ached so much she had resorted to carrying willow bark in her pouch, to chew on when she couldn't sleep. Her head hurt too. It was difficult to think when her head hurt and her visions had become weaker, which incensed Iaf, now that he needed her more than ever.

In quiet corners of the city, the dark alleyways and bazaars, people, not just the Unclanned, had begun to question Iaf's authority. After the heavy rains, damp had gotten into the granaries. Who should have been responsible for lining the granaries with extra layers of buffalo dung, who should have seen that the rains would be heavier this year? The Temple, of course. The priests. And the Goddess-Blessed.

The heavy rains was a development the Bloodstone had not shown her, but it was a serious one. With every spare piece of stock needed for the festival of Karani, the city had been forced to shut its free food stalls. It was ironic, considering that part of the significance of Karani was that it was a time to ensure that *all* people had full bellies. What good was taking food from the poor now, only to give it back to them in a few days at the harvest festival? But that was exactly what was happening. The priests did not want foreign dignitaries to see anything except the greatness of Meluhha, no matter what the price. Too many vassal states were refusing to pay their tithe already and the fear was that if they sensed that the city was weak, they may try to rebel even further.

But what did the priests know about suffering? Amongst the Unclanned, whole families were dying of starvation. Desperate, they had begun looting shops and stealing from houses. The Temple guards had been called on to arrest them. They offered little resistance, being hungry and tired, and were taken away in their dozens. In fact, they were happy to be imprisoned, as they would at least receive an evening meal in prison.

Things had gotten so bad that the Unclanned were looting members of the public in front of Temple guards, in the hope of being detained and given something to eat. But the Temple prisons were filling up. There had never been so much upheaval in the city, and now there was talk of forcing the Unclanned to leave and walk through the desert to get to Ocha, where they may or may not be received at the gates. For what if the Unclanned turned on decent citizens, just because they were not talented enough to join a clan, because they had missed a few meals? Who said it was their Goddess-given right anyway to be given food? Law-abiding citizens were forming their own groups, patrolling their own streets to ensure the safety of their families.

Meanwhile, there were whispers on the street that Iaf and his priests had grown fat with wealth from the merchants. Everyone wondered what the High One's purpose was. He had not improved the city with any new infrastructure, nor built another Temple in honour of the Goddess. For what reason was he amassing this fortune? Would it not be put to better purpose in building walls to keep the Unclanned away? The strangest symbol had begun to appear on many of the street walls. It was the jagged lightning bolt, the symbol of the One Horned God, painted in red. It was unsettling.

'What will Iaf do to Aal?'

She reached down for a pebble and tossed it into the river.

'Will he hurt her?'

'He will ... well, he won't hurt her. He will push her.'

Iaf was desperate for more Goddess-Blessed who had real visions, Jaya knew. He would make Aal embrace the Bloodstone before she came of age, if it suited his purpose. And if that happened, Aal would sicken quickly. She might even die if she had not the strength to use the Stone. 'He will force her before her time. She is too young. She is too young to survive it.'

He squeezed her hand gently. 'She is strong, Jaya.'

'We never had a choice,' she replied, surprised by how bitter she sounded. To protect Aal, she had endured a great deal. But she was losing her daughter.

She rubbed her temples. The headache was back. 'Aal is being influenced in that Temple day in and day out, meditating with the priests. The rest of us ... we are left to our own devices, as long as we do what he asks. But now he is teaching Aal to accept the religious doctrine, making it a part of the core of who she is. He wants to make her his. And foolish woman that I am, I have let it come this far.'

He began to rub her shoulders. 'She will not be so easily swayed, not with you as her mother, no matter how much time she spends there. She still keeps Al-Mien and I a secret, does she not?'

'Yes, but for how long?' It was another thing that worried her. She had been too loose in her talk in front of her daughter, too open about her friends and her intentions. Aal was so young, how could she possibly understand what must be kept secret?

Rafe was tossing pebbles into the river now. In the darkness, she could not see where they landed, but heard the soft plink as they hit the water.

'We need to wait until Karani, Jaya, as we agreed. It is only a few more days. There will be thousands of visitors in the city. We will leave amongst the throng of boats, and they will never find us in the confusion. But to leave now ... an errant boat will be easy to track.'

'But ...'

'Besides, I await Balbala the merchant, who has promised a pearl if I help him translate his negotiations with the Arraphans when they arrive. I know it has taken longer than expected, but every little bit is needed and this will help a great deal in buying us passage.'

'No, Rafe, we cannot risk it.'

He said nothing. In the darkness, she could not read his features.

'How is Al-Mien? I haven't seen him this week. He has not been meeting me here any more. I miss him.'

Rafe continued to pick up stones. He did not look at her. 'He has become obsessed with the birds by the riverbank. It is better to leave him to his own devices. He does not understand why he cannot see Aal any more.'

She stood up and sighed. The relationship between Al-Mien and Aal had had to end, for both their safety's sake. 'Rafe, why do you not listen to me? We must leave now. I don't care if we are a little short of gold. We are strong. We will survive on meagre rations. We will make our way, I know we will.'

He was twirling the pebbles in his hands. 'That is what I told Al-Mien when we made the decision to come here. And look how that turned out, Jaya. Besides, the Unclanned are talking.'

No doubt they were, now that they had started protesting. 'About what?'

He turned, his eyes glinting in the moonlight. 'About why it is that there is wealth being amassed by others, while we go hungry. Why the Unclanned cannot have the same rights as everyone else. Should a boy of only thirteen cycles truly be left to starve because he has not found a clan? What about those who come to this city, who have heard of its opportunities, but are barely let in through the gates simply because they are from another place? Isn't that what the vassal states pay taxes for? To be allowed equal opportunities in Meluhha? But it does not seem to matter that we have strong backs, that we can contribute, that we work hard. This place is devoted to the One Horned God, not to the Goddess. It is evil, how things work, how everything has a price.'

She took a step back and shook her head. What was Rafe saying? 'You are so angry. Always, so angry. I thought we were leaving. Together. I thought you cared about us, Rafe. Don't you?'

He finally stepped into the moonlight and she could see, in his eyes, that something had changed. He no longer looked at her as though she was everything to him. He looked cold and even more haunted than usual. 'Yesterday, I saw a mother leave her child by the steps of the seminary. A babe of but three or four cycles. The mother could no longer afford to feed him and so she placed him in Shakari's care. The child cried for so long that I thought the whole city would weep with him. But the priests never came out. Eventually, the seminary guards shooed him away.'

'What happened?'

'I took him with me to the Unclanned by the gates, to find his mother. But she had died on the walk back. She had been starving. It was too much for her. I cannot turn my back on such injustice, Jaya. Can you?'

She reached and touched his cheek, her fingers trailing against the hardness of his jawline. It wasn't fair. Hadn't she given enough of herself to this city? What did Rafe expect her to say?

He offered her a drink of wine from the flask he carried. She shook her head and he shrugged, drinking deeply. 'We might as well enjoy it, there is nothing left in this city to buy, even if we had the wealth.'

'Rafe ...'

'It is not just the Unclanned, Jaya. I've been speaking with the Crocodiles. *Your* friends. They have had enough of being pushed around by the priests and being forced to trade in Tiger territory. This is only being done to put them in their place. Iaf and the Tigers, they are one. The Crocodiles will join us, if it comes to that. So will the minor clans.'

His words made her heart race. 'Join us? Who is us? What is going on, Rafe?' Her mind went back to the night that Nor had pounded at her door, and to the time when she had spotted them in the alley outside the Street of Scribes.

She shook her head. She had let it go. She had not asked any questions because she did not want her moment of happiness to end. Had Rafe aligned himself with the dissenters? He could lose his life over those slogans!

He took her hand, holding it against his lips. 'It is better that you do not know who we are. Not if you want to leave now. I'll understand if you do.'

She pushed him away, stunned. 'Of course, I will leave. And I will take Aal with me and you will never see us again,' she said harshly. For the last moon she had waited for this man. And for what? Was he truly going to abandon her now, after all his promises?

He reached out again and held her against him, stroking her hair, even though her body was tense and did not yield. He spoke softly. 'In the mornings, by the main city gate, the poor come to scavenge, did you know that?'

She did not answer.

'They scavenge the bodies of the dead. The Unclanned, when they are completely defeated, sit and starve by the gate. There are so many of them, Jaya.'

She would not listen. She could not be held responsible for everyone's fate. 'Iaf should cancel Karani. There is food put aside for the festivities. He should use it to feed the people. No one need starve, Rafe.'

He shook his head. 'That's exactly what I am trying to tell you. Iaf will not sacrifice the festival for the Unclanned. He would rather we starved than have his nose cut off in front of all his distinguished guests, have his trade negotiations suffer in any way.'

'The land is plentiful,' she replied at last. 'There is fish in the river ...'

He looked angry now. 'We are not allowed to fish, or have you forgotten? Not without clan licences. We are not allowed to hunt either, not in any clan territory, nor go to orchards to collect fruit. We cannot work, not without clan permits, and the priests issue those, taking a healthy profit on top of their processing fees. The Unclanned are dying, Jaya. The priests may once have protected them, but Iaf no longer wants them in the city, not when our home councils are refusing to pay his steep demands each cycle. And why should they pay? What has Meluhha ever given us? The Tigers have plied him with riches and they no longer want to share their wealth with the Unclanned, or any other clan for that matter.'

'Well, half of the Unclanned are immigrants. If we could just get them back to where they came from they would have a chance ...'

'You can be such a stupid Cakk sometimes. Do you think people *want* to walk across the desert in the blistering sun? They come here because the places they have left behind are worse. The journey back to safe lands is perilous, as you well know or you would have undertaken it by now.' He was shouting.

She choked back a sob. Rafe had never talked this way to her before. But it was true that she had been so busy focusing on her own worries about Aal and the Bloodstone, she had not thought about the Unclanned, not for a long time. She knew, of course, of the horrors the Unclanned left behind when they came to the city. In Chanu, the priests took one child from every family as payment for their spiritual guidance. Those children were never seen or heard of again, perhaps killed in some ritual or sold to slave merchants, and so many families fled to Meluhha rather than submit. In the Northlands, women were bought and sold every cycle, like slabs of meat, their faces branded with the name of their owners. Only Meluhha stood out as a bastion of peace, of harmony, of freedom. And what a lie that was.

But what could she do? How many people was she supposed to help? She was tired. So tired. And she had Aal to think of.

'Rafe, we have a chance now. Will you throw all that away? Think of Al-Mien, if not me.'

They started to walk along the riverbank. For a moment, he did not reply. Then he took her hands in his, his eyes imploring her to listen. 'So what? So I should sit by while Iaf seizes more power? So that others, from the poorest to even the Goddess-Blessed, suffer? Look what he has done to you. You cannot even walk now without breathing heavily with exhaustion! Do you think I have not noticed how weak you are? And what about Aal, what is to be her fate? You think running away will solve anything? He will come after her with a vengeance that you cannot begin to imagine, and we will not have the resources to fight him off. I am thinking logically, Jaya. You need to do the same.'

She turned around and went back to sit down on the boulder, wincing slightly with the effort. She didn't want to know any more. It was too much. Her head was spinning. She was so tired she could not concentrate.

'Listen to me,' he pressed, coming closer. 'The people are scared of Iaf and the priests. Only a Goddess-Blessed can lead them.'

'Lead them where?'

But she knew where. She knew exactly what he was asking.

His eyes burned with that fervour again. 'You can convince them to overthrow Iaf. The Goddess-Blessed, not the priests, should be leading the people, and certainly not the Tigers. The people would listen to you. They would fight for you.'

'It's insanity ...' she whispered.

'Is it? Is it insane to want to help your people? All of your people? Are we not your people as well?'

She shook her head. 'You're wrong. They would never listen to me. Why should they?'

'You think not? It is not just the Unclanned that need justice, Jaya. Everyone is looking for someone to guide them. To save them. The others – you should hear the stories. The Buffalo clan, whose children can't access the Street of Healers because the Tigers have jurisdiction of that territory now and the Buffaloes will not agree to pay them a hefty toll price which would bankrupt them, they need justice, don't they? What about the healers themselves, who are eager to go to the lower city and help the Buffaloes, but for Iaf and his priests, who have warned them not to get involved or else suffer the wrath of the Goddess? They need justice too. And then there is your own clan who have fished in this very river for hundreds of cycles and who must now trade in Tiger-authorized market stalls, instead of here, by the river, where they can keep their own profits as they have always done. Don't they need justice? The priests are corrupt. They no longer care about this city. This city was built by the Goddess-Blessed, not by the priests. And yet, you are letting it be destroyed by men in pursuit of wealth. Men who are so corrupt they are not worthy of calling themselves Meluhhans. Stand up to them. You are popular in the city. You can lead the revolution.'

'Enough.' She sighed. 'Enough. I understand what you are saying. But I don't think ...'

He gripped her arms so tightly he caused her physical pain. She recoiled, but he held her even tighter. 'And what of you?'

'What of me?'

'Could you live with yourself if you abandoned the people for your own selfish reasons?'

She slapped him as hard as she could across the face. He reeled back, clutching his cheek. 'How dare you ... how dare you ... I have given up more than you can possibly imagine.'

He looked shocked by her action and anguished by his own words. 'Forgive me. Forgive me, please. I don't know what I am saying. It is almost as though the One Horned God had taken over my senses. I love you, Jaya, I love you.'

'I cannot do it,' she sobbed. 'I cannot do what you ask of me. I have a daughter to think about.'

'I know,' he said, caressing her hair. 'I know. I'm sorry. Shh ... I'm sorry.'

'We must not talk like this again. You must promise to stay away from the priests, even if you refuse to leave with me.'

He dropped his arms. 'This I cannot promise you.'

'What do you mean?' Her heart felt sick.

'The less I tell you, the better.'

'Again with this. Rafe ...'

'The less I tell you, the better, Jaya,' he repeated gently. 'You must protect yourself, as you said. And you must protect Aal. But the rest of us must also protect ourselves.'

He was scaring her now. 'What is it, Rafe? What are you planning? Who are you in league with? It is Nor, is it not? He is a dangerous man. I was stupid, so stupid, not to realize his power over you.'

He shook his head sadly. 'We will not meet again, Jaya. May Shakari bless you on your journey. I will do my utmost to ensure that the High One is not able to follow you. Whatever happens, know that you were loved, deeply, by one who was not worthy of you.' He kissed her then, roughly, his lips bruising hers. Then he let her go.

'Rafe,' she moaned.

But it was too late. He had already turned away and was walking along the bank. Her voice caught on the breeze. He could not hear her.

Chapter Twenty-Seven

KARACHI, PRESENT DAY.

The police van went over a speed bump, causing Nadia to lurch into the end of the bench. Her hip slammed painfully against the side. From the bench across, the cop smirked.

Nadia winced. Her wrists were sore, the cuffs had been put on too tight, but the cop refused to loosen them. He also refused to tell her where Liam was or where they were going. He simply sat there, chain smoking cigarettes, staring at her, enjoying her discomfort.

She ignored him, focusing instead on looking out of the small square window by her head. It was all she had. The navy blue metal interior of the van was stifling, it smelled like rust and vomit. She needed a distraction, and fresh air.

They drove for hours, stopping only briefly so the cop could jump out and take a piss on the side of the desert road. She heard the driver open his door and walk out too, and then they murmured to each other, before the cop climbed back in. They kept on driving.

She licked her lips. Her throat was dry from the dust. She hoped that they would reach the police station soon. How far could they possibly be? All she could see out of the window was the desert, and the odd bush or tree.

Hours later, when her whole body was aching, the van finally slowed down. She turned her head towards the window once more. She could see that a brightly painted truck, overloaded with mangoes, had overturned causing havoc and a snarling traffic jam on the road. She looked out for signs in English, and realized, in shock, that they were now on the main highway just before Karachi. The police were taking her all the way back to Karachi. Why?

She turned to examine the cop. He'd fallen asleep. He was actually very young, she realized, eighteen or nineteen, with a beard that made him seem older. His hand rested on his AK-47, his index finger on the trigger even as he dozed, looking so innocent that she almost couldn't believe he was the same jerk who had pushed his gun into the small of her back and cuffed her to the metal bar in the van. She looked out of the window again. They seemed to be nearing a town or village. She could see a toothless, wizened old woman, sitting on the side of the road, shielding herself from the sun with her dupatta, wearing rubber sandals that were blackened with dust. They went past paint-chipped wooden stalls selling soft drinks and fruit, and a billboard for Colgate toothpaste and Nurpur butter. She closed her eyes. There was nothing she could do, nothing she could do about any of this, except demand to see a representative of the British High Commission in Karachi. Jahanara would have contacted them by now, since Nadia had failed to check in with her. With that thought, she consoled herself just long enough to fall asleep.

She woke up when the van jolted over a pothole. The cop was awake too, looking bored. She looked out of the window again. They were now passing what looked to be several slum dwellings with corrugated metal roofs and small, unpainted brick houses which were crumbling in the heat. Where on earth were they? She could smell the sewage, which had seeped onto the dusty road. An empty plot of land was piled high with garbage, picked at by crows, and there was a large billboard. *Enjoy Pepsi.*

She took a breath. The whole drive now smelled like shit. Shit and sewage and unwashed bodies. Then they turned onto a much wider, more developed road at the end of which were some large white concrete blocks of apartments and shops. They passed a gateway of sorts, a wide sandstone entrance that simply said *Welcome. Lyari Town.*

She strained at the cuffs, panicking. 'You're taking me to Lyari?'

The cop picked at his thumbnail, saying nothing.

Oh God. The GoL. Lyari was where her father had his headquarters, Liam had said. Why else would they be driving there if not to take her to Sohail?

'Are you even a cop?'

Taking his time, he lit another cigarette, tossed the burnt match onto the floor and then looked at her. 'You foreigners always amaze me. Of course I'm with the police. But we have a hierarchy, same as your police force. I do what the District Superintendent tells me to do.'

'Well, there has been a mistake. If you take me to see him ...'

'If he wants to make some money on the side, who am I to stop him?' the cop continued, ignoring her. 'Those lunatics in their fortress in Lyari are paying a lot for you. You must be an important woman, to be worth so much. The DSP doesn't normally like getting his hands dirty with foreigners. Too messy, too many questions.'

Damn him. Sohail had connections everywhere, even in the police. How? And now what? 'Where's my friend? What did you do with him?'

The cop took a long drag, blowing the smoke directly at her. 'They took him to the thana. They'll scare him, rough him up a bit and then let him go. Nobody's paying anything for him, he isn't worth the trouble.'

'And if I pay you more? What if I promise you double what you're getting, to let me go?'

He shook his head. 'Too late. The DSP has already informed his Lyari friends of your arrest. He has a fondness for a prostitute named Mina. My guess is she's in his bed already and he's busy spending his finder's fee. Enough talking.'

There was nothing to do but try to dull her rising panic. If Liam was released, he would get help, wouldn't he? How long until he found her, until he realized what had happened? The van moved more slowly now, through narrow, compressed roads that were little more than alleyways. They passed hundreds of little shanty houses and children running in the streets.

'Almost there,' said the cop, stubbing out his cigarette. 'Don't give me any grief if you know what's good for you. I haven't eaten all day and I have a headache.'

They turned a corner and came to a slow stop. She craned her neck as far as she could out of the window, inhaling a mouthful of dust.

They were parked outside a small compound. In the middle of the slum stood a structure with tall concrete walls covered in barbed wire. So this is where her father had holed himself up for the last fifteen years. Like a rat.

The cop slid open the back of the van, undid her cuffs and pushed her out. Her legs protested as she emerged, blinking, into the sun.

The wanker was still smiling as he said something to a guard at the gate, who looked at her curiously. Then he opened the gate and the cop pushed her inside. The place looked like an army barrack. There was one long concrete bunker and a small house on the left. Is that where her father was? She was going to be sick. She doubled over and the cop tried to pull her up. As he did, she kicked him hard in the balls.

He cursed and doubled over himself.

She smiled in satisfaction, until she felt someone grab her from behind. Strong arms dragged her backwards towards the house.

Chapter Twenty-Eight

MELUHHA, 3791 BC.

The sun was only just beginning to fade, but already the mosquitoes were out in force. In the distance, the horizon was a sea of swirling red and orange dust. A sandstorm was brewing. It was time to go.

Jaya stood up and brushed down her tunic, which was already gritty and stiff. She had been leaning against the ledge of the balcony at the top of the Temple. It was the only place where she felt she could breathe. Iaf did not like heights. He never ventured there. As a result, neither did the other priests, worried about the patchy brickwork and the safety of the structure. It was the one place she knew she would be left alone.

She climbed down the stairs and returned to the inner sanctum, where Aal was slowly gathering her things after the last cleansing ritual. 'Hurry, child,' she said, anxiously glancing around. The priests were busy today for tonight the first dignitaries would arrive from Ocha and Arrapha. They were entering the gates of the city even now, amidst much fanfare, and there was much to be done before trade negotiations began. Karani ... supposedly a time to feed the city and yet, also an excuse for powerful men to come together and discuss business and politics. Only, this year there would be a great deal of argument as well, for Arrapha and Ocha, along with Dilmun, had decided to stop paying tithe to Meluhha. The whole city was talking about it.

Why should Meluhha accept immigrants from either Arrapha or Ocha if both cities were withholding their taxes, the merchants were muttering. Arrapha and Ocha were also demanding that their clan Elders be chosen by their cities, not sent to them from Meluhha. They wanted their own sons and daughters to be chosen to take on positions of power on their councils and Jaya sympathized with them. Why should they not have a voice? But Iaf was incensed, she knew. So very angry that he had beaten one of the new girls, Aska, so badly that she had to be taken to the Street of Healers.

Tonight would be a test. If Iaf could not win over the officials with food and wine, he would use harsher tactics. He might even kill them and set the whole region on the path of war. For isn't that what he had amassed all that wealth for? To build an army, if he needed one? To take over the region and ensure that he retained his power – and gained even more power – by bringing down the vassal states? It was all he cared about. Power. Power and control.

She rubbed her eyes and shook the thoughts away. She did not have time to dwell on all that. Not now. She stared at Aal and frowned. The child's eyes were lined with dark rings. She was as tired as her mother. 'Come on, you silly Cakk. Hurry.'

Aal looked annoyed. 'Mua, there is plenty of time to reach home before nightfall.' Her movements were slow and heavy, she seemed like she was ready to drop with fatigue. Iaf had worked Aal hard. She had been reading scripture today and learning the ways of the Uncovering ceremony, which, with the dance of the thirteen veils, was physically arduous for one so young.

Jaya took a deep breath and tried to keep calm.

She walked away, her arms crossed, watching the night torches flicker in the growing breeze. The sandstorm would be upon them in a matter of hours. It was this moment and this moment alone, where she could betray herself and everything would be undone. Anyone could be watching. She must not be in too much of a hurry. She turned around.

Aal had at last gathered her belongings – a small sack of incense, the bag of herbs and medicines, and the ritual robes of meditation which she had brought with her to the Temple that morning. The girl had no idea what was about to happen.

They were not returning home. When the stars reached high in the sky, she and her daughter would be on a boat, far away from here. It had all finally been agreed. She'd paid the bribe to Daku the oarsman, shaking the whole time, least he betray her to the priests. But he had agreed to help, demanding even extra, on top of the extra he had already fleeced from her, to take them at night, because it was more treacherous to travel without the safety of the sun. But Daku was a good navigator, he would stay along the shoreline and move to the open water when the sun rose. By the time Iaf thought to question their disappearance, it would be too late. She hoped the sandstorm would not prevent their leaving. They should move more quickly.

Her hands were damp, her body tense. Well, all that was natural, wasn't it? She was running away after all. Running from Iaf and the rest of them. From Rafe, running from him most of all, the man who had made her promises but had then broken them. She was furious with him, and hurt. And, more than that, she felt betrayed. How could he have abandoned her?

And yet ... and yet some small part of her knew that he was far more noble than she. Unlike her, he was standing up to Iaf, and standing up for what was right. Well, she did not have a choice, not any more. 'Hurry, Aal,' she said again, trying not to seem anxious.

Aal stood up and yawned. Thankfully, the child was too tired to truly question her mother's nervousness. These days, she fell into bed each night without so much as a sigh.

They made their way out of the antechamber, across the courtyard, which even now made her think of Iaf's rank breath and the smell of woodsmoke, through the dark corridors lined with more clan paintings, to the entryway, lit with firelight, where large wooden doors would open and take them to freedom. Jaya clutched her daughter's hand. They were close, so close now. But when they got there, the door was closed and bolted. She paused, panic-stricken.

The door was normally open until nightfall. The guards must have closed it because of the sandstorm. She lifted the bolt with shaking hands and pushed, exhaling deeply when it moved easily. Thank the Goddess. She pushed against the door. It was heavy wood, it yielded only a hair's breadth against her weight. But then she heard the trouble outside.

'But I want to see her,' someone was shouting. 'Aal, Aal, where are you? You haven't come to play with me. I want to see her, I tell you!'

She felt her daughter stiffen with recognition. It was Al-Mien. Aal turned to her in shock. 'You said we could not see them any more, Mua. You said they had to leave the city.' Her daughter's voice was heavy with accusation.

Jaya was too shocked herself and too preoccupied to answer. She pushed the door as hard as she could, but it was yielding very slowly against her. She could see only a little bit of the scene outside. There he was, Al-Mien, well, part of his shoulder and face anyway, looking furiously unhappy. The monkey, Pinar, sat on his shoulder, but there was something cradled, hidden in his hands. The Temple guards were amusing themselves at his expense. They were poking him with their spears and telling him to be on his way. 'But Aal is my friend and I want to play with her,' Al-Mien was insisting.

One of the guards burst out laughing. 'Listen to the cripple. Claiming friendship with a Goddess-Blessed. As if such a thing were possible.'

'But I have a present for her. Look.' He held out a little bird, a baby blue-and-green parakeet.

'Enough of this,' sneered Bas, who Jaya knew to be the cruellest of all the guards. He pointed his spear at the young boy's throat. 'Be off with you, cripple, before you give further insult.'

Jaya finally had the door open wide enough for her daughter to get through.

'Aal,' said Al-Mien in joy, recognizing her. He stepped forward, towards the door. 'At last. Look what I've got ...'

They gathered around him then, the guards, stopping him from moving any further. He strained against them and the parakeet flew out of his hands.

'Oh no,' he moaned. 'Oh no. Look what you've done. My present! My present!'

'Leave him,' said Aal. 'It is true, he is my friend.'

Jaya pushed at the door and squeezed through herself.

No one was listening to her daughter. In confusion, the guards had surrounded the boy, thinking he intended to harm a Goddess-Blessed. Then there was a shout and some colourful cursing. The monkey had launched himself on Bas and bit his cheek. The guard clutched his face, blood dripping from between his fingers. Furious, he grabbed Pinar and, with his large, beefy hands, he snapped his neck in two and threw the monkey onto the ground.

'No!' shouted Al-Mien, launching himself on Bas. 'I'll kill you, I'll kill you for that!' He pummelled the guard's face pathetically with his misshapen hands, sobbing.

Jaya and Aal tried in vain to intervene, but the other guards were in the way. They pulled Al-Mien aside like he was of little consequence. And then, it happened.

One of them drove his spear through the boy's stomach.

'Stop,' screamed Jaya, aware of nothing now, nothing except Al-Mien, of the look of stunned surprise on his face, of the way his lips were moving, as though he were still trying to talk. The guard pulled out his spear and walked away, and Al-Mien fell to the ground, his feet twitching.

Aal launched herself on the boy, weeping and calling his name. He smiled at her, smiled and held out his empty hand. Then he closed his eyes.

Jaya sank to the ground, her hand over her mouth. She crawled to the boy, incapable of standing up. Perhaps there was still a chance ... but she saw the blood pooling on the ground, she saw the wax of death already upon him as her daughter screamed and tried to revive her friend. In that moment, she saw it all. Nene's baby, crying, desperate to suckle, but left outside tied to the pipal tree to shrivel up and die, the time Iaf had blackened both Lal's eyes, the mother who left her child at the Temple and starved to death on the walk home.

Bas spat on the ground. 'Leave him, Lady. He was mad. An Unclanned cripple. He should have been killed at birth, instead of being a burden on others. Unclanned filth. We have enough of them on our streets, taking what's rightfully ours.' He walked away, his posture defensive.

She wept, her hand on Al-Mien's cheek. Silent tears, she held him against her. Al-Mien. He was such a beautiful, special boy. Al-Mien was dead. And once again, it was her fault. All her fault.

'No,' she whispered, rocking back and forth with his body in her arms. 'No, no, no, no, no.' She clutched his head with her fingers, bringing her cheek to his. 'No, no, no, no, no.' Someone was screaming. Was it her? 'I curse you, Bas,' she shouted at the retreating figure. 'I curse you and your family. Don't you walk away from me, you cur. I curse you, do you understand?'

She was aware, somewhere, of Aal holding her arm. She shrugged it away and turned towards the Temple, shouting even louder. 'I curse you, Iaf. Do you hear me? I curse you and all those who support you.' She turned back to the child, continuing to hold his cheek against hers, watching as the guards stood over her, looking stunned and unsure. 'And most of all I curse her,' she whispered. 'I curse the Goddess Shakari. I curse her and all of her family. I invoke the One Horned God. May he bring her untold suffering as she has brought me.'

It was enough, it was enough, because they had all heard it. Aal was gasping and crying. Bas was smiling in the distance. He knew ... he knew she had gone too far. She watched Iaf step outside, and when they came for her, she closed her eyes.

Chapter Twenty-Nine

KARACHI, PRESENT DAY.

The cop opened the door of the house and pushed her into some sort of living room, and then down onto a wooden chair. He cuffed her arms behind her and disappeared, his heavy footsteps thudding away. She was alone.

She tried to slow down her breathing, aware that she was on the verge of another panic attack. *Breathe. Just breathe, Nadia.* It wasn't working though. She was alone, handcuffed to a chair. She looked around, turning her head as much as she could.

From the corner of her eye she could see wall-to-wall bookshelves, stacked full, each book neatly arranged according to height. She couldn't make out the names, but she recognized several rows of repetitive lilac. Sohail's book, dozens of copies, like wallpaper.

In front of her were a couple of cane sofas and a coffee table, and in the right-hand corner was a desk with a lamp and some loose papers on it, and a pencil holder with some biros. It was all pleasantly nondescript – apart from the large GoL meditation orb on the table – and smelled faintly of cleaning polish. She could have been anywhere in the world, in any hotel or bed-and-breakfast. She shook her head, trying to blow off the hair that had fallen in front of her eyes. Then she jerked as someone reached out from behind her, caught a stray strand and pushed it behind her ear.

'Is that better?'

Her heart stopped. How well she knew that voice. How often she had ached to hear it when she was young.

'Sorry about the handcuffs,' her father said, coming to squat in front of her, his eyes full of sympathy. 'Unfortunately, Changhaiz the policeman said you were so worked up that it would be necessary to restrain you. You must know that nobody plans to harm you here, Nadia. It's good to see you, my daughter.'

He looked the same. How could he look the same? The slightly crooked, charming, seductive smile. The long black hair that was still thick and full and shoulder-length. The five-day shadow, now salt and pepper. Amber eyes that were always impossible to read, even know. And always, always an expression of calculation, as though he knew something she didn't.

'I wish I could say it is good to see you too, but we both know that would be a lie,' she said, raising her head in defiance. It took all her strength to ignore the sick feeling in her stomach. 'Hello Father.'

He shook his head, looking sad. 'I never wanted to involve you, you know. Not in any of this.' He stood up, reached into his pocket and pulled out a set of keys, which he dangled in front of her. 'I can remove the handcuffs, if you promise to stay calm. I don't want to fight with you, Nadia. You're my daughter. I love you. We're family.'

'What do you want?' It wasn't just fear she was feeling, she realized. There was anguish too. Anguish and ... and longing. Some part of her, some sick part of her yearned to have him love her, even now, even after everything. She looked away, disturbed. Sohail was a monster, never a loving father.

He walked behind her and started to massage her shoulders. She stiffened.

'Shh ... relax. I want us to understand each other, Nadia. Everything I did, I did for your own good, though I know you will find that hard to believe, with all the vile rubbish those care workers used to bias you against me.'

He still smelled of the peppermints he always used to stash in the front pocket of his jeans. He'd always been so deceptively benign. That's why people fell in love with him.

A memory came, unbidden. She was very young, perhaps six or seven. She'd had a fever and a hacking cough that would not go away and made her feel like her lungs were on fire. She could barely get out of bed. Father had refused to let her have any medication. The fever spiked, she had started to shake uncontrollably with the cold. He'd sat with her all night, pressing her head, massaging her shoulders, just as he was doing now. When morning came and the fever broke, he was gone.

She felt sick, Christ, she felt sick. But she was an adult. He had no power over her. Not any more. 'What do you want ... Sohail?'

He stopped the massage. He came and sat down on the sofa opposite her, rested his elbows on his knees and brought his index fingers together to his lips. It was his classic pose. She wondered now if it was an affectation he had picked up somewhere along the way. 'I wish you could understand, Nadia. It was for your own good. Everything I did, everything I am, what I strive for, it's to make the world a better place. There are forces at play you've never understood ...'

She rolled her eyes. 'Oh please. All these years of hiding, of skulking away, and you still haven't changed, have you? You murdered everyone in Mohenjodaro.'

'I didn't kill anyone. Your sister did. Such a shame really. Professor Webb was a loyal and faithful friend. His death has been quite hard on all of us.'

It took a minute to sink in. Webb. A member of GoL. Liam was going to be devastated. Though if she stopped to think about it, she supposed it made sense. 'You set the whole dig up, didn't you? The tablet ...'

He nodded. 'Yes, you're right. It's *his* tablet that you had in your possession, Nadia. Webb found it in Kisurra, in Iraq. He brought it to me a year ago. And we realized it was exactly what we'd been waiting for, sent to us to help illuminate the way to the Bloodstone. Say what you like about Karl, he was an excellent archaeologist, and a man who truly wanted to change the world for the better.'

'You ... you knew where the Bloodstone was because you deciphered the Indus Valley script using the tablet?'

He smiled and his eyes lit up. 'Once we could read the script, the whole city came to life. We read about the powers of the Bloodstone, but we also read that one of the Goddess-Blessed had become rebellious against the priests and had unleashed destruction on the city. Jaya. The Bloodstone was buried with her when she died. It was just a question of working out where to dig. The place is so massive, it took two months to find the right tomb.'

So it *was* Jaya's body they had uncovered. 'You sent Webb to retrieve it.'

He smirked. 'Gold star for you today.'

'You knew about the Bloodstone because Jahanara told you about it. About Jaya and the dreams.'

Now he scowled. 'Not so clever after all. That old crone taught me nothing! She never cared about me! The Bloodstone is my heritage. Do you think she was the only one who knew about it?'

Her arms were beginning to get stiff. She tried flexing her fingers. Maybe she should have let him remove the restraints, but she said nothing, even now not wanting to acknowledge his power over her. 'So did you know the Stone would kill all those people when it was dug up? How did Layla survive it? Why did you take her? What are you planning to do with her?'

'So full of questions, aren't you?' He got up and walked to the coffee table. She saw then the small teapot and cups in the corner. He lifted the pot and looked at her. 'Would you care for some? No? Forgive me if I indulge. It's been a long day.'

She jerked at the cuffs again, glaring at him.

'I'll take them off, Nadia, I told you. But you must promise to behave.'

'Where's Layla? What have you done with her?'

He took a sip of his drink, looking thoughtful. 'Layla is wonderful, isn't she? She was taken away from us far too early at the compound. Before I could teach her. The minute I heard that she was going to be studying archaeology, I knew she was the one. My *true* daughter. The one I could share my legacy with. She understands the need to re-examine the past. To unearth the truth forensically. To be open-minded. I wanted it to be her, who found it. I thought she would be able to control it. I suppose I must take some responsibility for that.'

'You're a liar,' Nadia said quietly. 'You were worried about what the Bloodstone might do to you. And so you wanted someone else to take all the risk. Why her?'

He said nothing for a moment. Then he put down his cup. 'So cynical. You've always been so cynical. I have read the scriptures of Meluhha. The ones left behind by the priests. The Bloodstone is wielded by a woman. A woman of the clan. Of the Blood. *Our* blood, Nadia. Our family. Why should we give up that birthright to someone else, someone we can't trust, who may use the power for their own gain? Layla would never do that. She can embrace my teachings, now that she has seen the truth of them for herself. She *will* embrace them and the world will love her for it.'

'You're so full of shit. You've taken her against her will.'

He raised an eyebrow. 'You've always been so ready to assume the worst of me. But that's not the case. She is here because she wants to be.'

'You're a liar! I saw the video. Her colleagues were burning. She would have wanted to be with them, to try and save them. She would have stayed until the authorities came.'

'Yes,' he said, nodding. 'When she opened the box, they burned. And she was the one who killed them. When she realized this, she was ... affected. She needed her father. I'm glad I was able to provide support and guidance at such a difficult and confusing time.'

Nadia inhaled sharply. 'You're going to try and force her to use the Stone again. That's it, isn't it? You'll be the puppet master, holding the strings, and Layla will do your bidding?'

'Do you never listen?' He scowled. 'Always so wilful. Always so disobedient! Even now, when I'm trying to bring you back into the family fold. The truth is, at first I didn't want to involve you because you don't deserve to be a part of this.' He leaned towards her, she could smell the peppermint again. 'You were never special enough, Nadia. Your mind could never expand enough to take in my teachings. I must say, I wrote you off a long time ago. I had assumed you would be drunk in a ditch somewhere. It was a surprise to me, when I started to follow your movements again, to learn that you had made something of yourself.'

'Sorry to ruin your plans,' she hissed, pulling at the cuffs one more time. The bastard things wouldn't budge. And now her foot had gone to sleep. She jiggled it restlessly.

'If you'll just calm down, I can take those off.'

'I won't give you the tablet, if that's what you're after. Not unless you let Layla go.'

He narrowed his eyes and smiled. 'Ah yes, the tablet. It was such a shame that Marianne turned out to be a traitor. A colleague of mine had a little word with her, you know, after your little ingenuity in getting the tablet. She had left it in the coat check for a journalist. Can you believe it? She was going to go public about what had happened in Mohenjodaro. And how stupid, too, to let herself be followed by you.'

'You killed her.'

He shrugged. 'Marianne was one of us, one of the first in my flock, in fact. She was a banker with a nasty addiction to cocaine when I found her. She lost everything because of it. Her marriage, her job, her home. I helped cure her of that addiction. I set her on a more worthy path. Unfortunately, she lost her way again when she was diagnosed with breast cancer. I told her to be patient. I told her I would physically manifest myself to the people again soon, and on that day, I would cure her. But she was selfish. She began to question my teachings. So when Layla killed everyone in Mohenjodaro, Marianne leaked the video feed to the world from our backup system. She made it public. She *wanted* people to know about the power we had found. And she stole the tablet from our London headquarters and left it for that journalist, because she wanted to bring GoL – bring me – to ruin. I couldn't believe it was her at first. But when her betrayal was confirmed, she had to be eliminated. If that journalist had gotten his hands on that tablet before our plans were set in motion ... well, that would have been a disaster.'

She tried to follow what he was saying, but it was all so confusing. 'Why? Why did Marianne have to die? What's the big deal about the damn thing? You deciphered the language, so why did you need the tablet?'

He trailed his elegant fingers along her cheek and she tried not to flinch. 'I didn't need it, Nadia. I just didn't want anyone else to have it. The Bloodstone is what will protect us from the Ancients, when they come to claim what is rightfully ours. They must not know the true extent of its power or what we are planning, until it is too late to stop us. The video leak was ... unfortunate.'

'Stop you? Stop you from doing what?'

'All in good time, my dear.'

'I won't give it to you. Not unless you give me Layla in exchange.'

He burst out laughing. 'Oh Nadia, you really are wonderfully precious. It was a silly thing to leave the Stone with your grandmother. Did you really think I wouldn't pay her a visit if I thought there was the slightest chance that she had it?'

She felt real fear then. Jahanara ... 'What have you done to her?'

'Oh, stop being so melodramatic, Nadia. I didn't kill her. She's my mother, after all. And anyway, she was happy to hand it over in exchange for my agreement that I wouldn't hurt *you.* It was a rather civilized reunion, after all this time. She's still an old battleaxe.'

'I have copies,' she blurted out. 'I sent photos of the tablet to many of my friends. If anything happens to me or Layla ...'

He frowned. Then he waved his arms in dismissal. 'No matter now. By the time they figure out what they have, it will be too late. By tomorrow, the world will have changed, Nadia. And my people will finally be free of the Ancients.'

'If you hurt Layla, I swear to God ...'

The mask fell then, his face finally showing the contempt she knew he really felt for her. 'I've had enough. I tried, darling, I really did, for your sake. But look at her, spitting and snarling like this. What am I supposed to do?'

Nadia blinked, confused.

She heard the footsteps first, then felt the presence behind her. She craned her neck, but couldn't see.

'You were right, Father. She doesn't want to listen.'

Nadia closed her eyes and shook her head. No. Not this. Not her.

Then the figure walked forward and everything stopped.

'Hello Nadia,' said Layla.

Chapter Thirty

MELUHHA, 3791 BC.

Slowly, insidiously, the trouble began. It started with a caravan from Magan, which was sacked just outside the city. Dignitaries and merchants were left tied up in the desert, burning in the sun, their livestock and goods hauled away. A few of their women had been taken as well, to be remarried or sold as servants as was the common practice. Luckily, Guljoo the trader happened upon the group before it was too late.

Guljoo was on his way back from bartering with the outer villages. He was leading a caravan laden with wild boar tusks which he planned to sell for a pretty profit in the market. The tusks would be bought by healers and soothsayers, and ground into a fine powder to be put into protection spells and amulets for strength and virility.

But then he came upon the group – the miserable sunburnt faces of the men, the few women and terrified children, sweltering in the heat with barely a tunic left amongst them.

It was later proclaimed by one of the freed merchants that Guljoo had spat on the ground, casually emptied his caravan of all the tusks and filled it with people. He brought the Magani to the city, but only once the desperate party had agreed to pay him triple what he would earn from selling his entire stock in the market. Otherwise, he said, he would simply leave them there to rot in the sun.

Such was a sign of the times. There was no honour. Not any more.

At least not according to Raka, the Temple cook. Raka was a kind, gentle sort of woman, thickset and old, with blunt hands and wispy white hair. She felt sorry for Jaya and had taken to bringing her sweetmeats at night sometimes. She told Jaya tales from the market, of all the goings-on outside the Temple, and of her own fears and woes, the terrible aches in her joints and the fact that her son, Felluk, had taken their only goat and sold it without her permission. Raka's allegiance to the Blessed was still strong, despite Iaf's edicts that this particular Goddess-Blessed was to remain in relative isolation.

Her visits were too infrequent for Jaya, who was desperate for any contact with the outside world. The priests largely ignored her, even though they used the antechamber for their meditations. They shuffled about in the mornings, prayed and left her again in the silence. To demand their attention would make things difficult for Aal, Jaya knew. And so she waited, quietly, her wrist attached to the wall by a long length of chain, twice the size of her body, long enough for her to be able to walk to the little mat they had brought in for her to sleep on, to suffer the indignity of opening her bowels in the clay urn in the corner, the urn to be taken away by Raka in the evenings.

The priests saw it all. They sneered at how low she had been brought down. But Jaya bore it without a word. She was calm now, and rational. Her fate did not matter any longer. It was Aal she cared about. And so she waited for Iaf to decide what he would do with her, and with her child. If she was certain she could break the chain, if she could reach Aal and flee, she would have done so. But for now, waiting was her only option.

Thankfully, she was not completely isolated. She begged Raka for news of her daughter every day, and the cook would quietly fill her ears. Aal still hadn't spoken, but she had eaten something that morning, a little buffalo milk and some cheese. It was some good news, wasn't it? At least the child was starting to feel better.

Jaya would nod. She accepted these morsels gratefully, for they were all she truly needed. Her days were spent obsessing over her daughter, over her well-being and her emotional state. She wondered whether Iaf would make Aal read the Bloodstone now.

She wondered too, about Rafe, about how he had dealt with the news of Al-Mien's death. Someone must have told him, someone would have recognized the child amongst the Unclanned, where his body was no doubt returned. Did he blame her, as she blamed herself, for the horrific events at the Temple that day? Just thinking about it made her cold and sick in the stomach. Al-Mien's expression, the stunned look on his face as the guard speared him ... it would never, ever leave her. *Forgive me, Al-Mien. Forgive me.*

Tonight, Raka had come to visit once more. Jaya leaned against the wall, thinking of Al-Mien, listening to all the news with half an ear, her arms wrapped around her unwashed body. Her hair was matted and brittle, her tunic was beginning to become rigid with the dust of the place. Her wrist was swollen from the heaviness of the metal bracelet which kept her chained to the wall. The fact that she had not been allowed to go outside and bathe was a testament to how low her status had become, but it was of little concern now. Iaf would hang her from the pipal tree, sooner or later. It was only a matter of time. So she would wait in the dimly lit antechamber, full of smoke from the mustard oil lamps and the fire torches. She would bide her time and stay where she was told. She would do anything in exchange for her daughter's safety. Just as she had always done.

She looked at the tray of sweetmeats Raka had brought. They made her stomach curl. So Aal still wasn't eating properly, was she? She must be so confused and so lost. Her friend Al-Mien killed and then her mother taken away from her by the priests who she had grown increasingly fond of. What could she say, what message could she send that would help the child garner her strength?

For the moment, she distracted herself with Raka's news.

There was tension and discord all over the city, Raka told her. The ongoing dispute between the Crocodiles and the Tigers had turned violent. The Crocodiles no longer brought their wares into Meluhha and anyone who ventured to the banks of the river was beaten up severely. The Crocodile clan demanded fairer prices and their own marketplace. The Temple would not listen, but without the fish caught daily by the Crocodiles, food was growing even scarcer.

'Things are very bad all around, Lady,' said Raka, shaking her head sadly. 'I don't know what's going to happen, I just don't.'

The city was holding its breath, it seemed. 'I don't know either, Raka,' Jaya said, stepping over the chain, and taking the old cook's hands. 'But I thank the Goddess for you and your kindness.'

The old woman seemed both absurdly proud and upset, for tears gathered in her eyes. 'Bless you, Lady, Bless you.'

It was a few days before Raka could spend any time with her again, and when she did, the news was even more troubling. A senior figure in the Tiger clan, a council member, had had his fingers broken by a gang. The gang stole his seal and used it to gain entry into Tiger territory. One of them hid in an old granary and, later that night, set fire to it as well as to the large storerooms in which the merchants kept their wares. Half the Tiger territory was in flames that night. And on the walls that remained, somebody had painted the symbol of the One Horned God.

This, said Raka quietly, offering Jaya a wet cloth to wipe her face, was the most shocking of it all. That a gang which followed the One Horned God had come so close to the Temple! 'They must be truly evil, Lady,' she whispered to Jaya, when she took away the cloth and the washing bowl she had smuggled in with her maize. 'They must be truly evil indeed. The Unclanned. It has to be them.'

Jaya always turned away during conversations like these. They pained her. She remembered too, her own words, shouted at Iaf in a moment of grief. She had cursed him, she had invoked the One Horned God. And she would be killed for it.

But the next night Raka came again to take away her toilet urn, and to tell her that the Tigers blamed the Crocodiles for the fires and swore vengeance.

Iaf was outraged. That much she saw for herself the following morning. Though they paid her little heed, priests raced in and out of the room for most of the day, using the antechamber as a thoroughfare between the gates and the courtyard where Iaf was meeting with senior council members.

It seemed her sins were forgotten or were being ignored, for Iaf had other, more pressing, concerns. Guards were dispatched to catch the gang of arsonists. The priests made a public declaration, calling for all able-bodied men from the neighbouring villages to come and protect the sanctity of the Temple against the followers of the One Horned God.

At the gates, Iaf declared that he had gold and copper to offer any man who could fight, and who would join the Cobras in protecting the Temple and its interests against this new blasphemous evil. Men were gathering in the fields outside the left gate of the city. Jaya knew what would happen next.

Iaf's army would march first on the Unclanned, getting rid of them once and for all. After that, he would take each city in the region, one after another, and install a new governing body with himself as head. Any city that refused to pay tithe would be brought down. He had told her this one night when he had come to lay with her, he had drunk too much wine and was in a rage. He warned her that she would pay for her blasphemy against him and against the Goddess, but then he had pummelled himself into her. The whole time, he had cursed her uncleanliness. But he had not unchained her, or let her bathe. Then he had disappeared, engrossed, she supposed, in everything that was happening.

There was little she could do, locked up here. She no longer cared what Iaf's plans for her were. There was always pain in her body now and she knew she would not be long in this world. She only wished to keep her daughter safe. And to see Rafe, one last time ...

But in the dimly lit, windowless chamber, there was little chance of either of those things happening. She was forced to content herself with her moments of conversation with Raka, of the frantic, whispered communications she asked the cook to pass on to her child, who she knew was in one of the chambers above hers. The one piece of wealth she had, the lapis lazuli necklace she had been wearing when she was taken, was given to Raka for safekeeping. Aal should have it.

She spent her nights pacing the room, or rather, the small corner of it that she could reach, anxiously aware of how alone she was, with the exception of the accursed Bloodstone. There it was, resting on its podium in its box, no doubt pulsing, as it always did. The heart of Shakari. She looked at the box, which seemed to be taunting her.

It was surprising how little she cared about offending the Goddess any more. Nene had been right. Shakari was vengeful, worse than the

One Horned God. She did not deserve Jaya's loyalty, for she had taken her family away.

Her brother Dar ... the thought of him, of his gentle teasing, the mocking smile and the way he splashed her in the river ... it made her long for them all once more. She remembered her childhood, of the days in which she woke up to easy mornings and lazy afternoons. She yearned for her family. Mua and Apa would know what to do, even now, Apa would have a plan to help her.

She felt her eyes linger on the Bloodstone. Perhaps ... Perhaps, she had been wrong, all those cycles ago, to swear never to use it for her own personal gain. She could find her family! She could ask the Stone to show her exactly where they were. She may never see them again, she may never escape the Temple, but at least she would know they were safe. Were her parents still alive? Had Dar found a wife? She closed her eyes and imagined his children. They would be stocky, like him. Stocky and strong, with teasing brown eyes and quick grins.

The next night, she begged Raka to bring her the Stone. The old woman looked terrified and backed away. 'I cannot do it, Lady. They will kill me for it.'

'It's all right,' she said, as gently and as soothingly as she could. 'I am Goddess-Blessed, Raka. The Stone is my birthright, not the priests'. If you do this for me, I will ask the Goddess to bless you, and the

Stone to take away the pain in your joints that keeps you up so many nights.'

Raka looked stunned. 'It ... it can do that?'

'Of course it can,' Jaya lied. 'Is it not Shakari's own heart? Though it will take time to work.' She felt no guilt over the lie. She would be dead soon and Raka would forgive her.

The old woman hesitated, looking doubtful. 'If we are caught ...'

'It will be but for a moment,' pressed Jaya. 'Besides, everyone has gone to bed. When I am finished, you can return it to the podium and no one will ever know. Shakari will bless you, Raka.'

It took some cajoling, but the other woman finally agreed. She lifted the box from the podium, with the Stone still inside. 'I daren't touch it,' she whispered, shaking. 'I would not want to be cursed for using it improperly. But I will do as you ask.'

Jaya took the box gratefully. Raka went to the door to stand watch, determined to look the other way as Jaya opened the box and stared at the jagged red stone with the pulsating lines. Shakari's heart. For a moment, she hesitated. Was this really such a good idea? But she and the Bloodstone were old friends now. They understood one another. What did she care about offending Shakari now, when all was lost? What did she care about being cursed, for hadn't she been cursed already?

She grew excited. It would not be just her family ... she could learn what was happening outside these walls. She could search for Iaf's army and get some sense of their numbers and strengths. Perhaps she could get a message to Rafe through Raka, warning him of their plans. And then maybe he would forgive her. She did not want to die knowing that he hated her.

She closed her eyes. Rafe. She could see him, the Stone would show him to her. Perhaps that would be enough.

She wondered, later, why Iaf had not thought to remove her from the antechamber where the Stone was kept. Did he think a mere chain would keep her from it? Perhaps he thought her too set in her ways, her fear of being cursed for using the Stone for her own benefit too strong for her to ever defy him.

But he was wrong. She held the pulsating rock in her hands once more and she felt its power, felt it probing her, her stomach twisting in on itself.

Show me my family.

There was Dar, on the boat, his arm against the sail. He was chewing on a stalk of water reed as he watched his parents walk down the riverbank, returning from Meluhha. The three of them ate a hurried meal of porridge and trout, and then sat while the sun set, watching the river grow silent. It was a perfect moment or would have been had the Bloodstone not pressed the vision further.

'I told them no,' said Tur'un, looking grey and tired. 'We will not leave her here. Not until she has recovered from her unhappiness.

Let Jaya settle first. It is a hard thing to leave your family and she is still young. In time, she will see how wonderful her life can be as a Goddess-Blessed. And then ... then if they insist upon it we will leave.'

Her mother nodded, tears gathering in her eyes.

Dar cleared his throat. 'I don't see why we must go. Our family is Clanned, we have been for hundreds of moons. This is our home. Besides, if Jaya doesn't want to be a Goddess-Blessed, why should she have to be one?'

'They worry that we will be a distraction, Dar. And it is an honour that your sister has been chosen. Who are we to question the will of the Goddess?' Her father finished chewing his bread, looking upset.

Her brother scowled. 'And what if we are a distraction? Are the Goddess-Blessed no longer allowed a family?'

Tur'un began to mend a frayed fishing rope, his blunt fingers working the knots with surprising deftness. He shook his head and sighed. 'It is politics. It is complicated. There is nothing more to be said, except that we have determined not to go to Dilmun. Not until Jaya no longer needs us.'

Dar got up. 'As you say. We will go and talk to her tomorrow. If they let us in this time.'

Jaya's heart ached for her family, now that she was reminded of them so vividly. She had forgotten about that scar Apa had above his eyebrow, the one from the time he had fallen from a tree as a child. She had forgotten that Mua smelled of the keekar leaves that grew along the river. She had forgotten ... everything. This is what joy felt like. Why had she waited so long to see them! And why was the Stone showing her an image of their past, not where they were currently? She longed to reach out, to touch them, but the vision was already changing, shifting in the wind. For there they were, the three of them, sleeping on the boat, immune to the noise of all its creaks and groans, of the way it swayed along the river breeze. Only, the creaking wasn't caused by the water this time.

Four men climbed stealthily onto the boat and under a blanket of stars, they slit the throats of her family as they slept. And then, showing no emotion whatsoever, they set sail. They wrapped the bodies of her family in sacks full of heavy stones. They dropped them into the river. Then they took the boat and continued on their way.

The water barely rippled with their passing.

In the dimly lit antechamber, Jaya awoke. She was lying on the floor, the Bloodstone still in her hands, mocking her, while Raka crouched next to her, looking terrified. *You wanted to see*, it seemed to be suggesting. *And now you've seen. You've seen that everything you have ever cared about is gone, destroyed because of you.*

Jaya started to shake. Then she began to scream and threw the Stone as hard as she could. It struck the wall and fell to the ground unharmed. The other woman, crying, retrieved it and placed it quickly back into its box. Jaya convulsed, clutching her stomach. Then she vomited all over the floor of the antechamber.

Chapter Thirty-One

KARACHI, PRESENT DAY.

'Layla.' Nadia stared. 'It's you.'

Layla reached out and put a hand on Nadia's knee. Her smile was shaky. 'You must have been so worried. I'm okay, Nadia. Don't be upset. Everything's going to be fine. Father, please, uncuff her. She must be so anxious and confused.'

Nadia watched Sohail give the keys to the handcuffs to her sister, who bent down, unrestrained her and then enveloped her in a hug. 'I've missed you so much. I've been so worried about you.'

Nadia was too shocked to hug back. 'Jesus, Layla, I thought you were hurt. I thought you might be *dead.* And the whole time, you were here with him? What's he done to you?' Layla had lost weight. She was tired, there were rings under her eyes. But other than that, she seemed to be okay.

But she looked uncomfortable. 'I'm so sorry about this, about everything you've been through. Come, sit on the sofa. I'll bring you some tea – I made sure they brought Lipton here especially for you. Have you eaten? No, of course you wouldn't have. What would you like?'

Nadia simply stared.

'Are you okay? I know you're surprised. It's a lot to take in, and Father didn't really explain things as clearly as he should have.'

And now her sister was brave enough to criticize their father? In *front* of him? Numbly, she let herself be guided to the sofa and watched Layla rush around, a bundle of nervous energy, bringing tea and biscuits, and then sandwiches, asking her every few minutes if she was okay. It was the sandwiches that made her blink, several times. Only an hour ago she had been eating dust and ingesting the second-hand smoke of a corrupt cop, chained to the inside of a van. And now she was being offered egg mayonnaise on white bread.

She drank the tea despite herself, feeling the caffeine come at her like a rush, reminded now, of how parched her lips felt. She said nothing, until she had finished. Then she put her cup down.

'Would you like another?'

She shook her head. Both Layla and Sohail were sitting on the sofa opposite her now, his arm resting casually across her sister's shoulders. What the fuck was going on?

'Layla,' she said, her voice on edge. 'Layla, what are you doing here? With *him*?'

Her sister looked down at her lap and played with her fingers. 'I know ... I know it's hard for you, Nadia. But Father has been right this whole time. It was such a shock to me when I realized he was telling the truth.'

'Whatever it is that he's said ...'

'The world is full of Ancients,' Layla burst out. 'I've seen it, Nadia. The Bloodstone is real. It called to me. I can't explain how, but it did. And I killed them. I killed them all. My colleagues, my friends.' She looked up, her face anguished. 'I didn't mean to. I swear it. You don't know how many sleepless nights I've had, how much of a burden it is, the knowledge of what I did, what I'm capable of ...'

'Shh,' said Sohail, patting her on the arm kindly. 'It's all behind you now, my child.'

Nadia wanted to wipe that smug expression off her father's face, but focused on her sister instead. 'Layla, that wasn't your fault. It was *his.* He knew the Stone was dangerous and he made sure you were the one to pick it up. He made sure Professor Webb gave it to you.'

'Father was just trying to keep everyone safe. He thought I could handle it.'

She couldn't bear the way his arm was resting on Layla's shoulder and how close he was to her. As if he had any right. 'He's lying, Layla. He's a fucking liar. He thought he would be able to control *you,* so he sent you to find the Stone. He has some crazy theory about keeping its power in the family.'

Layla looked troubled, but shook her head firmly. 'Listen to me, please. You're always so angry. You never just *listen.* The Stone, its power is undeniable. How could you ever argue again that ancient technology doesn't exist? It's mind-boggling, but it's all true. We're fighting against the oppressors, the ones that have used their knowledge of the past to take control of things. Father is the *good* guy, Nadia. His work has been so misunderstood. And I don't blame you,' she added quickly, 'for everything you thought about him. Without the right context and, of course, you were just a child ...'

Nadia glanced at her father now, who was calmly drinking his own cup of Lipton. He arched an eyebrow. 'I'm glad one of my daughters has understood my intentions.'

She tried to hold her sister's gaze and said slowly, 'Layla, Sohail's a psychopath. He's only been able to brainwash you because of the trauma you've been through. You aren't thinking clearly right now.'

'He didn't have to brainwash me, Nadia. I picked up the Bloodstone. I *felt* it inside me and I killed the people I cared about. How could you possibly know what it was like, seeing them die? I couldn't control it. Just think what would happen, if this kind of technology fell into the wrong hands. The only thing to do is keep it safe, so that,' she gulped, 'so that only we can wield the Stone. So that the Ancients can't control us any more. That's my destiny, Nadia. That's what I have to do.'

'Look at him,' Nadia snapped, pointing at Sohail. 'You're listening to a man who thinks people will learn how to heal themselves, Layla. He thinks we'll wake up one day and remember how to fly ...'

'And why not?' said Sohail, smiling. 'The Bloodstone gave the people of Meluhha great powers. Imagine what we could do with our knowledge of the world, with the technology that we already have. We could learn exponentially. Instead of the Bloodstone teaching us how to bind together bitumen and brick, we could ask it about complicated algorithms, about programming and mitigating the risks of climate change. Think about what all we could do, Nadia, if we had a Seer with the same abilities as Jaya to guide us. If we could make the Stone work again as a source of knowledge.'

'Yes,' said Layla eagerly, leaning forward. 'As a source of knowledge, as it once was. Not as a weapon, Nadia. We don't want to hurt anyone. Once we're safe from the Ancients, we'll figure out a way to turn it back to what it was, a gift sent to help humans evolve. You could help us, you could be a part of it all.'

'But it *is* a weapon, Layla. We know that from the writings on the tablet and from what happened when you touched it in Mohenjodaro. Whatever the Stone was before, whatever the dreams showed, it burns people now. And he' – now she glared at her father – 'will use it to get more power.'

Sohail raised his hands in mock surrender. 'Me? I have no control here. The Stone has called to Layla, not me. It is for her to decide what is to be done next. I am merely here as a conduit of the Light, a useful guide, as it were, on her journey.'

'And why am *I* here exactly?'

'Because Layla wanted you by her side,' he said, smiling blandly.

She didn't believe it. Not for a minute. 'He killed Jay, Layla,' she said quietly. 'Father killed Jay.'

She watched the pain set briefly on her sister's face, followed by a look of confusion. 'Why would you say such things? Father would never do that. He doesn't hurt people.'

Foolish, foolish girl. She obviously hadn't been listening to their conversation long enough to hear him admit to Marianne's killing. Nadia stood up and crossed her arms. 'I was there, Layla, when Jay was attacked and murdered by one of his henchmen'

Layla turned to Sohail, the question unspoken, her body tense.

Watchful. She was watchful, Nadia realized. Some part of her knew that he was a lunatic, even if she didn't seem capable of admitting it.

He shook his head. 'You see? This is exactly what your sister does. She's divisive. She tries to manipulate people. She did it as a girl on the compound and she's doing it now. It's heartbreaking to watch. I didn't kill anyone, Layla. I would never do that.'

'Oh, for fuck's sake ...'

'Nadia, where has this anger come from? Take it out on me, not on your poor sister. Hasn't she been through enough?'

'Layla, if you don't believe me, call the Metropolitan Police. And Jay wasn't the only one. There's a woman, a woman named Marian ...'

Sohail took Layla's hand. 'Please, please call your friend – Jay, was it? – and confirm it for yourself. Once you are satisfied that he is alive and well, we can move on.'

'Yes.' Nadia was nodding now. 'Call him and see if he answers.'

'But,' – and now her father was holding Layla's arm once more, looking into her eyes – 'when you do call him, just remember that the authorities will come after us. Everyone's looking for you. Everyone's looking for the weapon. They'll trace the call. Try not to give away too much information about our location or stay on the phone too long. I don't want to lose you again, Layla. I won't let them take you away from me. Nadia is right about one thing. What happened in Mohenjodaro was not your fault.'

Layla looked completely bewildered now.

'Here,' said Sohail, his eyes full of concern. 'Here's my mobile. Speak to him. Please.'

Layla had tears in her eyes now. 'No Father, I don't need to call him. Nadia is lashing out and saying hurtful things because she doesn't trust you yet.'

'Layla, this is nuts ...'

'Enough, Nadia, please. If you won't join us, then let us at least part as friends.'

Nadia sat down heavily. As though she was free to make her own choice, as though Sohail would just let her go. Could Layla really be that stupid? She looked up. Still, she could use that, couldn't she? If she called Sohail's bluff, if she insisted that he let her go in front of Layla, what would he do? Would he open the gates and let her out, in order to secure Layla's continued allegiance? Maybe, but if he did, that would mean leaving her sister behind. More likely, he would simply keep them both prisoner, or he would spin another bullshit story about how Nadia was at risk from the Ancients outside and Layla would believe him. Christ, it looked like Layla would believe anything at this point.

Her father was watching her, his lips upturned, as though he knew exactly what she was thinking. 'Layla, my dear,' he said, after a moment, 'I think your sister and I might need some time on our own, to talk things out.'

Layla got up, look relieved. 'Of course.' She leaned over and kissed Nadia on the cheek. 'Once you've seen the Stone, you'll realize that what he's saying is true and you won't be angry any more. It's real, Nadia. It's all real, and I have to believe that what happened, happened because we're meant to dedicate our lives to helping people learn the truth.'

She walked out of the room, leaving them in silence.

Sohail poured himself another cup of tea, his long, artisan fingers curling around the cup.

'What do you want?' asked Nadia quietly. 'You've got the tablet and you've got Layla determined to drink your Kool Aid, so what am I doing here?'

'I told you, Layla wanted you to be here.'

'Bullshit.'

He took a sip, watching her. Then he said, 'We're going back.'

'Back?'

'Back to Meluhha. I'm going to reclaim the city and rebuild it for the followers of the Light. The Ancients shall not enter it. And we will evolve far more quickly than anyone else on this planet. Because we have the Stone and it will tell us what to do, and it's wrath will befall those who seek to control us.'

'Jesus ...'

'Humans are intrinsically weak, Nadia. They will go wherever there is strength. The Bloodstone is strength and so am I. Our numbers will swell very quickly.'

'You're crazy,' she whispered, shaking her head. 'You're really crazy, aren't you? I always thought that the whole cult thing was a scam, but you really believe your own bullshit, don't you?'

He said nothing, merely sipped his tea.

'Why am I here?' she demanded. She could see from the corner of her eye that Layla had left the door ajar. Could she make a run for it?

'Tomorrow, I'll announce my resurrection to this world and my people will rejoice. Together we will make our way to the ruins of Meluhha. GoL members from around the globe will fly out here to join us in the promised land. We will finally be returning home.'

She shook her head. 'You don't really think you will get away with that, do you? The Pakistani government will never let you take over sovereign land, especially with the weapon you hold.'

'Exactly.' He was nodding. 'They'll come to stop us. Let them try. We have the Bloodstone. '

He really was insane. 'If you make Layla use that damn thing, a lot of people will get killed, can't you understand that?'

'If the authorities leave us in peace, we will not harm them,' he said dreamily.

She swallowed. 'You're hurting Layla too. The Stone is radioactive. We don't know how it works, how long she can be exposed before she gets sick. She could die, Sohail.'

'There are worse fates.'

She narrowed her eyes. 'Why am I here?'

He grinned, suddenly. 'The truth then. Your sister is weak. I wish it were not so, but she is. I see her hesitation, her horror, every time she looks at the Bloodstone. She is reminded of the events in Mohenjodaro and has not reconciled herself to the death of her colleagues. She wants to be a believer, but some part of her is holding her back.'

Relief could be so draining, Nadia realized in that moment. Her sister was still around, wrapped up somewhere in her own misery and confusion. Otherwise, Sohail would not be anxious about all of this. There was still a chance that she could reach her before it was too late ...

Sohail scowled. 'I'm worried that when the time comes, Layla won't have the emotional strength to turn the power of the Stone on the authorities, despite what she says.'

'So?'

'So you're my plan B, Nadia. If Layla can't wield the Stone, she'll have to be pushed into doing what is necessary.'

She raised her eyebrows. 'And how are you going to push her?'

This time his grin was easy. 'It's really quite simple. If she loses her nerve, I'll put a bullet in that very irritating brain of yours. I'm sure that keeping you safe will be motivation enough for Layla. We both know what a do-gooder she is.'

Chapter Thirty-Two

MELUHHA, 3791 BC.

Shouts from the street outside reverberated into the halls of the Temple. Jaya pulled Aal close. The little girl was sobbing.

'What is happening, Mua, what is it?'

She shook her head, stroking her daughter's hair. 'It's going to be all right, Aal. Just stay calm.' But that was a lie, wasn't it?

The city had gone insane. The Unclanned had lost all reason. They were killing indiscriminately now in a bid to get to the Temple and destroy Iaf once and for all. The Purification pool was red with blood, the streets lined with bodies. Iaf's army of recruits had crumpled against the onslaught of so many men.

She shivered. It was only a night ago that the Bloodstone had given her a vision that would haunt her to her grave, of her family's murder. She had not had time to send Raka to search for Rafe, to warn anyone of the strength of Iaf's army. She thought the Unclanned would be slaughtered if they tried to attack the authority of the priests. But the opposite was happening.

Inside the antechamber, those who were trapped waited in haunted silence, the terror shone in their eyes. The cook's assistant, the serving maids, even the odd Temple guard who had not fled with the priests ... everyone knew that the Unclanned were sparing no one, innocent and guilty. The mustard lamps continued to fill the space with smoke and, with the doors locked, the smoke stagnated, making them all choke. Everything seemed other-worldly and more frightening.

Jaya wished there were a window, a way to see what was taking place outside, a way to clear the smoke. She didn't know whether it was safer here, cornered in the back of the antechamber, or out there, where at least they could run. But run where? The Temple was surrounded by an angry mob, she could hear the door being splintered to pieces. The rioters would be upon them in moments.

Aal moaned and she held her daughter tightly, angry at how quickly the priests had rushed to save themselves. When it became apparent that the rioters had made it all the way to the Temple, Iaf had taken whatever guards were left and deserted his people. He had told the Temple attendants to hide, that he would return for them with more men, but Jaya knew that the High One had left to save his own skin. Thank the Goddess, Raka had unchained her and helped her find her daughter, though they had not been able to flee as those who remained had already barred the Temple doors.

Instinctively, her eyes glanced sideways, towards the shelves against the wall which held the meditation robes and incense sticks for the daily rituals. Under all that clothing was Iaf's most precious possession, and he didn't even know it.

Since the Bloodstone had shown her what had happened to her family, Jaya had decided to kill Iaf and rid this city of the menace of the priests and the Goddess who gave them their power. She'd asked Raka to bring her a sack of flour. She'd replaced the Stone with the flour in the box, making sure it was of roughly equal weight. And then, she'd made the trembling Raka put the box back on the podium.

Eventually, she knew, the theft would be discovered. But by then she would have found a way to destroy the Stone or found a more permanent hiding place. Raka had also brought her a kitchen knife. This, Jaya hid within her robes. She would use it on the High One, next time he came to visit. She swore to herself that she would watch the light fade from his eyes, watch him gasp his last breaths.

But it was not to be. Events in the city took over, things happening quickly.

It had started with the curfew. The Cobras and Iaf's new army had been sent to the trouble spots in the city to impose a strict edict. Nobody was allowed on the streets after sunset, not even the Tigers.

The city had complied. The market shut down. The dancing girls did not appear. Even the soothsayers and the astrologers closed their shops early.

The streets were tense. People were aware of the danger. The troublemakers who aligned themselves with the One Horned God would soon be at the mercy of Iaf's guards. Nobody wanted to be caught in the middle. Nobody wanted to anger the Temple.

But then, just as the sun disappeared below the horizon, a child, a little Unclanned girl who was resting at the gates with her parents, had broken free somehow, to chase a lizard down the street.

She was speared through the back by a Temple guard.

As one, the Unclanned rose, supported by the minor clans. They attacked the Citadel like swarms of angry bees, fighting, stabbing, killing, only to disappear into the heart of the city again. More slogans appeared on the walls, calling for the death of the priests, the death of Iaf, and even the death of the Goddess-Blessed. They adopted the One Horned God as theirs, because Shakari had forsaken them and was now their enemy. Anyone who did not join them would be slaughtered, they warned.

It was brutal. Neither side gave way. People began to flee the city or lock themselves in their houses, praying to the Goddess that nobody would break down the doors. All the dignitaries who had come for Karani had tried to leave, but most had been killed trying to return to their caravans.

The world had gone mad ...

They heard the door crash open then and Raka fell on her knees. 'Oh, Shakari be merciful,' she moaned. Jaya bent down beside her. 'Shh ... you are frightening the others. All will be well, I swear it,' she said. The old woman had risked her life to help her find Aal in those first initial moments of panic, when the girl was forgotten, locked in her chamber, when Jaya herself had been chained to the wall. The least she could do was provide a little reassurance.

'But we will die this day, Lady,' cried Raka, her hands on her head. 'They will be upon us soon and we will die. We have nothing to bargain for our lives with, nothing to offer them.'

'Shhh,' she said again. Raka was terrifying Aal. She was squeezing her mother's hand so fiercely that Jaya thought the bones might break. There was little she could do but leave Raka alone and go back to holding her child and stroking her hair, crooning softly. Aal's eyes were wide open with terror. Too much had happened. Too much had happened to her babe of only seven cycles. She had seen too much already, Jaya thought, with pain in her chest.

And who could blame her for her terror? One of the serving maids had rushed to the Temple with the news that the mob had already been to the Street of the Pipal Trees. Sarema was dead, her stomach had been cut open and a necklace of gold stuffed down her throat. The rioters had left the gold as a message to the people. Some of the others had been hanged outside their own houses. Lal's two children had been killed along with her. Someone had painted a slogan on the wall. *If they had any real powers, they would have known we were coming.* It was shocking.

'Mua,' shouted Aal.

The door to the inner sanctum burst open. The few Temple guards who were left were pushing through, along with some of the Unclanned, who were using sticks and bricks and pieces of flint to fight the guards' daggers and spears. It hardly seemed a fair fight, but there were many more of the rioters than guards, which evened the odds.

The Temple reverberated with the sound of curses and grunts as the men swarmed in, filling the room. Jaya shrank back, horrified, putting Aal behind her and hugging the cold wall. The Unclanned had streaked their tunics. They had used red dye to paint their own new seal on their shirts to identify one another – a crude beast with a horn in the centre of its forehead.

A man fell back, nearly on top of them, his neck spurting blood from where he had been struck, his body jerking. Jaya screamed and pulled her daughter towards the door. She passed the fighting men and was moving Aal forward, when she felt herself being dragged back by her hair. Her eyes watered with pain.

'Oh no, Lady,' grunted one of the Unclanned, a thick-jawed man with bloodlust in his eyes. 'You're the only one left who can read the Bloodstone. When we kill the High One and get it for ourselves, we'll need you.' He was strong, he tossed her onto the floor as though she were nothing. Aal came shrieking towards him, pummelling him with her small fists. The man grabbed her by the throat and lifted her into the air, where her arms and legs thrashed uselessly in protest. He examined her, a sick, twisted grin on his face. 'My own daughter starved to death by the gates only a week ago. She was beautiful. She was worth ten of you.'

It was difficult, but Jaya was back on her feet. 'Please, please, leave my daughter alone. She is an innocent ...'

'None of you are innocent,' the man snapped back. Around them, the others had cornered the few Temple guards, who were dropping their weapons and raising their hands in surrender, along with the maidservants. It was a futile gesture. One by one, they were slaughtered where they stood. A lone serving woman managed to break free. She raced towards the door, but the rioters ran after her, grabbed her from behind and slit her neck.

With horror Jaya realized that Raka had been pulled away from them. She lay on the ground, her body bent, her neck twisted, her eyes open and vacant. There was blood pooling on the ground where her stomach used to be. 'Stop it!' Jaya screamed. 'In the name of the Goddess, stop it!'

The man who had picked up Aal pushed her into the corner. 'Stay there until this is over. Don't worry, we have orders to keep you alive.' He spat. 'If I had my way, you'd be dead along with the rest of the Temple scum.'

Jaya clutched her daughter and they cowered in the corner as more Temple guards broke into the room. The fighting began in earnest again, but the Unclanned were still winning by the sheer force of numbers. Where had they all come from? She had no idea how many Unclanned there were in the city. All this time, she had had no idea ...

She did not try to move again. The man who had pulled them back was standing watch over them – letting the others fight. His left cheek was bleeding, and he had a large angry gash which ran from under his eye all the way to his jawline.

The man was cursing as the blood refused to stop flowing from his cheek. He spat on the ground once more and shot them a look of hatred.

Aal had stopped crying. She let out little sniffles but was otherwise silent, her face buried in her mother's arms.

Jaya looked on, her hand covering her mouth. The priests had taken most of the Temple guards with them. Those who were left had done their duty but they were few compared to the rioters. All the Temple guards were dead or lay dying. The rioters had spared no one, except her and Aal.

But there were many Unclanned bodies too. They had suffered heavy losses when they invaded the Temple. Those who survived were looking around, searching for things to loot. The Unclanned were restless now, unsure of what to do and where to go. They began to argue with one another – whether to leave now and chase after the priests, or wait for reinforcements. Should they dismantle the Temple, brick by brick? Nobody had the patience for that. One of them talked about setting fire to the whole place, another argued that it might be more useful as a base, a place of operations, a way to show the city that they were now in power.

The arguments were heated, the men tired but overexcited. Many were wounded and slouched against the wall. One was on the ground, his body convulsing. Some of the others were trying to staunch the bleeding from a wound in his lung. There was a discussion about whether there were any healers left who could be forced to help the man, and whether it was safe to even try to go and find them.

With the sheer number of bodies in the room, the living, dead and dying, and the smoke from the mustard lamps, Jaya began to feel ill. She let go of Aal long enough to wipe off the sweat that was dripping down into her eyes. Aal said nothing, looking agitated. But then, suddenly she jumped up and launched herself at the door, where more Unclanned had begun to enter the antechamber.

Jaya got up and ran after her daughter, shouting, 'No Aal, no!' The girl had become so frightened that she was trying to flee! The Unclanned men would kill her!

But it was not that. It was not that at all, she realized, as the men parted and bowed, as more men entered the room. For here were the leaders, the decision makers. And here, emerging from the shadows, wearing a headdress depicting a single horn, his chest painted red, standing amongst them all, was Rafe.

Chapter Thirty-Three

MOHENJODARO, PRESENT DAY.

Nadia opened her eyes. She moaned and massaged her temples, trying to sit up.

Where the hell was she? The air was stale and musty, and the room was full of grey shadows. Was she back in the Basement? No ... it was a ... container of sorts. A large wooden shipping crate – tall enough for her to stand in, with holes to let in air. She remembered now. It was the bloody chloroform. It had left her groggy, in some sort of perpetual dreamlike state. They'd drugged her, Sohail and that blonde-haired thug of his, the one she now knew was called Philip. He had smirked when he saw her shocked expression as he had entered the room. Only moments before, Sohail had calmly told her that he would kill her if Layla didn't use the Stone for him.

Philip's smirk had vanished though when she had asked him how his broken nose was. He had been more than happy to drag her out and toss her into Lyari's own version of the Basement, a concrete tunnel under the bunker. He grinned as he turned off the lights, retriggering every childhood panic she had ever had to endure.

How long had she been in there? She didn't really know. Just when she thought she wouldn't be able to take it any more, he had come and gotten her and dragged her into a van, informing her that they were going to Mohenjodaro.

She had tried to reason with him. Did he not understand what would happen if GoL claimed Mohenjodaro for their own? The inevitable showdown with the government would leave many people dead, because Sohail would never back down without a fight. But it wouldn't be him fighting, would it? Layla would be the target of the authorities. They would kill her. Or maybe she would kill them. People would die, GoL members would die. Is that what he wanted?

He seemed to find her anxiety amusing. In the van, he had sat next to her and stroked her arm as he talked to her. He reminded Nadia that she had already caused him a great deal of trouble and made it clear he was enjoying every moment of her discomfort. He talked about all the things he was going to do to her, once Father didn't need her any more. With one touch, he managed to terrorize her completely, though she tried very hard not to show it.

Philip had killed Jay. He was a murderer. Even though her skin had crawled when he caressed her face, she had forced herself to sit upright in her seat. Her stone-faced refusal to talk seemed to annoy him, so much so that only half an hour after waking up, she felt the sweet cloying smell of the rag on her face again, the same thing he had tried to drug her with in London. The world didn't go dark immediately though, not until he'd muttered something about her being a frigid bitch.

Now, she was awake. No – that wasn't quite right, was it? She kept waking up, only to fall asleep again, no matter how hard she tried to stay alert. She knew where she was – she had woken up here earlier, she now remembered that she had been here for some hours. She moved her hand around in the shadows, until she found the small bottle of water that they had left for her. She was trying to ration it, she had no idea how long she would be here and it was so bloody hot.

Nadia licked her cracked lips. She was hungry, and soon she was going to have to pee. How long had they kept her in here?

She sat up quickly when she heard the sharp sound of metal moving. She rubbed her eyes, disoriented.

It was Philip. His silhouette framed the entryway, but she could see the tray of food and the bottle of water in his hands.

'Where's my sister? Where are we?'

Philip stopped for a moment, letting his eyes adjust. 'The Enlightenment is upon us, Nadia. Layla is being prepared. People are arriving here, even now.'

'Here? So we've reached Mohenjodaro?'

'Yes.'

'You don't really believe that he's your messiah, do you? You've seen that he wasn't resurrected. He's been hiding like a rat all these years.' Her hands found the wall, and she stood and moved alongside it, as far away from him as she could get.

Philip shrugged. 'So?'

'So if you let me go, I'll pay you a hell of a lot more than he's paying you. You're a gun for hire, aren't you? Let me outbid him. Let's stop the fight that's about to happen.'

She could tell that she had made him angry. He dropped the tray on the floor and tossed the water at her. 'If you're still alive after this is over, you and I will have that little dance I've been promising you. Now eat up and I'll take you outside so you can piss. We're not animals here, you know.' He looked at her in disgust. 'You're starting to smell and even I have my limits.'

Chapter Thirty-Four

MELUHHA, 3791 BC.

Rafe entered the room slowly, one hand pressed against his stomach, his face pale and gaunt. It was only then that she saw the angry gash across his body. The gash ran all the way down from his stomach to his thigh. Jaya gasped and ran to him, placing her hands near the wound, feeling the swelling around it, the areas where the blood was still oozing. Some of the wound was pink, but parts of it were white, full with infection already. 'When did this happen? We must make a poultice quickly.'

He removed her hands. 'Calm yourself, it is nothing.'

She looked for any expression of welcome or gratitude that she was alive, anything that would tell her that she was forgiven for letting Al-Mien die, but his countenance was unreadable, made worse by the headdress that he wore which obscured his eyes and nose. He'd ignored Aal as well, giving her nothing more than a nod and a distracted pat on the head. She looked crestfallen.

Rafe walked past them to the centre of the antechamber, raising one arm. The men in the room grew silent. It was such a strange thing to see. All this time ... Rafe was one of the leaders of this revolt. She was used to thinking of him as a man who needed saving, a man who the world had abandoned. A boy, really, who the Goddess had tested with misfortune. And now here he was, plotting the downfall of the city. She began to think about the time she had seen him in the alleyway across the Street of Scribes. Had he been the leader of the revolution even back then?

She looked away, troubled. The Unclanned had killed too many innocents. They were demons, just as the High One was. Was Rafe there when the mob strung up Lal and her children? Was he there when all the families who resided on the Street of Dentists had their throats cut open, the children too? She began to tremble. If he was, she did not want to know, she did not want to know him like that.

Jaya sat down next to her daughter. Aal was curled up with her knees to her chest. She listened as Rafe spoke.

'My brothers and sisters, the city is ours, but without the priests, we have nothing. The people will not follow us, and we will be at risk every day of Iaf raising another army. He has fled with the priests and three hundred men. They are trained fighters and can survive much hardship in the desert.

They have much wealth. If they recruit, it could be enough to destroy everything we have fought for.'

'What do we do?' shouted one of the men. 'If we don't kill the High One, he will receive aid from a vassal state and return. This city is ours now. I'll see it burnt to the ground, rather than given back to the priests.' There were grunts of agreement, the odd curse and mutterings.

Rafe nodded, wincing with pain, crossing his arms. 'It is a good question. I propose that we leave sentries to guard the Temple. Let us scour all of Meluhha for our enemies. We will burn everything on the Street of Boat Makers and on the river, so the fat ones cannot escape by water. We'll raid all the houses in the Citadel. If anyone is brave enough to hide Iaf from us, it will be the Tigers. Take their women and children. Line them up in the square. We will kill them if we have to.'

'No!' shouted Jaya. She got up and stepped forward, looking at all the men, the weather-beaten, blood-soaked men with revenge in their eyes. 'You cannot kill all these innocents! You are not the priests. You must stop this madness. How many enemies do you wish for? How many orphans are you creating?'

The man with the wound on his cheek, the one who had been guarding them, spat at her. She felt his anger, the spittle, hit her chin. 'Goddess-Blessed whore.'

She wiped it away. 'Rafe,' she said simply. He had to listen. He just had to.

'Enough,' shouted Rafe, raising his hand again. This time though, he trembled slightly with the effort. The wound was bad. Very bad, she could see it now, it was starting to look lumpy. 'This woman speaks the truth and she is one of us. We cannot murder the whole city. Nor can we contain it by fear. We will not kill women and children, not if we can help it.'

She sighed. It was something, at least.

Rafe hesitated, then seemed to come to a decision. 'The hour grows late, the fighting has been long. We will not find anyone in the dark. We will rest here until sunrise. We will treat the wounded. In the morning, we will pay homage to the One Horned God by joining Nor's people in the market square. Together, we will hunt down the priests. I promise you, we will exact retribution for what they have done.'

There were mutterings and rebellious voices, but the men got busy quickly. Some were sent to the Temple kitchens, to see what food, if any, was left. Others were lying flat on the ground in relief, exhausted by the day. Still others gathered water and coverings. Someone had broken into the wine room and soon there was an atmosphere of boisterousness, as the men got steadily drunk.

Jaya's eyes kept going to the shelves in the corner, praying that nobody would discover the Bloodstone. She kept vigil, ready to leap up and grab it if necessary. But no one glanced in its direction. Eventually, she slumped against the wall, Aal in her arms. She was exhausted. She closed her eyes.

Some time later, she felt Rafe shaking her. He held out a bowl. 'The child must eat.'

It was porridge. She sensed the hard stares of the other men. They were curious, perhaps, about why Rafe treated her with courtesy. It made her uncomfortable, but she took the bowl gratefully and woke Aal. Her daughter protested, but Jaya spooned the food with her fingers directly into Aal's mouth. Aal ate her fill and then fell asleep once again, her head resting on Jaya's knee.

Rafe came to sit with them. He was sweating badly. 'Your wound is festering,' she whispered, not wanting to wake her daughter. 'We must see to it. If we leave here and go to the Street of Healers, we can find what we need.'

Rafe looked away. 'It doesn't matter. I am not long for this world, Jaya.' He had his own bowl of porridge of which he ate small spoonfuls without any real pleasure.

'Rafe ...' she cried out, anguished. 'You must not talk like this. We can heal you ...'

'It does not matter any more.' He turned to her. 'I long to be in the Upworld, to be reunited with my family, don't you understand? But,' he hesitated, 'do you think Shakari will give me leave to enter?'

She said nothing, but he allowed her to take his hand.

'Even if I am damned, I do not regret what has happened these last few days, Jaya. I cannot regret it.'

'I am so sorry,' she burst out, the tears coming hot and fast. 'I am so sorry about Al-Mien. I ... there was nothing I could do, it happened so fast. But if he had not come looking for us ...' she trailed off.

He sighed. 'He would have died in the market square that day, if it had not been for you. I had my brother with me for many glorious days. We were happy, were we not, in the Street of the Pipal Trees?'

She nodded, not trusting herself to speak, overcome.

'Tomorrow you must leave,' said Rafe, wincing as he shifted position. 'I will ensure that there is a boat for you. It will not be safe here, not for a long time. Food will be scarce for many moons. Trade with the vassal cities will stop. You must be protected. Find your family.'

'They are dead,' she told him. 'I saw it in the Bloodstone. Iaf killed them a long time ago.'

He squeezed her hand then. 'I am sorry, Jaya. I am truly sorry. I should have ... I should have let you go all that time ago. Take your child and flee this accursed place while you can.'

For the moment, she contented herself with this, that he only wished the best for her, the two of them, sitting side by side as they used to, soothed by the pleasure of each other's company. The truth was, she would not be long in this world either, she could tell by the pain in her bones, but why trouble him with this? Tomorrow she would find someone, her old friend Anarki perhaps, and beg her to take in Aal and treat her as one of her own. It pained her to think about leaving her daughter. But as long as Aal had a good life, nothing else mattered.

Slowly, all the noise died down. The men were tired. They were falling asleep. Jaya closed her eyes, listening to the sound of Rafe's laboured breathing, feeling as though her heart would shatter under the weight of all the death and destruction.

She did not know when she fell asleep, but she awoke to a commotion. A boy had burst into the antechamber. 'Rafe, come quickly,' he yelled.

Rafe sat up, startled. 'What is it?'

The boy looked fear-stricken. 'The Temple guards ... the priests! They have returned. It was all a ploy, Rafe, it was an evil trick!'

Everyone was up now, up and arming themselves. The room was in chaos. Aal awoke as well. The boy was telling Rafe about the discovery of a tunnel, directly under the Temple. The priests had hidden there with their guards.

'They waited until we were all trapped inside and now they have come out. There are more coming out still, from a large drain by the Purification pool. I counted many hundreds. It was all a ploy to lure us here.'

Rafe looked at her, the shock clearly visible on his face. 'Did you know?'

'I swear I didn't,' she cried. 'I swear it, Rafe.' Aal sat up and put her hand over her mouth.

Rafe frowned. 'Call reinforcements. We have men all over the city. Nor's men are in the market square.'

The boy shook his head. 'But ... we cannot get out to call them. Besides, nobody will get here in time. We thought we had taken the Temple. The others are clearing the warehouses and it is the middle of the night. They have probably gone to sleep. They will not hear us if we shout.'

The silence was deafening then, the men growing anxious.

Rafe picked up a spear and left the antechamber. She got up to follow him but he pushed her back down. 'Stay with Aal.'

They waited, saying nothing.

He returned a few moments later, his expression pinched and white. 'It is Iaf. What Ayan said is true. The High One lured us here. They have fire torches and are threatening to light them. There is no way out, not with so many of them blocking the door. They will burn us alive if we stay.'

The men were truly agitated now, kicking and cursing furiously, pledging to storm out to die in the moonlight, instead of in the

Temple, pledging to take many of the priests down with them.

Rafe ignored them and came directly to her. 'The High One offers us free passage, if we give him but one thing.'

'What?' she asked. There was something strange in the way he was avoiding her eyes.

He exhaled deeply, looking completely and utterly defeated. 'Aal. He wants Aal.'

Chapter Thirty-Five

MOHENJODARO, PRESENT DAY.

Nadia emerged from the container, blinking in the sunlight, squinting until she got used to the glare. All around her, there was the movement of hundreds of people.

They were standing at the far side of the easternmost section of the ruins, right next to a tall pipal tree. Mohenjodaro looked completely different from the site she had come to with Liam only a couple of days earlier – she assumed it had been a couple of days, but she had lost track of time. Men, women and even children raced about with purpose, trampling over ancient bricks. There was stuff everywhere.

She could see that multiple containers had made it to the site, not just the one she had been locked in. Large groups of men were helping to pull them off trucks and lower them into place, and people were turning them into temporary accommodation for their families. The makeshift boundary of ropes and cement bags set up by the government was being replaced by the heavy shipping crates, and anything else that members of GoL could find. Chairs. Stools. Empty cooler boxes and old tyres, an old camper van and a few cars. They were marking out their city and they seemed so damn cheerful about it. Some children were playing games in the dirt with twigs and pieces of stone. Others were climbing trees or racing about, while their parents set up tents and listened to music. She could smell weed, stagnant and heavy in the heat of the day. People greeted each other with hugs and kisses – some had clearly not seen each other in a long time, while others were total strangers, offering each other Light blessings. A woman had her arms raised and was swaying to Bob Dylan with her eyes closed.

'Come on,' muttered Philip. 'There's a makeshift latrine further ahead. You can use that.' He pulled her up the hill, towards the main ruins. She followed reluctantly.

When they had climbed up a bit, she had a broader view of the site. She stopped in shock. There were tens of thousands of people, far more than she had ever thought possible. It was a swarm, with people milling all the way down past the ruins and near the main road. GoL members were setting up camp everywhere, adults directing the movement of supplies, while kids were carrying lilac flags with the GoL symbol – two hands, clasped together, emitting rays of yellow light. There were water coolers and even food stalls – she caught the smell of barbecued meat. Local merchants were wandering amongst the crowd too, selling everything from little candies, to combs and mosquito repellent, looking amazed at their good fortune. GoL members were buying up all their wares.

Members seemed to have travelled from across the globe. A group of Japanese men were paying a fruit-wallah selling fresh mangoes from a wooden platform which hung around his neck, while under the shade of a large tree, a trio of twenty-something women were speaking Italian. There seemed to be many more Pakistanis, some clearly locals from Larkana who had come along to see what all the commotion was about. They were enjoying the spectacle, but looking confused.

'How the hell did these people get here? How did Sohail orchestrate all this? And how come the army let them through?'

Philip laughed. 'Father was right. You really are stupid. Do you really think this happened overnight? This has been years in the planning. Senior members around the world have been secretly readying our people. The logistics were quite challenging, especially since it had to be done quietly. And in Pakistan – it's not been easy, you know, establishing networks, bribing the right authorities. The police, the army. Even the politicians.' He spat on the ground. 'And what has all that bought us? The appearance of spontaneity. The Enlightenment. All it takes is a little showmanship, a little song and dance, and this bunch will believe anything.'

'But you don't believe it, do you? Why are you here?' she pressed. But she knew the answer. This man liked power. He was twisted, and he liked to dominate. Mohenjodaro – the cult – was his perfect playhouse. 'You're going to die here, you know. We're all going to die here if you let this madness continue.'

Philip ignored her. 'Hurry up. You have five minutes. I'm not a damned babysitter, and as you can see, there's plenty to do.'

She used the makeshift latrine – which was really just three pieces of canvas resting against an old wall of the ruin to cordon off space – and tried to ignore Philip, who had followed her inside. There wasn't much here except a few dug-out holes in the ground, and a line of buckets of water and soap. The place was already well used and stank horribly. She grabbed a bucket and the soap, doing her best to wash away the grime on her face, reluctantly pulling away when her captor barked at her to finish up.

Outside again, there were more people. Somebody was passing out leaflets about GoL, which she ignored. 'What now?' she asked.

Philip pushed her forward. 'You're going back into your hole until we need you. Father's orders. He doesn't want anything to happen to you.'

'Try not to look so disappointed,' she muttered. She could see the Stupa in the distance and make out a few figures, overseeing the work below. Was Sohail there? Was Layla?

'Take me to Sohail,' she said.

Philip scowled. 'Shut up and move.'

She turned to look at him, determined to swallow her fear. 'Or what? You can't hurt me, you just admitted it. Now take me to see him, there's something he needs to know.'

But he wanted to hurt her, she could tell that much from his expression. He was torn by his desire to put her in her place, and his need to do what was best for Sohail.

'Come,' he muttered crossly, pulling her towards the Stupa.

There he was. Sohail. She could make him out as they got closer. He was gazing into the distance, standing still despite the hive of activity around him, wearing his classic blue jeans and crisp white kameez. Someone was setting up a wooden stage on the Stupa itself, as well as a sound system. She could see some cops, carrying speakers and carpets, helping out.

What the hell! Why were the police helping GoL? Surely even Sohail didn't have the funds to bribe so many cops.

Sohail sensed her there, because he turned and stared, his expression as calculating as ever. He watched as they climbed towards him, and said nothing until she was right in front of him. 'Well?'

'I have a counterproposal for you,' she said.

He arched an eyebrow. 'I'm not sure you're in any position to barter here, Nadia.'

'Let me use the Stone, instead of Layla. Save her. You love her, you said yourself she was your true heir. I'll keep using it for you until I die, and she'll live, believing in you. It's a win–win situation all around. Let me use the Stone.'

His laugh was one of amazement. 'So you can turn it on me and my people? I don't think so. At least Layla would never do that.'

'I wouldn't either. There are too many innocent people here. Children.'

Now he scowled. 'But you wouldn't kill the authorities when they come for us either. You would simply give them the Stone. Do you think I'm stupid?'

'You don't really want me to answer that, do you?'

'Why are you wasting my time, Nadia? Can't you see that there's enough going on here? Anyway, we don't even know if the Stone will work for you.' He motioned below. 'My people are getting ready for the Enlightenment, I have so much on my plate. You're distracting me from important work.'

'Then let me talk to Layla. Where is she?'

He shook his head. 'You're not going to be able to pull her away from us. Not now.'

She felt the desperation then, and hated herself for it. 'I've come to beg you, once more, to reconsider. I don't know how you managed to get all these people here, with the aid of the police no less. But things are going to get nasty and you know it. Do you really want your followers to die for you?'

He made a show of rolling his eyes. 'You really are so boringly predictable. We've discussed this already and we have nothing more to say. Philip, kindly take her off my hands, as you had previously been instructed to do.'

Philip looked murderous. 'She said ...'

'She says a lot of things. Take her back. It won't be long now. We've alerted the media, they'll all be here soon.'

'Yes, Father.'

This time when he yanked her, he practically pulled her arm from her socket.

'I won't stay quiet,' Nadia shouted. 'I'll tell all these people they're going to die if they stay here.'

Sohail shot her a look of irritation. 'Go ahead. My people are prepared to die for me.' But he clearly had second thoughts because then he said, 'Shut her up, Philip, until we're ready. There's enough to keep us busy here.'

Philip grunted his agreement and practically dragged her all the way back to the container, opened the latch and tossed her in. He slammed the door shut. She breathed heavily. Arsehole. She got up and began to kick and punch at the walls, venting her frustration.

She heard footsteps and then he was back. 'Shut up,' he barked. 'You're scaring people outside.'

She didn't see the glint of the syringe in his hand until he was on her, until she felt the sharp, stabbing pain in her neck and the world began to swim. 'What ... what is that?'

'Relax, Nadia.' He laughed. 'This is way better than the chloroform. Enjoy the ride.'

Chapter Thirty-Six

MELUHHA, 3791 BC.

She would not give up her daughter.

Rafe was whispering into her ear, reminding her that Aal was Iaf's daughter too. The High One would not harm her, he valued her too dearly. In fact, Aal would be safer out there than she was in here, where she would burn with the rest of them. He spoke urgently, trying not to draw any attention.

The men were restless and anxious. They wondered why no decision had been made about storming the guards outside. Surely a few of them would survive, if they ran? Some of them were still drunk and singing bawdy songs, even as they took out their cocks and peed all over the Temple floor. Others were glaring at Rafe and Jaya suspiciously. Some were praying, but to which God, it wasn't clear.

The man with the gaping wound in his stomach had died. Already his face held the shrunken expression of a corpse, his legs were bent in an awkward angle, for the others had moved him to the top of the pile of bodies. Nobody had bothered to close his eyes – they stared at the ceiling with a pained expression.

She looked at Aal. The child was sucking her thumb, something she had not done since she was a babe. She rocked back and forth, lost in her own world. Jaya too had never felt so lost and so helpless. And so very angry. For Rafe to even consider asking her to give up Aal!

She pushed Rafe away with as much force as she could muster. 'You really are a child of the One Horned God for talking thus. You will not have my daughter. I will kill you first,' she hissed.

'Calm down,' he whispered frantically, as a few of the others began to take notice. 'I am trying to be rational, but if the rest of them hear about Iaf's bargain, they will throw her out right away. And they'll kill you, just out of spite.'

She looked at the men. Many of them had begun to pace the room, waiting for orders. They would have cut her throat if it were not for Rafe, she knew that. She represented the Temple, and they would not listen to reason. But outside, the High One waited. It was amazing to think that anyone would trust his promises. He would take Aal and then he would burn the Temple down anyway. They were in danger. Either way, Aal was in danger.

'Jaya,' said Rafe urgently, taking her arm. 'I feel myself weaker. I do this not for myself, but for everyone here. Aal will not be harmed, I promise you.'

She looked at him, painfully aware of the truth of his words. Some of them at least. Rafe would not be long in this world, he wore the same grey pallor as the man in the corner. His breathing was heavy and the trail of sweat going down his face made her heart soften and cry out. She touched his cheek. Rafe. Her Rafe. He would be dead soon.

Well, she would join him shortly after. But to leave Aal with the High One would be to consign her to a fate worse than dying here.

And then she remembered. Iaf still thought he had the Bloodstone in his possession. He had not checked the box. Otherwise, it would be the Bloodstone he would be demanding.

She looked at Rafe and at the others, suddenly hopeful. 'What if there was another way,' she said. 'What if we had more to barter with than our lives?'

'What are you saying?'

'Come with me, I will show you.' She held out her hand and, after some hesitation, he took it.

Chapter Thirty-Seven

MOHENJODARO, PRESENT DAY.

Nadia was dreaming again.

The images were murky. They rippled in and out of focus like something viewed under water, filtered through translucent greyness. A pair of outstretched arms, china hands cupped together in offering. And then a face, half concealed in semi-darkness. A face that was, and wasn't, Jaya's.

'You were supposed to save us,' said the face. It had Jaya's heavy features, somehow transposed onto a porcelain doll whose visage was cracked and decaying. It was Jaya without any eyes, with bloodless lips moving in a vacuum without colour.

'Jaya,' she replied, her own voice heavy with grief. 'I'm so sorry.'

'Too late now,' hissed the voice. 'You're too late.' The face dissolved and the cupped hands were full of liquid which overflowed and turned everything the colour of rubies.

'Nadia!'

She felt her body move. Strong arms, shaking her.

'Nadia. For God's sake, wake up.'

She turned on her side. What did they want from her now? A second later, she felt her stomach heave and she vomited.

'Jesus Christ. Are you all right there?'

When she opened her eyes, it was painful, even in the darkness. The lids felt heavy.

'Come on, drink some water, darling. That's right. Sip slowly. You'll feel better. We have to flush your system. God knows what they've done to you.'

She touched her neck and winced, and then looked up. Liam's face swam in and out of focus. She sighed with relief. 'I was wondering when you would make it.'

He looked relieved himself and a little worse for wear. There were yellow bruises on his cheek and he had a large scrape under his chin. His knuckles were bloody.

He saw her looking and smiled ruefully, raising his fists. 'Those coppers had a bit of fun with me when they picked us up.'

'Are you ... okay?' Her voice was hoarse.

He nodded. 'They thought they could intimidate me just enough that I would leg it back to Ireland and leave you to your fate. But then they realized I was one of the archaeologists on the dig and panicked, and let me go.'

'It's good to see you,' she said.

'No, don't sit up so quickly. I don't know what they gave you ...'

Her head spun. 'Syringe ... He injected something ...'

'Maybe a strong sedative. Whoa.' He moved out of the way as she threw up again, and then reached over, raised her head and gave her more water. 'We've got to get you out of here, quickly'

Nadia drank gratefully. 'Have you seen what's happening outside? There are GoL members everywhere. And somehow, the police and the army aren't stopping them.' Her whole body felt thick and immobile.

'Yeah, I saw. Sohail told the army that he wanted to have a festival of light on the ruins for his followers. The place has been used for events before, which is sacrilegious, to be honest with you. But he paid enough of them off that they didn't care if he destroyed the place. He paid government officials off too, and promised to set up some sort of conservation fund after. He's loaded, your father.'

'But the excavation site ...'

'They razed the site to the ground. All evidence gone. They were getting ready to open this place up to the public again anyway. Too many conspiracy theories buzzing about – they wanted to show that it was the Taliban who had kidnapped the team, and what better way than letting people see that there is nothing here to gawk at? So in a way, the timing was good for them. I don't think they're really bothered by the fact that your dad is a cult leader. He's been living among them for years and never caused any trouble. Did you see how many people are here? Many of his most devoted followers have been travelling over the last week to be here.'

'How did they know he was alive?'

Liam shook his head. 'They didn't, until the day before yesterday, when he announced his "resurrection" to the world, ironically, via a YouTube video. But his most loyal followers were told that there would be a big gathering in Pakistan this week, and that if they truly believed, they should start to make their way here. He's been planning this for a long time, and now of course, they think their Enlightenment is about to happen.'

Her head was really throbbing and she struggled not to vomit again. Her father and that bastard Philip. They'd kept her drugged for God knows how long. 'How ... how do you know all this?'

He winked. 'I got a little friendly with the janitor at the police station. He had all the gossip. People never watch what they say in front of the cleaners.'

'Well, your janitor friend doesn't have the whole story. Sohail is planning to stay here. To rebuild the city for his people. If they try and stop him, he's going to use the Bloodstone and kill everyone.'

He raked a hand through his hair. 'Christ, I knew it had to be something ...'

'The authorities must know by now that Layla is Sohail's daughter. And she was the last person to hold the Stone. Yet he's here, unencumbered.'

He shrugged. 'The GoL is considered to be full of benign loonies around here. I don't think anyone is taking them seriously at the moment. I think they really believe they are here for a festival. That will change soon enough.'

When she tried to stand up, she clutched the wall. 'My body feels like it's made of lead.'

'Just keeping sipping on the water.'

'How did you get here?'

Liam grinned and bowed, bringing his hands together and then to his chest. 'The blessings of the Light upon you, friend.'

'You posed as one of them?'

'Easy enough to do, with the swarms coming in. I slipped in with an English family that had sold their car to purchase plane tickets to Pakistan. Amazing, what these people will do for your father. Even now, everyone knows that their leader has been resurrected, but nobody gets what's really happening. They know that the Enlightenment is upon them, but they don't really understand what that means. They think they will be transported to the Light, the poor delusional saps.'

'They don't know about the Stone?'

'No. Nor about your family and their dreams. That he's kept to himself. They don't even know why this place is special, but it's where "Father" has called them to gather. The GoL are pretty organized, I'll give them that. Apparently, they had buses lined up at the airport for all the foreign "pilgrims" who were arriving. This has been orchestrated over a very long time.'

She sipped some more water. 'How did you find me?'

'I spotted that bastard – blondie from London. I followed him around for a bit. I saw him unlock this door and come in. When he left, he locked it again, so I figured there was a good chance you were inside. I couldn't get in though. Too many people hovering around. It was an hour before the coast was clear, but I couldn't get the lock open. I had to use a rock to smash the hinge on the door.' He winced. 'It was a bit of a bugger, actually.'

Nadia's legs still felt like jelly. She began to walk with his help, but had to stop and rest after every few steps. 'How are we going to get out of here? '

'Just give it a few more minutes. Try and keep walking, build up the circulation. Look,' he said, 'I'll help you get somewhere safe, somewhere where you can hide nearby. I'll come back and find Layla. I've got the jeep hidden just off the main road. It's about a mile away. Between us, Layla and I can support you over that distance. Do you know where they're keeping her?'

She was about to tell him that Layla was here voluntarily, when she heard a scraping noise. They both froze.

Philip stood in the entryway, a look of surprise on his face. But he recovered within seconds and launched himself on Liam. With unexpected agility, Liam sidestepped and punched the other man twice in his torso in rapid succession. The *whoosh* of his breath made it clear that he was winded. Philip took a step back warily, circling Liam. 'I'm glad we get a do-over,' he panted, with a look of hatred on his face. 'This time, I'm going to kill you.'

Liam said nothing, his eyes following the other man, waiting for his move. It came swiftly. Philip lurched forward and landed several blows on Liam's face and ribcage. He was heavier and used his weight to propel him forward, pushing Liam into the wall of the container, grabbing his head and slamming it into the wall.

'Fuck you,' Liam grunted, as the other man grabbed him by the neck. He tried to push Philip away, but was having little success. He lifted his knee and hit Philip in the groin instead.

Philip doubled over. Liam grabbed him by the back of his head and kneed him in the stomach. He groaned and fell forward, but recovered quickly and managed to grab Liam from behind as he tried to get past. Within seconds, he had Liam in a chokehold. Liam was struggling, turning blue, his hands clawing Philip's arms, gasping for breath.

'No!' screamed Nadia, rushing forward.

She looked frantically for a weapon, something she could use to pull Philip off. He was straining now, trying his best to strangle Liam from behind, to stop him thrashing around.

It was then that she saw it. Philip had brought another syringe with him. The fight had dislodged it. It had fallen on to the ground, right next to their feet. Both men were cursing now. She ran towards it, praying that she would be fast enough. Philip grabbed at her the moment she reached them, but lost his grip on Liam, who turned and began to pummel him hard so that he lurched backwards.

In that moment, Nadia struck. She picked up the syringe and in the same movement, plunged it into Philip's neck. She watched the stunned expression on his face as he stopped, pawing at the needle. And then Philip's eyes glazed over and he collapsed, face down, onto the ground.

Liam spat out blood. 'Sweet dreams,' he muttered.

Then he looked at her and smiled. 'Well, looks like your legs are working again. What do you say we go get your sister?'

Chapter Thirty-Eight

MELUHHA, 3791 BC.

Jaya pulled the Bloodstone out from its hiding place, careful to leave it covered in the grey cloth she had wrapped it in.

'If I touch it, it will most likely take me into a vision,' she warned Rafe. 'I am not strong enough to read it. It will probably kill me this time.'

Rafe took it from her, but even its meagre weight seemed like such a burden to him. He would not let Jaya make him a poultice, but she had covered his wound with strips of cotton dipped in camphor. They were yellow and stained already, and beginning to smell.

'Give it to the priests and let us be done with them,' said Jaya, gently wrapping his hands around the Stone. 'Let us be done with them, Rafe, and live out what moments we have left together. The High One values this more than anything. He will let us go – let us all go – in exchange for this jewel.'

Rafe hesitated.

'What is it?' she asked. She did not want whatever time they had left to be full of regret.

He looked so sad when he gazed at her, so sad and so tender. 'What guarantee do we have that the High One will keep his promise and let us go once we give him this?'

'I ...' She hesitated. There was no guarantee and knowing the High One as she did, it was right to doubt his word. But surely the Bloodstone ... surely he would not break his word about the Bloodstone? He would risk being cursed by the Goddess if he did.

With some difficulty, Rafe took the Stone to the podium, ignoring the curious looks of the others. What was he doing? Then he held out his hand to Jaya. 'I wish it were not so, but you must stay strong and you must read it. It is the only way. Tell us if the High One means to double-cross us. Tell us if there is another way to escape. You and I will soon be reunited in the Upworld, Jaya. But Aal must live.'

She swallowed. The Temple was silent, its occupants shocked. The Bloodstone was here, with them. Every man had heard Rafe's words and yet none spoke. They watched though, with hooded eyes and exhaustion, and perhaps with a kindling of hope. It was Aal who made the noise, Aal whose sobs could be heard in the night sky.

As much as it pained her, Jaya knew that Rafe was right.

Jaya stepped up to the podium, her fingers caressing the cloth around the Stone. If she touched it, if she called upon its power, it would be for the last time. She would not have the strength to continue. She knew this, she knew this in some deep part of her that the Bloodstone had ignited, all those cycles ago. Shakari was calling her home. And yet, and yet ...

She looked at her daughter and then at Rafe, who was leaning against the wall now, wheezing. Aal shook her head, her body heaving with the anguish. 'Please, Mua, stay away from it. It will hurt you. I can tell.'

'Aal, this is for the best. You must be strong. This is for the best. Remember how much I love you.' Her hands trembled.

If there was even a chance that Aal could escape from here, to live a life away from Iaf, she had to try and find it. Otherwise, everything was lost. She took a deep breath, and unwrapped the Bloodstone, trying her best to ignore her daughter's crying.

'No, Mua!' shouted Aal.

But Jaya was somewhere else now, the Bloodstone entering her core, searching, pulling, taking every bit of what was left, before revealing its secrets.

Chapter Thirty-Nine

MOHENJODARO, PRESENT DAY.

Nadia kept her head down, hoping she wouldn't be recognized. Luckily, her father's followers were too distracted to pay them much attention. Sohail had appeared on the Stupa with his hands raised in the air. His stage was finally ready. There was even a large screen behind him, filming him for those who were too far away to make out his features. Many of his followers had never even seen Father in the flesh before. There was music pumping – rhythmic drums that sounded primeval – which dulled as his mass of followers encircled the main ruins. Sohail was wearing a headset with a mic attached, and he had changed into black jeans and an orange kameez. His beard looked freshly oiled, too, or maybe just slick with sweat.

Nadia stopped and stared. She had never seen her father wear anything but white before. The colour grabbed at her. Something ...

'My people,' Sohail began, 'it is good to see you again. May the blessings of the Light be upon you.'

'And upon you,' they replied, bringing their hands to their chests and clapping once.

Nadia blinked. She had seen all this before, and recently. Why was this so familiar?

Sohail's eyes shone with love as he gazed down at his followers. 'As you can see, I walk amongst you all once more. I have returned to this realm because the Enlightenment is upon us. Children, it is time to take our place in the world.' He spread his arms wide. 'This ruin we now walk upon was once a great city. It was the home of the Light Bearers. The Ancients have tried, for centuries, to keep us away from here, because they know what power lies underneath. But now I reclaim this land for a new City of Light. For *our* city, Meluhha. We will live here and we will prosper, developing skills and powers that most humans can't even begin to imagine. Welcome to your new home.'

There were excited mutterings after this, and some confusion, as GoL members tried to process what he was saying.

He raised one arm and waited for the chatter to die down. 'I'm certain you will have questions and I will answer them all before this day is done. Know this. I have reclaimed the power of the Light, despite the obstacles set against us. We are now the most advanced humans on this earth. As time progresses, I will teach you how to harness your power, to heal yourselves, to read others' minds. To become invisible. To build great things and dream up new philosophies. If the Pakistani government and its cronies leave us in peace, then we will exist within the demarcated territory we have established here today. If they try to stop us, to prevent us rebuilding our City of Light, then I will unleash my wrath upon them and they will see how powerless they truly are. Because we are the guardians of the Light.'

Widespread applause and wolf whistles followed this remark, with GoL members hugging each other and grinning.

'Do they even have a clue what the feck he's on about?' Liam whispered.

She shook her head. 'I doubt it. But I don't think it matters.' She wiped the sweat off her forehead with her shirtsleeve and looked around. 'We have to get to the Bloodstone. Wherever it is, that's where Layla will be. We have to take it from her.'

Liam clenched his jaw. 'That's not the only problem we have. Look.' He pointed to the west.

She could see two figures in khaki pushing their way through the crowd. The army was here. Two men with an air of authority, but also with youthful countenances – which made her think they were of middling rank – made their way up to the Stupa. Nobody stopped them. Sohail watched with narrowed eyes as they approached. He spoke with them for several minutes, his hand over his mic, the army men talking urgently, their expressions shielded by the aviator sunglasses they wore. Were these the guys that had put their necks on the line by letting Sohail have his 'festival' here? Clearly, they had just realized they had been duped and were about to get into big trouble with their superiors.

She watched them stride off the stage, their anger visible.

Sohail addressed the crowds once more. 'My children. It has begun already. Those two men are members of the Pakistani army, come to disperse us. No, let them pass. I have respectfully explained to them that we are not going anywhere.'

More whistling and clapping, though a little muted this time. GoL members seemed confused about what it was that was happening. More disciples were arriving every few minutes, which was adding to the confusion.

Sohail must have sensed this, because he cleared his throat. 'Now is not the time for anger, my children. We will spend the next few hours in guided meditation. Then we will celebrate our homecoming. We will feast and we will dance and we will rejoice in this moment. The rest can wait.' He clapped his hands on to his chest and his followers did the same.

It came to her then. The orange and the black, the ritualistic clapping. 'He's doing what the priests of Meluhha used to do,' she told Liam. 'He's wearing their clothes and invoking their rituals. Why?'

'Who cares,' Liam said, grabbing her hand. 'Let's go follow the army guys. See how many of them there are.'

'Why?'

'So we can work out what they intend to do next.'

'We need to find Layla, Liam. That's the most important thing.'

He stopped suddenly. 'Nadia, Layla isn't here.'

'She isn't?'

'No. Sohail would never jeopardize his own life, would he? The Bloodstone kills people who are within half a mile's radius or so. People further than that are spared.'

'How can we possibly know that ...'

'Because otherwise Layla would have killed Mushtaq and everybody else in the nearby villages when she first picked up the Stone. And the people of Larkana, and the men selling souvenirs by the entrance of the ruins – that's just over half a mile away from where the Stone was found, and her reach was not that far. There's a kill zone to this thing and it can't be more than half a mile.'

'Unless that was a fluke, her first time holding it ...'

'The forty-four bodies that were found ... they were all within a half-mile concentric radius. There were no bodies found beyond that. Nobody else was killed by it when it was unleashed the last time. We've excavated enough to learn that.'

'This is a huge assumption ...'

'Maybe, but your father is operating under the same assumption that I am. The Bloodstone will be somewhere near the entrance to the ruins, away from Sohail and his followers, but close enough to the main road to kill anyone who tries to come here from Larkana.'

It made sense, she realized, as she wiped away more sweat. Christ, it was hot. But it was a big gamble on Sohail's part to assume he would be safe from the Stone if he stood just over half a mile away from Layla. Perhaps he intended to move even further away if there was a showdown. Knowing what a coward he really was, he probably had a jeep waiting to take him to safety.

They made their way back through the ruins, past the large, oversized replica of the Priest King that stood sentry at the edge of the old city, and back to modern civilization – the main street with its souvenir shops and restaurants, and the Mohenjodaro museum. The whole place was full of GoL members.

'Even if you're right,' said Nadia, gesturing, 'all these people will be within the kill zone. They'll all die.'

'Your father doesn't care about that,' Liam replied, his teeth clenched into a smile as he put his hands together and bowed – a devotee had come and put a garland of orange and black around his neck.

'The blessings of the Light upon you, my friend,' he said, watching the other man disappear into the crowd. He took off the garland. 'Here. Put it on. We have to blend in.'

She shot him a look. 'Are you saying you're blending in better than I am?'

'Well, to be honest with you, you look like you've emerged from inside an elephant's arsehole.'

She couldn't help but laugh as she put on the garland. 'All right then, let's find Layla.'

The place was so densely packed that it took them about fifteen minutes to walk the length of the main road.

Liam pointed. 'Look, the colonels are there.'

He was talking about the two army men, who were lounging by the entrance to the site – an imposing brick gateway with mock Meluhhan script that was meant to look like English lettering spelling out the word *Mohenjodaro*. It was the gateway, the turning from the main Larkana road into the ancient civilization.

She stopped. 'Why are they just standing there?'

'I reckon they're waiting.'

'Waiting? Waiting for what?'

He shrugged. 'Orders, perhaps? Let's look around.'

They walked some more in the sweltering heat. 'Layla will be somewhere in the shade,' Nadia said suddenly. 'If she's keeping an eye on the road, she'll have found a shady spot. She burns easily, the sun gives her headaches.'

He scanned the crowds and nodded. 'There's a pipal tree just right of the large Dancing Girl statue by the gardens, near the museum. Layla sometimes went there when she wanted to escape from the dig and be alone. She would be able to see the main road from there.'

'Show me,' said Nadia.

They were only moments away from the museum and the statue of the Dancing Girl to the right of it, so they turned around and walked slowly, careful to remain as hidden as possible. It was tough. There were crowds of people to navigate, and they had to keep their heads down. They smiled at bowing strangers several times, and Nadia's heart constricted when she watched a father carrying his little daughter on his shoulders. The little girl was beaming at the world, excited. There were so many innocent people here ...

Liam put his arm out, stopping her from stepping forward, and whispered, 'Look.'

There she was, shielded from view by the Dancing Girl herself. You had to walk by and around to really notice Layla. If they got any closer, she would see them approach. She was sitting under the tree, absent-mindedly caressing an ancient copper box.

Nadia swallowed. She knew what was in that box. 'We have to move.'

'Careful now,' said Liam. 'We don't want to spook her. Walk slowly.'

But then they were distracted by the roar of engines. Nadia stepped back to get a better view. The army had arrived. Not just two colonels, but trucks full of soldiers who pulled up at the entrance, jumped out and began ordering people to disperse. Some GoL members were pushing them back and telling them to get off their land. Others were simply ignoring them and carrying on.

Layla stirred.

'She's heard them,' said Nadia urgently. 'She's going to try to stop them now.'

'Come on,' Liam said. He took her hand.

She let him guide them, her heart thudding. They crossed the garden and walked past the statue, until they stood in front of her. 'Layla,' she said gently.

It was a mistake, she knew it the moment she stepped forward. A man came towards her, smiling. He was tall and young, black-haired, wearing jeans and an orange kameez. He held a gun in his hand. 'He said there was a good chance that you would come,' said the man, still smiling. 'Shall we step away?

Layla was staring at her. 'Nadia? What are you doing here?'

'Stay focused, sister,' said the man, turning towards Layla. Then he jerked his head. 'You two, come with me.'

Liam stepped forward. 'Go ahead and shoot, you gobshiite. How long do you think before those soldiers over there see what's happening? They'll be here before my body hits the ground and then they'll get the Stone.'

The man paused, calculating. Then he smiled. 'Layla, open the box now. It's time.'

'No,' said Nadia, walking forward, extending her arms slowly. 'Layla, I know you don't want to do this. Give me the box. Please Layla. Give it to me.' Layla hesitated and Nadia could see her grip the copper box more tightly. From here the beautiful etchings of a goddess's fury were visible.

It was strange, but she wanted to touch the box. She wanted to see the Stone for herself, to feel it in her hands. It was like a compulsion ... she felt sick. Was this how Layla had felt when she had lifted the Stone out of its box the first time? Was it some sort of addiction? But Layla caught her gaze and held the box away sharply.

'Why do you want it, Nadia? It's mine. It was meant for me.' A passing GoL member gave them a curious look.

But now there were more noises from the entrance. One of the colonels was on the roof of a jeep, speaking through a loudspeaker, telling GoL members that they were breaking the law and that they would be arrested if they didn't leave the area immediately.

The man put his arm on Layla's shoulder and gave her a reassuring smile. 'Layla, you know what you must do. Focus your energy on those who are on the road and on those who try to prohibit our goals. They must die, you know this. It is the only way that the Ancients will fear Father. It is the only way to prevent them killing more innocents. We have to take away their power for good. You understand, don't you?'

And then he sidled up to Nadia. His right hand curled into her side, pressing his gun close into her flesh. He was smiling, to make sure she understood. If Layla didn't do as instructed, Nadia would die.

Layla didn't even need to see the gun. 'Yes,' she said, nodding, looking so eager to please. 'It is the only way. I'm going to open the box now, Nadia. Then the Ancients won't have any power left.'

Liam stepped forward. 'Layla. We worked hard to find you. I know ... I know this isn't what you want. Layla, you'll kill everyone here, including your sister. This isn't you.'

She seemed surprised to see him. 'Liam?' Her hand trembled over the box.

'Enough of this,' said the man. 'Use the Stone or I'll kill your sister.'

'I'll die anyway,' Nadia snapped, not taking her eyes of Layla. 'Listen to me. Father was going to use me as a bargaining chip, to make you do what he wanted. He was going to keep me near him and threaten to kill me if you didn't do as he asked, because he knows you're not a killer, Layla. He told me so himself. But now I'm here, and if you use the Stone, I'll die. Liam and I will both die, and so will thousands of others.'

Layla looked anguished. 'If I don't ... if I don't then millions will die, Nadia. This power, it's not for the Ancients. They'll destroy us all if they get their hands on it.'

She watched Layla's fingers play with the box. She watched her press and heard the click. She saw the throbbing, pulsing thing inside. Layla looked up. 'I ... I don't know wha ...'

And in that moment, Nadia threw herself on her sister, even as she heard the gun go off, and saw Liam moving from the corner of her eye.

But it was too late. Already, the Stone was doing something, she could feel heat along her shoulders, her skin was hot and clammy. She reached out, reached out, and grabbed the Stone from her sister's fingers. She felt it touch her skin, felt it caress the edge of her fingertips. It was enough. Enough for her to see.

Jaya had the Stone in her hand. She felt her own life ebb away even as she focused her mind. *Will Iaf keep his promise? How can I save Aal from him?* The Stone was showing her something ... something was happening. Iaf had found out that she had tricked him, that she had taken the Stone out of its box. And he was furious. Let them all die, he was saying. Let his daughter die as well, if it was necessary. At least, the Stone would still be there in the morning, immersed in the ashes of the Temple. He would start again. He would take back the city and start again.

Layla cried out, shocked now. She launched herself on her sister and they wrestled, each one refusing to let go of the Stone. But Nadia held fast. Somewhere in the background, she heard the anguished screaming of thousands of people. She didn't have much time.

Jaya felt herself fall, she felt the Bloodstone roll out of her palm, and she heard her daughter screaming. Listlessly, she tried to pick it up again. But her body wouldn't move. She sighed. It was over. 'He has already lit the torches. It is too late for us,' she whispered.

She barely had the strength to watch the men race out of the antechamber, ready to fight their last battle, calling for Iaf's head, promising to take down a hundred priests for each one of them. Only she and Rafe remained, along with the dead bodies, along with those who were dying. They listened to the shouts, the sound of metal scraping against metal, of good men crying in pain. With great difficultly Rafe came and lay down next to her. He clutched her hand. 'I am sorry,' he said, his eyes full of pain and regret. 'Forgive me, Jaya.' And then, with barely a shudder, he was gone.

Layla would not let go. 'You lied, Nadia! Father was right. You're an Ancient. You're trying to destroy the Light!' They tumbled together onto the ground, oblivious to the screams of those around them.

'Aal,' whispered Jaya. The child was scared and sobbing, holding her hands over her ears. Jaya lifted her own hand and shakily caressed her daughter's cheek. It was getting harder to draw breath. 'Go. Go now. It is not too late. Iaf will not harm you. Give him the Bloodstone, it will make him happy. And one day, one day when you are old enough, be brave. Be braver than I was and run away from here. Promise me. Leave now, Aal, and do not look back.'

She stopped, she stopped just for a moment. 'Layla, this is not who you are,' panted Nadia. 'You are not a killer! Listen to me. You are my sister. I love you. Please, listen to me. Let go, Layla, let go.'

But Aal would not leave. Instead, she banged her head against the wall and screamed. Jaya could not bear to watch. The child seemed to have gone mad. Oh, what horror was this for a mother to see!

'Aal, please,' she cried out. 'Be calm. Leave before the fire burns you.' Eventually, the screams subsided and Aal drew deep, shuddering breaths. Then she picked up the Bloodstone.

'Thank the Goddess. Take it now, Aal. Wrap it in the cloth and take it to Iaf. Do not linger, they have already started the fire and you will be trapped in here. Run.'

But Aal ignored her mother. She remained where she was. She wrapped her small hands around the Stone and scrunched her eyes tight. 'Show me how to kill them,' she whispered. 'Show me how to use the Stone to make them burn, the way they want to burn us.'

'Aal, no!' said Jaya, struggling to sit up. But it was too late. It was too late, because her little girl had her eyes open now, and she was smiling as though she had discovered all the secrets of the Universe. And then she lifted her arms.

For a minute, she had the Bloodstone solely in her hands. For a minute, her sister had been too weak to hold on. And she did the only thing she could think of. She threw it as far away as possible. When Layla ran after it, she smashed an elbow into her sister's face.

They were burning, their flesh was melting off their bones. Aal could see them. She watched Iaf scream in shock and in pain, she watched the way he stamped his feet. She smiled. As though that would help him. She had all the power now. The Stone had shown her how to use it. The High One had taken her away from Mua. And then he had hurt her. Did he think she could not see how he hurt her mother? Mua was dying because of him. He had killed Al-Mien. He had killed Rafe. He had killed Nene. Everybody she loved was dead. Her fury drove the Stone, it drove the fires, and she could see in her mind's eye the men fall outside the Temple. She could see that brute of a guard, Bas, crying out in pain as he dropped on his knees. So many tried to flee, so many ran down the streets, but she followed them, walking out of the Temple, followed them and watched them all die, even those who came out of their houses, watched them falling where they stood or as they ran down the road. Good. Good. Let them embrace the Goddess in the Upworld. All those who had brought her so much pain. The priests had hurt her mother and they had killed Nene's child. They had locked her in the Temple and taken her away from Mua. The Unclanned were no better. They had killed Raka. They had killed Benha, Lal's daughter, her best friend. And Rafe, even Rafe, had wanted to send her back to the priests to protect himself. So let them all perish. She stepped further into the street. Let them all perish.

And then she heard Jaya's voice in her head.

Aal. It is enough. Please. It is enough.

She stopped and blinked. She knew, in that moment, that her mua was dead. She turned back. The Temple was burning, the flames had already reached the second level. No. No. Oh Goddess, no. Her mother was gone. She sank down on her knees and began to howl.

Layla fell to the ground and moaned. Nadia ignored her and ran to the Stone. But there was someone else here. She blinked, stunned, staring at the shoes, the body that blocked her way. She looked up. So he had seen them after all and he had followed them. Of course, she should have expected it.

'Not this time,' he said, a gun in his hands. 'You're too late, this time.' The Stone lay at his feet. He bent down to pick it up.

'Wait,' she whispered hoarsely. She was only just beginning to understand. The orange-and-black clothes, the ritualistic clapping, the hatred of his own mother – a hatred which he developed after Jahanara told him about her dreams about the girl with the chipped tooth and black braided hair ... She should have connected the dots a long time ago. 'Wait. The Stone is radioactive. It can harm you if you use it, you know that.'

He paused, straightening himself. 'I have no choice any more. Thanks to you. Get up, Nadia.'

'You've dreamt of him since you were a child, haven't you? It's not just Jahanara's dreams that you heard stories of. *You* dreamt of *him.* You don't have to do this, you know.' She stood up warily.

His expression was sharp, curious. 'What do you know about the dreams?'

'I have them too.'

'Jahanara told you about them, obviously. I would have known if you had dreamt of ... her.'

'Jaya. Her name is Jaya. I kept the dreams from you. I suppose I always knew that you would try and take Jaya away from me, if you knew.'

He looked furious. 'Jaya.' He spat on the ground. 'Jaya again. Well, I suppose this explains your wilful disobedience and your refusal to understand. Jaya has corrupted your mind, as she did my mother's. Perhaps that is why Layla is so pure. Jaya left her alone.'

There were shouts from the street. Soldiers had fallen out of the trucks, clutching themselves and moaning. GoL members were on the ground too, stunned, looking confused and terrified. The soldiers didn't understand what was happening, where the threat was coming from or why the burning had stopped. They burst into the museum, looking around, barking orders. She did not dare turn around to check if Layla and Liam were okay.

She focused on her father. It stood to reason, she supposed, because Aal would have lived. She would have to have lived, because she would have had to have children. That was the only way that the dreams ... the memories could be passed down from Jaya. And if they were passed down from Jaya, they could just as easily have been passed down from Iaf as well. Perhaps it was the Bloodstone that made it all possible, that affected their genetic code in such a way as to retain the memories of others.

'You dream of the High One,' she said quietly. 'You dream of Iaf. What a horrible thing it must have been, to have him in your head all this time. No wonder you went insane.'

'You want to talk of madness?' said Sohail, waving his gun in her face. 'Jaya was a whore who single-handedly brought down an entire nation. She destroyed everything in her path and turned the High One's own daughter against him! Imagine what humiliation he had to live through. He offered her the world and she threw it in his face. The Bloodstone was his, not hers.'

'No,' she said, shaking her head, aware now, of the shouts coming in their direction. Some soldiers had seen the gun, they were yelling at Sohail to put it on the ground, but he was ignoring them. 'You're wrong. Iaf took what didn't belong to him. The Bloodstone was meant to be used for the good of the city, not for a priest's whims. He wanted power and he took it, and now you're doing the same. And nothing will have changed. Thousands of years later, and nothing has changed.'

Her father pointed the gun at her head. 'I should kill you now. I should watch you die, before I burn these bastards.'

'Go ahead.' She shrugged, as though it was of little concern. Better a bullet now, than being burnt alive later.

'No,' he said suddenly, shaking his head. 'You should burn too. I want to watch you suffer.' He put down the gun and picked up the Stone at the same time.

She felt the pain in her body, she doubled up with the shock of it. The fire ... she could feel it already. She was burning from the inside!

'It's over, Nadia. It's over,' he said, the pleasure evident in his voice.

There was yelling and a curse. From behind her, someone barrelled into her father. It was Liam. But then Liam started to pant and stumble. Something was wrong with him. He was injured, she could see the burn marks on his skin.

She crawled on the ground. GoL followers were yelling again, panic-stricken and in pain, and nearby several soldiers were rolling in the earth. Parts of them were on fire.

She saw the gun, the gun her father had left on the ground.

She took the gun with shaking hands. She pointed it at her father. 'Stop it,' she screamed. 'Stop it now.' But he was lost in the Stone, lost in the pleasure of what he was doing, his eyes crazed, a strange smile on his face. 'All this time,' he said. 'All this time it was waiting for me.'

She closed her eyes and squeezed the trigger.

Chapter Forty

MELUHHA, 3791 BC.

She buried Rafe two days later. It took that long for the Unclanned to remove the rocks and debris from the burnt ashes of the Temple. They laboured through the night, watching her with pained and wary expressions as they unearthed bodies for her inspection. Perhaps they thought she would kill them next. Well ... she might. She just might, if they tried to cross her. See if she didn't.

She sat up with them, that first evening, her body slowly blackening with the soot, her clothes heavy with smoke. She felt the smoke filling her lungs, drying her throat, but she did not leave. Neither did she sleep nor eat. She cradled the Bloodstone distractedly, waiting. The evening was still but for the deep grunts of the men, and the sound of rock being scraped and pulled. Everything hung on a knife's edge. Everyone waited.

When they pulled him out, it was nearly dawn and she knew immediately that it was Rafe they handled so roughly with their thick hands. There were fragments of his tunic still attached at his shoulders, and some of the bandage her mother had wrapped around his stomach was still sticking to his ribcage, fluttering like a ribbon in the slow breeze. Unravelling. Rafe's skeleton, charcoal black now, seemed to be smiling to itself, the jaw partially open, slightly twisted to the left. An inner joke. A laugh at everyone else's expense, so unlike his true self, so unlike the furrowed brows and tense expression he usually wore as he stared at her and Al-Mien suspiciously, wondering what mischief they were getting up to.

It must have been the pain which contorted his jaw like this. She touched his skull when they brought it to her, her fingers trembling. Pain and sadness. Aal swallowed and looked away. She was glad Al-Mien was in the Upworld, taking care of his brother. Al-Mien would be making barley broth or chicken stew with apricot, stirring the heavens with his delicious morsels. And Rafe would enjoy them, she supposed. Perhaps, for the first time, he would be smiling. Not just a skeleton smile, but a real one. Perhaps Mua was with him, enjoying the stew as well.

She wiped away a tear. The heaviness in her heart was unbearable. She wished she had died with them. She wished that the Bloodstone had not shown her that there was no Upworld and no real Goddess. She wished it had not shown her the truth.

It took another day to find her mother's body and by then Aal could barely stand. She was reeling with shock and fatigue and hunger. Nobody offered her anything to eat. She supposed she could have asked them to bring her food – they would have done as she bid – but the truth was that she felt ashamed. Many of the men clearing the debris had lost loved ones in the ... incident. They only toiled at the remains of the Temple to appease her. Some of them had begun to whisper that she was a reincarnation of Goddess Shakari herself. They had initially feared her, but now many reacted by revering her instead. It was easier, she supposed, to worship her than question why someone so small could gain so much dominance over them.

It was inevitable that she would close her eyes, inevitable that she would need to sleep. And inevitable that one of them would try to take the Bloodstone from her and would burn for it. She gathered them then, in the square. She knew it was a strange sight, a little girl, standing above an entire city. But she was not a little girl any more. Every moment with the Bloodstone aged her. Every moment it gave her knowledge beyond her years. She had learnt more in her few days with the Stone than many of them would understand in their lifetimes.

She looked at the people in the square. They were Unclanned and Clanned alike, the odd priest, uncomfortable in the crowd, wondering when his throat would be slit. She had decreed earlier that there was to be no more killing. Neither were the bodies of the dead to be collected. Instead, they would be buried as they lay on the ground. Their bodies, she explained to the people, carried sickness now, the power of the sun's rays. They would make others sick too. The houses along the Street of the Temple were to be abandoned. The place would be turned into a mound of the dead instead. Mohenjodaro. They would warn others not to disturb it, lest they too became ill.

But not the bodies in the Temple. Not Rafe. Not Mua. She had Rafe buried next to Al-Mien in the paupers' cemetery, without any fanfare or flourish. She knew now that it mattered little what objects the graves would need for the soul to carry to the Upworld.

But Mua ... Mua was different. It took the metal workers fourteen days to build the casket, the carvers heating the lead so that the warnings could be written on it. The lead was important. It would protect those who followed from the sickness the Stone brought upon them.

She had decided what to do finally because she now knew how the Bloodstone worked. She knew it was not a soothsaying piece of the Goddess's heart. Instead it was technology, as simple to those who wielded it as a brick baked in the kiln was to her people. It was *intent*. The priests had wanted the Bloodstone to predict the future and so it had. She had wanted the Bloodstone to cause harm to those who wanted to harm her and so it had obliged. *Intent*. Such a simple thing. Such a powerful thing.

As she sat there during those first two lonely nights, watching them dig out the bodies, waiting for her mother, she learnt much about the Stone. It was created by people, not Gods. People like Mua. People like Rafe who had once lived on this earth. A commonplace device. A manifestation, a magnification, of their will. In those great times, men and women could come together and manipulate their own thoughts and desires. They used the stone, and many like it, to talk to one another. To move their bricks of metal using simply the power of their minds. To see the future too, that was true. To cure what ailed them, allowing the Stone to search their own bodies in ways she had not yet begun to understand. Intent. That was all it was. The ability to control the air around them, their very environment. An implementation, a processing device. But those people – the people who used the Stone – had developed an ability to resist the power of the sun, and so to resist the sickness of the Stone. It did not take from them, the way it took from Jaya and the others. It did not make them ill. In the end, they used the Stones, the many, many Stones they had, for war. Until they died and nothing remained save this one piece of their world.

She dropped her gaze. If only they had known. If only Mua had known. They could have asked the Stone how to prevent their becoming ill. They could have asked it to change their bodies perhaps, or give them powers of strength or cunning, or vanquish their enemies. They could have used it in so many different ways. Instead, they wasted it on fortune telling, on soothsaying. She had been the first person who, in her anger, demanded something more from it. And now it would be gone for good. It was for the best, for everyone.

'Come closer,' she shouted, as they gathered. 'For I am but seven cycles old and have a small voice.'

There were nervous giggles at that.

She held out the Stone. 'I have communed with the Goddess Shakari. I am her physical manifestation in this land. And she has decreed that there are to be no more priests and no more Goddess-Blessed. The clans will be dismantled, for we have done little to celebrate her in joy when we have divided and pitted ourselves against each other.'

There were murmurings now, dissatisfaction amidst the crowd. A child began to wail and was boxed on the ears.

She waited until their attention focused on her once more. 'The Bloodstone will be buried with the body of my mother, Jaya, the last of the Goddess-Blessed. I have placed a curse on it. Believe my blood oath. Anybody who touches it from this day hence or comes near it will be burned alive, save those of my blood. Anyone who dares to touch me will also burn and suffer the worst of fates – their bodies will be covered in pustules and their skin will fall off. You have seen what I can do, so question this at your peril.'

She listened to the shocked gasps, watched a woman place her hand across her mouth and shake her head, horrified. The last statement had been for effect. Who would dare to cause her harm now? But as for the first, it was true that she had made this final request of the Bloodstone. Let only those descended of her blood wield this power. It was unfortunate, but it was for the greater good. A way to protect those who came after her, to teach them to keep their distance. She asked instead that the Stone pass her memories to those who came after her. Let her children, and their children, remember what had happened here so that they had the strength to protect others from the Bloodstone, should the need ever arise.

She raised her hand, speaking softly, aware of how they stared at her, unsure of what to make of her. 'Today we will bury my mother. And then you will choose Elders amongst you to lead you. Everyone will have a vote. Everyone will have a say. Then you will never see me again.'

There was shocked silence at this last statement. It shocked her too, to say it out loud. The truth was, she had found the tunnel under the Temple where Iaf had hidden with his priests. There was enough gold there for many lifetimes. Iaf and his corruption. Well, now he had learnt that no amount of gold could have protected him from her anger.

She would pay a caravan leader enough that he could retire after one trip. She would disappear. Perhaps she would go to Arrapha, to see the land of her friend's birth. She would take on a new name. Everyone would see her for what she used to be: a child. No harm would befall her, not if she was careful. In time, perhaps, she would remember how to live and be brave, as her mother had wished her to be. For what was a worse curse than knowledge, at such a small age, when her body was nearly as helpless as a babe's?

She felt the bitterness rise as she watched the people's expressions. They believed her. They believed her capable of anything. She was a demon. How could she blame them for believing that? She knew that many cycles from now, they too, would disappear. Without the Bloodstone, the city could not dominate. Others would thrive in its place. That was the nature of things, she understood that now.

Later that day, she watched as the bones of her mother, now as dry as the stalks of wheat that grew along the edges of the city in the summer, were buried in the earth, along the bank of the river where the bula dolphins came to play. It was a good spot. Mua would like it.

She whispered her goodbyes, some part of her longing to throw herself on her mother's body. She placed the Stone in the casket, in a specially built box that Akba the carver had made. The box would warn people of what was inside, its carvings showed that death followed any who unleashed the fury of the Stone. The warnings on the casket told the whole tragic tale. Only a fool would open it now.

The wind was still, the heat unbearable. A fly played along her nose, crawling down her face. She shooed it away. Nobody had come to the burial. She was alone, save the gravedigger. He nodded and moved aside now, shuffling along with his stick, giving her time to grieve for her mother.

She pressed her palm against the dry earth. One day, she knew, others would come. They would not heed the warnings. Perhaps they would not even understand them. The Stone had shown her a woman, a beautiful woman with an innocent soul, a woman who would unleash its power once more. One of her own blood. So be it. It could not remain hidden forever.

She closed her eyes. She made sure again that the Stone understood what she demanded most from it. She demanded memory, knowledge of what had happened to be passed down amongst those of her blood, those with the dust of Meluhha in their fingernails. Those who were strong enough, would always know this story. Perhaps that way the warning would continue to pass through history, for as long as there were people here. Perhaps that way she could help that woman, when the Stone was revealed once again to the world. It was all she had the power to do.

She slumped down. She was exhausted. She had spent too much time with the Stone. She forced herself to stand. Slowly she walked away from her mother and the dusty silence of the grave by the river, shrouded by the shade of a lone pipal tree.

It was time to start again.

Epilogue

KARACHI, PRESENT DAY.

A parakeet flew into the garden and pecked lazily at the grass. She watched it for a few moments, enjoying the distraction.

Jahanara shifted in her chair. 'You don't see many of those here any more. It's mostly just crows now. All the pollution.'

'Hmmm.'

They sat together on the veranda in companionable silence, drinking their tea, enjoying the easing warmth of the day. The quiet. The quiet was the best thing of all.

Nadia scratched at the scab on her cheek. Six weeks on, and it was the last of the burns, but it itched furiously. One last physical reminder of everything she had endured. That they had all endured. Had it only been six weeks?

Her grandmother took a sip of her tea and then turned to look at her. 'It's going to be all right, you know.'

She glanced at the old woman, the woman with the gnarled hands and slender frame, the woman whose eyes were looking back at her now, full of concern.

She nodded. Did Jahanara think that she was upset because she had killed her father? The truth was, she felt little remorse. She had shot him because she had not had a choice. If he had been allowed to continue, they would have all died. She did not feel horrified by her actions. She did not feel unjustified. The truth was far worse. The truth was, she felt nothing at all. She chewed her lip. But just because she did not feel remorse did not mean that she wanted the legacy ... the burden of being the woman who had killed her own parent.

She had been calm enough after she had shot Sohail, to drop the gun. She had had the presence of mind to step over his inert body and pick up the Bloodstone. She thought about running before the army caught her, but she didn't think she would get far. She was amazed at herself, at her own logical thinking. She had killed her father, and here she was, able to behave rationally.

She did the only thing she could think of. She held the Stone in her hand once more and willed it to stop working. To play dead. She had realized, during the tussle with Layla, that the Stone could do a lot of things. It was some sort of artificial intelligence, a machine, a computer that could magnify its users' intentions. And so she had opened her mind to see for herself what it was capable of. At first, she felt the Stone resist. It was probing her, twisting along her body. Wanting a piece of her. But she held on and made her intent clear. *Nobody should have this kind of power.*

When they came for her, she told them that she had disarmed the thing. They wanted to know how, and how it could be 'reset'. She told them it couldn't be reset, that it had run out of energy. That was a lie. Anyone could get it working again, if their intent was stronger than hers, if they had any genetic ties to Mohenjodaro. But it wouldn't be easy, because they had no clue how the thing worked. They'd threatened her, of course. The authorities, the intelligence services. Her and Liam. But it was difficult to arrest them, especially after reluctant GoL witnesses confirmed that she had been kidnapped by her father, helped by corrupt cops. The army, the police, the intelligence services ... none of them wanted that kind of publicity.

She cleared her throat. 'I saw a green parrot here this morning. It was quite large.'

'Yes, they come sometimes. They like the almond tree.'

They sat in silence once more.

Later, she heard footsteps behind her. Layla walked out onto the veranda, still wrapped in her blanket. At once, the hollow feeling began to ease and her throat felt less constricted. Layla was doing so well. The first-degree burns on her face and upper arms had healed. She had put on weight, looking more and more like herself.

She shifted on the cane sofa, so Layla could sit down, taking in every inch of her, still longing, instinctively, to touch her, to make sure she was okay. She was so fucking fragile.

The first few days after the events in Mohenjodaro had been the worst. The authorities had taken Layla away, along with many senior GoL members, including a man named Philip Abbott. The media had had a field day. The world's most notorious cult leader had re-emerged to take over an ancient city which he thought belonged to him. Then he had set off a white phosphorous grenade on his own people. Sohail Hussain had been behind the disappearance of the original Mohenjodaro 8. Journalists speculated that Sohail Hussain must have connections to the ISIS, which had its own store of white phosphorous from the stockpile the Americans had left behind after the war in Baghdad. Anything was for sale these days, media pundits had announced. Nobody was safe when you could practically buy a chemical weapon on eBay.

White phosphorous was the party line, and amazingly enough, the media had accepted the story. The fact that there had been no actual explosion, nothing to be seen from the sky or residue left afterwards to measure or pick up didn't really matter, not by the time the intelligence services were done spreading misinformation. In the absence of any tangible alternative, the white phosphorous story worked nicely for the authorities, who bent the facts to accommodate it. Anyone in the immediate vicinity had been far too busy trying to survive to really know what had exploded, but they all had burn marks to show off. GoL members were filmed leaving Mohenjodaro in tears, sobbing at the loss of Father. Without him, they were rudderless. They were victims, just as much as Layla was.

Just as well they had decided to cover the whole thing up, Nadia decided. Because using her silence as leverage is what saved Layla in the end. The government had taken Layla in for questioning. They hadn't even given her a chance to get medical treatment for her burns. Perhaps that had been what ultimately destroyed Layla's fragile mind: the flock of army, police, and later, intelligence officials who locked a woman with painful injuries in a small room for several hours and demanded answers before they would treat her. Sohail Hussain was dead. There was nobody left to blame for the 'incident' at Mohenjodaro, except the one woman who had originally held the Stone in her hands and watched while her colleagues burned.

Thankfully, the powers that be decided the whole thing was better off covered up. They would have made Layla disappear – lock her up somewhere – but for that pesky sister of hers. Nadia refused to get treatment for her own injuries until she knew Layla had been released. She threatened to go to the media and tell the truth. She had too much media visibility to simply vanish, so she became a thorn in their side.

When Layla was finally released, Jahanara had come into her own, refusing to leave her granddaughter's side. The Stone had taken its toll on Layla. She was weak and her injuries took longer to recover from than Nadia's. Plus, she was reeling, psychologically, from everything she had gone through. Jahanara held Layla's hair back as she vomited into the toilet. She spoon-fed her granddaughter vegetable soup. She sang her songs, told her stories about her childhood in Karachi, laughing and making jokes. She kept Layla sane and her demons at bay. And seeing her sister so well cared for ... well, it kept Nadia sane too. At night, they would sit quietly on the veranda and Nadia would tell her stories of her life in the compound, of how their father had manipulated people and how he had convinced them of his power. It helped Layla, she thought, to realize she was not the only one who had fallen under his thrall.

Nadia sipped her tea, not looking forward to the rest of the day. They had reached another tough crossroads. Liam would be here soon. They'd agreed that it was time to make Layla face the truth about Jay. She didn't want to, Nadia knew. She would take that burden onto herself, as though it were her fault he had been killed. Well, Layla was strong. She had survived Sohail. She would survive this discussion.

She heard the car honk and watched the gates being pulled open. It was Liam. He jumped out of his Land Cruiser and came towards them, a smile on his face. She felt relief. She had come to rely on this man and it felt strangely ... comfortable.

Liam had been the most seriously injured by the Stone, though he had also recovered the fastest. He was limping slightly – the burn on his calf was second degree, rather than first. She frowned, thinking about how close they had come to dying. A few more seconds and things would have been so much worse.

He took off his sunglasses and put his hands on his hips. 'Well, is that not the most fetching picture? All my girls sitting in the sunshine. How are you doing, ladies?'

Layla's face lit up. She was used to Liam coming now, at all hours, to play checkers or watch a movie, or just sit with her when she was tired.

'Hello Layla,' he said, giving her a kiss on the cheek. 'I'll be right back, I'm starving. I'll go grab something from the kitchen, shall I?'

'I'll come and give you a hand,' said Nadia quickly, getting up.

They walked into the house together, but she guided him into the library, closing the door behind her. The ancient ceiling fan was still rattling, the dust still everywhere, though she had begun to clear out the books, begun to catalogue them, and clean the shelves, before putting them back.

'Well?' she said.

He walked to the window, staring at the coconut trees outside. 'Philip Abbot has been charged with Jay's murder. The investigation into Marianne Riviere's death has also been reopened and the authorities are confident he'll be charged with that too. He's being extradited even as we speak.'

She exhaled and nodded. 'Thank you, Liam.'

He turned and smiled at her, and her heart skipped a beat.

'Are you really hungry or did you just want an excuse to tell me this in private?' she asked.

He grinned. 'Famished. You know, if we're going to be here for a while, I think we need to do a better job of stocking the fridge. There aren't even any coco pops. And Layla loves coco pops. Me, I'm a steak man myself. Steak and chips will do me any time.'

She stared. 'You're staying then?'

'Are you kicking me out?'

'No,' she said hurriedly. 'Of course not. It's just ...'

He took her hand. 'Come on, you silly woman. Let's go eat.'

And just like that, her heart felt lighter.

Author's Note

Very little is known about Mohenjodaro, but it is truly the most breathtaking place I have ever visited. I have taken some liberties with its history for the sake of my plot. The city dates back to 2500 BC, not 3800 BC. However, recent efforts to date the site suggest it might be much older. These studies are not yet conclusive. The seals that have been found so far have only short pieces of text on them, not long ones, which has made it exceedingly difficult to decipher its language.

The people did not worship a one-horned god, though they did appear to worship a mother goddess, and there is evidence of a male deity wearing a two-horned helmet. A one-horned animal motif, like a unicorn, appears on numerous seals. No poetry or tablets were buried in any tombs, and the area around the site is less remote than I have made it out to be. What has been excavated thus far shows a society that does not seem to have had a military, and which was far more prosperous and equal than I have suggested. If there were temples, they have not revealed themselves yet, unless the Granary was in fact a place of gathering, as some researchers have suggested.

It is true that approximately only 10 per cent of the site has been excavated, and that over forty bodies were found fleeing from some unknown fate. Photos of those bodies can be found online and in the Mohenjodaro Museum.

Archaeologists have never been able to tell us what brought about the city's decline.

David Davenport did write a book entitled *Atomic Destruction in 2000 BC,* and it was references to that book which first piqued my interest in setting a thriller in the Indus Valley. Many of Sohail's beliefs in this novel stem from the Forbidden Archaeology movement. The specific examples used by his cult to prove that human beings have lived on earth for billions of years came from the books and writings of Graham Hancock, David Hatcher Childress, and Michael A. Cremo and Richard L. Thompson. I will leave the readers to make their own minds up about the veracity of their claims.

Acknowledgements

Halfway through writing this book, I was diagnosed with cancer. It was a difficult and exhausting period, but I was blessed to have many, many people who helped me through it, and so now you'll have to bear with me while I thank them all. I owe a big dose of gratitude to my family – the incredible Waddling Warducks and the Jals – everyone should have a family like mine and the world would right itself. But thank you particularly to Lubna Khan, Nina Khan, Damien Phillips, Tia Noon, Fahad Khan, Mariam Saeedullah, and Alyia Yusuf, who all went beyond the call of duty. I must also thank my sisters-from-another-mother, Kamila and Saman Shamsie. Kamila particularly, who now has first-hand experience of visiting every hospital in north London.

Thank you also to Anoushka Beazley, who kept me sane, Jumana Dalal who flew out to be with me, and to the following people whose love and support touched me deeply: Erum Sultan, Farid Azfar, Taniya Zaffer Khan and Raaheen Mani (nobody can pull off a hospital dance routine quite like those two), Ayira Khan, Adnan Noon, Marie-France Phillips, Aisha Rahman, Deepak Sathe, Osman Hadi, Mahnaz Hadi, Gillian Slovo, Duncan James, Jill Henry, Sarah Trueman, Max Beazley, Lulu Nana, Harriett Gilbert, Tahmima Anam, Lillian Jensen, Annie Lodge, Jemima

McDonell, Alketa Xhafa Mripa, Lulzim Mripa, Dr Dermot O'Flynn, Dr Evadney Keith, Ann Herreboudt, Rachel Holmes, and the City University Writing Crew that is Simon Edge, Glenda Cooper, Sarah-Jane Checkland, and David Evans. Thank you also to Jamia Biswas and Ghulam Jaffar for all the childcare, which made this possible, and to my darling Poker Sharks of West Hampstead, who made me laugh, a lot.

My deepest gratitude to my publisher, Diya Kar Hazra, and my agent, Margaret Halton, the entire team at Pan Macmillan, particularly Sushmita Chatterjee, and to the people who provided me with early feedback on parts of the book, some of whom are mentioned above, while the others are Mahvesh Murad, Rosey Strub, Jonathan Myerson, Kamiar Rokni, and Alexandra Shelley. For the archaeology, I turned to Egyptologist extraordinaire Dr Salima Ikram. Thank you also to Dr Michael Jansen for telling me about his lifelong work in Mohenjodaro, and to Eileen Kernaghan, whose magical Indus Valley novel, *Winter on the Plain of Ghosts,* proved to be really inspiring.

Finally, I must thank the one person who makes it all worthwhile, every day. My beautiful son Rohan, who is a never-ending source of joy. I love you.